FIVE ZERO TRIPLE TWO

SOMEONE'S ALWAYS SAYING GOODBYE

CRYSTAL LAKE PUBLISHING

TO

THE BIEN HOA BOYS

FIRST AIR COMMANDO SQUADRON

SOUTH VIETNAM

OTHER BOOKS BY JACK HARVEY

AC-47 SIDE FIRING GUNNERY
(USAF TECHNICAL)

CROPDUSTERS

SELF RIGHTEOUS
ARROGANT & UNTOUCHABLE

ISBN 0– 9651647-4-8

LCCN 99 096123

Gayle Martinez
Editor

PROLOGUE

The neighbors came trickling in the newly mowed cemetery like people under some kind of sentence--farmers in their best overalls, a few of the more prosperous with coats, and neckties, sweat trickling down their florid faces. Their wives walked along-side, dabbing at their eyes with soggy handkerchiefs, their starched, freshly ironed dresses already beginning to wilt. A grim faced, widow Cumrine brought up the rear, upswept hair still perfectly in place, clutching a bible to her breast with white knuckled hands.

They milled about, uncharacteristically subdued, some politely motioning others to go first as they gradually assembled next to the grave site. Finally, the preacher raised the book, cleared his throat, and began to read.

Behind them, a meadowlark sang, its cheerful notes seemingly out of place. Through it all, John Cramer stood stoically, trying to ignore the strangling grip of the first necktie he had ever worn, and the heat of a blazing sun burning through his new black suit. He fought desperately against the urge to cry, reminding himself that he was, after all, nearly eight years old and therefore expected to be a man about things like this. Women could cry, men could not.

His gaze never wavered from the two shiny metal caskets sitting side by side above the deep hole in the ground. He passionately wished he could see his parents just one more time, but the terrible effects of the head-on collision had ruled that out.

The presence of the neighbors angered him. It seemed intrusive. He wasn't sure why that was, but some of them were already referring to him in hushed, secretive tones as an orphan, and the title grated against his tortured nerves like a subtle, whispered insult.

After what seemed like an eternity, the preacher's voice wound down to his final, empty words. The crowd stirred, then milled about self consciously, mumbling to each other, and conveying final condolences to bereaved relatives. After that, they scattered aimlessly, slowly drifting away from the gravesite.

Still he stood there, staring transfixed at the coffins until he noticed the persistent tug on his hand. His aunt's voice jolted him, prodding him with her clipped, impatient words. "Come on, John. It's over. It's time to go."

He turned reluctantly, following her with halting steps--looking back over his shoulder, watching the workmen as they lowered the caskets into the void. It seemed a heartless, barbaric thing for them to do. He wanted to rush back, and put an end to it.

He had to do something dammit! His agony translated into rebellion and he struck out the only way he could, stopping suddenly, planting his feet, and trying to tear his hand from his aunt's grasp. "I don't like this," he shouted in helpless frustration. "It's not right! It's not fair! I won't take it anymore. I want to go home!"

She looked at him coldly with her usual tight-lipped stare. "You're going home, John. You'll live with us. Your house is our house now."

"I don't want to live with you!"

She leaned downward, thrusting her scowling face toward him until their noses nearly touched. "I don't want you to live with us either!" she snapped. That's just the way it has to be."

The words burned into him, filling his chest with a terrible, searing ache. She turned, and yanked on his arm, pulling him after her. He stumbled along, his eyes fixed on the front end of his uncle's Model A. The radiator on the old Ford wavered, then melted away as a flood of tears washed out his sight, and spilled down his cheeks. He was alone now. His mother, and father were gone. His family was gone. The good part of his life was over, and he knew that nothing would ever be the same for him again.

CHAPTER ONE

Cramer woke up suddenly, gasping for breath, and fighting to drive the nightmare from his mind. Finally, he wiped the sweat from his face, clenched his teeth, and slammed the side of his fist on the floor. Why? Why, after all these years was it back?

Early morning light filtered into the dimly lit room, and he fixed his eyes on the ceiling tiles, trying to find comfort in their neat, orderly pattern. After a few minutes, he sat up on the bare, polished hardwood, winching from the pain and stiffness in his back.

He stretched his neck, and looked through the bottom of the window, noticing that the snow had stopped. His reflection stared back at him, uncharacteristically somber, and glowering, black hair, wavy, and short cut, with premature flecks of gray. A stubble of beard confirmed his need for a shave.

The dark mood of the dream still gripped him, and he shook his head, trying to rid himself of it. Finally, he reached behind him, grabbed the rolled up flight jacket he had used for a pillow, and stared at the bold silver letters beneath the senior pilot's wings. Cramer, John D. Captain USAF.

Muscles in his forearms rippled as he tightened his grip on the wad of nylon, fighting to drive the message home. That's who you are, dammit! That's what you are. You're not some helpless kid anymore. Your parents are dead. Dead and buried. It's been twenty five years, for Christ's sake. You ought to be over it by now.

Still, the mood of the nightmare lingered, filling him with a gnawing sense of dread. How it had haunted him in his youth. Each time it came it was the same--vivid, merciless, and agonizingly real, forcing him to relive that horrible day at the cemetery over, and over. But suddenly, after he and Sandy were married, it left. He never had it again. Maybe that was the connection. Now she was gone, he was alone, and the nightmare was back.

His eyes swept the once cheerful room, now drab and empty. Damn. She didn't even leave him a chair to sit on. His gaze shifted to the nearly empty whiskey bottle an arm's length away. Not even a glass to drink out of. Why would she do that? Just...strip everything? Did she hate him that much? She never showed it.

He ran his fingers through his hair, and shook his head. It made no sense dammit! The only thing he wouldn't do for her was get out of the Air Force. How could she expect him to do that anyway? He'd been in since he was seventeen...didn't know anything else.

Fourteen years he had invested. Seven years enlisted, Korea, OCS-- Pilot Training, not to mention the other schools. Had his own crew, and just made instructor pilot. What was he supposed to do? Throw all that away? Why? Just because he had to pull Reflex Alert in Greenland for a couple of weeks a month, and do a 3 month tour overseas every year?

Sure there were separations. So what? A lot of people had that, truck drivers, salesmen, merchant seamen, offshore oil workers. Nobody's life was perfect. What did she expect?

He jumped at the sound of the doorbell. Damn bell--always hated it. Should have had it changed. He struggled to his feet, feeling the stiffness in his joints as he walked to the stairwell, and slowly descended the steps to the foyer.

It was worth the trip. When he opened the door, Janet Shaw was standing there with a coffee pot in one hand, a couple of mugs in the other, and a sympathetic smile on her pretty face.

"How did you ring the bell?" he asked.

Her smile broadened. "Pushed the button with my nose."

He chuckled, "You nurses are a resourceful lot. But your nose is too nice to be pushing buttons. Anyway, it's good to see you. Come in."

She brushed by him, smelling fresh, and looking great in her starched white uniform.

He followed her into the kitchen, watching as she sat the mugs on the counter, and poured the coffee. When she handed him the cup, and looked up at him, it almost made him catch his breath. Her short black hair, and dark eyes were even more striking when she wore white.

"You look beat, John."

He nodded, rubbing the stubble on his face. "I am beat. It's a long flight from Sondrestrom to Otis in a KC-97. A half pint of whiskey, and sleeping four hours on the floor didn't help much either."

"You should have knocked on our door. We have an extra bed."

He shook his head. "I appreciate the offer, but it was two in the morning. Besides, when I realized what had happened, I didn't want to talk to anyone."

"I can understand that. Do you want to talk about it now?"

He looked despondently around the barren kitchen. "Not much to talk about, I guess. Looks pretty final to me."

CHAPTER TWO

The two days Cramer had off after returning from Greenland seemed like a week. He killed half a day moving into a room in the Base Officers Quarters, then went by the Housing Office, and turned in the keys to his apartment. With that out of the way, there didn't seem to be much to do.

How could that be, he wondered? Otis was a sprawling base, left over from WW II, filled with Beetle Bailey barracks, an expansive flight line, BX, Commissary, military clubs, picnic areas, and tree-lined walkways, but somehow, it all seemed empty now.

After he got back to his room, he tried to read, but couldn't concentrate, tried to watch television, but couldn't get interested. And the time...God the time...it...it just, dragged. For hours he sat there, motionless, caught in a dark stupor, watching the polished brass pendulum of the wall clock swing back and forth, listening to its loud, rhythmic tick.

Finally, he roused himself, got up, and looked out the window. Snow was falling in heavy, sodden flakes, already covering every flat surface in sight. That ruled out going into Falmouth or Boston. Why take the chance of sliding off the road?

He thought about going to the club, and getting drunk, but rejected that. In his current state of depression, he'd probably over do it. Four or five drinks was one thing--a dozen was something else. No sense in doing the slobbering drunk routine. Might as well face it. He was alone now. An orphan again. He shook his head, fighting down the sinking feeling in the pit of his stomach. To hell with that. Somehow... somehow, he'd work his way out of this.

At 0800 the third morning, duty mercifully called, and Cramer snapped out of his depression. Cheerful, he wasn't, but at least he felt resigned to the situation. There hadn't been a word from her. She was gone for good. Bailed out. Hauled ass.

Might as well enjoy the silence. He'd hear from her lawyer soon enough. The good part was, he didn't let her talk him into quitting the Air Force. Sooner or later, she'd probably have left anyway. If she wanted to go, she could always find a reason. At least this way, he still had his career. He couldn't go home, but he could damn sure go to work.

After a short drive to the flight line, he walked into Squadron Ops, and checked the huge status board on the far wall. There his name was, lead pilot for a flight of four tankers, scheduled to offload to a flight of B-47s in the central Wisconsin refueling area called Simpson Hill. Might as well get psyched up for it, he figured. Time for a dress rehearsal.

He went to his locker, got out his parka, and picked up his briefcase, feeling the heft of the overstuffed satchel. Damn thing ought to be heavy. There was a lot of crap in there. Two Sears catalogue-sized volumes of the

KC-97 Pilot's handbook, a thick loose-leaf with countless SAC flying regulations, and the tanker version of the Strategic Air Command Tactical Doctrine. Books, books, books! When he was a kid, he never dreamed there'd be so much study in being a pilot.

On the way out, he approached the squadron coffee shop, noticed the enticing aroma, and decided to stop in for a little human contact. As he entered the room, a thin faced, solemn looking Master Sergeant Kroft leaned on the bar, and nodded cordially. "How's it going Captain?"

"Okay. Coffee fresh?"

"Yes sir. Just made it."

A tired looking, T/Sgt Dobbs, obviously just back from a flight, and needing a shave, turned on the last stool, and asked, "What's the latest from Sondrestrom, captain?"

Cramer poured half a cup. "Nothing different there. Can't say as much for home though. While I was gone, my wife bailed out on me." He set the pot back on the hot plate, and added, "Stripped the damn place. Took everything but my sense of smell."

Kroft shook his head. "Welcome aboard captain. You're the latest in a growing line. Johnson and I, went through that months ago. It's like some kind of epidemic. Maybe we ought to form a club."

Cramer nodded, then realized he didn't feel like talking about this, even if the other two did have the same thing in common. The wound was too deep, too private, almost overwhelming. He drained his still steaming coffee, feeling it burn on the way down. After that, he made his excuses and left.

Once outside, the cold air hit with a shock, and he walked awkwardly through foot deep snow, struggling laboriously toward the nearest plane in a mile long ramp full of four engine, KC-97s.

The sun bounced off their shiny aluminum, almost giving him a headache, and he squinted as he viewed them. They looked so peaceful, in the cold morning light. Sitting there silently, in a neat, orderly row. A long line of aerodynamic weight lifters--snow piled high on thick aluminum wings, their fat, rounded, double decked bodies, waiting patiently for broom wielding mechanics, and the de-ice truck to make them flyable again. Two miles across the field, near an underground bunker, sat six more just like them, that group kept perpetually ice free, full of fuel, cocked, and ready to go. The lesson of Pearl Harbor was long since learned. Russians be damned. They wouldn't catch Curtis LeMay's bunch asleep, and off guard on Sunday morning.

Moscow would try though. Through any means available. And it looked like they had the means. The world's largest, and most insidious espionage system, a fleet of long range bombers, and now, a growing arsenal of ICBMs that made ours look puny by comparison. And the bastards never let up. Always sinister, and forever threatening. Probing

6

every angle, looking for any weakness. Senator Scoop Jackson had it right. Said they were like hotel burglars, prowling every corridor, and trying all the doors.

Finally, he reached the first plane, and opened the lower forward entrance door, exposing a row of steps on the backside of the hatch. He climbed aboard, stomping his feet on the way up, carefully knocking the snow from his boots. Once inside, he went up the ladder, through the floor hatch into the main cargo compartment, then stepped into the cabin and slammed the door behind him to keep out the draft.

God, it was cold! A trail of wispy fog marked his breathing as he squeezed between the navigator, and engineer's stations, and eased himself into the aircraft commander's seat. Sunlight filtered through the thick layer of snow covering the panorama of windows in the huge, round nose, lighting the cabin with a soft, translucent glow. It was a nice effect, and he welcomed the privacy. For the next couple of hours, he'd be flying only in his mind, and the fact that he couldn't see out, would add to the realism, isolating him from the bustling distractions of the sprawling ramp outside.

Normally at this time of year, he would have studied at home--but now, he no longer had a home, and the frigid cabin seemed preferable to the loneliness of his BOQ room. Anyway, if he used his imagination, and concentrated, practicing emergency procedures in a tanker cockpit was almost as good as a couple of hours in the flight simulator.

He slid the seat forward, adjusted the rudder pedals, then fastened his seat belt, and shoulder harness--exactly like he'd do if he were flying. Finally, to set the mood, he scanned the scores of instruments on the pilot's panel, grasped the ice-cold yoke in his left hand, placed his right on the throttles...and started the disaster movie in his mind.

Thirty minutes later, his feet felt like blocks of ice, but he ignored the discomfort as he mentally flew the plane through a continuing series of hypothetical, life threatening emergencies. Engine failures, runaway props, electrical failures and fuselage fires, each compounded by subsequent problems with hydraulic and mechanical systems.

For each fancied catastrophe he took the proper action, touched the correct levers, tapped the right switches, and made the required calls over his dead radio to an imaginary formation, crew, and Air Route Traffic Control. Following each procedure he methodically turned to the books, and checked carefully, item by item, making sure he had done everything properly.

Each review was a dress rehearsal, preparing him for the worst, and renewing his knowledge. Over the years, he'd performed well, and his expertise had not gone unnoticed. The Squadron had upgraded him as soon as he qualified for the next higher position, Co-pilot, Aircraft Commander, and finally, Instructor Pilot. Now, he often served as formation leader, with more senior pilots flying behind him.

Two hours later he felt nearly frozen. Finally, he closed the thick book, put it back in the satchel, and left the plane, heading for the Officers Club. Something to look forward to. Good food in a fine setting. Padded, linen tablecloths, fine china, the best in silverware, and comfortable chairs, with soft music in the background. Made a man feel good, just to be there.

Today he selected roast beef, mashed potatoes, (no gravy), fresh steamed asparagus,(where the hell did they get that at this time of year?), rolls and coffee. In the end, he passed up desert. Too much self indulgence was not a good thing. Following lunch, he drove back to the Base Officers Quarters to catch a nap before his mission.

The door closed softly behind him as Cramer's eyes swept the room. Large, and nicely furnished, with modern, walnut, Scandinavian furniture, and a small refrigerator, it was more than comfortable. When he was an enlisted man, a room like this would have seemed opulent. It should have made him feel good, just being here--a status symbol attesting to his rise through the ranks. But now, it seemed little more than an unhappy reminder that he no longer had a wife, or a home of his own.

The thought gripped him, tightening his chest. God! He was alone again. Forever separated from the only person he had been close to since the death of his parents. And he hadn't even seen it coming. How could he have been so stupid?

He needed to rest before tonight's mission, but hesitated to lie down, concerned that the nightmare might return. Would he have it for the rest of his life? God, what a depressing thought. Could a psychiatrist help? No. Hell no! That was the worst idea he'd had yet. An Air Force shrink would yank him off flying status at the first hint of a mental problem. His flying career would be finished. Hell, they might even force him into medical retirement. Then he'd have nothing. No family, *and* no career.

He gritted his teeth, and clenched his fists. Damn her! Why did she do this to him? He'd always done everything he could for her. Why couldn't she see that?

He took a deep breath, and his anger slowly subsided. To hell with her. He'd done alright before met her...he'd do alright again. She could ruin the marriage, but she damn sure wasn't going to ruin him.

He walked over to the bed, sat on the edge, and unlaced his boots, kicking them off before laying down on top of the covers. It was a relief to stretch out.

Tonight's mission could be tough. Northeastern winter weather was treacherous. Even under ideal conditions, a night air refueling in an eight plane formation, was a dicey operation with a high potential for disaster.

There was only one way to handle that. Concentrate on the job, and worry about the personal stuff later. He felt the tension leaving him as his muscles relaxed. Finally, he took a deep breath, and felt himself drifting into sleep. A short while later, he was eight years old, back at the cemetery, watching those caskets going into that God-awful hole in the ground. He woke up suddenly, in a cold sweat, gasping for breath and threshing around in twisted clothes.

CHAPTER THREE

Twenty six thousand feet below, a snow covered landscape gleamed softly in the moonlight, its rolling fields, and scattered woods punctuated by widely separated farmhouse lights. Inside the cockpit, a blast of hot air warmed Cramer's feet, but his hands were cold.

The refueling had gone well. No one broke radio silence, and the bombers had their designated offloads. He banked slowly left, and the three KC-97s he was leading, followed, making a sweeping 45 degree turn, so they could move out of the B-47s' way. Once clear, the trailing quartet of six engine jets, increased power, bolted ahead, and quickly left the plodding, 300 mile-an-hour tankers behind.

He tightened his grip on a handful of knobs, pulled back the throttles, and four, 3500 horse, 28 cylinder, radial engines changed from a screaming roar, to a peaceful, contented rumble.

"Engineer's Throttles," he said.

"Roger sir."

Cramer picked up his heading, punched on the autopilot, and began to relax. Behind him, the other three tankers would be slipping into an in-trail formation, holding one mile separation between planes, with each pilot maintaining position on his APS 42 radar.

Lieutenant Joe Dixon, tall, lanky, with blond hair, and a surprisingly boyish face turned his wafer switch from HF to interphone, then looked across the aisle-stand. Cramer knew that look.

"What's the problem?"

"Otis is still socked in, captain. The Squadron Command Post says we've got to divert to McGuire."

"Bullshit!" Cramer barked. "The ceiling at McGuire is 500 obscured, with a mile visibility. It's forecast to go to 300 and a half, and could easily go below minimums. Plattsburg is perfect! 8000 overcast with ten miles. We only have two choices for alternates, and barely enough fuel to make one of them. "

Dixon ripped a sheet of paper off his knee-pad, and nodded, "I know captain. You want to talk to them?"

"You're damned right!" Cramer reached down to the center aisle-stand and switched to HF. "Clamshell control, this is Granville two six."

"Two six, go ahead.

"Since home station is below minimums I'm taking my formation to Plattsburg, over."

The duty controller came back immediately, his exhausted patience reflected in his condescending tone. *"Granville two six, be advised we checked with the Plattsburg housing office. They may not have quarters for your crews by the time your flight arrives there. There's plenty of housing at McGuire. If you'd think about details like this before you make your decisions, perhaps you'd make the best choice the first time. Over."*

Cramer slammed his fist on the armrest. "Listen to that paper shuffling dumb ass! In ten minutes we'll be at the point of no return. We've got a choice between one alternate or the other. McGuire weather is rotten. If it deteriorates, we'll be nearly out of fuel, with no place to go."

Dixon gave him a wary look. "I know captain. But Major Snyder is the senior controller tonight. You know how he is. He won't appreciate you bucking him."

Cramer snorted, "That paper shuffling prick isn't leading this formation. Snyder's a second rate instrument pilot with screwed-up judgment, and no guts. When the squadron moved north to the Cape, he couldn't handle the weather, so he ran to the Command Post, and got him a nice, safe, desk job. Now that he's safely out of the fray, he wants to tell everyone else how to fly."

Dixon looked doubtful. "You could be in trouble if you buck him."

"We could be in a hell of a lot more trouble if I don't," Cramer said. He squeezed his mic button. "Clamshell, I'm really not concerned about what kind of pillows we'll have under our heads tonight. I'll let my crews sleep in the street before I choose 300 and one, over 8000 and ten. This formation's going to Plattsburg. Granville two six out."

CHAPTER FOUR

Captain! Dammit captain, wake up!

Cramer jerked his arm free, opened his eyes and saw Dixon standing over the bunk, looking down at him, blond hair tousled, his youthful face worried.

"You OK captain?"

"Yeah," he mumbled. "I'm alright. Gimme a minute. I'll sort it out. It's just...its confusing. I don't usually wake up there."

Dixon straightened up to his full six-two, towering over the bed. "What are you talking about?"

"The nightmare," he said sheepishly. "I usually don't wake up until I get in the car, and she slams the door."

Dixon shook his head. "I don't understand."

"My aunt...she's..." He waved irritably. "It's a nightmare dammit. No big deal. I've had it since I was a kid. It's...it's just a dream."

"You've been having recurring nightmares?"

He threw back the covers, swung his feet to the floor, and sighed. "Yeah. Don't make a big thing of it. I thought I was over it years ago. But, after Sandy left, it came back. So what? I lose a little sleep now and then, that's all."

Dixon gave him a worried look. "I dunno, captain. If I was you, I wouldn't tell anybody about this. Someone in Headquarters might jump to the conclusion that you're...well, you know...unstable.

He took a deep breath. "Joe, you've gotta stop taking those damn psychology courses. All that night school is fogging up your mind."

Dixon sat down on edge of the overstuffed chair, dangling his hands between his legs. "Maybe so captain. But I'd keep quiet about this if I were you. SAC's hypersensitive about combat crewmembers with psychological problems. You know the bit. We're all part of the nuclear team. That kind of crap."

Cramer rolled his eyes, and looked away. "I know."

Screams of children running down the hallway broke into the conversation.

"Must be some dependents in here," Dixon said. "Probably a spill-over from temporary family quarters. Sounds like they're leaving."

"Thank God for that." He reached into the top of his boots, and grabbed his socks. "To hell with it. I'm awake now." He looked at Dixon. "You ready to eat?"

Dixon smiled, and grabbed his jacket. "I'm always ready to eat. Which way's the mess hall?"

"Mess hall your ass," Cramer grumbled, as he slid his socks on. "I didn't go to officer's training so I could eat in the friggin' mess hall. Ate there for seven years. Let's go to the Club."

12

Dixon gave him a sly smile. "The mess hall's cheaper."

He chuckled, "Dammit Joe. This isn't Aviation Cadets. You're an officer now. Start living like one."

After breakfast, they left the Club, and headed for the flight line, with wisps of foggy breath trailing over their shoulders as they walked. Damn! Otis might be cold, but Plattsburg was an absolute bitch in winter. Almost as bad as Dow. Why would anyone voluntarily live here, and put up with this climate? Suddenly he noticed Dixon was wearing a light jacket. Poor bastard, looked like he was freezing.

Passing through the perimeter gate, they returned the guard's salute, and Cramer stopped short, staring at an airplane parked just beyond the first hangar. He wiped his nose on his glove, sniffed, and pointed. "A B-26? Where the hell did that come from?"

"I thought they were all retired," Dixon said, his voice quivering as he shivered.

"This one isn't." Cramer said. "Look at it. Bomb shackles under the wings, and eight fifties in the nose. Not just the tubes, the guns are actually in there." He ran his eyes over the plane admiring the lines. Sleek, and deadly looking, with two powerful, tightly cowled radials—had a small internal bomb bay, provisions to hang more ordinance from the wings and even had a streamlined rear gunner position with twin fifties.

"P...Probably flying it to some museum," Dixon mumbled through chattering teeth.

Cramer shook his head. "No. Not this one. The markings are wrong. They're up to date. This is an active airplane." They started walking toward it, and he ran his eyes over the plane, as they drew closer. "In WW II, these babies could out perform a lot of fighters," he said. "I watched them operate in Korea...always dreamed of flying one."

"Fa...fat chance captain."

"This is really strange." He glanced at Dixon. "Something's going on here by God, and I want in on it!"

Dixon wrapped his arms around his chest, and shivered harder. "You know what they s..say, captain. Nobody g...gets out SAC."

"Maybe they don't try hard enough."

Dixon gave him a wary glance, hunched his shoulders and slipped his hands into his jacket pockets, his face nearly beet red now. "This could be a lousy deal, captain. Volunteer for something out of SAC, and you'll make yourself look like a mal-content. The head shed's sure to retaliate. Look at what they did to Benson."

"Who says they'll know I'm looking?"

Dixon sniffed, and shrugged. "You'd have to go to Headquarters, do...do research, or at least ask questions. If you make any kind of an official inquiry they'll g...get wind of it. How can you f...find out anything, without t...tipping your hand?"

Cramer pointed to the plane. "That son-of-a-bitch didn't fly itself in here. The pilot's gotta be around somewhere. He'll know what the score is.

"Yeah, but h...how you gonna find him?'

"He's probably still asleep in the BOQ." Cramer pulled one hand out of his jacket, and checked his watch. "Get the crew together, and meet me at the airplane in an hour."

"Sounds g...good to me. Whatever you say, captain."

They exchanged salutes, and parted company. Cramer turned, and walked briskly toward Base Ops. Once there, he pushed through the double doors and surveyed the large room. Felt good inside. A little musty smelling, but nice and warm. Not surprisingly, since it was Sunday morning, the place was nearly deserted. Only one sleeping clerk slumped in a chair behind the counter. He looked to the right, and scanned the huge status board covering the wall behind the dispatch station. Neat, orderly columns listed scheduled departures, and arrivals, with the last column showing the name of each pilot in command. There it was. The only B-26 listed. And the pilot's name?...Fuller.

He turned, and headed for the door, mumbling softly to himself, "I hope you're a light sleeper, Fuller. 'Cause you're about to get your lazy ass rolled out of the sack."

He knocked louder the second time, nearly bruising his knuckles. Finally a muffled voice responded, "Come in."

Cramer turned the knob, and the unlocked door opened, as a sleepy eyed man with brown, crew cut hair sat up in bed, letting the covers slide to his waist. Better be careful here. Even half asleep, this guy looked tough. Tight skin over a well muscled torso, with battered, rugged facial features resembling veteran middle weight, Tony Zale.

Next to the bed, a gray B-4 bag lay open, like a giant, filleted oyster, its disorganized guts of black socks, and tangled underwear spilling onto the floor. To the left, a flying suit with captain's bars hung over the back of a chair.

He closed the door behind him, as Fuller, rubbed his eyes, scratched his head, and mumbled with surprising civility, "What can I do for you?"

"You the pilot on that B-26?"

Fuller's head snapped up. "B-26?"

He grinned. "Come on man, it's the only B-26 on the Base Ops board, and the pilot's name is listed as Fuller." He gestured toward the chair. "Even with your flying suit hanging upside down, I can still read your name tag."

Fuller shook his head. "I can't talk about this. It's classified."

"So what? I'm an Aircraft Commander in SAC. We're awash in classified shit. I've got a Top Secret Security Clearance."

14

Fuller gave him a so-what look. "Maybe so. But you don't have a need to know this."

"Dammit, give me a break," Cramer said. "I'm looking for another job. I've been in SAC all my life.

"What's wrong with SAC?"

"It's the most iron-assed command in the Air Force. Every time we turn around we get a check ride, or some kind of fucking test. Bust one, and your career hits the skids. We're working seventy...sometimes eighty hour weeks. No time for a social life. I might as well be a monk--haven't had a date since my wife got fed up, and left."

Fuller seemed to be buying it, so Cramer softened his tone. "Hey, it's obvious you're ass deep in some kind of special mission. I don't care what it is. If it involves flying a B-26, I want in on it."

Fuller took a deep breath, looked down at his lap, and pursed his lips. "Sounds like you need a change," he said. Finally, he looked up. "Fair enough. When you get back home, go to Wing Personnel. Tell them you want to volunteer for a project called Jungle Jim." He pointed his finger and scowled. "But don't--by God, don't you *dare* tell them where you heard about it."

"Thanks," Cramer said. "I owe you a beer."

Fuller grinned, and chuckled, "A beer your ass. You owe me a case."

CHAPTER FIVE

He turned the knob, and opened the door to a surprisingly large room that smelled like a stale ashtray. Nothing fancy about Base Personnel, not at Otis anyway. An obviously remodeled, wooden, WW II building, furnished with listless clerks, battered file cabinets, and clacking Underwoods. Inside, cigarette smoke hung in the air like a London fog as a half dozen clerks pounded typewriters, shuffled forms, and tended to their specialty.

To the right at the receptionist's desk, a chubby, pimply faced, female two striper looked up. "Can I help you captain?"

Cramer nodded. "I'd like to request an assignment."

"What kind of assignment, Sir."

"Classified. Who handles those?"

She turned, and pointed behind her. "Sergeant Peters. Last cubicle on the right."

He thanked her, then walked down the aisle, reading the placards and name plates on each desk. Inside the last railed off cubicle, a skinny, dark haired sergeant named Peters still had a piece of tissue plastered to this morning's shaving cut. He made a half-hearted effort to rise as Cramer stopped in front of the desk. "What can I do for you captain?"

Cramer motioned for the clerk to remain seated. "I want to volunteer for a project called Jungle Jim," he said.

Peters smiled weakly as he sank back into his chair. "I'm not familiar with that project Sir."

"That's what I figured you'd say."

Peters' eyebrows lifted as he made an obvious effort to look innocent. "I don't even know where to look captain."

He leaned on the desk, and looked down at the man. "Sarge, don't bullshit me. I'm not a novice at this game. I've got a right to request any assignment I'm qualified for. It's your job to take care of the paper work. I'll give you some time to look this up, but I'll be back."

He turned, and left the building, already modifying his plans. Obviously, a more subtle approach was needed. Ordinarily, an enlisted man couldn't withhold information from an officer. But info about classified projects could be kept secret, unless the officer had a need to know. The sergeant could side-step him forever on this one, with no fear of reprisal. In this situation, banging on doors, or pressing his nose against the glass was no way to get anywhere. He needed to become less of an outsider. Familiarity might breed contempt, but it could also build camaraderie, and a bridge to opportunity.

In the following days, he dropped into Personnel for random visits, studying the bulletin board, and checking on other openings, seemingly shopping around. During each visit he managed to engage Sergeant Peters in conversation, and encouraged him to air his gripes, adding his own examples of how, he too, had experienced frustrations during his enlisted service.

Gradually, the sergeant's attitude softened. Finally one afternoon, he met Cramer at the Coke machine in the break room, requested confidentiality, and admitted in a subdued voice, that there was indeed, a program called Jungle Jim.

Major Evans stopped tapping his pencil, took his feet off his desk, and sighed as he shifted position. The overhead light reflected off his bald spot as he leaned over his blotter, looked up and shook his head.

"I've got to hand it to you captain. I've never seen anyone more determined to get into a program. Apparently, if I don't get you out of here, my people are never going to get anything done." He leaned back, turned to the right, and barked, "Sergeant Waggoner!"

The tortured spring of a swivel chair squeaked in the adjoining room, and seconds later, a tall, lanky, red haired staff sergeant came through the archway. "Yes sir."

"Make out an application for project Jungle Jim for Captain Cramer."

Waggoner drew his head back, giving himself a hint of a double chin as he gave the Major a skeptical squint. "According to the shoulder patch on the captain's flying suit, he's a SAC crewmember."

"So?"

Waggoner shrugged, and turned his palms up. "Sir...you know what I mean. That command holds onto their people no matter what. With all due respect, it's a waste of time. They'll shit-can it for sure."

The major scowled, tore a page from his scratch pad, then reached out and handed him the paper. "Sarge...let the latrine orderly worry about the shit-can. You type the form."

"Whatever you say, sir." Waggoner took the page, and nodded at Cramer. "Come next door captain, we'll give it a shot."

Cramer smiled at the major. "I really appreciate this sir."

Evans leaned back in his chair, put his feet on his desk, and folded his hands in his lap. "Thanks. But don't get your hopes up, Captain. You're not the first SAC crewmember to come in here looking for a way out of that tyrannical Command. I don't know of a single one who's made it."

The flight planning room smelled as musty as ever, when Cramer entered, looked up, and scanned a number of listings on the board, looking for his name. Damn. There it was. Another tour in Greenland. This time a week early. He went to his in-basket picked up his flight plan, lifted the cover, and scanned page one. En-route, there'd be a night, air refueling with a B-47, just west of Newfoundland.

Dixon came up behind him, unzipped the left arm pocket of his flying suit, and extracted a lighter, and cigarettes. "Heard anything about that assignment?"

He shook his head. "It's still too early."

Dixon flipped the lid of his Zippo, thumbed the wheel, and set fire to the end of a Winston, as he stretched his neck, and looked at the form. "For Chrissake, captain. Look at that fuel load. We'll be lucky to get there with dry tanks."

Cramer waved the smoke away from his face. "If you're looking for an easy job, get out of SAC."

"Fat chance."

Their navigator, Captain Don Morino, tall, perpetually calm, and darkly handsome, came into the room, sat his satchel down, reached inside his briefcase, and pulled out a fistful of forms. Cramer sat down across from him, opened the performance section of his dash one, and the crew began their usual, mind-numbing slog through the flight planning charts. Two hours later, he stuffed the completed paperwork back into his briefcase, and nodded toward the break room.

"Let's go have some coffee," he said.

Once seated around the horseshoe shaped coffee bar, they talked about the job. Even though he'd done this countless times, Cramer still looked forward to it. It was one of the few perks he could count on. In a way, it didn't figure. He'd always wanted a family, and these guys were the only family he had. And now, he was doing his best to leave them. Well...family or not, he still had to do it. The specter of that B-26 wouldn't stop haunting him. It wasn't just an intriguing plane anymore. It was a symbol of change, a chance for adventure, but most of all...a way to escape--start over--alter the course of his life, and leave the memories of Sandy, and Otis behind.

Would it all work out? There was no way to tell. Maybe the ponderous, plodding bureaucracy of Air Force Personnel was already printing his name on a set of orders...or perhaps, it simply chewed up his application and spit it out.

CHAPTER SIX

It was pitch dark, and near freezing as Tech Sergeant Martin flopped down on the boom pod ironing board, squashing the thin, cold-soaked mattress against his belly. Thank God he'd be there for less than half an hour. He brought his panel to life, lifted the ruddevator control stick, took the weight off the boom latch, then reached over, and unlocked it. After that, he lowered the boom to the in-flight trail position.

With every breath, he blew a thin fog, and his boom mike already felt cold, and clammy against his lips. Martin worked the controls, flying the long silver pipe around the envelope, making a circle, checking freedom of movement, and his gauges. The big tanker reacted, wallowing in a gentle, fish tail motion.

He pushed the extension lever, telescoping the heavy pipe outward, moving it to the 10 foot, ready for contact position, then punched a button, checked the blue Ready light, and peered into the darkness, searching for the incoming bomber.

Nav already had it on his equipment. They'd be radio silence all the way. In close, pilot director lights on the tanker's belly would do the talking.

Martin smiled smugly. Best enlisted job in the Air Force. No other non-com got more respect, or more responsibility...and the flying pay wasn't bad either.

The navigator's voice crackled in his earphones, "He's here, boomer." Martin lowered his head alongside the ironing board, tipped it back until his neck hurt, peered out the black window, and searched the darkness.

Finally, there it was, sliding in--a slender, sinister looking, shadowy hulk, the scream of its six jets wiped out by the thunderous roar of the '97's huge, straining engines. Here she came, moving closer, the faintly lit, open slipway door forming a tiny platform protruding from her nose. Not much to aim at--no margin for error.

Three thousand pounds of hydraulic pressure, ready and waiting, enough to ram that big, stainless steel nozzle through a solid brick wall. Night or day, good weather or bad, smooth or bumpy, it made no difference. From this point on, the ball was in his court. Screw it up--miss the slot-- punch a hole--things would explode, and people would die.

Martin waved the boom gently, up and down, signaling ready for contact.

Now he could look down into the bomber's cockpit--the dim glow of the jet's instruments reflecting on a shadowy, ghost-like figure deftly working the bomber's controls. Golden oak leaves on gray-clad shoulders meant he was either an old man of 35, or some bright young captain with a spot promotion. Whoever he was, he was good. In she came, closer, ever closer, until he parked her there, like she was some kind of permanent fixture.

Martin lined it up, and made his move. Pressure hissed through lines as the long shiny tube reached out for its fragile objective.

The bomber wallowed softly as the nozzle grounded on the slipway door, and Martin slid it home with a soft, satisfying thunk. Panel lights jumped from blue to green. Up front, the engineer moved his lever, sending a thick stream of JP-4 gushing into the bomber at twelve drums a minute.

Finally, she was full. A puff of vapor blew from the slipway, as the boom disconnected, then telescoped inward, and thunked against the stop. Martin held the boom to one side, and watched her slide slowly backward, losing herself in the darkness. Man, what an airplane. A no longer thirsty, nuclear laden phantom, roaming the dark, in a secret, cocked and ready prowl.

Below them, Frobisher Bay looked dark, and foreboding, its icy, windswept surface still hidden in the earth's shadow. Finally, the first faint glimmer of daylight cracked the horizon to the southeast as they crossed Hall Peninsula, and made their way over the frigid, wind tossed waves of Davis Strait, on the north side of the Labrador sea. Thirty minutes later the Navigator gave Cramer a new heading to Sondrestrom, and they continued flying eastward with a feeble, slowly evolving sunrise off to the right.

Weather reported a solid overcast as they approached the isolated base situated ninety miles inland on the edge of an ice choked fjord. Sondrestrom was a mean-assed place to get into, with a mountain rising steeply at the end of the 9000 foot runway. Had to land on the first try. No go-arounds there.

The reported 3500 overcast with three miles visibility, was barely good enough for the weather. Cramer reduced power, and began the high altitude portion of his let-down in clear air, with the engineer grumbling fitfully about carb heat, and trying to keep his engines out of the icing range.

Power had been reduced, and airspeed changed, so Cramer reached for the elevator trim wheel, and rolled in an adjustment to ease the heavy feeling of his controls.

The complex demands of physics, and aerodynamics were relentless. Changes in pitch--power--airspeed--weight, or center of gravity--all required adjustments in trim. If someone walks to the back--trim. When they walk back front, trim again. Ignore the process, and the controls became unbearably heavy, requiring a frenzied, distracting effort to catch up.

Passing 12,000 feet, they plunged into cloud, and the universe closed in on them, its boundaries now defined by cold soaked aluminum and frosted glass. Shuddering, choppy little jolts pounded them, and Cramer noticed a faint, sporadic chatter as his instrument panel danced in its dynafocal mounts.

Finally, Approach Control handed them off to GCA. The controller came on, and Cramer followed the nerve soothing directions of his monotone voice, making the necessary changes in heading, and altitude.

Several minutes later, they rolled out on final, descending below the weather into a gray, dismal box canyon. Ahead, the mountain towered ominously, an intimidating, insurmountable, snow covered dead end.

The airstrip seemed badly misplaced, its topography distorted by rugged terrain. From the approach end, snow packed asphalt climbed a hill, rising steeply--90 feet in the first one third of its length, before leveling off for the remaining 6000. On low final, the uphill grade rose above them, hiding the remaining mile, making the strip appear far too short.

He ignored the illusion, closed the throttles, and flared, touching down smoothly at the 1000 foot marker. The uphill roll killed much of their speed, and after topping the crest, he reversed the props, and stayed off the brakes, as the plane lost momentum. Finally, he needed power just to make the turn-off.

He taxied slowly, mindful of the slippery footing as the crew ran their checklists. Nearing the ramp, he turned cautiously into the parking area, following the waving, orange wands of a fur lined, parka clad Sergeant standing on hard packed snow. Dense puffs of breath rose above the parker's frosty mask as Cramer eased carefully into the spot, and stopped with a light touch of brake.

The instant the last prop stopped turning, the ground crew surged forward, pulling bulky heaters, and insulated tarps to protect the engines from the sub-zero cold. At 53 below, engine oil doesn't stay fluid for long.

Following shutdown, everyone grabbed their bags, and boarded the heavily insulated bus. Cramer sat in front, as the roaring, double heater fought a loosing battle against the cold. Visibility through side windows was restricted, reduced to a narrow three inch strip by added insulation. Only the windshield was left unchanged. A prudent concession to the driver's need for an unrestricted view.

Outside, Sondrestrom looked as bleak, and depressing as ever. Across the runway the new glass, and aluminum, Danish hotel was off-limits to horny, American G Is--though their protective presence was reportedly much appreciated. American airmen might be drunken, and uncouth, but they were a hell of a lot better than anyone the Russians would send.

On the American side of the runway, more than a dozen, drab wooden buildings of varying size, lined snow packed streets, squeezed in between the flight line and the cliff above the ice choked fjord.

The bus drove slowly, heading toward the old, wooden Danish hotel that now served as the SAC flight crew quarters. Once there, everyone grabbed their bags, scrambled off the bus, and hurried inside, eager to escape the brutal cold.

Balding, round faced, Staff Sergeant Kroft sitting behind the counter, nodded cordially, and held up a key. "Room seven this time, Captain. I'll bet you could hardly wait to get back huh?"

Cramer dropped his bags, reached across the counter, and took his key. "I don't mind the peace, and quiet Sarge, but you ought to do something about getting a few women up here. I could use the company."

Kroft grinned as Cramer picked up his bags. "You're out of luck captain. The nearest available woman is 135 miles away, and she probably wouldn't give you the time of day...unless you had a dead seal under your arm."

"Damn. Now you tell me. If I'd known that, I'd have brought my harpoon."

Kroft gave him a sly grin. "I could loan you my binoculars, and you could stand in the snow and maybe catch a glimpse of the Danish Commander's wife. I hear she's a real beauty. 'Course I can't vouch for that personally. He never lets her come near us."

"Sounds like a smart man," Cramer said. He turned, and started down the hallway, lugging his bags, and searching for room seven.

Everyone made jokes about the hotel's chaotic floor plan. Some rooms were nearly isolated, connected by windowless, meandering corridors that cornered at odd angles, destroying a man's sense of direction, making rapid egress during an alert, a by guess, and by God proposition. What a screwed up place. Finally he found his room, squeezed inside, threw his heavy bags on the bed, and scanned the tiny cubicle. Warm air from the overhead vent poured down his neck, but at floor level there was frost in the corners.

Well, at least it was private. With thick insulation, and widely separated rooms, he wouldn't have to worry about disturbing anyone if he had the nightmare.

He'd have to be careful about that from now on. Dixon was right. Even if most people overlooked it, there'd always be those who'd run their mouth, and exaggerate his problem. If you were trying to outdo someone, casting doubt on their mental stability was a sure way to cut them down. The charge alone, could end his career.

CHAPTER SEVEN

Cramer zipped up his parka, checked himself in the full length lobby mirror to make sure there was no exposed skin, then left the building. Ten steps out the door, he could already feel the brutal cold creeping into his multi-layered winter gear. Ahead, a few blocks away, the small, wood-frame Officers Club was visible in the street lights.

With no wind, the short walk ought to be safe enough, he figured. Underfoot, the snow was hard packed, and his heavy boots made muffled, clunking sounds as he took each step. The hair in his nose was beginning to stiffen, already frosty from his frozen breath.

Beyond the club, sat the small Base Exchange, the feeble light from it's one, tiny, ice encrusted window shining like a ghostly, glazed over beacon. Normally reserved for American service men, here, exchange rules were modified. In accordance with a local Danish Status of Forces agreement, the Eskimo population was allowed to buy any American goods they could afford--an understandable concession to a hardy, but impoverished people living on the raw edge of a brutal environment.

Greenland Eskimo children grew up early. Those who managed to survive, possessed stoic courage, and awesome determination.

He remembered last summer, when the BX officer pointed out a 13 year old Eskimo girl, barely four feet tall. She stood next to her five year old brother, the both of them staring wide-eyed at a show case filled with marvels from America.

The two of them had traveled unaccompanied, 135 miles from their village, in a fragile skin boat, paddling down the rocky, wave swept, southwestern coast of Greenland, then up the long, uninhabited Fjord to Sondrestrom. More than three days they'd spent getting there, including three, nearly freezing, arctic summer nights, sleeping huddled together, on wet rocks, underneath the shelter of their overturned boat. Endured all of that--just to buy their beloved, thirty year old mother, treasures from America--a dozen genuine, stainless steel needles, and a few precious yards of printed, woven cloth. What an incredible illustration of love, and family devotion. When he compared it to the relationship he'd had with his aunt, and uncle, the contrast left him in awe.

Suddenly, he realized he had passed the club. He stopped, turned woodenly, like an overstuffed robot, and back-tracked toward the building. Once there, he reached for the handle, pulled the heavy door open, then slammed it hard behind him, as Lester Lanin's rendition of Moonlight Becomes You, played on the juke-box.

Small by Stateside standards, the Club was nevertheless well done, with two moderately sized rooms decorated in excellent taste. In the middle of the horseshoe shaped bar, rows of fine crystal, and an admirable selection of brand name booze lined the well stocked shelves.

He took off his heavy outer wear, and hung it up. Damn. Nothing in the Arctic was done without a struggle. Finally, feeling pounds lighter, he stepped over, eased onto a stool, leaned on the padded armrest, and tossed a twenty on the finely polished walnut. "Gimme a CC and soda," he said.

A solemn looking, blond headed, Sergeant Peters, ten months into his tour, was moonlighting behind the bar. It was interesting to see the contrast between the way he looked now, and the way he was when his one year ordeal began. Formerly up-beat, and cheerful, he now moved like an automaton, his expression emotionless with that deep winter, long distance stare. He listlessly poured the drink, sat it on the bar, then silently took the money. Cramer reached for the glass, and took a sip. Good. Rich. Heavy on the booze--light on the soda. Just right. He'd better damn well enjoy it. Tonight would be his last snort until he got back to Otis. The rules were strict. On alert, no booze for the crews. Even worse, the prospect for female companionship was zero. He shook his head, and sighed. It was going to be a long two weeks.

Next morning, Cramer, and his men sat quietly in the theatre with five other crews, as the Reflex Commander, a slim, gray haired, ramrod straight, Lieutenant Colonel Givins, wound down his briefing. Givins, turned his head slowly, his eyes sweeping the room. "As usual, immediately after this briefing, all pilots, and navigators will take a thirty question test on Positive Control procedures." His eyes narrowed as he added, "I remind you...the only acceptable grade is one hundred percent!"

Major Clifford's fuzzy cheeked, gawky looking, new navigator, slowly raised a hand, and the colonel recognized him with a curt nod.

"Sir, that seems a bit austere. What if we just make a mistake? I mean like inadvertently marking the wrong answer?"

Givins' look hardened. "That's tough shit lieutenant. A wrong answer, is a wrong answer. Make just one, and you, and your entire crew will go before Major General Clark, for what will, no doubt, be a monumental ass chewing, and the subsequent demotion of your aircraft commander to co-pilot status."

"But sir..."

The colonel barked, "RTFQ! Read the fucking question! And by God, you had better double check your answers. There are no second chances on this. Do you understand?"

The lieutenant sank slowly into his seat. "Yes sir."

A sardonic smile covered his face as Givins scanned the crowd. "And now for the good news kiddies. Perhaps you noticed that sleek looking KC-135 sitting on the ramp when you did your preflight this morning."

An enthusiastic rumble filled the room. Givins chuckled. "Isn't she an inspiring sight? Four gleaming jets. Swept-back wings. They tell me a B-47 has to literally beg her to slow down during refueling. Something for all of us to shoot for, right?

"Damn right colonel!"

Givins' expression twisted into a cynical smile. "Well...sad to say, she's not here on a motivational tour. Early this morning, from inside her guts she puked out a group most foul and evil. A dastardly band with hearts as cold, and dark as the long nights of winter. The vermin are upon us lads. CEG slithered in here last night."

"Jesus Christ!" The room reverberated in a storm of grumbling, and mumbled oaths. Givins chuckled, "Yes indeed...SAC has done it again. The highly revered Combat Evaluation Group from SAC Headquarters has paid us a surprise visit. Now isn't that lovely?"

Major Thorn, his face florid, stood up, and shouted angrily, "What the hell are those bastards doing up here? That's all we need, a bunch of professional hatchet men coming in to fuck all over us. What are they gonna do, launch us and give us a checkride?"

The colonel raised his hand to quiet the room. "No! No, they can't launch you. Your alert posture is too critical. But they will expect a briefing. I hope you studied your assigned mission thoroughly."

"How much time do we get for review?" Thorn asked.

"You've had your time for review, major. There'll be no more. You brief immediately following your positive control test."

Cramer leaned toward Dixon. "That's what I like about this outfit. They never run out of ways to play, you bet your ass."

CHAPTER EIGHT

Cramer flinched as a full colonel burst abruptly through the door, followed by a glowering light colonel, two majors, and a captain.

"Tenhut!" His crew rose, each man assuming a rigid brace, staring blankly ahead. The team, looking as friendly as Gestapo, scanned them as they walked by, then took their seats in the front row.

The colonel broke the ice. "At ease gentlemen, take your seats. Captain, you may begin your briefing immediately."

Cramer stepped to the front of the room, turned his back to the blackboard, and faced the glowering team.

"Gentlemen. Assume we have just been alerted, and have reached aircraft. The cocking checklists have already been run. The co-pilot copies the alert message. The navigator, and I copy as well, and all three check the code, then verify its authenticity by comparing the results. If everything checks, we know the launch order is valid. The war is on." He turned, snapped his pointer against the map, and looked back at the inspectors. "After starting engines, we takeoff with a fifteen second interval between aircraft, and depart Sondrestrom, with each plane picking up the route for its own particular mission..."

After the first few minutes, his apprehension vanished. He could do this by God. Why not? He'd been in tankers longer than any son of a bitch in this room--learned the business from the ground up, from the back of that Goddamned greasy old plane to the front. No one in here knew more about tankers than he did, regardless of what they wore on their shoulders. They might ask him a trick question, and trip him up, but as long as they stuck to pertinent facts he had them by the balls.

He continued for 20 minutes, the sound of his voice filling the room as he described each succeeding phase--cruise to rendezvous, refueling, and clearing track, as well as landing at the planned recovery base. Following that, he covered the route to the alternates, plus bailout, and ground assembly of his crew if both bases were blown off the face of the earth before he reached them.

The unsmiling panel stared at him, silently, intently, mercilessly, waiting...almost daring him to make a mistake. Finally, he summed up. "Are there any questions gentlemen?"

The full bird nodded, and awarded him a tight-lipped smile. "Good briefing captain. Now let's deal with a hypothetical. You arrive at your aircraft after being alerted. While running to your plane, your boom operator slips on the ice, and falls backward, cracking his skull open. You try to rouse him, but he doesn't respond..."

"Is he dead?"

The colonel's smile broadened. "Yes. Yes, let's say he's dead. What do you do now?"

"I'll drag him over to the side so we don't run over the body when we taxi out, and I'll continue the mission, sir."

The colonel snorted, "Why? What the hell for? Your boom operator is dead, captain. Who's going to make the hookup? Who's going to refuel your bomber?"

"I will sir. I'll have my co-pilot fly the plane, and I'll make the hookup."

The colonel gave him a skeptical, sideways look. "Oh Really? We select the best NCO's in this command, and train them for months before they make their first unsupervised hookup. What makes you think you can do it cold turkey? How many hookups have you made?"

"Over 650 sir. I'm an ex instructor boom operator."

The colonel's jaw dropped, as a shocked silence filled the room. Finally, he laughed, and shook his head. "Talk about surprise. I walked into that one with my eyes open."

Now the weasely looking, Light Colonel with the wire frame, glasses wanted to play. "Could we have the rest of the crew leave the room colonel?" he said. "I have a confidential question for the captain."

The colonel nodded, and Cramer's crew, clearly relieved, got up and left.

As soon as the door closed behind the last man, the light colonel cleared his throat. "How well do you, and your navigator get along captain?"

"Very well sir. I consider him a friend."

"Do you know his wife?"

What was this asshole driving at? "Yes sir. She's...she's a fine woman, and a good mother."

"You're acquainted with his kids too, I take it?"

Cramer nodded. "Yes sir."

The junior colonel looked craftily at the ceiling, pursed his lips, then looked back at him. "Let's say you're on the way to meet your bomber. Your navigator comes up behind you, and puts the barrel of his thirty eight behind your ear--says he doesn't want to refuel a bomber that's going to kill a million people. Tells you to dump the bomber's fuel, and abort the mission. What's your reaction?"

He shrugged. "It's not a tough call, colonel. Our bomber might be scheduled to take out a Russian outfit that could kill three or four million Americans."

"Granted. But obviously, your navigator doesn't give a shit about that. How do you convince him to change his mind."

"If he's gone that far, I probably can't. So, I'll tell him I feel the same way he does. After that, I'll ask him to go back to his seat, and figure out a heading to Sweden. When he turns to leave, I'll pull out my thirty eight, put three shots in the middle of his back, and continue the mission according to flight plan."

The full bird rose abruptly. "Gentlemen, we've taken enough of this crew's time." He nodded curtly. "Congratulations captain. You passed this test. But don't get complacent. There'll be a lot more tests in your future. And you'd better be ready when they come. In SAC, everyone's career hangs by a thread."

Cramer snapped to attention as they filed out. After the door closed, he paused, making sure they were gone, then left the room. In the hallway, he stopped in front of Dixon, and shook his head. "What a bunch of pricks. I wish Sandy could have worked for this outfit for just one day. Maybe she'd have understood why I lavished so much attention on my friggin' job."

CHAPTER NINE

The front had passed the Cape just after dark, and a million stars were out when Cramer slammed the door of his Buick, and walked eagerly toward the Club. Talk about cold. First Sondrestrom, now this. Snow crunched under his feet as he walked, and he shivered under his heavy coat, wondering if he'd ever get warm again. It was hell coming out on a night like this, even if it was Saturday. But, two dry weeks on Reflex was enough. Cold or not, it was time for a drink.

Noted for its food, and entertainment, the Otis Officers Club was a busy place. Tonight, there'd be a band, and that meant unattached women. Maybe he'd get lucky.

Once inside, he headed for the bar. Sandy haired, athletic looking, Captain Al Greenwood, one of the Squadron's navigators sat on the corner stool, slowly stirring his drink--had on his favorite outfit--medium brown pants, gold tie, and dark brown sport coat. It seemed like a long time since they were second lieutenants on Major Johnson's crew.

As he approached, Greenwood looked up, waved him over, and asked with a crooked smile, "How was Sondrestrom?"

"Worse than usual," he grumbled. "This time we had a visit from CEG."

Greenwood chuckled. "Heard about that. Nasty bunch of bastards huh?"

Cramer grunted as he slid onto the stool, and put one elbow on the bar. "I can't figure it out. Did those guys become assholes after they got that job, or were they always that way?"

Al shook his head. "Who knows? Kinda like the chicken or the egg riddle huh?"

A chubby, bald headed, red jacketed bartender approached, and Cramer ordered a CC, and soda. Greenwood raised his eyebrows. "No doubles tonight?"

He shook his head. "I've had enough of that. Can't stand the hangovers. Besides, getting hammered isn't going to bring her back. It's time to move on." He looked sideways at Greenwood, and moved to change the focus of the discussion. "You still getting married next month?"

Al tipped his drink up, swallowed, and smiled faintly as he set the glass on the bar. "Yep. Hope it works out better than the first time. Anyway, she says she'll be different than Lisa. Claims she can handle the separations. We'll see."

Cramer winced as a trumpet blast announced the band's opening number, ending any chance for a conversation that wasn't a shouting match. As he finished his second drink, he noticed a stunning girl in a tight, brown knit, dress, sitting with a middle aged couple. After the old folks got up to trip the light fantastic, he made a bee line for the table, and asked her to dance.

She smiled sweetly, and rose slowly, revealing a form that was nothing short of breath taking. As they worked their way through the crowd, he belatedly realized she looked a bit young.

On the floor, she moved in quickly, pressing herself against him like a long lost lover. The firm curves of her youthful body aroused him, and his organ hardened. Good God! A teenager on his first night out, and all he could think about was how good she felt moving against him.

Finally he got himself under control, and began the get acquainted routine. The specifics were less than encouraging. She looked like high school kid, because that's what she was. Fifteen years old, by God-- wouldn't be sixteen until spring, and as predatory as any woman he ever met.

When he loosened his grip on her, she tightened her grip on him, pressed her pelvis against him and gave it a little twist, to make his arousal complete. By the time they were into the third number, sweat trickled down the side of his face, and he felt like everyone in the club was watching. Finally the band took a break, and he walked her back to the table. As she slid into her seat, he thanked her, and told her she was a terrific dancer, then quickly excused himself, and slipped quietly back to the bar.

As he took his seat, Greenwood turned his head, and smiled evilly. "Nice looking girl."

He felt his face getting warm. "Yeah. She's a little young though."

Greenwood chuckled, and gave him the needle. "She didn't seem to mind the age difference."

"I'm not getting involved with a teenager," he grumbled.

"Maybe your neighbor would like a shot at it."

"Neighbor?"

"You know Stan, the F101 pilot. The one who's married to that good looking nurse."

"You mean Janet Shaw?" Cramer said.

"Yeah, her husband." Al cocked his head to the right. "The one sitting at the corner table holding hands with Bedford's wife."

He leaned back, and looked past Greenwood. "That's par for the course for him," he said. "He's tried to make out with every wife on the base, including mine. Officer's wives, enlisted wives, it makes no difference. He's persona non grata in every quadraplex on the base."

The blast of a trumpet marked the band's return, ending any possibility for further conversation.

An hour later, Cramer downed the last of his third drink, and scanned the room. Three women were just sitting down a couple of tables away. One looked particularly interesting, so he got up, walked over and asked her to dance.

She was a good looking woman, trim, with brown hair, and a nice

30

smile. Not beautiful, but neat, and well groomed. Danced well too. When the band changed pace to a slow number he did the get acquainted routine.

At first it was a tough go. He'd been out of circulation for so long it was difficult to relate to a strange woman. She solved the problem by breaking the news that she, and the other two women, were girlfriends of the musicians. When the second number ended, he thanked her, squeezed her hand, and escorted her back to her table.

He slid back onto his barstool, and ordered drink number four, noticing for the first time that the barkeep gave it an extra little jolt after the shot glass had already run over. Nothing like having friends in the right places.

What the hell, two weeks on alert with no booze, he figured he had it coming. Unfortunately, something else was nagging him now. He punched Greenwood lightly on the shoulder.

"Dammit why'd you have to mention Janet Shaw? Now I can't get her out of my mind."

Greenwood smiled evilly. "So...you've got the hots for Lieutenant Shaw, you lecherous bastard. Shame on you. She's a married woman, and you're sitting here wallowing in carnal desire. Lusting for her firm young flesh."

Cramer laughed. "No, dammit. It's not that. I mean it's not only that. She's a great person. Really! One of the nicest people I've ever met. I lived next door to her for two years." He waived defensively. "Yeah, sure I was happily married, but that didn't make me like Janet any less."

Greenwood raised his eyebrows. "Sounds like you may be in love, ol' buddy. You've had just enough booze to loosen up, but you're not so drunk you don't know what you're saying."

"You're not going to tell anyone are you?"

Greenwood reached out, and gripped his shoulder. "Did you tell anyone about the secretary I was rooming with in Torrejon?"

"Of course not."

"Then why would I tell anyone about this?"

Cramer slid off the barstool. "Well, that's a relief. Anyway...I've got to go to the boy's room. After that, I think I'll look around."

Greenwood nodded, and gave him a little wave. "See you later."

After Cramer came out of the restroom, he checked the small lounge. The place was packed, but on the far side, Janet Shaw was sitting, with two other women. She spotted him, and waved. It was the only invitation he needed. He crossed the room, nodded cordially to the others, then looked at Janet. Looking at Janet was easy to do. The tough part was making sure he didn't over do it.

"Do you have time for a dance with an old friend?" he asked.

"Of course." She excused herself, stood up, and he fell in behind her as she made her way to the dance floor. That alone, made it worth the trip.

Nobody walked like Janet. This woman was graceful. She didn't twist, or jiggle, or clack along with that tiny little stagger like most women in high heels, she just...glided. She was neat, and trim, and her short black hair, and dark eyes made an alluring combination. Everything about her seemed to fit in with everything else. But the nicest thing about her was the way she acted, the way she treated people.

The band started a slow, dreamy number, he took her in his arms, and she moved with him like she could read his mind. They danced like that for two more numbers. Finally, he looked down at her, seeing her lovely face in the soft light, her eyes closed, and he kissed her softly...and she didn't pull away, she held it. But finally it was over, she turned her face, held her lips to his ear, and said softly, "I liked that John, I really did. But we can't do this. And even if we could, we couldn't do it here."

In the following months Cramer didn't see Janet again. Not much surprise there. He didn't live in family housing anymore, and she seldom went to the club. She worked long hours at the hospital, and his schedule was becoming increasingly demanding. Regardless of that, she'd made it clear she had no intention of becoming involved with him, so he did his best to concentrate on other things.

Cold War tension was building rapidly. Following the Cuban missile crisis, SAC increased the pressure on its already overburdened flight crews, and off duty time all but vanished. Now, with alert, simulator, ground training, and a busy flying schedule, he was spending 80 to 90 hours a week on duty.

The long awaited request for Project Jungle Jim, was never answered. Finally, restless in what seemed like a dead end job in aging tankers, he decided to apply for KC-135 school.

Admittedly, it was a long shot. Not all of his extensive experience in KC-97s would be considered when he competed for the new assignment. Pilot applications were standardized, and seldom took the unusual into account. Few enlisted crewmembers went on to become pilots, and the system gave no special recognition to the background of those who did.

The rest of the personnel clerks in the room were sitting on straight backed, ass numbing chairs, that after a few hours must have seemed like torture racks, so it was hard to figure how a two striper rated a padded, tip back, swivel model.

The skinny, young freckle faced clerk looked up at him, and said in a smug, condescending manner, "Captain, the minimum pilot time for a KC-135 aircraft commander's seat is 1500 hours. You're only ten hours above that."

"So?"

32

The arrogant little asshole leaned back in his chair, and tossed his pencil on the desk, with an air of finality. "Sir...even the best qualified applicants have been waiting two years or more."

Cramer struggled to hold his irritation in check, and keep his voice even. "Stick time isn't the only thing that makes a good pilot."

The two striper gave him a dismissive wave. "Maybe so Captain. But I don't know what else you can cite to justify selection."

He stepped forward, and pointed at the typewriter. "Try this. I've been in KC-97s for ten years, and served in every crew position except navigator. It's time to move on."

The Airman, shook his head. "Sir...that's not going to help."

"It'll damn sure get their attention." Cramer leaned on the desk, pointed to the form, and scowled. "Goddammit! Enough of this. Shut up, and do it!"

The clerk jerked himself erect, machine-gunned the letters into the proper space, then snatched the paper from the roller, tipped his nose up and snipped, "This was a wasted effort, Captain. You don't have the chance of a snowball in hell."

"We'll see," Cramer grumbled. "We'll see."

CHAPTER TEN

It was hard to believe, but obviously, somewhere in the dark, sinister corridors of SAC Personnel, someone had a heart. In less than thirty days, the application for jet tankers came back approved, and Cramer gleefully began to pack his bags.

Training would be in two stages. First, he'd go to Atwater, California for six weeks of ground school, and after that to Roswell, New Mexico for a final six weeks of flying training.

He applied for leave time, requesting a thirty day delay en-route, and began the trip with high expectations. On the second evening, he spent the night in Fort Wayne, Indiana, then left early the next morning for Wabash, anticipating a nostalgic, three day stop in his home town.

Wabash, the first electrically lighted city in the world, hadn't changed-- a tree lined, mid-western, industrial town of twelve thousand, situated on the banks of a river with the same name. Stepped up in three levels, from south to north, its downtown area covered a few blocks in the middle tier.

At nine AM he parked his car across the street from the Eagles theatre, descended the outside basement steps of the Indiana hotel, and entered his old hangout. The Indiana Billiards, looked the same, smudged walls, massive pillars in the middle of a huge room, and four still surprisingly attractive pool tables.

A closed cigar box still rested in its customary place under the glass counter top, with, no doubt, an illegal punch board hidden inside--the arrangement common knowledge to all who gambled--including the police. Nevertheless, small town justice did occasionally, extract its toll. Every three or four years an apologetic cop would come down the stairs, and make an arrest. The owner would pay a small fine, the law would have been served, and life would go on. Even in straight-laced Indiana, the people were grudgingly granted their minor vices. It was nice to know some things never changed.

On the far side of the room, a long, ruled blackboard held the results of last fall's final World Series game, and a dust covered ticker tape silently waited to supply the stats of the coming season's events. In front of that, four circular card tables with green felt tops, their outer perimeters marred by burn stains inflicted by carelessly laid, then forgotten cigarettes.

Behind the counter, a lanky man with dandruff sprinkled hair, ignored the room as he leaned against the wall, cleaning his finger nails with a pen knife. Finally, Cramer laid some change on the counter, took a Coke out of the cooler, and quietly drank it, as he watched a pair of scruffy looking tree trimmers shoot too hard, miss their bank shots, and insult each other with profane good humor.

Eventually, he tired of it, and left, walking the streets, looking in store windows and searching the sidewalks for anyone he knew. After an uneventful hour, he stopped at the sweet shop for a cup of coffee. The same industrious Greek, still hustled behind the counter, and the place looked as clean as always, but no one he knew came in. He killed another hour just wandering around, then ate an early lunch in the Rock City Restaurant. It had been a long time since he'd had a pork tenderloin sandwich, but he resisted the urge for a second, and held himself to a single Bud.

Following lunch, he drove out of town on state road 13, and eight miles south, turned onto a gravel road. A couple of miles later, he crossed the rusty old bridge, high above the Mississinewa. On the far side, the small village of Somerset still looked neat, and serene.

The school had been great--three story brick, with twelve grades, a peaceful, all white student body, and dedicated teachers who actually managed to educate the kids. And now, a grateful, government was going to show its appreciation by building a dam, and covering it with water. His family was gone, and now, even his school would disappear. Suddenly, he felt an emptiness sweep over him. He was becoming a man with no roots.

Other than the scenery, the trip had been a bust so far. He hadn't seen a single individual he knew well. Obviously no one had put their life on hold waiting for the great John Cramer to return. He felt like a stranger in the place where he grew up.

Finally, the nagging in back of his mind couldn't be put off any longer. He turned onto the gravel road leading to his uncle's farm, heading for a visit he dreaded, but knew he had to make.

During the three mile drive, the farms he passed, appeared unchanged--most of them, close to the road with two story, twenties style houses, graveled driveways and meticulously maintained barns.

The home place was never the same after his folks were killed. How his aunt, and uncle got it, he wasn't quite sure. Maybe the judge was on the take...or...maybe, he was just taken in. Bible thumpers always put on a good act. They knew when to be on their best behavior. Most were fearful of power, and quaked in its presence. Government or God, it made no difference.

He remembered how they acted in the judges chambers--warm and considerate--loving--caring. He could still hear their words echoing in the walnut paneled, high ceilinged room. "We'll give him a good Christian home," they said, in that whining, ass kissing tone.

He shook his head. Poor bastards. It never got better for them. They spent their lives quivering--waiting for the Devil to come out of the ground, and drag them to Hell. Small wonder they took their fears out on him.

He remembered what Sunday's were like...especially when the preacher came. They really grilled him then, made him perform. He'd try to keep quiet, but they'd force him to talk--ask questions--make him recite. Inevitably he'd make some minor verbal transgression, and they'd respond with shocked faces, and stern lectures. Warnings about wholesome thoughts,

35

and getting right with God. After his uncle died, it only got worse.

Passing the neighbor's farm, the formerly red barn, was now painted white. Other than that, little had changed. Finally, here it came...the property. His pulse quickened, pounding in his chest, and temples, and he hated himself for the re-action. Somehow, it seemed almost cowardly, this...apprehension, that bordered on fear. For God's sake, what was there to be afraid of? Just a spooky old house, and a cranky old woman.

Resentment filled him as he did his best to concentrate on the scenery. In the southeast corner, the old Sycamore was still standing, now minus a couple of limbs. A quarter mile beyond, he slowed, and turned into the driveway.

A mangy, yellow dog rushed from the hedge, chasing beside him, growling, and snapping at the front wheel. He stopped, shut off the engine, and the mutt backed off, still barking viciously. He sat there quietly, wondering if it would bite.

Finally he turned toward the house. God, it looked awful. Run down--peeling paint--the rotting center post dangling from the sagging porch roof, its adjustable foot, long since rusted away. Upstairs in the front room, a crack zig-zagged across the window, ending in a three inch hole. Bird strike? Who knew? High on the steeply pitched roof, two slates were hanging precariously, cocked at a crazy angle, waiting to slide free, and shatter with the others on the stone walk below.

He remembered how homey it looked when his parents were alive. Now, it seemed foreboding, sinister...almost haunted.

His stomach ached. The urge to go seemed overpowering, but somehow, he couldn't leave. By now she must have seen him. He'd have to go in.

36

CHAPTER ELEVEN

Ten minutes, and still no sign of life. Damn dog hadn't missed a beat--still yapping like he'd never stop. Finally, Cramer opened the car door, stepped out, and snarled, "Shut up you son of a bitch!"

The mutt let out a yelp, tucked his tail, and slunk away like a whipped puppy. It figured. That's just the kind of dog they'd have.

He went up the flagstone walk, stepped on the porch, and knocked. Nothing happened. A minute later, he knocked harder. Finally the chintz curtains parted, and a muffled female voice croaked, "Who is it?'

"It's me, John."

The door opened a crack, and she peered out suspiciously. "Who?"

For Chrissake, he thought, she doesn't even know who I am. "It's me, Aunt Mary, your nephew...John. You know, the kid that used to live here." For a moment he considered saying something to soften the remark, but decided to let it stand.

"Oh...well...I wasn't expecting anyone."

"If you had a phone I would have called first."

"I don't need a phone," she snapped. "When I want to talk to someone I go to the store, or go to church. I don't need to talk to anyone else."

He took a deep breath, and struggled to keep his voice even. "Aunt Mary, are you going to let me in, or are we going to stand here, and talk through a crack in the door?"

"Oh well...I guess I can let you in."

She opened the door--barely. He squeezed through, and brushed by, then walked over to the big, round kitchen table, pulled out a chair, and sat down in his old place. The rancid smell of burned grease coming from the blackened skillet on the wood burning range, offered irrefutable proof that her prowess in the culinary arts had not improved. When he looked up, she was still standing there, holding the door open, staring at him with that perpetually sour look. "I don't have any coffee made," she grumbled.

"That's OK," he said. "I don't want any coffee."

"Well, what do you want?"

He had an overpowering urge to scream--I want out of this fucking place!--instead, he shrugged, and said quietly, "Nothing. I just came by to see how you were."

She said nothing. Finally she closed the door, and turned toward the table. He watched her as she moved. Nearly white headed, slightly overweight, wrinkled frown lines covering her perpetually sour face, the picture of a worried Christian, ground down by a lifetime pre-occupation with death.

She was only in her mid fifties, but she shuffled, stoop shouldered, and doddering, like an old lady. Well why not, he wondered, she acted like an old lady when she was thirty.

She pulled out the chair across from him, and sat down without scooting up to the table. Obviously she wasn't planning on him staying long. He figured that was one thing he could help her out with.

"So, how have you been?" he said.

"Fine. I eat good, and I go to church every chance I get." Her eyes narrowed and she gave him a penetrating look. "Do you go to church?"

There it was again. She hadn't changed a bit. "No. No I don't go to church. I'm never going to church again."

She leaned toward him, scowling fiercely, and snapped, "Then you're going to hell! Do you want to go to hell?"

"Sure don't. Too many preachers down there."

She glared at him, speechless, teeth clenched behind thin, white lips.

He'd had enough of this. He damn sure wasn't going to sit here, and argue religion. He waited a minute, then stood up, and said, "Well, I just came by to see how you were doing. You look good."

She said nothing, just sat there with that scowl on her face, watching him walk toward the door. He turned the knob, and looked back at her. "Take care of yourself. Good-by."

Still she said nothing, and the scowl never left her face. He went out the door, then closed it behind him. As the latch caught, he let out his breath. Suddenly a weight lifted from his shoulders. There was one good thing about this, he figured. He'd never have to do it again.

He left Indiana the next morning, traveling leisurely toward California, while admiring the scenery. The first day he indulged himself by eating lunch at a good restaurant. The meal was so enjoyable he decided to stop only at the best places along the way. Why not? He was an Air Force captain on flying pay. Money wouldn't be a problem. His divorce was final now, and Sandy hadn't asked for alimony. Greed had never been one of her faults, and she still had her career as a teacher. It was time to stop worrying about her.

This was America's heartland, hard working, conservative, and homey. Along the way, dozens of well kept, small towns, showed the pride of the people. In rural areas, farms with well tended fences, and neat, set aside woods, reflected the frugal, hardworking lifestyle of the residents. The fields looked seasonally dreary--still wet from melted snow and early spring rains, with corn stalks broken and shredded by last fall's mechanical picking. No matter. Soon they'd be dry enough for plow, disk and harrow—the dark, rich soil worked to the proper texture for planting. Shortly afterward, bright green shoots would break through the surface, seeking the sun in an age old cycle of renewal.

Crossing the bridge, high above the Mississippi, he drove slowly, marveling at the expanse of the rain swollen river, fascinated by an impossibly long line of barges being pushed by a straining tug boat. Later that day, he raced a short distance on one of Americas' slowly evolving interstate, highways. What a way to travel, and wouldn't it be great when all were finally finished?

The next morning he got up before sunrise, and drove a long stretch on route 66, then stopped for the night at a first rate motel in Amarillo, Texas. The place had a nice lounge, with a good band, and he bought drinks, and danced for a couple of hours with a sultry looking, dark haired girl in a short skirt, and cowboy boots. She had great legs, and her outfit showed them off with stunning effect.

She was attractive, pleasant, and a good dancer, but her questions made it obvious she was looking for mister right. It would have been easy to lie to her, and make her think he was moving into the local area, but he decided against that. His Air Force career made it unlikely he'd ever see her again. She probably wanted a family as much as he did, and he wasn't going to lie to a woman about something that important.

The evening ended in a short goodnight kiss, with her left arm around his waist, and her right hand holding the open door of her pickup.

Atwater was a neat, orderly town with clean streets, well kept shops and bulging, colorful groceries filled with the agricultural abundance of California. He arrived there with two weeks of leave time still unused, and decided to spend it wisely.

The base officers quarters were full, so, armed with a non-availability certificate, he rented a well furnished, one bedroom apartment in town. Entry was through a private driveway bordering on a small, wooded lot. If there were any children about, they were exceptionally quiet, and he rarely saw the neighbors. It was a good place to study. All things considered, it was a fortunate break. On base, he would have been lured into the club scene, and no doubt would have enjoyed himself immensely. But here, he could tend to business with few distractions.

The KC-135 was new on the line, and had already earned the reputation of being a demanding aircraft. It was big, complex and fast, and the Air Force rated it as--unforgiving--particularly on takeoff. With only 1500 hours of pilot time in his log, he knew he'd have to get the most from his schooling, or he'd never be able to command the plane. Training had to come first. He couldn't get that by making the rounds of bars, and clubs, so his social life would have to wait.

The day after arriving, he went to student supply, and checked out his flying manuals. After that, he spent the next two weeks of his leave pouring over the two thick books for twelve hours a day.

Castle Air Force base became one of the least memorable in his career. In spite of being well manicured, in his mind, it consisted of little but the classroom he spent so much time in. Lunch was gleaned daily from peanut butter, and cracker machines in the hallway. In the end, his Spartan lifestyle paid off, and he finished the rigorous ground school, a close second in his class.

When he transferred to sprawling, semi-arid Roswell, for the six week flying course, providence smiled. Short, thin and sandy haired, Major Bates, his instructor pilot, proved to be a man of unusual talent. Bates' knowledge of the huge tanker was awesome, his flying skill admirable, and his ability to communicate, remarkable. The Major's expert instruction, coupled with Cramer's exhausting, off duty study schedule, produced commendable results, and he finished at the top of his class. Following graduation, he and his new crew, were assigned to Columbus, Mississippi. Career-wise it was a move upward. The social prospects were something else.

Columbus was a small, dry, bible-belt town of less than twenty thousand. Available women were hard to find. There was a small, religious, girls' school there, but Cramer felt that at age thirty two he was too old to date girls in their teens. Besides, he doubted if they'd be tolerant of his views on religion, or his intemperate lifestyle.

The remainder of the social scene was either well hidden, or non-existent. Nothing was going on--no community functions--and worst of all, no bars or clubs. The fact that he couldn't even buy a girl a drink, or invite her to dance, put a severe crimp in his chances to meet women.

There was an upside. Normally he had two days off each time he finished an alert tour, and his schedule at Columbus was surprisingly predictable. Now there was time to deal with the psychological problem that had plagued him for so long.

Three months after his arrival, he finished an alert tour, and drove to Jackson. He checked into a motel with a good restaurant, ate a leisurely lunch of fried catfish, baked potato, and coleslaw, then returned to his room, and searched the yellow pages. There were a surprising number of psychiatrists in town, but he finally selected one, and made an appointment for a session following his next scheduled alert tour. He felt better immediately. After a year of worry, and fitful sleep, there was hope he might end his now infrequent, but still recurring nightmare.

CHAPTER TWELVE

The receptionist, an attractive, neatly dressed, brown haired woman in her early thirties, looked up, took off her glasses, and smiled, as Cramer entered the office.

"Good morning Mister Stevens," She said. "Nice to see you again. Doctor Phillips is with another patient. He will be with you shortly." She gestured toward the pricey looking, overstuffed chairs. "Make yourself comfortable."

He nodded, then reached across the desk, and handed her a plain white envelope. "Any change in the fee?"

She opened the envelope, took out the hundred dollar bill, looked at him sympathetically, and said softly, "You know, Mister Stevens, a doctor-patient relationship is strictly confidential. There's no danger in using your right name, and paying by check."

"Humor me," he said. "The people I work for won't be understanding about this."

He turned, and sat on a nearby chair, then leaned forward, and picked up one of several copies of *Yachting* lying on the coffee table. The magazine was exceptionally well done, obviously dedicated to giving the impression that boating was something everyone did. He wondered how many patients the good doctor had to see to finance his passion. He leafed listlessly through it, overlooking the articles, and concentrating on barely clothed, attractive females, provocatively posed on expensive boats.

Finally, a sniffing, dumpy looking, middle-aged woman came out of the doctor's office, wiping her eyes with a handkerchief. She passed the receptionist, ignored her good-by, and walked by Cramer, apparently without noticing him.

The instant she was gone, the receptionist nodded. "The Doctor will see you now Mr. Stevens."

The smiling shrink met him on the other side of the door, and shook hands like they were old friends. "Nice to see you John."

Dammit, the man just didn't look like a psychiatrist--Hollywood handsome, wavy blond hair, clean shaven, athletic--not a day over forty.

Cramer eased into the chair facing the massive mahogany desk. Dr. Phillips sat down, leaned his elbows on the desk top, and pressed his finger tips together, making a pyramid with his hands. "Have you had the nightmare since our last session?"

He shook his head. "No. The last one was a little over a month ago."

The Doc leaned back in his chair. "I see. John...I'm going to be straightforward about this. Fortunately, even though you refuse to give me your real name, at least you've disclosed your background, and what you do for a living."

The Doc opened his hands expansively. "You are, as far as I can determine, a stable, well adjusted adult, who manages to function quite well in an extremely demanding, and unforgiving environment. You are not sick. Granted, you have a problem, but you are definitely not sick. My other patients are sick!"

He fought back his irritation. "Doc...this is not a minor problem."

Phillips shook his head. "I'm sorry. I didn't mean to sound like I thought it was...but...

Cramer slid forward in his seat. "But hell! I'm not just having nightmares. I'm reliving the death of my parents over and over."

Phillips nodded, waved his hand, and gave him an eye-lid fluttering, condescending look. "I understand."

Anger welled up in him, and he spoke through gritted teeth, "No dammit, you obviously don't understand. You don't understand at all! For you, it's a dream. For me, it's real! I can see those caskets over that damned hole in the ground--feel the sun burning through my clothes--the sweat tickling down the side of my face." He hooked a thumb over his shoulder. "There's a meadowlark singing behind me, and the sound of thunder in the distance. There's nothing vague, or wispy or dreamlike about this. It's real, Goddammit. Real! And I'm only eight years old. A sick, bewildered, helpless little kid, living through it for the first time!" He shook his head, and snorted. "Jesus! I went through that two or three times a month...for years. Then, suddenly, after I got married, it stopped. What a relief. But now it's back, and I want the son of a bitch turned off. Permanently!"

"Of course you do. Believe me, I'm not making light of your problem." Phillips leaned forward, laid his arms on top of the desk, and clasped his hands, interlocking the fingers. "Part of your distress may be caused by your own frustration. I sense an inner dissatisfaction because you..." Phillips paused, and waved a hand, searching for the phrase "...you think a real man should be able to handle a situation like this."

"That may be part of it."

The Doc shook his head. "I don't believe you're being fair to yourself. You're not giving adequate consideration to how difficult your position was when all of this began. The catastrophic loss of both of your parents could hardly have come at a worse time in your life."

Cramer shifted irritably in his seat. "Other kids loose a parent, and seem to be able to handle it."

The Doc tipped his nose up, turned his head slightly and raised his eyebrows. "Maybe they don't handle it as well as you think. You don't know what's going on in their mind."

"True."

"Have you ever met anyone who lost both parents at the same time?"

"No."

The Doc stabbed a finger at him, and scowled. "Your tragedy was doubled! And it occurred when you were only eight. Old enough to be fully aware of the horrible consequences, but far too young to cope. Completely dependent on the understanding, and compassion of your aunt, and uncle, and they failed you miserably. In fact, they made things worse."

"You've got that right."

Phillips shook his head. "Leaving the cemetery that day, your Aunt's declaration that she didn't want you to live with them, was incredibly insensitive, and ill-timed. A vicious, final twist of misfortune's knife."

"I'll never forget it, that's for damn sure."

Phillips glanced down, staring glumly at the top of his desk. " I'm constantly amazed at how unspeakably cruel people can be." He looked back at Cramer. "They took you in, fed you, housed you, and clothed you. But they showed no affection, and made it obvious you were an unwelcome burden in their lives. Worst of all, they treated your nightmares as though they were something to be ashamed of. They made you feel weak, and inadequate, because you could not overcome them...which, of course, may actually have helped perpetuate the dreams."

Cramer scowled. "They raised me Doc, and maybe I should be grateful. I tried to be. I kept telling myself it was better than an orphanage. But I was never sure about that."

Phillips leaned back in his seat. "There was no love, no sense of family, no home. The terrible, void in your life was never filled."

"You're damn sure right about that."

The doctor squinted, cocked his head, and pointed a finger. "But then, you got married. You were no longer abandoned--no longer alone. You had a wife who loved you, and a home--a real home. The void was filled, and the dream disappeared."

"Are you saying that if I get married again, the nightmare will stop?"

"Not necessarily. But, it may. I doubt that you could marry just anyone, and make it work. I think the crucial elements would be love, and a feeling of stability in your relationship."

"Okay, suppose I get married, and the nightmare stops? Then what? What happens if I get divorced again? Then the damn thing starts all over again, right?"

Phillips propped his feet up on the desk, and folded his hands in his lap. "That doesn't necessarily figure. To begin with, most divorces don't come about the way yours did. You had no idea your wife would leave you. Her departure was a shock--as sudden, and unexpected as the loss of your parents."

"Could that be what started things again? The shock?"

"Perhaps. That coupled with the feeling of loss, and abandonment."

"What else could cause it?"

"With different people, different things. Nightmares can also be caused by unrelenting stress, or excessive use of alcohol." Phillips pointed his finger, and gave him a grim look. "Watch the booze John. Too much can cause problems.

Finally, the Doc took his feet down, stood up, and walked around the desk. "John, I repeat, I don't believe you're sick. And frankly, I don't think this is something I can talk you out of."

Cramer looked up at him. "So, what do I do now? Just...give up?"

"Of course not. Time may be your greatest ally. What may solve your problem is how you manage your life from this point onward. Try another doctor if you wish. Whatever happens, I wish you the best of luck."

Cramer stood up, shook hands, and thanked him, then turned, and left the office. As he walked to the elevator, he had the feeling that nothing had been solved, and couldn't help wondering if it ever would be.

CHAPTER THIRTEEN

He glanced around the well appointed, nearly deserted club, then glumly watched the lanky, crew cut bartender, mix his drink.

"Roger, I don't know when I've seen an Officer's Club this dead," Cramer said. "Don't you ever have any women in here?"

The barkeep, resplendent in white shirt, black bow tie, and cummerbund, leaned forward, and sat the drink in front of him. "You mean, unaccompanied?"

"Yeah, that kind."

Roger stepped back, and shook his head. "Probably the last time that happened was World War Two. I'm not sure. I was in grade school then."

"How the hell can a guy meet a woman in this county?" Cramer grumbled. "There aren't any bars. They don't have any of those decadent things like dances, where people move in close, and actually touch each other. There aren't any social functions. How do they get acquainted?"

Roger leaned back, put his elbows on the back-bar, and interlocked his fingers, clasping his hands in the center of the cummerbund. "Well, if you're not in school, about the only place I can think of is church. Why don't you join a church?"

He shook his head. "Anything but that. I was raised by bible thumpers. I'm not going through that again for anyone. Not even if I have to date a hooker."

Roger chuckled, "Sorry Captain, we don't have any of those either. Rural Mississippi is not noted for it's night life. To tell you the truth, if I wasn't already married, I'd get the hell out of here."

"That's not an option for me. SAC holds on to it's people like a miser clutches a bag of gold. I'm stuck here." He glanced over his shoulder, then lowered his voice. "I'm not just horny, I'm tired of living by myself. I'd like to be part of a family again. Have a home. You know, like...real people."

Roger nodded, giving him a sympathetic look. "I know what you mean Captain. I batched it for a couple of years. Gets lonesome as hell."

Cramer's social life remained stalled, and it appeared there was little he could do about it. As far as the town of Columbus was concerned, he was apparently perceived as a foreigner, and there seemed no way to change that. The local population spoke with a deep southern accent, and his GI modified, mid-western dialect branded him as an outsider, the minute he opened his mouth. Whenever he tried to strike up a conversation with an attractive woman in a drug store, or restaurant, his initiative was invariably met with a polite, but distant response.

He suspected part of the problem may have been that local people viewed the military as temporary residents. Before Columbus was a SAC base, it had been a pilot training facility. The majority of students stayed only six months before moving on, and few of the local residents bothered to develop relationships with people they considered transients.

At Otis, his unit had been socially active, and there were always parties at the club, or in someone's house. The Columbus Wing was entirely different. This bunch lived like hermits.

He found himself traveling to increasingly wider locations, in search of a social scene that offered more opportunities to meet women than he found locally. Unfortunately, the closer, medium sized towns like Tupelo, Meridian, and Tuscaloosa, seemed just as socially restricted as Columbus. He spent one rare, three day break in New Orleans, but its tourist trap look, and rat-race pace offended him almost as much the prices. Anyway, hookers were never his style.

Silent Sands of Gulfport. A second rate name for a barely passable Motel. Cramer turned off the shower, slid the glass door back, and stepped out of the tub. Green. Good God. Every thing was varying shades of green-- the tub, the john, the sink--even the floor tile. Damned architect must have been color-blind. He stepped over, and opened the bathroom door to let some of the steam out, then grabbed a towel, and dried himself off. Finally he folded the towel, reached up, and did his best to wipe the condensation off the mirror.

"How was the shower," Alice called.

He looked through the doorway. Finally off her back, she was propped up in bed, with both pillows behind her, and the sheet lying casually across her pelvis, her well formed breasts in full display. Wow. She might not be a rocket scientist in the brains department, but she was certainly attractive, even with her short, brown hair a tousled mess.

"Shower's fine," Cramer said. "I tried to save some of the hot water for you." He squirted the shaving cream, and spread it over his face, treating himself to brief glances in her direction.

She leaned to her left, reached over to the night stand, and stubbed out her cigarette. "Your a considerate guy," she said. "That's probably one reason you're so good in bed." She sat up straight, coughed, blinked, then smiled at him, and added, "I really enjoyed it. You're even better than Bob."

He stopped his razor mid-stroke, and stared at his reflection in the mirror. "Who's Bob?"

"My husband."

He snapped his head around. "You're married?"

She waved her hand. "Sure. Isn't everybody?"

"How come you don't wear a wedding ring?"

She looked at him smugly. "I do, usually. Took it off last night. It's in my purse."

46

"Oh." He looked back in the mirror, and began another stroke, pulling his mouth to the side to tighten the skin. "What's your husband do?" he mumbled.

"He's a vice cop."

The razor slipped from his grasp, clunked off the edge of the sink, and clattered on the tile floor. Alice fell sideways, laughing hysterically, and pounding the bed. Finally, she straightened up, sniffed, wiped her eyes, and said, "I'm sorry." She stifled a little giggle, and added. "God, if I knew fooling around was going to be this much fun, I'd have done it sooner."

He leaned down, retrieved his razor, and looked up at her. "Your husband's a vice cop?"

Her smile broadened. "Not really. I just said that to see how you'd react. He owns a bar." She giggled again, pointed at him, and shook her head. "Oh God. You should have seen the look on your face. This is great. Who said revenge is a bad thing?"

He held the razor under the tap, rinsed it, then turned his head, and looked at her. "Revenge? You did this for revenge?"

She tilted her nose upward. "Sure. Why not? He's always screwing around. Why can't I?" She squinted, "So what? How come you're worried about it?"

He looked back at the sink, and turned off the hot water tap. "Well, for one thing, the thought crosses my mind, that for your purposes at least, revenge unrevealed, will be no revenge at all."

"What's that supposed to mean?"

"You won't have real revenge unless he finds out about this. That's the only way you can effectively get even. He hurt you, so you want to hurt him." He shook the razor dry, turned his head, and looked at her. "You're going to tell him aren't you?"

She tipped her nose even higher, and looked at him sideways. "Not exactly. I won't make it that obvious. I'll wait a couple of days, then confide my little secret to Alice."

"Who's Alice?"

She frowned, looked down, and ran her hand across the sheet. "She's supposed to be my best friend. But she's the one he's been screwing." She blinked several times, wiped her eyes, sniffed, then looked up at him, her expression defiant. "It'll be a nice coup for her. She can tell him, and stab me in the back at the same time." She shrugged, looked down at her lap, and said softly, "In the end, it'll all work out, I suppose. After the divorce, he'll get Alice, and I'll get the bar."

"That might not work out the way you think," Cramer said.

"Why not?"

He reached for the towel, and began drying his face. "If you're also guilty of adultery," he said, his voice muffled by the fabric, "you may lose your tactical advantage in court." He shrugged, and lowered the towel. "On the other hand...maybe not. What the hell do I know? I've only had a couple of business law courses, so I'm no Clarence Darrow."

She cocked her head. "Who's Clarence Darrow?"

"He was a famous lawyer, you know...from the monkey trial."

She squinted, and her voice went up two octaves. "They put a monkey on *trial*?"

"No! Not really. It was...it was an ideological conflict between evolutionists, and some church group." He waved his hand. "It's not important. Happened a long time ago."

Her expression softened. "Oh." She paused, and gave him a sly look. "So, anyway, maybe we could do this again. You know, in some other town, if you'd be more comfortable."

"I dunno," he mumbled, as he finished drying his face. He lowered his head, reached up and rubbed the towel on the back of his neck. "It's...it's hard for me to get away. I'm on alert fairly often, and I fly a lot too."

"So? Maybe I could come to see you. Where are you stationed."

"Uh...Lake Charles," he said, keeping his eyes on the sink. "Lake Charles, Louisiana. Unfortunately, I won't be there much longer." He glanced at her. "This was probably my last night out before I go overseas."

"That's too bad. Where are you going?"

"Uh...French Morocco."

She squinted. "Where's that?"

"Northwest Africa," he said as he began putting his gear back in the kit. "Hell of a place. Outside of Casablanca, nobody speaks English. Sand everywhere." He shook the kit down, zipped it shut, and added, "Country's a bitch to get around in. No roads. I'll be stationed way out in the boondocks."

After they got dressed, he checked out, bought her breakfast at a nice restaurant on the beach, then made his excuses, kissed her good-by, and quietly drove toward Columbus, re-running the experience through his mind.

Certainly, the night had been enjoyable. An undeniably pleasurable experience that at least provided sexual relief. But his primary objective remained unfulfilled. Damn shame. She wasn't real bright, but she was still a nice girl. Unfortunately, she was already married. And now, she'd been cheated on, so she was running around on her husband. She'd probably be bitter for the rest of her life. Not much chance for a stable home, and family there.

Opportunities to expand Cramer's social horizons continued to be elusive, severely curtailed by the demands of his profession. When he wasn't flying, a significant portion of his time was spent on two week alert tours at home station--a common lifestyle in the Strategic Air Command. At bases world wide, atomic blast resistant, underground alert facilities, with living quarters, libraries--and even movies--housed SAC alert crews.

In spite of being undeniably first class in accommodations, flight crews irreverently dubbed the facilities--The Mole Hole. There, booze was forbidden, but at least everyone ate well. Sometimes too well. The food was hard to resist. Expertly prepared dishes from French, Chinese, and Italian menus, supplemented a full range of traditional American fare. He soon discovered he had to watch his weight, and increase his exercise in order to stay fit.

Following alert tours, he flew--on average--two missions per week. Ground training, flight planning, and a relentless battery of scheduled, as well as no-notice tests, filled the remainder of his time. Most sorties lasted from seven to ten hours, and the day before each flight, he, his co-pilot, and navigator, spent nearly half a day just flight planning the coming event.

Nearly all missions simulated war time operation. Consequently, crews were expected to operate the 135 on the razor thin edge of its capability. Fortunately, SAC had spent mega-millions testing the new KC-135, and its charts were surprisingly accurate. Scores of complicated graphs were used during flight planning, challenging the crew's concentration, as pilots, and navigators meticulously followed a plethora of closely spaced, intersecting lines, some straight, some curving, in order to arrive at a figure that if, incorrect, might well produce a deadly result.

Maximum weight takeoffs were especially critical, requiring meticulous calculations for temperature, field elevation, wind direction and velocity, as well as runway gradient. Water injection to increase engine thrust was normally used, but only above a certain temperature. Below that, water injection would ice up the engines.

SAC took a dim view of late takeoffs, regardless of the cause. Wing, and Squadron Headquarters, passed on the demands to the crews and insisted they make every departure an on-time takeoff. Eventually, it all rested on the shoulders of the man in the left seat.

Prior to one mission, a cold front passed ahead of forecast time, and the mercury plunged, forcing Cramer to dump 600 gallons of distilled water on the taxiway. The plane sat near the runway, engines at idle, as a thick stream of water built a spreading pond beneath the plane, while both pilots frantically flipped through performance charts in a desperate effort to re-calculate take-off data. In spite of that, they made their scheduled departure time.

Max weight take-offs were a gut wrenching experience for flight crews, and nothing short of spectacular to the casual observer. Anytime a tanker max weight takeoff began, even seasoned mechanics dropped their wrenches, and gathered in little clusters to watch the spectacle unfold.

During its two mile ground run, the fuel laden giant accelerated slowly at first. But momentum built rapidly as runway markers passed with increasing frequency until she was roaring down the runway like a runaway freight--black smoke pouring from screaming, water injected engines--furiously spinning tires still firmly rolling on concrete, and the end of the runway approaching at an alarming rate.

At the last possible instant, the pilot brought the nose up, not less than ten, nor more than twelve degrees, and the screaming, two hundred mile an hour juggernaut rolled yet another thousand feet before finally breaking ground--only two, heart stopping seconds from the end of the runway, and total disaster.

To Cramer, it always seemed that this time they were dead for sure, and he was invariably surprised when they made it. Once airborne, however, with the gear and flaps up, the huge jet accelerated quickly, and climb out was far quicker than in the KC-97.

Fuel management was made deliberately demanding in an obvious effort to train crews to achieve maximum range by getting the most from what they had. Once aloft, tension mounted. Judicious adherence to speed, power, and optimum altitude was essential. It seemed a never ending struggle.

Fuel consumed by the tanker, and offloaded to the receiver caused tremendous changes in aircraft weight, altering performance markedly. By mission's end, the now, nearly empty tanker flew like a different plane.

There was, however, one particularly satisfying factor in all this. Now, during air refueling, staying ahead of receivers, was no problem. During one mission, he chuckled when a B-47 pilot broke radio silence, and grumbled, "Slow it down a little, dammit!"

All things considered, he reveled in the speed, and performance of the 135, and took pride in his ability to fly her. But as pleased as he was, he still wanted out of SAC, and the social vacuum of Columbus.

Unfortunately, the way things looked, the only way he'd get a transfer was to leave the Air Force, or die, and eventually he began to wonder if he was doomed to a solo lifestyle.

The Mole Hole dining hall gleamed with its usual immaculate ambiance, shinning floors, first rate furnishings, and fine dinner ware. Behind the serving line, white clad cooks, the best SAC could muster, worked in a kitchen that sparkled like a hospital operating room. No disgruntled banging of pots, or rattling pans here. These cooks were dedicated, taking pride in serving the sharp, deadly edge of America's military.

Cramer sat down at the table, and took a slurp of steaming coffee, feeling the brew burn all the way down. Dark haired, Second Lieutenant Martin, his new co-pilot, ran his hand over the tablecloth, a look of grudging admiration on his boyishly, handsome face. "Almost as good as fine Irish linen," he said. "I've got to give them credit. They give us nice stuff in here."

50

Their navigator, Captain Bill Tilden, tugged irritably at the neck-band of his green scarf, and gave Martin a steely eyed, glowering glance. "Screw the fancy trimmings. Just once I'd like to have a whole hour of free time to myself. No test--no ass chewing, and no ground training."

Cramer chuckled. "It never stops. What Air Division doesn't schedule, Second Air Force does, and SAC adds to that."

Martin lit a cigarette, and blew smoke toward the ceiling. "I can't believe I was dumb enough to ask for this."

"Why did you?" Cramer asked.

Martin shrugged, laid his cigarette in the ash tray, and picked up his coffee cup, holding it with both hands. "I'd heard all this great stuff about SAC. You know--how they were keeping the world free--holding the Russians at bay. How was I supposed to know? When you're in Pilot Training, they don't tell you the bad stuff."

"Well, now you know," Tildon said.

"Yes sir. Like there's no time off. You never get to see your family, and there's somebody riding your ass every minute."

"Looks like you've got it figured out," Cramer said.

Martin's brow furrowed. "At least in the Training Command they didn't start every meeting with an ass chewing, or some kind of fuckin' test. These guys never let up!"

Cramer smiled. "All SAC crewmembers labor under the burden of lofty expectations. As far as the head shed's concerned, nothing's ever done good enough, or fast enough."

"The family problems seem insurmountable," Martin grumbled, shaking his head. "My wife is constantly bitching 'cause I'm never home. I'm getting to the point where I hate to call her at night."

"She needs to adjust her attitude," Cramer said. "Tell her to enjoy what she has. If we start pulling alert overseas, she's gonna see a hell of a lot less of you."

"God!"

Tildon took the toothpick out of the corner of his mouth, and laid it in his saucer. "That's not the worst of it," he said. "Make even a minor mistake, and it'll never be forgotten." He took a sip of coffee, and looked at Cramer. "Speaking of mistakes, what did they decide about Shumski?"

"No formal charges. The Division Commander's gonna let him resign."

Tildon set his cup down, picked up his toothpick, and threw it into the ash tray. "Holy shit, John! He's got twelve years in. The man was on the major's list, and now they're pushing him out? Just like that? From an ace to an ass, in two strokes. And neither one was his fault."

Cramer shrugged. "That's not the way they look at it. The AC is responsible for his crew, and what goes on in his airplane. This isn't baseball. In SAC, it's two strikes, and you're out."

Tildon's face flushed, as he gritted his teeth, scowled, and slapped the table. "It's not right dammit! That alert incident wasn't his fault. He was filling in for another AC. The navigator was the one who took the alert vehicle off by himself, and caused them to get to the airplane late."

"They took that into consideration," Cramer said. "If it had been his crew that busted an alert, they'd have downgraded him to co-pilot right then."

Martin gave them a baffled look. "They're throwing him out for being late? Just once?"

Cramer shook his head. "There's more to it than that," he said. "Three weeks after he busted the alert, the poor bastard comes in for a landing, makes a beautiful touchdown, and the airplane sits on it's ass."

"That wasn't his fault," Tildon snapped.

"Not directly," Cramer said. "But Shumski was the aircraft commander, and he's the one who's ultimately responsible."

"What happened?" Martin asked.

Cramer took a sip of coffee, and sat his cup back in the saucer. "After they refueled the bomber, the co-pilot closed the wing tank transfer valves to stop fuel flow into the aft body tank. Unfortunately, one of the valves failed to close."

"A ten thousand to one chance," Tildon grumbled.

Cramer nodded. "True. But still no excuse. Anyway...while they were coming home, the wing tank with the open valve continued to drain fuel into the aft body tank, and the center of gravity went beyond the aft limit. When Shumski touched down, she tipped backwards, and sat on her ass. He ground up an awful lot of aluminum before he got her stopped. They were lucky she didn't burn."

Martin threw his hands up. "If the valve failed, how could they have prevented that? Wouldn't fuel have drained into the body tank anyway?"

"Sure," Cramer said. "But if they had checked the aft body tank gauge, they would have seen there was too much fuel in it. They could have dumped enough in-flight to correct the CG before they landed."

"They ought to have lights on the panel to show what position the valves are in," Martin said.

"I agree," Cramer said. "They ought to, but they don't."

"So how can you tell if a valve doesn't close?"

"You have to periodically check the fuel level in the aft body tank," Cramer said. "If it starts to rise, you've got a valve open somewhere. Shumski's co-pilot forgot to check. But Shumski was the aircraft commander, and he's the one who's ultimately responsible. So...he's the one they're throwing out."

"That doesn't seem fair."

"Welcome to SAC, lieutenant. Someday you'll be an aircraft commander. Then you can get your ass reamed when someone on your crew screws up."

"Well, at least that's something I won't have to worry about for while. Maybe before that happens I can get a transfer. Is there any way I can get out of this command?"

Cramer snorted, "I don't know. Suicide might work."

CHAPTER FOURTEEN

Cramer signed for the top-secret satchel, locked the flap, left the vault, and walked down the hall to the study room his crew already occupied. After entering, he locked the door behind him.

The small room was made for study. No distractions. Plain, tan walls, no notices, no threats, and no slogans--about the only place in SAC, other than the latrine, where one could find that. In here, the plan--the assigned mission--was everything.

He put the satchel on the table, inserted the key, opened the hasp, and passed out the proper folders to his co-pilot, and navigator.

A half hour later, a knock on the door interrupted them. He pointed to the jumble of forms scattered about the table. "Put everything back in the satchel."

They collected the papers, re-folding forms, closing books, and stuffing them back into the kit. Finally, Tildon locked the case, nodded, and Cramer opened the door.

A grim faced, Major Valedes stuck his head in the room. "Sorry to interrupt John. I just got a call from the Squadron Commander. He wants you in his office right away. Take your kit back to the vault, and get up there pronto."

"Did he say what he wanted?"

Valedes shook his head. "No. But it can't be good news. I've never seen them delay an alert tour for anything."

They entered the long, one story structure with his crew trailing behind in single file, their footsteps echoing off the finely polished tile. Cramer looked over his shoulder, and pointed to his left. "Wait for me in the coffee room."

Ahead, in obvious anticipation of his arrival, a grim faced, first sergeant held open the doorway to the Commander's office. Well, what the hell, first sergeants always looked grim. It was part of their job.

The sergeant nodded briefly as he approached, then motioned him inside, and closed the door behind him.

Lt Colonel Jorgensen sat behind his desk, heavy brows drooping over penetrating blue eyes, the gray barely noticeable in his short cropped, blond hair. Behind him, a photograph, with a decades younger Jorgensen standing, second from the left, in a line-up of WWII aviators posing in front of a B-17.

He stopped, snapped his heals together, and saluted. "Cramer, John D, Captain, reporting sir."

Jorgensen, returned the salute, and motioned for him to sit down.

He eased into a chair, his apprehension building.

The colonel leaned back in his seat, looking glum. "Captain, I want you to know the Wing Commander, and I, have pulled every string we could think of, in an effort to save your ass."

Cramer felt his stomach churn.

Jorgensen shook his head. "This is a done deal. There is no appeal. This crap came down, *by name*, from the Secretary of The Air Force." He shook his head woefully. "Can't be changed. It's your turn in the barrel."

The colonel leaned forward, dropped his gaze to the paper on his blotter, and cleared his throat. "Captain Cramer, it is my unpleasant duty to inform you, that you are hereby reassigned to the Third Air Commando Squadron in some Goddamned place called...Ben...Ben...is it Hoyia? In some fucked up little country called South Vietnam...where the hell ever that is."

Jorgenson looked up, obviously baffled. "How in God's name do they come up with this shit? An Aircraft Commander on a SAC Combat Crew...spotless record...and Air Force Headquarters shafts him with some off-the-wall, dog shit assignment to East, Bum-Fuck Asia?"

Cramer took a deep breath, and struggled to mask his elation. Hot damn! Jungle Jim. JUNGLE JIM, by God. It finally came through. Unbelievable! A long-ago, long shot, played out on Sunday morning in the Plattsburg BOQ...and finally...here it was. After all this time. Oh my God.

He was out of Columbus. Out of SAC. Out of the most iron assed, unforgiving outfit in the Air Force, and off to Southeast Asia on some kind of wild, crazy-assed adventure. He felt like a kid on Christmas morning. It was all he could do to keep from jumping up, and turning cartwheels around the room.

Jorgensen raised his hand, and shook his head. "I know. I know, John. It's a shock. But you've got to deal with this. Hey, what the hell...maybe it's not as bad as it sounds."

Cramer nodded, looked his commander in the eye...and lied like hell, "Gee Colonel, I sure hate to leave SAC. It's been like a second home to me."

CHAPTER FIFTEEN

HURLBURT FIELD, FLORIDA

The penetrating smell of the urinal deodorant disk was so strong it almost took his breath away, as Cramer pointed his penis toward the shiny porcelain, finally relaxed and directed the stream downward toward the drain. Man! Talk about relief. Dammit, he should have known better. Three cups of coffee before any orientation briefing was just plain asking for it. Those things always went on forever. Maybe someday he'd learn.

Oh well, no wonder he had to piss so bad. He could hardly contain his excitement. Adventure was obviously in the making.

Hurlburt Field was different, a small specialized base, with widely separated, recently renovated buildings. One hangar standing, another being planned. In spite of it's auxiliary status, there was a small, well stocked BX, a theatre, and an NCO club. Across highway 98, fronting on the inland waterway, a newly constructed Officers club nestled among a number of well kept shade trees.

The flightline hardware looked like holdovers from WW II. Vintage planes, that were perfect choices for various low profile, low budget conflicts around the globe--twin engine B-26s, C-47s, and C-46s, as well as a number of A1Es, recently cast off by the Navy, and recycled by the Air Force. The latter, a seemingly unlikely choice, had a huge, radial engine, and had already proven itself to be a phenomenal weight lifter, as well as a cheap, and able killer of communist insurgents. The T-28s had already been phased out of course, but nobody was even talking about jets. Why waste the good stuff on half-assed wars?

Cramer shook it off, zipped up, washed his hands, and hurried through the door. Outside, the grounds were green, and well kept. He strode briskly on the recently poured walkway, enjoying the gentle off-shore breeze, and the soft rustling sound of wind blowing through towering pines. Ahead, loomed Group Personnel, where legions of dedicated, pencil pushers were filling squares on hundreds of forms. With a bit of luck, and a careful application of judicious bullshit, maybe he could trade his C-47 seat, for an assignment to B-26s.

He looked across the briefing table, as Captain Jim Gibson, blond, balding, and six three, smiled at him.

"I almost wish I was back in SAC," Cramer grumbled. "Thought I could get into B-26s...never dreamed I'd end up in C-47s."

Gibson leaned back in his seat, grabbed the diagonal zippers of his breast pockets, and pulled his sweat-soaked flying suit away from his chest. "Maybe that wasn't such a bad break. If you'd got what you wanted, you might have been one of the guys who pulled the wings off his airplane."

Cramer shook his head. "I never figured they'd tear the wings off a B-26."

"Nobody else thought so either. They were so sure it wouldn't happen, they had to do it three times, before anyone believed it."

"I didn't hear about that."

Gibson squinted. "Why would you? It wasn't something they wanted to advertise." He picked up his smokes, shook one out of the pack, stuck it in his mouth, lit it, and blew the smoke to one side. "Anyway, enough of the what-ifs. The B-26s are grounded, and you're stuck in C-47s. Might as well get used to it, John. You're not having any more trouble in this plane than a lot of guys.

Cramer slammed his palm on the table. "I still don't get it! I grease the wheels onto the pavement, keep everything under control, hold her right on centerline, and then, just as the tail comes down, all hell breaks loose."

Gibson nodded. "Sounds like an accurate assessment of the way it's gone so far."

Cramer threw his hands up. "The minute the tail comes down, the son of a bitch heads for the side of the runway. I slam in the rudder to correct, and it takes off in the other direction. All I get is an endless series of S turns that get progressively wilder. In every one of my first twelve landings if you hadn't jumped in, and saved my ass, I'd have gone into the bushes."

"I know, I know." Gibson made an obvious effort to suppress a chuckle. "Don't worry about it. Trust me, things will fall into place before long. What the hell...the rest of your work has been top notch. Don't let it get you down. Any pilot trained exclusively in tri-cycle gear aircraft is going to have trouble with a tail-dragger. They're squirrelly on the ground."

"You're not just trying to make me feel good?"

Gibson shook his head. "Trust me. After a couple more missions, everything will fall into place, and you'll get the hang of it. Anyway, tomorrow, we've got a briefing at 0700. In addition to takeoffs and landings, we do our first sneaky Pete, low level navigation."

"Sounds like fun."

"It is." Gibson said. "You'll love it. Before you're done, we're going to show you how to fight dirty, break every rule in the book, and get into, and out of, any friggin' country in the world...undetected!"

"That ought to come in handy."

"It will. We'll also teach you how to land at night, without lights, in places where there's no airstrip at all, as well as dropping people, and supplies behind enemy lines." Gibson reached across the table and punched him lightly on the shoulder. "Cheer up John. You're a natural for this crap. You've got the makin's of a real, low life son of a bitch. You're going to fit right in with the rest of us."

"You've made me feel better already."

Gibson grinned, and snapped the briefing book closed. "Good. Now, what you need, is a little diversion. Go to the Dirty Bird, tonight. Have a few drinks, maybe pick up one of the local lovelies."

"Sounds like good advice. I could use a little female companionship."

"Atta boy. Do it up right. In the morning, we'll teach you how to fly with a hangover."

Cramer chuckled. "You're too late. I already learned that in SAC."

The Seagull sat next to the water near the southeast corner of Brooks bridge, and was the most popular night spot in Fort Walton Beach. The prices were reasonable, the food was good, and the drinks were first rate. Cramer had already made it his unofficial, off duty home.

Tonight, he intended to eat first, but as he walked through the bar, he noticed a couple of women sitting near the far wall. The blond was obviously occupied, talking to some half dressed guy on the last stool, but the other girl just sat there, looking pensively into her glass.

Cramer slid onto the seat next to her. Early twenties, attractive and trim, with short brown hair, she was dressed in a bare midriff, loose fitting, sleeveless cotton top, and white shorts. Legs that almost made him catch his breath. She turned her head, and smiled, her straight, white teeth, perfectly matched. Wow!

"Hi," he said. "How are the martinis?"

She shrugged. "I guess they're OK. I don't really know. This is the first one I ever drank."

"Don't be too quick to judge. They're an acquired taste."

She gave him a wry smile. "I can believe that."

Cramer raised his hand, and the barkeep set the glass he was polishing on the shelf, and came over. "What can I get you?

"Make mine a CC and soda, and give the lady whatever consolation drink she wants."

"Thanks," she said, and pushed her half empty glass toward the bartender. "I'll have a gin, and tonic this time."

Cramer liked her already. With a little subtle probing he learned her name was Betty, she was living in Pensacola, recently divorced from a sailor, and had a young son who was currently living with her mother in North Dakota.

As they were finishing their third drink, her girlfriend turned, and said, "Eddie and I are going back to Pensacola. Do you mind driving home alone?"

Betty shook her head. "No, I'll call you tomorrow, after I get out of class."

"Okay. Talk to you later."

After the couple left, Cramer pushed his glass to the back edge of the bar, and looked at her. "Do you want another, or would you like to go for a ride along the beach?"

"The beach would be nice. It's a clear night so it ought to be pretty. I love it there. Even when it's dark. Just sitting there listening to the surf is a treat."

He paid the bill, and they left. In the parking lot Betty stopped by her car, locked the doors, and they walked over to his Buick.

He pulled off the road and parked, being careful to keep his wheels on the narrow strip of hard-packed oyster shells. Not surprisingly, there were no other cars in sight. Ft Walton Beach was a small town, and this far down the island there were seldom any people, even in the daytime.

He shut off the car, turned out the lights, and rolled down the window. The half-moon lighting seemed just right. The surf was subtle, the water whispering in over off-white sand, then receding in a slow, gentle wash-back.

He reached for her, and she turned in the seat, then lay across his lap with her head cradled in the crook of his left arm. She felt good there. Everything about her felt good, and he kissed her for a long time before he gave her a chance to say anything.

She looked up at him, and said nothing, so he kissed her again, and moved his hand under her dress, feeling her smooth firm thigh. She shifted in the seat, opening her legs slightly and he slid his fingers up to her crotch, feeling the warmth of her slick nylon panties. She squeezed her legs together gripping his hand as a soft purring moan came from her throat.

She put her hand on his cheek, looked up at him, and smiled. "I'm really not this easy," she said softly. "It's just that it's been such a long time, and you're so damned attractive."

She reached up, pulled his head down, and kissed him. He moved his hand up, caught the waistband of her panties, pulled downward, and she lifted her hips to help him out.

Hurlburt's Air Commando School was the most straight-forward military course Cramer had ever attended. Here, bullshit was held to a minimum, and the curriculum was surprisingly logical. His new tactical doctrine followed common sense rules, and the old C-47 was comparatively simple. By the end of the second week, he already knew his aircraft systems, and had studied the tactical procedure manual from cover to cover.

After the first few landings, his problems with aircraft directional control vanished, and he found he could fly the old plane surprisingly well.

In SAC his normal duty week had covered 80 to 90 hours. Here, he could seldom fill forty. Suddenly, there was more opportunity to enjoy himself than he had ever had in the Air Force. He quickly overcame his initial feelings of guilt, and eagerly took advantage of the situation, falling into a satisfying routine, frequently driving to Pensacola to pick up Betty, or meeting her in Ft Walton.

Other than night flying, his schedule closely matched her classes at Pensacola Junior College. She was a terrific girl, good natured, easy to talk to, and fun to be with. They toured the area on nights, and weekends, going to the beach, or driving the coastline, dropping in at small bars, and restaurants all along Highway 98 from Panama City, to Pensacola.

Privacy required some adjustments. Betty lived with a roommate, and his BOQ was off limits to females, so most of their love making took place in his car along deserted stretches of the beach--or--whenever they both had the next day off, in a motel. He liked her. He liked her a lot, and inevitably began to wonder if they could resume their relationship when he returned from Vietnam.

It was a nice motel, pale tan cement block, with a small restaurant, barely thirty yards off the Gulf. The room was rather small, but at least the bath was clean, the beds were comfortable, and the furnishings looked nearly new. The air conditioner wasn't running, and Cramer could hear the surf pounding outside, its energy magnified by a distant hurricane now veering westward toward the gulf coast of Texas.

A pole light at the edge of the small patio lit the room with a soft, feeble glow. He propped himself up on his elbow, and looked at her. Betty was lying on her back, staring at the ceiling with the sheet barely covering her navel. In that position her breasts looked nearly flat, and he decided that even if she had been flat chested, it wouldn't have made much difference.

She glanced at him, and smiled. "What are you thinking?"

"I was wondering if maybe we could see each other again, after I get back from overseas."

"That would be nice. But I have to tell you, I'm going back to North Dakota as soon as this semester is over." She reached up, and touched his cheek with her fingertips. "Would you consider getting out of the Air Force, and coming up there to live?"

He shook his head. "I can't do that. I've got too much time invested. Besides, I want to stay in the Air Force at least thirty years. It isn't just a job. It's...it's like home. Even in SAC, as bad as that was, I never considered quitting."

She nodded. "I understand. But I have a home too, John. And I've got to go back. If there's anything I learned being down here, it's that I can't stand being away from my family."

She rolled on her side, doubled up her pillow, and looked at him. "It was awful when I was married to Denny. He'd get sea duty, and I'd go down to see him off. Everywhere I looked there were people being separated--people crying. He'd go out to sea, and leave me, and no matter how many people were around, it didn't help. I still felt alone. I missed North Dakota, and my family. Military life is too hard. There's too much separation. Someone's always leaving. Someone's always saying goodbye. It's heartbreaking. I can't live like that anymore."

He nodded. "Well, at least we have a few more weeks together."

"Thank God for that," she said, then reached up, pulled his head down and kissed him.

CHAPTER SIXTEEN

He usually slept well, but tonight, Cramer awoke in a cold room. It had been unseasonably warm that day, and he failed to anticipate the effects of a fast moving cold front. Hours earlier, he had gone to bed with the temperature control on the window unit still set at its lowest point.

By now, he was fully awake, and feeling depressed. A street light filtered in through the partially open slats of the Venetian blinds, and he looked around the dimly lit room. Not bad. Nicely furnished, with full maid service. No iron bunks with thin mattresses, and sagging springs here. Sure beat sleeping in an open bay barrack with 30 other guys. Thank God he'd hung on through OCS instead of telling them to shove it, as he almost did a thousand times.

He rolled on his side, doubled up his pillow, and irritably stuffed it under his head. It didn't help. Obviously, sleep was no longer an option. Finally, he stood up, grabbed the blanket, and wrapped it around himself, then walked over to the window unit. As he turned up the thermostat, the compressor disengaged with a heavy thump, and the cold blast died.

He turned, and sat down in the overstuffed chair, putting his feet on the footstool. Damn! He hated it when he felt like this, drowsy, irritable, obviously in a state of post alcoholic depression. Sure he'd feel better in the morning, he always did, but for now, he was down in the dumps.

Too bad it wasn't daylight. At least then, he could get up, and go to breakfast. After that, it would be hard to fill his time. Betty would be in school, and he wasn't scheduled to fly until evening.

He'd never had this problem in SAC. Those bastards worked him so hard he never woke up early. And he sure as hell never got bored.

Still, there were things he liked about his old command. Having a crew was one of them. At least with a permanent crew, he had a surrogate family, a feeling of social stability that he hadn't experienced since he left.

Admittedly, there were other good experiences associated with SAC. He'd never felt at home in Columbus, but Cape Cod was an enjoyable assignment. Nice in spite of the weather. There were a lot of fond memories he could draw on, and Janet Shaw was the best. He thought of her often-- still had the picture he took of her at that housing area block party.

Was she was still at Otis? Still married? Did she ever think of him? Would he ever stop thinking of her? Damn, he'd give almost anything to see her again.

Maybe...maybe when he got back from Vietnam...if he got back...maybe he could take leave, and go to the Cape and see her.

He laughed. What a stupid idea. How the hell could he do that? How would he explain it to her husband? Hey Stan, remember me? Your old next door neighbor--big hero, home from the wars--back to covet your lovely wife. For Chrissake. That wouldn't work.

He shook his head, and ran his fingers through his hair. Dammit! Why was he so depressed? He couldn't put his finger on it, but something was missing. He felt...uneasy. It didn't figure. He was breezing through school. Acing the course. Soon he'd leave on an adventure most men only dreamed of.

Professionally he was ready. But personally he wasn't. The trouble was, he didn't want to give up Betty. He'd miss her. Miss her a lot. In spite of that...he didn't love her. And she never claimed she loved him. It was as if they both held back, knowing the life that each of them needed, would never work for the other.

Somehow, that didn't help. Right now, if he could do it, he'd keep everything the way it was. But the system was relentless. He had volunteered to go to war when his life was completely different than it was now--but he had volunteered. And he was going. Whether he was ready to or not.

Both engines were operating smoothly, grumbling with that satisfying rumble that radials make at cruise power. An anemic, washed-out red bathed the instrument panel. Cramer checked his altitude at 200 feet as a small cluster of scattered lights appeared through the trees, swept by and vanished behind them. Ahead lay a blackened void.

Gibson tapped his shoulder. He turned his head, seeing the sweat on the side of Gibson's face glistening in the faint glow of panel lights.

"Good run," Gibson shouted. "Your navigation was damn near perfect. You split the sprawling metropolis of Bruce right down the middle. OK, what's next on your flight plan?"

"I'll hit the coast, and head for Hurlburt."

"Fine. When we get there, you can make your first blackout landing on that sorry assed dirt strip. Feel comfortable with that?"

"Fine with me. I'll watch you close. Try to do it just like you."

Gibson turned his head, and grinned. "No demonstration, John. You're doing the first one."

His mouth dropped open. "Now wait a minute. Standard procedure. You demonstrate the first one, I get to watch."

Gibson laughed. "Why demonstrate? What's to watch? There's nothing to see. The only thing out there will be three pencil flashlights. Might as well fly it yourself. Don't worry. I'll talk you through it."

A few minutes later, the first lights along the coast became visible. Finally, they crossed highway 98, and Cramer rolled into a steep bank, turned 90 degrees right, and followed the shoreline, a quarter mile out over the water. Along the shore, widely spaced lights marked the location of isolated homes and businesses. At long intervals along the highway, the headlights of an occasional car stabbed through the darkness. He sped up his cross-check. Even out here, altitude control was critical. With no moon, the water was a dark void beneath them. With only 200 feet of altitude, it would be easy to become distracted, and let her settle in.

Cockpit temperature was warmer now, so he slid his side window the rest of the way open, feeling the increased buffet of warm, sodden air on his face, and upper body. Out here, in the dark, sensations seemed magnified-- the rumble of engines, a slight vibration in the yoke, and an even stronger drumming on the balls of his feet, coming from the rudder pedals. Suddenly, the shore lights ran out, and they barreled along, recklessly, flying in a black void--the altimeter the only hint of how close they were to the water. He sped up his cross check, nailing heading, airspeed and altitude.

"One more mission after this one," Gibson shouted. "A couple of airdrops, and a dozen blackout landings to go. You're the best student I ever had. It's been like a vacation for me. I hate to see you go."

Minutes later the lights near Brooks Bridge came into view, giving him the first hint of something familiar. Gibson laughed, pointing as they swept past the Seagull. "Too bad they don't know it's you, John. They'd probably wave. You left enough of your money with them."

The lights of Fort Walton passed quickly, and Gibson jerked his thumb to the right. "You know where it's at?"

Cramer shrugged. "Pretty close. Studied the map. But I've never seen it before."

Gibson laughed, "So what? You won't see it this time either. Nothing but those pencil flashlights." Gibson slapped him on the shoulder with the back of his hand. "Hey, don't worry. Follow the procedure. You'll do fine."

"Before Landing Checklist," Cramer said.

They ran the checklist, and suddenly a small cluster of lights swept beneath them. "That the IP?" he asked."

"You bet. Now look around," Gibson said, pointing out the blackened windshield. "Search the dark. Sweep your eyes back, and forth, about 60 degrees on each side of the nose. We've got to be getting close. When they hear you coming, they'll point their lights directly at you, no matter which way you go. Everything else depends on you."

Cramer pointed through the windshield. "Is that them? About a mile out?"

"Probably. Not much else out here, is there?"

"Gear down. Flaps a half."

Gibson ducked down, and moved the levers, as Cramer adjusted power. "Play this for real John," Gibson shouted, still bent over as he snapped the ring over the lock. "You've got three desperate men out there, hiding from the enemy." He sat up straight again. "They've been waiting for hours-- maybe days--praying to God that you'll show up. What are you looking for?"

"Two lights on the approach end, sixty feet apart," Cramer said.

64

"Twenty five hundred feet beyond that, should be another light in the center of the end of the landing area."

"That's right. What would that look like?"

"Three corners of an invisible triangle."

"Right again. And now..." Gibson pointed, "that's exactly what you see, isn't it? It's got to be them. Well, it's either them, or those nasty little bastards on the other side trying to suck you in, and capture your ass."

"Comforting thought."

"Okay John, looks good. Start turning final when the first two lights are near the two o'clock position, around a half mile out. Just about...now! When you roll out on final, the far light should appear to be slightly above the middle of the front pair. After that, adjust your power, and make like you're sliding down a shallow glideslope."

"Gimme full flaps." Gibson worked the lever, as Cramer rolled in trim, relieving the building pressure on his elevators. He could feel her slowing now, and double-checked his airspeed. "How's it look?"

"Looking good, John. Remember, the lights on the approach end are sixty feet apart, two thirds of your wing span. That'll help your perspective. Makes it easier to judge distance." Gibson chuckled, "Dark sumbitch out here ain't it. Okay, getting close. Here come the lights. Ease your power back, and start your flare."

Cramer closed the throttles just before the lights swept beneath them as Gibson continued coaching, "Ok, focus on the far light, keep her nose up, and let her sink. Hold it. Hold it. Forget the grease job, dammit, just bomb her in. She can take it."

Suddenly, the wheels slammed on, with a neck snapping jolt, lofting them back into the air. Cramer kicked rudder, fought to center the far light and kept her straight. The second bounce was softer, and the third time she touched, she stayed. They rumbled along in the darkness, feeling the wheels jolting over uneven ground. He touched brakes cautiously, then gradually increased pressure as the distant light rushed toward them. After the tail wheel touched, he increased back pressure, got on the brakes harder, and held it like that until they stopped, well short of the end light.

Gibson punched him on the shoulder. "Look at that! What did I tell you? Blind as a bat, John. But you're down in one piece, and you only used two thousand feet."

Cramer let out his breath. "Man, that was the hairiest Goddamned thing I've ever done in an airplane."

Gibson chuckled, "Don't worry. The next one will be easier. It'll never be a piece of cake, mind you, but the first one is always the hardest. Really makes the old bung-hole pucker huh?"

"A demonstration first, would have been nice."

"I figured you didn't need it. What the Hell, you've aced everything else in the course."

He shook his head, "Gibson, you've got to be the craziest son of a bitch in the Air Force. I'd never trust a student that far."

Gibson grabbed his shoulder, shook it and laughed, "You think I'm crazy? Wait 'till you get to Bien Hoa, buddy. There's a whole bunch of crazy bastards in that outfit. But don't worry. You'll fit right in. The tough part will be gettin' through the year without bustin' your ass."

The tiny civilian terminal looked strangely out of place on the sprawling Eglin complex. Few military bases had such an arrangement, but Eglin's primary mission of flight, and weapons test, dictated a need for convenient civilian transportation to arms industry experts and Defense Department bureaucrats in Washington.

A high, thin overcast blocked most of the sun's rays, and the temperature was down in the high eighties, as the small, twin engine airliner made a wide 180 degree turn, then rolled to a stop, 50 yards in front of them. Behind them, an eager stream of outbound passengers poured from the air-conditioned terminal and headed for the plane.

Betty squeezed Cramer's hand, and looked up at him. "You'll write me, and let me know you got there, OK ?"

"Sure. I'll send it to your mother's address. By the time I get to Vietnam, you'll probably be back in North Dakota."

She took a deep breath. "I'm leaving in the morning," she said. "Going home for good. Haven't seen my little boy for such a long time, and I miss the rest of them too."

"Must be nice to have a family like that."

"It's big, but it's always been close." Her voice broke, and she blinked back the moisture in her eyes. "God this hurts. I didn't want to go through this again, but here I am." She squinted up at him. "How can military people live like this? Having to leave each other, spending so much time apart. It's heartbreaking. Someone's always leaving. Someone's always saying good-by"

"Its not easy."

She looked down at the ramp, and shook her head. "Too tough for me. I'll miss you John. But it has to be this way. It would never work for us. I can't stand being away from my family, and you wouldn't be happy out of the Air Force."

The last of a dozen passengers neared the airliner's rear stairs, and he reached for her. "Well, I've got to get aboard. These last two months have been terrific. I'll never forget you."

She looked up at him, tears welling in her eyes, her voice trembling, "I won't forget you either."

He kissed her, making it a long one, feeling her soft curves as she squeezed against him. Finally he stepped back, lifted her hand, and kissed it. "God bless you Betty. I hope you have a long, and happy life."

He let go of her hand, and started walking backward, reluctant to lose sight of her. She gave him a little wave, her chin quivered, and she called to him, "You be careful John Cramer. You be careful, you hear?"

CHAPTER SEVENTEEN

BIEN HOA AIR BASE, SOUTH VIETNAM

They landed on a hard surface runway, rolled along paved taxiways, crossed a pierced, steel planking ramp, and finally parked in a fitting location for a lowly transport assigned to a fighter outfit...a muddy, weed infested lot.

As soon as the decrepit, C-47 rolled to a stop, the other passengers, obviously old timers, got to their feet, and stampeded for the rear. A tired looking loadmaster, dressed in a faded, badly worn flying suit, removed the cargo strap tied across the empty door frame as the passengers crowded around him. Once the exit was clear, most jumped to the ground before he could get the flimsy, portable stairway in place.

Cramer unfastened his seat belt, picked up his bags, and walked carefully down the greasy, declined slope of the cargo deck. Tail wheel airplanes...damn things were all alike. Hard to handle, and downright inconvenient on the ground. Couldn't even walk in 'em without being careful.

Sweat trickled down the loadmaster's florid, pock-marked face, as he smiled. "Well Captain, you've just survived the most boring seven minutes of flying in Vietnam, the fabled Bien Hoa--Tan Son Nhut Courier." His grin widened as he cocked his head, and stabbed a finger at Cramer's chest. "Before you leave here, you'll know every tree, and bush out there. Uh...you are a C-47 pilot ain't you?"

"How could you tell?"

"Easy. You've got that, I've been screwed look about you."

Cramer chuckled. "You're a perceptive man Sarge."

The sergeant reached for his bags. "Here sir, I'll hold your stuff until you're outside."

He descended the steps, then turned, and reached up as the loadmaster handed him his luggage. When he turned around, he nearly bumped into an officer who had suddenly materialized behind him.

A slim major with sunken cheeks, beard stubble, and deep set, bloodshot eyes, stuck out his arm. "Captain Cramer, I'm Major Keller, your operations officer. Welcome to the Junk Air Force."

Cramer dropped his right-hand bag and shook hands. "Thank you sir."

The major, dressed in a badly worn, sweat stained flying suit, leaned over, and picked up the awol bag, then gestured toward his Jeep. "Throw your shit in back. I'll give you a ride up to your quarters."

What a start. A personal reception from a superior officer? In a war zone? Remarkable.

After the bags were loaded, they climbed aboard, and Keller turned the jeep around, then slowly drove out of the weed infested lot, jolting and splashing through several mud holes along the way. Cramer held on tight, doing his best to stay in the seat. Damn, it was hot.

Finally, they reached the concrete portion of the ramp, and Keller shifted gears and nodded toward a line of A1Es, armed with bombs, and rockets. "Intelligence says there's a VC outfit near Tay Ninh," he said. "They're expected to attack tonight. We're gonna throw 'em a little party."

"Do you fly much over here, Sir?"

Keller gave him a tired glance, and nodded. "I flew last night, flew this morning, and one of those back there is mine for tonight. Yeah...yeah, we fly a lot. Everyone flies a lot. FACs, fighters, or transports, it makes no difference."

They drove off the flight line onto a narrow gravel road. Keller shifted to third, and they rolled along, leisurely at 25, passing a line of buildings with peeling paint, rotted door-frames, and broken windows. Mud-holes infested the road, and waist high weeds grew everywhere. On each side, sprawling, 80 foot trees, draped with sinister looking mosses and vines, lined their route.

"Don't let the looks of the place get you down," Keller said. "This is the Vietnamese area. We live in a fenced-in compound a little farther on."

Cramer shook his head, and snorted, "Damn place smells like a shithouse."

Keller flashed him a sardonic smile. "Our ARVN allies seldom bother to piss indoors. Wherever the urge strikes them, they just whip it out, and drain their sump."

A half-mile later they came to the American compound, where neat rows of white huts, trimmed in green, filled a large area behind a tall, heavy wire, hurricane fence. Keller stopped at the gate, showed his pass to the ARVN guard, returned his salute, then drove inside.

On the right, two men in sweat stained flying suits came out of a low, slat sided building, one slicing open a letter, with the other already reading. Well, now he knew where the mailroom was.

They idled slowly along, passing a line of huts on the left. On the right, a long low building offered shade to a wrinkled, barefoot Vietnamese woman, wearing what looked like black pajamas, as she dumped steaming water from a huge aluminum pot. The odor of hot spices, and a clatter of rattling pans came from the setting, betraying the site as the mess hall. Things were coming together. All he needed now, was a place to get some booze--and a place to sleep it off.

"I've already assigned you a hut," Keller said. "Put you in with Bishop and Williams. Figured you already knew them, since they were in the class ahead of you at Hurlburt."

"Glad to hear it, sir. I like both of those guys." He looked away and scanned the area. The huts seemed clean, as well as functional, and the streets were free of litter. Other than a faint, pervasive odor of mildew, there seemed little to complain about.

They rolled to a stop in front of hut 124, and Keller turned off the jeep, stepped out, and grabbed a bag. Cramer took the other two, and followed him.

Once inside, the major dropped the bag next to a freshly made bunk. "This is yours," he said. He unzipped his left breast pocket, took out a small notebook, glanced up and said, "Hang on for a minute. I've got to check something."

"Yes sir."

Cramer took the opportunity to survey his new home. Apparently, utility was the primary objective here--a sturdy, sub-tropical structure with peaked roof, and louvered sides, hinged at the top so they could be propped open for increased ventilation. Under the louvers, screen wire ran all the way from the bare wooden floor to the eaves. The size, about fifteen by twenty, seemed more than adequate for four men.

One thing was certain, the decor would never make the pages of *House Beautiful*. A metal frame GI bunk, under mosquito netting, occupied each of the four corners. On the west wall, an obviously home made, boxy looking desk, fashioned from scrap lumber was secured to the framework by bent over nails. Near the center of the room, a crudely constructed table, was tastefully matched by four scruffy looking, discarded ammunition crates that apparently served as chairs.

Keller interrupted the survey. "What do you think?"

Cramer gave him a thumbs-up. "Beats hell out of the year I spent in tents in Korea."

The major managed his first real smile, then unzipped the small pocket on the left arm of his flying suit, and took out a pack of Luckys. He shook one out, set fire to the end, and exhaled the smoke.

He seemed about to speak, then paused, and pulled a small piece of cigarette paper off his lip. Finally, he looked at Cramer, his craggy face reflecting an obvious fatigue. "Okay, Captain. I'll dispense with the usual bullshit about this being the greatest outfit in the Air Force, and get to the point. You're here because somebody thought you were a pilot with skill, initiative, and enough guts to do a difficult job."

Keller looked away for a moment, and stuffed the smokes back into his sleeve, then zipped the pocket shut, and looked back at Cramer. "In this outfit, all flying regulations are waived. We only have two rules--do the job, and try to stay alive. The details of how to accomplish that, will be left up to you. That's all the orientation you're going to get! Are you ready to fly?"

The sudden, question jolted Cramer. "Uh...yes sir. Just as soon as I change into my flying suit. You don't want me to fly in khakis do you?"

70

"Captain, I don't give a big rat's ass if you fly in jockey shorts, and shower clogs, just as long as you fly."

"Yes sir," Cramer said, reaching for his briefcase. "I'll be ready as soon as I get my checklist." He wondered why Keller smiled when he said that.

CHAPTER EIGHTEEN

Bill Bishop, the good natured, chunky, gray haired, just turned forty, ex B-47 pilot he knew from Hurlburt, met him coming in the door of hut 124, and they shook hands warmly.

"Nice to know someone who's an old hand here," Cramer said.

Bishop, now only slightly overweight, grinned. "I'm not an old hand yet, but after a month, I'm at least checked out. It's good to see you, John."

Cramer held up his checklist." Obviously, there's no need to lug this around anymore." He turned, and threw the small booklet into the corner.

Bishop chuckled. "I see they gave you the FNG treatment."

"FNG?"

"Fucking new guy." Bishop smiled, and gave a little shrug. "Don't worry, it won't last long. In a few days they'll treat you like an old hand."

Cramer shook his head. "Man…what a reception. The Ops Officer meets me at the plane, gives me a ride up here--bores me with an orientation that must have lasted thirty seconds, then drives my ass back to the flight line, and puts me in the right seat of the same airplane I just came in on."

"Don't waste much time do they? How was the flying?"

"Different! The big some-bitch in the left seat didn't even say "hi." I couldn't even get the checklist open before his hands were darting all over the cockpit--the left engine starts, she rolls ahead--the right engine starts-- and I'm still looking for my friggin' headset. Before I can call the tower, we're off the ground. He levels off at sixty feet, and blows the leaves off every Goddamned tree between here and Saigon. When we leave Tan Son Nhut, it's the same shit all over again. After we get back, he shuts her off, smiles, sticks out his hand, and says, 'Hi, I'm Don Wilson."

Bishop gave him a wry smile. "He's your new section chief."

"That's encouraging," Cramer said, as he looked around the room. "Where's Mark?"

"On a trip to Ban Me Thout."

"Where?"

"Bammy Too." Bishop shook his head, and chuckled, "Don't ask me to spell it." He reached out, picked his gun belt off the table, and began strapping it on. "Anyway, I've got an evening run to Soc Trang. See you later."

Cramer looked at his watch. "Time to check out the club, I guess."

Bishop reached for his hat, and nodded to his left. "Fifty yards that way. Take the walk to your right, and then the first left. You can't miss it. Except for the field ration mess, and latrine, it's the biggest building in the compound. See you later."

Bishop turned, and left. The screen door slammed behind him, banging twice before staying closed.

Cramer looked around the room, noticing a small metal picnic cooler sitting on a stand in the center of the west wall. He walked over, and lifted the lid. Inside, a surprising assortment of soft drinks, and mixers crowded a large chunk of ice. Above that, at eye level, a dusty wooden shelf, sagged wearily under the weight of several, forty ounce bottles of brand name liquor and a stack of cheap plastic glasses.

"Not bad," he mumbled. "Think I'm gonna like it here."

Inspection finished, he went out the door, and walked slowly between the huts. It felt a bit cooler now. Not much over 90. At the crosswalk, he turned left, and stopped momentarily, staring at the building ahead--the first, one room Officer's Club he'd ever seen.

Nothing fancy about this one. Screened openings without glass ran across the entire front. It wasn't hard to figure that anytime it rained, and the wind blew, it was going to be wet inside. He resumed walking, and the babble of voices coming from the room diminished as he approached. Obviously, he'd been spotted.

First impressions were important, and the next few minutes would be crucial. He climbed the steps, removed his cap, opened the door, and stepped inside. All conversation ceased, as the occupants focused their attention on the fucking new guy. Cramer faked a lack of concern, turned his head slowly, and let the suspense build as he surveyed the sparsely furnished enclosure.

The arrangement was, to say the least, stark. With no interior paneling, the 2x4 frame was obvious. On the back wall, a badly scarred dart board hung from a rusty spike, while overhead, two rattling, fly specked ceiling fans made wobbly, unbalanced circles as they feebly stirred the smoke-filled air. Underfoot--dirty black heel marks, and scattered deep abrasions covered an unfinished, plywood floor.

Round wooden stools, surrounded the horseshoe shaped bar, and above the register crowding the west wall, a huge cardboard sign screamed out in red letters, "Beer ten cents, Mixed Drinks a quarter. Drink faster. You're losing money."

Inspection completed, he smiled, and nodded to the crowd. "Can't stay long, chaps. Just dropped by to get the name of your decorator."

The room roared with laughter. He relaxed, slid onto a nearby stool, and ordered a round of drinks.

In spite of predominantly bad weather, and junky equipment, the Group functioned smoothly. There were no assigned co-pilots. Incoming C-47 pilots were upgraded to Aircraft Commander after an initial checkout that seldom lasted more than a few weeks. Once qualified, both pilots swapped seats on succeeding legs of a mission, and the responsibility of command rested on the shoulders of the officer on the left.

Although surprisingly brief, Cramer's checkout was grueling, and thorough. Each day he made from three to four runs, in a hectic schedule that was clearly designed to give maximum exposure to his new work environment, and familiarize him with the country. By the end of the first month, he had landed on, or air-dropped over, more than 60 locations. After that, his initiation was deemed complete, and he was allowed to select flights on his own, taking any that were not yet chosen from the morning's listing. Obviously, getting to Operations early, had its rewards, and he took advantage of his farm boy heritage by rising before daylight and beating the other pilots to work.

The diversity of missions was awesome. Some went to conventional airfields with paved, well lighted runways. Others to soggy Delta outposts with rutted, dirt runways only inches above the water table-- still others, to isolated, Special Forces camps surrounded by jungle, and towering mountains. In those places he squeezed the old plane onto narrow, washed-out strips that pounded her unmercifully, taxing his skills to the limit. Some locations had no airstrip at all, so heavy packs of food, medicine, and ammunition were kicked out the open side door, at altitudes just high enough for the cargo chute to open, and make one swing before the bundle thudded to the ground.

Most days began, and ended, in a desperate struggle with the country's predominately bad weather. In the morning, fog covered low lying areas, making low visibility approaches into poorly defined airstrips a high stakes gamble of guess, and gasp. By 10 AM, the fog burned off, and the crews enjoyed a brief period of decent weather. Early afternoon brought high humidity, with the heat of a blazing sun spawning thunderstorms at an incredible rate. Before long, the entire country turned dark, as billowing black cumulus boiled upward faster than a rattling old C-47 could climb. After that, there were only two choices--punch through, and ride it out, or take her down on the deck, and hug the trees, in a desperate, life threatening gamble to stay visual, and find the destination.

All six of the American crewed C-47s, bore the insignia of the Vietnamese Air Force, and were on loan from the impoverished host country. Filthy, metal fatigued, and junky, they were doggedly maintained by a pitifully few, sleep deprived American mechanics, who stumbled through an endless string of sweat soaked, thankless days--improvising this, and jury-rigging that.

Flight crews fared little better. Flying in rain, water poured in through the poorly sealed windshield, cascading over the pilot's knees, running down their legs, and filling their boots with a toe squishing, icy bath, drug down from the stratosphere.

Calculated risk became his way of life. By the end of the first few weeks he had encountered more dicey situations, and survived more close calls than he had experienced in his entire career. In spite of that, his prayers had been answered. This was indeed, the great adventure he had hoped for, but he could not escape the disquieting conclusion that his survival until the end of his tour, was far from being a sure thing.

Streaks of lightning, door rattling thunder, and gully washing rain, filled the compound as Cramer rubbed the back of his neck, paced the floor, then looked at his watch for the tenth time. Damn! Happy hour had already started.

Cold mist dampened his face as he opened the door, and peered out. Mold. You couldn't help smelling it. Always the damn mold. God, what a country. Run down, diseased, and decadent, with some of the shitiest weather on earth.

Oh well, a man had to do, what a man had to do. He shuffled his feet, feeling for firm footing, then lunged into the deluge. The cold rain washed over him, soaking him as he ran, stretching his legs to the limit, feet pounding in sodden, rhythmic splashes.

Approaching the corner, he slowed, then rounded the slippery bend in careful, prancing steps. Soaking wet was one thing, covered with mud, another. Finally, he reached the steps, jumped to the top, turned the knob, and barged into the room.

Thirty pilots, and a half dozen navigators filled the club, talking and laughing boisterously as they crowded around the bar--making jokes, and telling war stories.

A cold spray drifted in through the screens, floating all the way to the back wall. Those nearest the windows kept their backs turned, blocking the mist by hunching their shoulders, and clutching their glasses close to their chest.

Cramer, elbowed his way through the crowd, with dribbles of cold runoff spattering behind him on the plywood floor. Time was wasting. For one fleeting hour, drinks were a dime. Getting drunk might be fun, but getting drunk cheap, was an opportunity.

He crowded in on the far side of the bar, threw down a waterlogged, ten cent script note, and yelled above the roar. "Gimme a CC and soda!"

Steve Davis a muscular, A1E pilot with wiry brown hair, clapped him on the back, sending an explosion of droplets skyward. Davis leaned close, and yelled above the din, "Where the hell you been, John? You've already missed the first round."

"Yeah I know," Cramer shouted. "I was waiting for it to stop raining, but I finally realized that wasn't going to happen."

"Damn John, I'm disappointed in you, letting a little water stand between you, and demon rum. Show's a serious lack of dedication."

Cramer nodded. "Don't sweat the small shit buddy, it's only a temporary lapse. I'll catch up. Anyway, how'd it go with you today--kill any bad guys?"

Davis shook his head. "Naw. Only one mission. Flew cover for a couple of C-123s making air drops north of Plieku. Talk about dull shit. How about you?"

"Made a couple of runs. Ban Me Thout, and Vung Tau in the morning. Soc Trang this afternoon."

Davis gave him a warm smile. "You're hitting your stride John. Been here for more than a month. Not an FNG anymore. They tell me, you're flying your ass off. Getting a reputation as a hard worker."

"This is the most interesting assignment I ever had," Cramer said. "The airplanes are junk, but I love the work. Never had anything like it."

Davis took a sip, and sat his glass on the bar. "Yeah, it is different. That's for damn sure. I'm eight months into my tour, and I'm not bored yet." He nudged Cramer's arm. "They tell me, you flew KC-135s in SAC."

He nodded. "Sure did."

Davis gave him a sly smile. "Must be quite a change. From sleek shiny jets, to worn out Gooney Birds."

"What the hell. If you gotta fly junk, you might as well fly old junk, right?"

Davis feigned surprise. "Junk? Never heard that before. Apparently you don't get misty eyed, and nostalgic about C-47s like some of the other guys. To hear them tell it, the airplane's some kind of friggin', national treasure."

Cramer raised his eyebrows. "Well, maybe they're right. I have to admit a certain reverence for the old girl. Lot of history behind her, you know? In fact, every once in a while, in the evening, I like to sneak down to the parking area just to pay my respects. It's almost like some kind of...religious experience. Standing there in the weeds, with the mosquitoes chewing on my ass--mud oozing over the tops of my boots--drinking in the sight of that worn out, battered old wreck." He lifted his hands, made a frame, and peered through the hole. "There she is...silhouetted in the setting sun...mud spattered, corroded, oil soaked, and junky, but damn, she flies good." He gave Davis a sly look. "Talk about responsive--only takes 50 pounds of pressure to ease her into a gentle turn."

Davis chuckled. "Bet you can hardly wait to get to work in the morning."

"Cramer nodded. "You got that right. Wonderful work environment. Filthy cockpit. Tangled plumbing. Rusty pipes. Popped rivets, wheezing engines, rattling sheet metal, and a rate of climb that gets all the way into double digits."

Davis clapped him on the back, sending a shower of drops flying. "Glad to see you've found your niche, buddy. Met your destiny, by God! Our boy John." He made a grand, sweeping gesture. "Born to be in C-47s!"

Cramer grinned, and chuckled. "You asshole. I wouldn't slam a shit house door that hard."

CHAPTER NINETEEN

Mark Williams, the good natured, youthful looking, captain with reddish-blond hair led the way as Cramer followed him into the dingy, musty smelling C-47 section. Behind the twelve foot counter, a towering, Captain Don Wilson turned from the scheduling board, and laid down his grease pencil. Six--five, and grouchy looking, the man was in fact, a grumbling, but good natured pussy cat. Today he even managed a slight smile. "Back in record time. You guys don't fool around."

"Nice to know we're appreciated," Cramer said.

"You got a reward?" Mark asked.

Wilson gave them a smug smile. "Matter of fact, I do. Easy run. Grab a bite, pack a bag, and be back here, ready to go to Tan Son Nhut in an hour. "

"Why pack a bag?" Cramer asked. "It's less than twenty miles over there."

"Tan Son Nhut's only the first stop. You'll be hauling a State Department civilian to Bangkok. Unless, you want me to give the trip to someone else." Wilson cocked his head, and squinted. "I could send you to Muc Hoa."

"No!"

"Hell no!"

"Somehow I knew I could depend on you guys."

The Tan Son Nhut ramp appeared unusually quiet, as the crew crowded together, huddled in the shade of the overhanging wing tip. Farther down the ramp, near the terminal, a red and white, World Airlines 707 was loading passengers. But where they were parked, there was no activity at all. That was the way the head shed liked it. Get too near a main terminal, and international travelers might wonder what a bunch of Yankees were doing flying a Vietnamese, military C-47.

The Engineer, Tech Sergeant Thompson, stroked his handlebar mustache, and looked suspiciously at Cramer. "It don't figure, Captain. Why would some high level civilian from the State Department fly with us. Those people always go first class."

Cramer raised his eyebrows. "Maybe the ambassador blew their travel budget in a crap game. "

Williams pointed across the ramp. "Here comes a limousine. Must be our passenger."

"Well it's damn sure not the ambassador," Cramer said.

"How can you tell?"

"There's no cute little flag flying over the front fender."

Williams gave him a skeptical look. "You're not going to call us to attention are you?"

Cramer snorted, "For a damn civilian? You've got to be kidding."

"S'pose it's the President?"

"For that damn civilian, I'll make an exception."

The limousine slowed, then came to a stop forty feet in front of the plane. The crew reluctantly left the shade, and walked toward the car. A uniformed driver stepped out, and held the rear door open. A head of wavy, blond hair emerged, and the engineer said softly, "Holy shit! It's a broad."

A shapely, well tanned leg followed, and she tipped her head back as she exited, then straightened up, and looked them over. Thompson mumbled softly out of the side of his mouth, "Make that a good lookin' broad."

She walked toward them, beauty in motion, radiant in a yellow, knee length dress, with white high heels, and matching handbag, moving with a self confident grace that was downright intimidating.

Cramer stepped forward to meet her, and she extended her hand, stunning him with a dazzling smile. "Hi, I'm Nancy Alderman. I'm with the State Department. I'll be your only passenger."

He took her hand, feeling her soft, gentle grip. "Miss Alderman, I'm your pilot, John Cramer." He pointed toward Mark. "This is your other pilot Captain Williams. The two enlisted swine are Sergeants Thompson, and Procopio, our Engineer and loadmaster."

Her smile faded. "You call your Sergeants swine?"

Cramer grinned. "Why not? Williams and I, are both former enlisted swine, so we're familiar with the breed."

She smiled again, and he vowed to keep her that way. They walked slowly toward the aircraft, exchanging remarks about the heat. Suddenly, she stopped, and her mouth dropped open as she stared at the plane. "Good Lord! They told me it might be a little shabby, but this is ridiculous."

Cramer put his hand lightly on her shoulder. "Don't be too concerned about her looks, mam. She hasn't had a bath for a while."

"Looks like she hasn't been washed since she was built!"

He gave her a weak smile.

She squinted at him, and pointed toward the mud spattered, landing gear. "What's that red stuff running down that pipe?"

"Uh...just a little hydraulic fluid mam. Seals are a bit worn. Don't worry, Sergeant Thompson filled her this morning. We won't run out."

She nodded toward the Vietnamese insignia. "Is this a VNAF plane?"

Mark butted in, crowding past Cramer, giving her a kiss-ass, ingratiating smile. "Yes mam. They let us use their stuff while we're, ah...advising them."

"Spare me the advisor con, Captain. I work for the same government you do. I know what you guys do."

Cramer cleared his throat, and gestured toward the door. "Uh, perhaps, we should get aboard mam. Sergeant Procopio will give you a hand up.

Watch your step now. This ladder's a bit shaky. Not really suited for high heels.

She reached up, took Procopio's hand, then paused, and looked back at them. "Can we ease off on that 'mam' stuff, guys? As far as rank is concerned, it's a draw. My GS rating is the same as Captain. Call me Nancy."

She turned, and climbed the shaky ladder with only a slight wobble to her white pumps. Williams watched as she ascended, peering up her dress like a leering lecher, and rolling his eyes skyward.

Finally, Cramer, and Williams climbed aboard while Thompson led her up the greasy incline, holding on to her arm. Behind them, Procopio fastened a tie-down strap in a Z shape across the gaping entrance.

Nancy eased herself into the forward bucket seat, as Thompson asked, "Do you smoke mam?"

She shook her head.

"Well that's fortunate," Thompson said dryly. "We like to keep our cabin smelling fresh."

She fumbled with her seat belt, and giggled, "Smells fresh alright. Like a garbage dump." She suppressed another chuckle, then looked up, and nodded toward the rear. "Maybe you should close the door Sarge--you know--so we can go?"

"Sorry, mam...there's no door."

Her eyes darted around the cabin, and she laughed nervously, "What do you mean, no door?"

Thompson pointed to the tie down strap across the opening, "I'm afraid that's it."

She squinted. "The door is just a strap?"

He nodded. "Yes mam. Just a strap."

She looked around, apparently bewildered. "This has got to be the most beat up, foul smelling, piece of crap I've ever been in...and now, you tell me there's no door? "

"'Fraid not."

"Good Lord!" she giggled. "And I used to complain about Eastern Air Lines." Suddenly, she lost it, doubled over, and laughed until tears ran down her cheeks.

The crew stood there helplessly, trading embarrassed little smiles.

Finally, she got herself under control, straightened up, searched her purse, found a hanky, and wiped her eyes. After that, she blew her nose, shook her head, and chuckled, "Damn that Benish. I'll bet he's behind this. Donaldson was probably in on it too. They said they'd get me." She smiled up at Cramer. "Oh well, this ought to be a real experience. I might as well enjoy it."

"We'll do our best to make it a memorable occasion," Cramer said. He motioned toward the cockpit. "Tell you what...instead of sitting back here, why don't you come up front. We don't use a navigator on this run. You can sit in his seat."

"Why thank you." She shot a nervous glance at the gaping rear doorway, then unfastened her belt, and followed him forward.

As they went through the cabin door, Cramer waved his hand expansively, highlighting the filthy, grease stained cockpit. "As you can see, no effort has been spared to make this a pleasant workplace."

He pointed to a tangled maze of tubing, and valves. "Sam Starbuck, the head plumber at Ellis Island, designed the hydraulics. The instruments are from F. W. Woolworth, and the cockpit lighting was done by Coleman."

He pointed to a battered metal case. "We even have a radio. This particular unit was, in fact, original equipment on the world's largest ocean liner. A dedicated seaman removed it just in time, saving it from a watery grave, during that unfortunate incident with the iceberg in the North Atlantic."

As Thompson showed her to the navigator's seat, Cramer took the left pilot's seat, Williams, the right. The left engine was started, the proper switches positioned, and the right engine was subsequently cranked. A slight fumble with the mixture control produced a resounding backfire, causing everyone to jump. Williams snickered, and slapped Cramer on the shoulder with the back of his hand. "Nice move, asshole" he chuckled. "We got one of the wheels on board, and you backfire an engine."

Cramer felt his face getting hot as he grumbled, "Aw shove it up your f…f….foolish ass."

CHAPTER TWENTY

The smoke in the room was as thick as a London fog, and Cramer silently thanked God he'd broken the habit years ago. The one solitary bulb overhead couldn't have been more than 20 watts, so reading labels on the bottles behind the bartender was nearly impossible. Couldn't tell the CC from the cheap stuff. Maybe that was part of the plan.

It had to be the loudest band in Bangkok, but Mark Williams seemed to thrive on the music. He leaned toward the pretty, brown skinned girl on his left, shouting something in her ear that was either funny, dirty or both. The girl tipped her head back, laughed, and clapped him on the back.

Cramer took another sip, sat his glass on the bar, and glanced to his right as a sultry looking girl in a tight fitting, white dress walked toward him. The contrast between her flawless brown skin, and white fabric was electrifying, but he shook his head, and she veered away, passing behind him in an obvious quest for a more likely prospect.

He downed the last of his drink, then put his hand on William's shoulder. Mark snapped his head around. "Hey John, loosen up. There's a lot of action in here. Enjoy yourself."

Cramer leaned toward his ear, and shouted, "I've had it with this noise. I'm going back to the hotel."

Mark gave him a sly grin. "She won't be there John."

"Who?"

"You know who, asshole. Nancy. The one you've got the hots for. The one you couldn't take your eyes off of. Why waste your time? We've got plenty of good looking women right here. Forget her. She's probably at one of those fancy-assed receptions with some limp-wristed, State Department pansey "

"Screw you, Williams. I hope you get the clap."

Mark grinned, and squeezed the girl. "Don't rush me. I'm working on it."

Cramer slid off his seat, and patted him on the shoulder. "Enjoy yourself. I'll see you later. I'm going back to the hotel."

A couple of speeding cars and a smoking, garishly painted, diesel truck whizzed by on the other side of the cab, as Cramer struggled out of the tiny Datsun, and stepped onto the sidewalk. He reached into his pocket, pulled out a wad of cash, and fumbled through the unfamiliar money. Once it was sorted out, he paid the driver, turned around and walked toward the hotel entrance. A uniformed doorman clicked his heels, reached out, opened a massive, gold framed, glass door and grandly waved him inside.

The expansive, high ceilinged lobby was opulent--inlaid panels, expensive carpet, hand carved exotic wooden tables, and overstuffed furniture covered with the finest fabric. Thank God for per diem, he thought, if I didn't get that, there's no way I'd stay in a place like this.

He walked into the main lounge, and headed for the far end of the dimly lit bar. Piped in Thai music was playing softly over the intercom. Nice touch. Played with seemingly mis-strung instruments, softer was usually better with that stuff.

Ten seats beyond the entrance, the bar made a 90 degree turn. Any of the three seats on the end section, would give him a good view of the room...if his eyes ever adjusted to the light.

As he sat down, a tall, Caucasian bartender approached, resplendent in a brass buttoned, red jacket. Cramer ordered a CC, and soda. The man nodded cordially, then turned to an impressive array of bottles, selected one, and poured. They weren't into charity here. He got an honest shot, and not a whisper more.

He took a sip, and scanned the expansive room. The first time around he missed her, but suddenly, there she was, sitting with two couples at a circular table near the back.

Her back was to the bar, and more than likely, she hadn't seen him, so he sat quietly, looking things over, trying to determine if she was with someone. After a few minutes, the featured quartet returned, and he noted with satisfaction that none of them played the trumpet, so conversation would at least be possible.

One couple at her table got up to dance, and his hopes rose momentarily, then sagged when it became obvious the other pair wasn't going anywhere.

To hell with it. Indecision was the father of failure. It was time to make his move. All he'd suffer was a little embarrassment if she turned him down. He'd survived that before. At least this way, he'd know, one way or the other. He downed his drink, eased out of his seat, and circled to the right, approaching so he'd be in her line of sight, and she would, hopefully, give some indication she was glad to see him.

It worked better than expected. Suddenly, her face lit up with that terrific smile, and she waved.

Nancy introduced him to the overweight, obviously married couple at the table, and he promptly forgot their names. Suddenly he felt clumsy-- awkward--almost overwhelmed. God, she was gorgeous.

Dammit, he had to snap out of this, or he'd ruin everything. He forced a smile, and ask her to dance. She accepted, rose from the table, and he finally began to relax.

By the time the third number was over, he knew she'd be in Bangkok for two more weeks. Following that, she was going back to Saigon on the airlines. More importantly, he also learned that she, and another girl from the embassy, shared a house in one of the few good neighborhoods in Saigon.

82

She danced well enough to make him look good, and he marveled at her sense of humor. It was hard to believe a woman like her wasn't attached.

He looked down at her. "Is there any chance you could throw caution to the winds, and tour the city with me?"

She answered gently, "I'd like to, but I'm more or less committed to stay with the group for the evening."

He quashed his disappointment, and tried another angle. "I've got to go back to Vietnam in the morning, so this is my only night here. Is there anyway I could see you after you're back in country?"

"Can you get time off?"

He nodded. "Unless something unusual comes up. I'm flying more than most of the guys, so I can take a break if I give them notice."

"Great. When we get back to the table, I'll give you my number at the Embassy, and the house. You can usually get through to one place or the other." She gave him a sly look. "Who knows, I might even be able to come out to Bien Hoa to see you."

"You know what base I'm from?"

"Of course. I even know what outfit you're in."

How could that be, he wondered? As far as he knew, she hadn't asked any of his crew. "Well...I'd like for you to come out sometime, that would be nice. But I'm not sure you could get on base."

She smiled, and answered quietly, "I can go anywhere I want over here. On that base, or any other."

The way she said it, he knew she wasn't kidding.

CHAPTER TWENTY ONE

The out of balance ceiling fan wobbled erratically, fitfully stirring Sergeant Saunders' thinning blond hair. Saunders smiled as he poured a healthy shot of CC, then splashed a dash of soda into the glass. "Congratulations on passing your IP check Captain."

Cramer picked up the drink, took a swallow, and tossed Saunders the required twenty five cents in script. "Thanks Sarge. Good drink."

Saunders moved to his left, and brushed a few wisps of hair out of his eyes. "Pouring straight shots is my specialty. It's a gift."

"How'd you get this job?"

Saunders leaned forward, and put both hands against the back edge of the bar. "Volunteered. What the hell. It's nice to have something to do after I get down from flying. And the extra money comes in handy." He smiled faintly. "I've got a girl friend in Saigon. You know...pay her rent...buy her groceries. Keeps her off the streets."

Cramer looked to his left. Donald Jenson, a slender, newly promoted captain with brown, crew cut hair, finished his beer, put the empty on the bar, and gestured for another. Saunders retrieved the empty, tossed it in the trash barrel, and put a fresh brew in front of the captain.

Jenson winced slightly as he pried the tab up. The beer gave the expected pfzzzt, and he put it to his lips and took a drink.

"I hear you fly U-10s," Cramer said.

Jenson's cheeks puffed out, as he nodded, swallowing with obvious difficulty, and blinking his watering eyes. Finally, he answered in a hoarse, half-strangled voice, "As a matter of fact, I do."

"How do you like it?" Cramer asked.

Jenson wiped his lips, and dried his fingers on the leg of his flying suit. "For an ex fighter pilot it's damn sure a change of pace. Single engine, unarmed planes are not a great way to travel in this country."

Cramer squinted. "Must get hairy sometimes, those psy-war missions especially."

"You've got that right. There's a jungle full of enemy soldiers with small arms, and automatic weapons out there. I have to fly around at low altitude, and insult the little bastards with a line of bullshit spewed from a loud speaker. Guess how well that goes over."

Just then, Captain Steve Davis walked in, looking refreshed, obviously just back from the shower, his still damp, straight brown hair combed back, and for once, plastered down on the ends. Cramer called to him, "How was the trip to the Philippines?"

Davis took the only remaining empty seat across the horseshoe shaped bar, and shook his head. "I thought that A1E was slow, but I'll never ride in a C-47 again. Damn thing just hangs in the air."

"How'd everything go at Clark?" Cramer asked.

Davis gave him a sly grin. "Miserable as hell. A real punishment. Air conditioning, plush clubs, swimming, tennis with the wives club, all those beautiful flowers, and manicured lawns--you know, a real pain in the ass. One disappointment after the other."

Cramer chuckled. "My condolences."

Steve picked up his drink, and looked sideways at him. "Of course you know all about that, don't you. You C-47 guys really have it rough. Flying all over Southeast Asia like a bunch of fucking travel agents on holiday-- high rise hotels, fine restaurants, high class bars."

"Hey, it all evens out," Cramer said. "You guys get the medals, we get per diem, and travel."

Steve smiled, and shook his head. "It's a damn shame how they treat you poor bastards. Trouble is, it's all wasted on a guy like you. You're just not refined enough to appreciate it. You belong here John. You're a back country kind of guy--real Bien Hoa riff-raff. "

"Glad you enjoyed your trip. Where'd you stay? One of those Quonset huts, or the BOQ?"

"You know that thing they call the motel?" Davis said. "The one with three corridors?"

"The U shaped building with the bird shit running down its side?"

Davis took a sip, and nodded. "Only two bathrooms in the whole damn place. Both of 'em at the end of the corridor? Did you ever stay there?"

Cramer sat his glass down, and leaned one elbow on the bar. "Yeah. The rooms aren't bad, but it's a little inconvenient going all the way down the hall, and around the corner, just to take a leak."

"That feature caused me a problem," Davis said."

"How so?" Cramer asked.

"I flew over with Mark, and Denny. Mark and I, had the corner room, Denny, the one next to it. After we checked in, we're standing out in the hall trying to decide whether to go to the club, or take in a movie."

"Tough decision."

Steve took another sip, and nodded. "We're standing in the corridor discussing options when a door pops open down the line, and this gorgeous chick comes rushing out with nothing on but a thin, shorty nightgown."

The room went suddenly silent, as Davis stifled a grin, and his eyes swept the bar. "So, anyway, this broad bursts out of her room, turns in our direction, and starts running flat-out toward me. Man she was something. Beautiful face, fantastic body, great legs, and I can see she's got nothing--I mean *nothing* on under that little bitty nightgown."

Cramer grinned, looked down at the bar and shook his head. "Some guys have all the luck."

"Ain't it the truth?" Davis said. "All my life I've been eat up with envy 'cause stuff like this happened to other guys, but never me. But this time,"-- he slapped the bar--"this time, by God, it's my turn. Here she comes," he shouted, spreading his arms wide. "Running full tilt, with a look of desperation on her face, like she just can't wait to get to me. So I open my arms to take her in, and just then, she rounds the corner, sprays shit across the toes of my shoes, and hauls ass for the bathroom."

The room roared with laughter, as Cramer shook his head. What an outfit. Every evening something like this was going on in here. Bawdy humor, self-deprecating jokes, and an endless series of spell-binding war stories. God, he loved this place. These guys were like family. For the first time since Sandy left, he really felt at home. Sure it wouldn't last forever. But for now, just being here was enough.

Captain Don Wilson rose from his desk, picked up the paper towel lying on the counter, and wiped his face as Cramer walked into the sweltering C-47 section.

"When are you going to get air conditioning in here?" he said."

"Probably the same day Hell freezes over," Wilson grumbled. He stooped low, reached under the counter, brought out a short stack of papers, and tossed them on the counter. "Finally got your IP orders. Congratulations. Martin said your checkride was letter perfect."

"Thanks," Cramer said. "Uh...do you suppose I could have a couple of days off?"

Wilson looked surprised. "Why not? You've been working harder than anyone in the section. Make the most of it. When you get back, I'm sending you to Nha Trang for a couple of weeks. They'll fly your ass off up there."

Cramer chuckled, "Now won't that be a refreshing change of pace?"

It was cloudy, and surprisingly cool as Cramer sat under the ceiling fan on the hotel veranda, sipping his drink. On the sidewalk below, a few yards away, a beggar woman with crossed, withered legs, sat on a cushion strapped to her bottom--scooting along--making her way, by propelling herself ape-like, on rag wrapped knuckles.

Finally, she stopped below him, and looked up, a woeful expression on her deeply lined face. Cramer reached in his pocket, leaned over, stuck his arm through the railing, and handed her a hundred P. She award him a beetle nut blackened smile, took the money, and croaked her thanks in a raspy voice.

Across the street, a skinny, tubercular looking cop, snarled at her, and pointed his nightstick down the street. She gave him a fearful look, stuffed the money into her blouse, and scooted away, head down, shoulders hunched, arms pumping, her deformed body swinging like a pendulum with each onerous stride. Cramer watched until she disappeared around the corner. God, he wondered, what must her life be like? A social untouchable in a third world country. What a sorry-assed place.

86

Minutes later, at the other tables, all heads turned, as a car pulled up, and he marveled at how anyone could make getting out of a cab look that graceful. Nancy, smartly dressed in an above the knee, white dress, with tan high heels, and clutch handbag, closed the door, and started up the steps. He walked over to meet her.

She smiled when she saw him, and a flutter of excitement stirred in his chest.

"Hi," she said. "Been here long?"

He smiled back at her. "Long enough to check in, and call you. You look great. How was your tour in Bangkok?"

"Interesting. On the other hand, the ride back wasn't nearly as interesting as the ride over."

They laughed. He pulled out a chair, and she sat down. A waiter, dressed in black trousers, white shirt, and black bow tie, arrived, obviously nervous, and in a hurry. Nancy asked for a Martini, and Cramer ordered another whiskey and soda.

"How was your stay in Thailand?" he asked.

"Wonderful!" she beamed. "I loved it there. The people are so...different."

"Sure beats this place," he said. "Cleaner, more relaxed, and no war."

She opened her hands expansively. "It was like...a vacation. I didn't realize how adjusted I had become to this country."

Minutes later, the waiter brought the drinks.

"What have you been doing for the last two weeks?" She asked, as he paid the man.

He closed his wallet, leaned sideways, and slipped it back in his pocket. "Flying."

"A lot?"

He nodded. "Day, and night."

"Are you short handed?"

"Not really. We have six airplanes, and twenty pilots. Even with all planes in the air, there are still eight pilots on the ground."

She cocked her head, and gave him a puzzled look. "Then why do you fly so often? Do you like it that much?'

"I like it. But what I really wanted, was to earn a few brownie points, so I could get time off, to come and see you."

She smiled, showing white, perfectly lined teeth. "That's very flattering. I like that." She looked down, picked up the toothpick holding her olive, and gently stirred her drink. "Have you ever been to Circle Sportif?"

"No. I'm not a member. I don't play tennis."

"Neither do I," she said. "Certainly not in this climate. But that's not all there is to do there. Anyway, it would give us somewhere to go after lunch." She looked up at him. "I can get you in as my guest."

"Fine."

She looked down at her drink. "Why did you go to so much trouble to see me?'

"I like you. Not just the way you look...the way you act. I was really impressed when you got on board that dirty old plane. All dressed up, and obviously expecting something better. But you made the best of it."

She looked up, and the corners of her eyes crinkled. "I have to admit, it was quite a shock."

"You had to know how good you looked in that outfit," he said. "Most women would have had a fit. But when you sat down in that greasy old wreck, you didn't fuss about getting dirty. You laughed. You got a kick out of it. Made us all feel better."

She took a sip of her Martini, gave him a steady look, and said softly. "You're an attractive man, John Cramer. Different. Something under that rough, hell for leather exterior makes you different. I haven't figured out what it is yet, but when I do...I don't think it will be much of a problem."

After lunch, most of the small shops were closed for siesta, so they strolled around the city for a while. Obviously, Saigon had seen better days. Many of the downtown buildings were well done examples of French Colonial architecture, but now, nearly all had peeling paint, and stains from polluted air. They wandered aimlessly, through the siesta hour, looking into store windows, and the open, but grated and chained doorways of small shops--crowded to the ceiling with goods decorated in garish oriental colors. Finally, Nancy suggested taking a cab to Circle Sportif. Cramer agreed. It made no difference where they went, as long as he could be with her.

Airplanes had taken him around the world. He'd been in a lot of clubs, and Circle Sportif didn't live up to his expectations. Not surprisingly, the French colonial influence was present in the decor, but the furnishings were beginning to look a bit worn. On the other hand, he had to admit, it was a tad fancier than the Bien Hoa Officers Club.

They watched a couple playing tennis for a few minutes, then lost interest, found a quiet table, and talked, mostly about the situation in Southeast Asia. Nancy was obviously well schooled on the area. She questioned him--at times almost quizzing him--about the places he'd gone, and his impression of how the war was impacting them. She seemed surprisingly familiar with a number of small villages in Vietnam, and Laos. Well, why wouldn't she be? She was an analyst. No doubt studied a lot of that stuff. Probably had an office in some embassy back room with reports, and field studies stacked to the ceiling.

Finally she suggested they go by her house, and meet her roommate. He agreed, relieved to be able to get up, and move around. The ride lasted less than ten minutes, and the cab stopped at a large, single story dwelling in a neighborhood, that in Saigon at least, would definitely be considered upscale. There was even a hint of lawn with some red, and yellow flowers in front, and he wondered wryly who mowed the grass.

After they got out of the cab, he paid the driver, then turned, and took a better look at the house--certainly unusual for Saigon--modern looking--sitting in the middle of a half dozen others with the same architecture.

"Maybe I should have joined the State Department," he said. "You seem to live a lot better than I do."

She looked at him, and smiled. "You might be surprised at some of the places I live." It sounded so casual, he barely noticed.

Once inside, she introduced him to Margaret Sullivan, her room-mate. Margaret was a stunner. Early to mid twenties, slim, and well tanned with short black hair, and surprisingly blue eyes. It occurred to him that if he had met her first, he would not have hesitated to ask her out.

Nancy showed him around the dwelling, a spacious house with a kitchen, dining room, and a large, rather sparsely furnished living room. Other than that, the tour made little impression. He was totally pre-occupied with watching her--had to struggle to keep from staring.

One fact came through loud and clear. There were two bedrooms, with a huge bath between them. The arrangement obviously afforded each of the women a considerable amount of privacy, and he made a mental note of that.

Nancy broke into his thoughts. "I like to eat early in the evening, how about you?"

"All GI's like to eat early."

"Care to suggest a place? Something unusual perhaps?"

He nodded. "A fighter pilot friend is going with a Chinese girl. She runs a pizza parlor near Tu Do street. It's clean, and the food is good. They have all kinds of food, not just pizza."

Nancy looked at Margaret. "Want to join us?"

Margaret shook her head. "I'll take a rain check. Ron and I are going to a reception."

Nancy looked back at Cramer, and smiled. "A Chinese pizza place? Even if I wasn't hungry, I'd have to see that. I'll call a cab."

As usual, the place was crowded, almost rumbling with the sound of subdued conversation and the clatter of plates and silverware being removed from the only un-occupied table in the place. Like better class Chinese restaurants all over the world, it was decorated mostly in red, accentuated by the traditional sculptured gold figures, and Chinese writing. The clientele, half oriental, and half civilian clothed, American G. I. were determinedly engaged in satisfying their senses--drinking their fill, and stuffing themselves with an awesome variety of food. Shortly after they entered, Cramer noticed Steve Davis, sitting in back with his girlfriend, Kim.

Kim, a stunningly beautiful Chinese in her mid twenties, had a good sense of humor, and a nearly flawless proficiency in English. He introduced Nancy, and accepted Kim's invitation to stay for drinks, and dinner."

Shortly after they sat down, a middle aged Oriental man with greasy, parted in the middle, slicked-down hair, came in with a pretty Asian girl. Kim looked around the table, and nodded toward the man. "Mister Wu" she said quietly. "Mister Wu likes American movies. Gangster movies."

The man, dressed in dark pants, a white, open at the collar shirt, and dark vest, motioned for the young woman to take a seat. Once the girl was parked, he turned, and approached Kim's table, giving a greeting in what sounded like Chinese. He gestured toward the girl, and said something to Kim.

She glanced coolly at the young woman, and answered quietly, "I know of this girl. Her experience has been mostly in bars. When customers drink too much, she often has trouble with their change. Even drunk people do not like to be cheated."

The man, obviously annoyed, grumbled in Chinese, and Kim replied, "I speak in English so my friends will know the nature of this meeting."

The man stepped back a couple of paces, started to turn away, then paused, and added something. Kim shook her head. "I've been to that butcher shop. There is no ice, and the place is never cleaned. The origin of the meat is suspect. On that street...dogs just...disappear. I want nothing from that place."

The man turned, and walked to the front, then motioned curtly to the young woman, and they left.

Kim's face softened. She made a subtle gesture, and a waiter suddenly appeared at the table.

Everything worked. The food, and drinks were excellent, and the conversation lively. Before they came in, Cramer had promised himself he wouldn't overindulge, but he ordered sweet and sour pork anyway.

Nancy and Kim, seemed to get along well from the start, though Nancy now seemed the more reserved of the two. Both were obviously well versed on Southeast Asian current events, and compared notes on a surprising number of Vietnamese towns he had never heard of.

At eleven, Nancy said she had an early morning schedule at the embassy, and the session ended. Once outside, they took one of the cabs parked nearby. Nancy gave the driver the name of Cramer's hotel, and the cabbie pulled away from the curb.

She leaned back in the seat and smiled. "I enjoyed that, Cramer. Your friends are interesting people."

He smiled back, and nodded. "Glad you liked it."

"Kim seems like a good manager," she said. "Obviously a woman who knows how to get what she wants." The smile turned mischievous. "She seems quite taken with you."

For a moment, he was taken aback by the remark. Unsure how to respond. Finally, he said, "Nothing's going to come of that. I don't fool around with my buddies' women."

She nudged him with an elbow and laughed, "Don't go serious on me. I was only kidding."

Time was getting short, so he took her hand and kissed it. Her response was encouraging...so, he kissed her on the lips. Suddenly, urges he had suppressed for far too long, boiled to the surface, and he struggled to keep himself under control.

When the embrace ended, she leaned back, and smiled. "I wondered when you were going to get around to that." This time she moved first, and kissed him.

He felt himself tremble. When she pulled away, he tried to sound casual, but his voice shook. "Want to stay with me tonight?"

"That's an attractive offer, but I've got to get up early."

"Promise me if I don't badger you, you won't think I don't care."

She winked, and patted him on the leg. "Don't worry. I know you're serious."

"Okay," he said. "I'd better ride home with you, then go back to the hotel. At this time of night, it's not safe in this town."

"That isn't necessary." She opened her handbag, and held it up so he could see inside. The dim glow of passing lights swept across the purse, and he caught a glimpse of a small, black automatic nestled among cosmetics, and folded tissues.

"I'll be safe enough," she said.

The cab rolled to a stop in front of his hotel, and Cramer gave the driver enough money to cover the trip to her place. After that, he turned, and kissed her again. When he got out, and closed the door, she rolled down the window. He put his hands on the bottom of the window frame, leaned in, and kissed her once more, briefly. After the kiss ended, he straightened up, and she suddenly looked away, staring out the windshield, seemingly lost in thought. The pause lengthened, and still she sat there, apparently pondering something. Cramer began to worry he might have done something to offend her.

Finally, she turned her head, and looked up at him. "Life can be short," she said, softly. "Maybe it's time to live it. Can you can spend another night in Saigon?"

"Sure. I don't have to be back until noon, day after tomorrow."

"Good," she said. "Check out of here tomorrow, and bring your things by the house. I should be home by four."

CHAPTER TWENTY TWO

As the cab drove away, somewhere in the distance, a dog barked, the urgency of its warning, nearly lost in the noise of an airplane passing overhead. Cramer walked toward the house, pulled out a handkerchief, patted the sweat off his forehead, and did his best to ignore the gnawing sensation in the pit of his stomach.

There'd be a lot riding on the next few minutes. Maybe he shouldn't have let the cab go until he knew he was on solid ground. Oh well, too late now.

He went up the steps, and knocked. A minute later, a young Vietnamese girl dressed in blue jeans, and a white, gold brocaded, oriental top, opened the door, and charmed him with the most infectious grin, he had ever seen. "You Captain Cramer? You John?"

He smiled back. "Yes."

She rolled her eyes, and giggled. "Miss Nancy right. You very handsome." She stepped back, pulling the door open farther, then held out her hand. "Come in please. Give me your bag. I put in Miss Nancy's room."

Cramer handed her the bag. "What's your name?"

"My name Lon. I work here for miss Nancy, and Margaret. I like very much. Very good job."

He followed her to the door of a spacious bedroom. High over the massive, dark stained bed, an off white mosquito netting hung from a thin wooden frame, its bottom tucked neatly under a thick mattress, covered with light blue sheets. At the foot of the bed, a thin, yellow blanket lay neatly folded.

Lon set his bag beside the dresser, then stepped over, and grasped a large porcelain wall switch. She clenched her lips, and turned it with an obvious effort, bringing forth a loud, irritating clack. The ceiling fan eased into lethargic life, revving up slowly--peaking out at about 50 RPM.

Lon smiled at him. "Very nice room," she giggled. "I think you like it here. You want coffee?"

"Uh, no thanks."

She giggled again, and Cramer followed her out of the room as Margaret stuck her head around the corner of the other doorway. "Hi John. Nice to see you again. Nancy called just before you got here. She'll be home in a few minutes."

She stepped out of the room, fastening her watch band as she walked, looking great in a white blouse, short black skirt, and high heels. "I'd stay and talk," she said, "but I have to be at the embassy at four."

"What do you do there?"

"Work in the communications section. Nothing glamorous. Handle messages, stuff like that. I like it. It's interesting." She smiled and waved. "See you later."

After she left, he looked around the living room. Large by any standard, it had a polished, stained plank floor, with three large throw rugs and a comfortable looking, leather couch. A huge mahogany chair, fitted with a couple of thick cushions, sat next to an end table displaying a two month old copy of, *U.S. News and World Report*. What a find. It was more current than anything he'd seen in months.

He was still reading when a car stopped outside. As he looked up, the car door slammed, and the vehicle pulled away. The clacking sound of high heels coming briskly up the walk, held him transfixed. Anticipation built. Finally, the knob turned, and she swept into the room, slamming the door behind her.

A determined smile covered her beautiful face as she walked toward him, calling over her shoulder. "Lon, You can go home now. I won't need you until tomorrow."

He stood up, and she came into his arms, kissing him hungrily as Lon called from the kitchen. "Yes mam."

They were still holding the kiss when the back door slammed. Finally she broke the embrace, tipped her head back, and said, "Do you still get to stay until tomorrow?"

"You bet."

"Great." Her expression turned serious. "No more games. Let's get comfortable." She led him into the bedroom, closed the door, and locked it. She turned around, kissed him, and began pulling the back of his shirt tail out from under his belt. Suddenly, he was trembling all over.

He reached up, fumbled with the clasp behind her neck, pulled the zipper all the way to the lower stop, then raised his hand, slipped it under the elastic in her panties and slid his fingers downward, feeling the thrill of her smooth firm flesh.

Cramer lay on his back, naked, bathed in moonlight coming through the window, with the faint rattle of the ceiling fan almost drowning out the soft sound of her breathing.

He shifted carefully, propped himself up on one elbow, reached out, and tucked the mosquito netting in further. He stared down at Nancy, her beautiful, slender body made even lovelier in the dim light. She opened her eyes, and looked at him sleepily.

Might as well tell her, he figured. He hadn't done it yet. Held back both times. First, because he was afraid of...God knows what...then because he didn't want her to think he was just saying it in the heat of passion. Sudden? So what? There was a war on dammit.

He leaned down, and kissed her gently on the mouth, then lifted his head, and said softly, "I love you Nancy."

She smiled back at him, her sleepy eyes barely open. "I love you too,

John." Then she squeezed his arm, and went back to sleep.

He lay there, looking at her, bathed in the soft glow of moonlight. Suddenly, he felt vulnerable. This wasn't like what he had with Betty. This time he was out of control--in love with this beautiful, brilliant, perpetually cheerful girl. And it came at a time when he was in the most precarious situation he had ever been in. A time when he had less control over his life than ever before.

It could all blow up in an instant. He knew what it was like to lose someone, and he didn't want it to happen again...but he knew that it might.

There were a million ways he could lose her over here--even if he didn't get killed. He could be wounded, and sent to the hospital at Clark. Or back to the States. Or, he could be transferred. Or...she might be transferred. In any of those situations, he'd be powerless to control events, and they'd be separated...probably forever.

Now, he knew what it was like to be caught up in a war, and have to worry about something other than his own survival. It wasn't just the danger, the shooting, the risky flying. It was the helplessness. The inability to manage events that seemed perpetually out of control. Suddenly, the two weeks he would spend in Nha Trang seemed like an eternity.

CHAPTER TWENTY THREE

Lieutenant Colonel Grayson, the Squadron Commander stood behind both pilots, gripping their seat backs, his swarthy face grim, hovering over them like some kind of high powered flight examiner. He leaned forward, and shouted in Cramer's ear, his breath still laden with a lingering hint of alcohol. "Where the hell is this camp?"

"It's about an hour out of Nha Trang sir," Cramer said. "Not much farther."

"Damn I hope not. I've got to be back before dark. Got a meeting with the Group Commander at 1900. He's hell on people being late, even if they have a good excuse."

They approached the camp from the southeast, skimming just beneath the low ceiling, squeezing in between the weather, and hills. Finally Cramer spotted the canyon, and made a steep left turn, as they roared in over the east rim. He could feel the Colonel pulling even harder against the seatback now, stooping down, craning his neck, and looking out the open side window for a better view of the gorge.

Gia Vuc seemed almost serene from this altitude, a medium sized camp, nestled in a deep, moderately wide canyon, with surrounding cliffs rising on both the East, and West sides.

"I can see the damn camp," Grayson shouted. "But where the hell's the airstrip?"

Williams reached across the cockpit, sticking his hand in front of Cramer's face, as he pointed out the left side window. "We usually land in the grassy area just beyond that cone shaped hill."

Grayson scowled. "I can see the fucking hill Captain, but what I want to know, is where you're going to land this rattling piece of junk."

"There, Colonel. Just beyond the hill."

"Are you shittin' me? There's nothing there, but mud holes, brush and weeds."

Mark grinned up at him. "I'm not saying you'd want to put your trusty A1 in there, Colonel. With those skinny, little tires, she'd probably sink to her belly. But we can make it."

"You're not supposed to land on anything shorter than 2500."

Williams shrugged. "Uh...actually Colonel...in here...we fudge a little. But that's OK. The terrain rises at the far end, so the uphill run shortens our ground roll."

Grayson gave him a suspicious look. "What about that cliff at the end?"

"Nobody's gone over it yet, sir."

"Make damn sure we're not the first."

Cramer reached out, adjusted the knobs and levers, then looked outside, and continued circling left, skimming low over the ridges, checking the camp to see if it was still in friendly hands.

Unpainted, open sided, wood frame huts with corrugated metal roofs made up the primary structures. Narrow, well trampled trails of bare earth ran erratically through the brush and tall weeds, connecting each of several buildings. On the South end, a large mortar had been newly installed, adding to the camp's defense options.

The signs were good. No houches burning, no holes blown in roofs, and no fresh craters in the ground. The ARVN flag still flew, and everyone walked around normally, though a few troops did look up and wave. Finally, yellow smoke billowed upward.

"There's the signal," Cramer shouted, rolling out of the turn. "We're going in. Give me gear down, and half flaps."

Williams grinned mischievously, answering in a falsetto voice. "Now sir?'

"Now, Goddammit!" Cramer snapped his head to the right, saw William's infectious grin, and laughed. "Don't screw around. We've got the Squadron Commander on board. He's gonna think we're nuts."

"Think hell, I'm convinced."

Williams ducked to his left, and began the complex ritual of lowering the old fashioned landing gear, manipulating lever, lock and snap ring. Finally he raised up, and set the flaps to one half, while Cramer shoved the mixtures rich, and set the rpm at 2300. They descended into the gorge, with the airspeed bleeding off slowly, and the cliffs seemingly higher, and ever more threatening.

"Full flaps. "

Williams set them, as Cramer trimmed the elevator, rolling the small, grimy wheel in quick, wiping motions, relieving the control pressure. Finally, he pushed the prop levers to the forward limit, rolled hard left, into a 60 degree bank, and began a steep, diving, 180 degree turn.

With the throttles nearly closed, hot, humid air buffeted in through the open side windows, while the prop blades made staccato, slathering sounds, as they lazily coasted on the back side of the power curve.

Forty five degrees from final, he closed the throttles completely. The engines changed from a low rumble, to a gentle mutter, and the descent increased significantly.

On final, he rolled wings level--nose pointed just above the hill, coming down in a steep dive. Atop the cone shaped hill, ARVN troops hugged the ground, and waved, as the plane swept low over their isolated outpost. He rolled in a little more elevator trim, with the airspeed hanging on 75, and the ground rushing up to meet them.

Passing a hundred feet, he pulled back the yoke, began his flare, opened both throttles halfway, and the engines gave their expected, hesitation, cough...then sudden roar to life, loading the elevators with air, just in time to bring the nose up sharply.

They hit with a neck snapping thud, just beyond the threshold, and lofted back into the air. He shoved the yoke forward, spiked her back on, and stepped on the brakes. She slewed wildly, lurching sideways, skidding, and slipping, first one way, then the other, as the distant cliff rushed toward them.

She was bouncing hard now--tires thudding over a boggy, uneven surface, with geysers of muddy water exploding skyward, and the prop tips whapping the tops of tall weeds, throwing mangled patches of greenery back across the wings. Gradually, feeble brakes, skidding tires and dragging brush, killed their momentum. Finally, he brought her to a stop, a hundred feet short of the cliff.

He expelled his breath, let go of the yoke, reached down and dried his hands on the legs of his flying suit. "Man! Always an interesting arrival in here."

Williams punched him lightly on the arm, and chuckled. "You made it look easy,"

Cramer, unlocked the tail-wheel--looked over his shoulder, stepped on the left brake, and slowly brought power up on the right engine. Clumps of weeds, and grass swirled behind them, churning backward in the prop blast, as he swung around sharply to the left, with the roar of the engine echoing off canyon walls. Once straight, he locked the tail wheel, and taxied back, wing tips waggling erratically as she wallowed over uneven ground--following a freshly made trail of muddy tracks, and mangled greenery.

The Colonel stooped, tipped his head back, and squinted out the narrow windshield. "I had to see this for myself," he said. "That PACAF inspector you brought up here last week was raising hell about it. I thought the son of a bitch was lying." He clapped his hand on Cramer's shoulder. "No more Gooney Bird jokes, lads. You bastards earn your money."

Cramer barely heard him. One more leg. Just one more leg, and he'd be back at Bien Hoa, grabbing a cab, and hauling ass for Saigon. He could hardly wait to see her.

CHAPTER TWENTY FOUR

Cramer burst into the hut, nearly bumping into Bill Bishop in the process.

Bishop, freshly back from the showers with a towel still wrapped around his chunky waist, chuckled. "How was the two weeks in Nha Trang?"

"Busy."

He unbuckled his gun-belt, hung it in his new wall locker, then unzipped his bag, and turned it upside down, dumping a pile of dirty laundry on his bunk for the cleaning woman to take care of.

"How was the flying?" Bishop asked.

"Hot and hairy," he said, stepping over to his new foot locker. He bent down, opened the top, took out the tray, and shoveled fresh laundry into his bag. "Weather's always bad in the afternoon, and the Special Forces are always out of everything. No matter how hard you work, or how many chances you take, it never seems to be enough. Everybody flies their ass off during the day, and gets drunk every night."

Bishop smiled. "Nice to hear it hasn't changed." He watched as Cramer zipped his bag shut. "Looks like you're in a hurry John. Do these frenzied preparations have anything to do with that girl from the State Department?"

"Yep." Cramer turned toward the door, stopped, snapped his fingers, then stepped over to the booze shelf, and grabbed a 40 ounce bottle of Canadian Club.

As he stuffed it into his bag, Bishop grinned. "Mark says she's real knockout. According to him, she's got you so stirred up you wouldn't even buy those poor bar girls up north a drink."

Cramer lifted his bag, and headed for the door. "Williams is an evil minded little prick...can't think of anything but pussy."

Bishop raised his eyebrows. "Obviously you have more noble objectives."

"Damn right." He opened the door, stumbled down the steps, and caught himself just in time to save his dignity.

As soon as he heard the car stop, he folded the paper, laid it aside and stood up. That had to be her. She was already two hours overdue.

When she opened the door, and stepped inside, he couldn't believe it. Camouflage fatigues, muddy boots, and a 9mm automatic strapped to her side. Her sweat streaked face was smudged, and dirty. Her hair, tightly pulled back, with the ends tangled, was sprinkled with dried mud, and broken twigs. She looked beat, barely able to make it. What the hell was going on?

Her face broke into a mischievous smile. "You seem surprised. You expected someone else?"

"No...I...uh...how come you're dressed like that?" Cramer said.

"I got tired of going formal." She moved in close, slipped her arms around him, and looked up. "I had to take a field trip. Sorry I didn't have time to change."

She kissed him, and his mind snapped back on track, focusing on more important things. He ran his hands over her, feeling the warmth, the soft, barely yielding firmness of her curves, the response of her pressing against him. His heart pounded, and his organ hardened, cramping within the confines of his clothes.

Finally, she pulled her head back and smiled. "How about a drink and a shower? I could use both before we do anything else."

"Sounds good to me."

They walked into the kitchen. She pulled out a chair, and wearily sat down at the small table, watching, while he arranged the bottle and glasses, then poured the drinks. He handed her a glass, then took his seat, and a welcome sip of CC. After he put his drink down, he reached across the table, and took her hand.

Her eyes crinkled. "You're shaking."

He laughed, and answered in a trembling voice, "I'm all stirred up. Excited. Can't keep my hands off you."

Her smile broadened, and she chuckled, "Considering the way I look, that's a lot better than I expected." She tipped her drink up, and finished it in three swallows, then put the glass back on the table. "I hope Lon put clean towels in the bathroom."

He nodded. "She did."

"She reached out, and squeezed his other hand. "Good. Let's do it. I've got to get this dirt off."

They walked into the bedroom, and he closed the door, and locked it. When he turned around, she had already unbuckled her belt, put her gun on the small table in the corner, and was undoing her fatigue blouse. He shed his clothes slowly, dropping them on the floor as he watched her undress. Finally she was nude. She walked over to the shower, reached in, turned on the water, and adjusted it for the right temperature.

She was already washing her hair when he stepped in, and closed the door behind him. He watched her as she tipped her head back, rolled it from side to side, her eyes closed, letting the shower wash over her face, and hair. Finally she wiped the water from her eyes, blew the drips off the end of her nose, then moved over, so he could get under the flow. This time, she soaped her hands and ran them over him. That did it. He couldn't wait any longer. He stooped, reached out, and locked his hands together under her bottom. She put her arms around his neck, and sprang up, circling him with her legs.

He adjusted his grip, then lowered her slowly, feeling the hot, sensual pleasure of her sliding down over him, enveloping him. He backed her into a corner, moving slowly, as warm, soothing water washed gently over their undulating bodies.

CHAPTER TWENTY FIVE

Things were heating up in country. Almost before Cramer knew it, he was scheduled for another tour in Nha Trang. Although flight crews were rotated, the section now kept two airplanes up there permanently, flying exclusively in support of the Special Forces.

Nha Trang was one of the better looking cities in Vietnam, situated in a picturesque setting. To the east, the city fronted along a wide, coarsely grained, brown-sand beach. A couple of miles offshore, hilly islands offered a landscape that each morning's sunrise turned into a beautiful, soul stirring scene. To the north, and west, distant mountains provided a pleasing backdrop to what was still, a surprisingly peaceful area.

Off duty time was pleasant, and civilian transportation cheap, provided mostly by wiry cyclo drivers, pedaling their shaded, tricycle rigs with remarkably stoic endurance. Living near the beach, the crews had easy access to the better restaurants, and bars, with enough free time for an occasional dip in the surf. Certainly, it was the best duty station in country. But it all had a price.

They were supposedly nearing the end of the wet season, but mountain flying out of Nha Trang remained dangerous, and demanding, with the weather, a constantly threatening factor. Mornings were invariably foggy, with mountain passes hidden in clouds. By ten AM, the fog would dissipate, giving them a brief period of good flying weather. Early afternoon, built puffy, white cumulus that billowed rapidly upward, then slowly turned black. Once mature, the thunderstorms peaked above forty thousand feet, then expended their awesome, stored-up energy in dark shafts of rain, buffeting winds, and jagged streaks of lightning.

Cramer flew two missions a day, with many of those scheduled for multiple destinations. Inland, with a pitifully few, weak and unreliable navigational aids, most sorties were a tension ridden gamble. On early morning flights, they searched through fog shrouded, canyons in a desperate quest for ill-defined objectives. The nerve wracking specter of flying head-on into an unseen hill, haunted them constantly.

Once the destination was found, the flight, more often than not, ended with a risky landing on some barely adequate airstrip. Short, rutted, and rough, they pounded the planes mercilessly, and he marveled at how much punishment the junky, old transports could take.

In mountain camps where no strip was available, they air-dropped supplies, flying the narrow canyons, in tight, racetrack patterns, banking 60 degrees or more, staying just high enough above the trees for the chutes to open, and make one swing before the bundle thudded onto the ground.

In the cargo compartment, during airdrops, sweating kickers staggered through turbulence, fighting to keep their footing on a greasy aluminum deck, as they wrestled heavy bundles to the gaping doorway, then shoved them out, when the green light came on. With no safety harness, and too low for a chute of their own, not one ever complained.

In spite of everything, the system worked. Seldom did bundles land more than a few feet from the marker, and even among the squadron's fighter pilots, Bien Hoa's C-47 crews gradually earned respect for their tenacity, reliability, and air-drop accuracy.

Major Gifford, the Detachment Operations Officer, came through the straw thatch door of the tiny, Officers club perched atop Army Headquarters in downtown Nha Trang. As the door flapped shut behind him, he leaned down and stubbed out his cigarette on a coffee table ash tray. Six-two and muscular, with brown crew cut hair, he was beginning to show just a bit of a paunch, the result of spending far too many hours complying with the continually increasing demand for never ending reports. Gifford, straightened up, walked by the comely Vietnamese bartender, ignored her cheerful greeting, and headed straight for their table.

Cramer downed the last of his drink and set the tumbler down as Mark Williams grumbled, "Oh shit!"

Gifford looked down at them, his face grim. "Shit is right."

"What's up, Major?" Cramer said.

"You guys fit to fly?"

"Yes sir. Only had one."

"That's good. Instead of going back home in the morning, we'll send you back tonight. On the way, we need a flare mission for a flight of A1Es coming out of Bien Hoa."

"What's the deal?" Cramer asked

"Bunch of sampans sneaking down the Coast. Probably heading for the mangroves down south. Never saw a big flotilla use such an obvious route before. We'll try to make sure they don't do it again." Gifford leaned over the coffee table, unfolded a map, laid it out, and pointed. "Your FAC will meet you here. When you get close, he'll let you know what to do." He tossed a torn piece of paper on top of the map. "Here's the frequency you'll work on. Grab your navigator and go. The enlisted men are already alerted. Good luck."

The tiny, single engine Cessna orbited below them, its red, rotating beacon piercing the darkness with monotonous regularity. Cramer turned his head, and looked at the dim image of Williams sitting in the right seat. "Man it takes balls to fly one of those things over this jungle at night."

"Williams nodded. "They can have that friggin' job. We get in enough trouble flying this thing."

The radio crackled, as the bird dog checked in. *"Lighthouse, this is*

Pointer. I'm a mile north of the target, turning inbound."

"Roger Pointer," Cramer said. "I'm right behind you. Did you read that, Rattlesnake Leader?"

"Snake one, Roger. Turn on the lights, and we'll get to work."

"Roger." Cramer moved his wafer switch to interphone. "Ok loadmaster, stand by to drop."

"Roger sir."

He checked his airspeed, and began a series of shallow turns in an effort to stay behind the Cessna.

The lead fighter called, *"This is Snake One. I'll do a three sixty until the target's lighted."*

"Roger."

A mile to the East, the coastline was nearly indiscernible. Below, the muddy, multi-streamed, brush choked Delta, stretched in front of them, barely visible in the quarter-moon light. As the Cessna passed over the largest inlet, the pilot called, *"Flares now!"*

Cramer adjusted power, motioned for Williams to raise the flaps then turned his wafer switch to interphone, and called. "Flares now!"

"Flares away."

Cramer rolled into a steep left bank.

Behind them, a pair of 2 million candlepower, magnesium flares lit, flooding a mile wide circle of tangled mangroves, and winding waterways in near daylight.

Below, a long line of Sampans floating in trail, were suddenly exposed, like deer in the headlights, drifting southwestward. Shouts of glee came from the fighters, as the first of the heavily loaded boats began to turn, making a desperate, slow motion quest for the doubtful cover of overhanging brush along the inlet bank.

Rattlesnake one bored in, and for an instant, it seemed the lead boat might make cover before the battle started. Suddenly, rockets streaked toward the flotilla, changing the equation. One splashed harmlessly in the water, but the other hit with a flash, dead center on the lead boat. A huge, secondary explosion resulted, billowing rapidly upward in a roiling, churning mushroom of dirty red flame, and oily black smoke. On top, a face up, arched back body trailing lifeless, rag-doll limbs, rose briefly, then seemingly sank back, and was quickly engulfed in the still rising holocaust.

Seconds later, the concussion hit with a rivet popping, neck wrenching jolt, rocking the old C-47 viciously. On the water, shock waves spread in ever widening rings, pitching, and bobbing the other floats, as all along the procession, tiny, match stick figures began diving over the sides.

Events became a melee, FAC, fighters and flare ship--working in unison. The flares drifted slowly, swinging lazily in their chutes, as roaring A1s fell into a deadly, determined effort, diving, swooping, and zooming, in a rhythmic, orderly sequence, dispensing their seemingly inexhaustible stores of ordinance, while the muddy brown water slowly became saturated with splintered wood, floating bodies and burning debris.

Finally, all remaining boats were afire, and the snarling, slab-sided, fighters began their clean-up. The fighter boys were into it now--enjoying their work. Killing was their business, and business was good, and they gave it that extra flare, that extra flash--sweeping high, rolling up past vertical, doing a wing over, then diving down, rolling out, lining up, and firing-- sending multiple rows of yard high splashes stitching across the water, that climbed the banks in bright red flashes, and disappeared into the mangroves.

"This is one load that won't make it through," Williams yelled. "There'll be damn few survivors in that bunch."

"I don't feel sorry for them," Cramer shouted. "In a couple of days they'd have been all over the Delta attacking villages with that shit."

Williams clapped him on the shoulder. "Great way to end our tour, John. After this, Bien Hoa's gonna seem dull."

Cramer grinned. "Won't be dull for me. I've got unfinished business in Saigon."

The sun was just coming up when Cramer leaned over the seat, and paid the cabbie, then picked up his bag, and stepped out of the car.

As the Renault pulled away, he felt the clammy, early morning dampness on his skin, smelled the dank odors of Saigon, the wood smoke, the mildew, the mold. An hour from now the air would turn blue with exhaust fumes as hordes of people hurried to work in cars, diesel spewing trucks, and a legion of sputtering motorbikes.

The sound of the cab faded in the distance as his footsteps echoed off the flagstone walk. He climbed the steps eagerly, filled with anticipation, seeing the door already opening.

A red eyed Lon peered out, clapped her hand over her mouth, then turned, left the door ajar, and ran toward the kitchen. His heart sank.

He stepped inside, and closed the door behind him. A grim faced Margaret came into the room.

"What's wrong ?" He said.

Margaret bit her lip, tears welling in her eyes. "It's Nancy."

"What's the matter?"

"There's no good way to say this." Her shoulders sagged. "She's dead."

His mouth dropped open. "What?"

Margaret sat down suddenly, collapsing backward onto a chair, sobbing. Cramer stood there dumbfounded, nearly overwhelmed, looking helplessly around the room. "Dead? How...how the hell can she be dead? There's gotta be some mistake!"

Margaret shook her head, tears streaming down her cheeks. "There's no mistake. She was ambushed."

Anger welled up in him. "Ambushed?" he shouted. "For Christ's sake what are you telling me? How the hell could she be ambushed? In a Goddamned cab coming back from the embassy? On the street? In a restaurant? Where?"

"It didn't happen here...not in this country. She was part of a group, six of them...God...I shouldn't be talking about this..."

She stopped suddenly, wiped her eyes, sniffed, then continued in a calm, almost detached voice, gripping her soggy hanky, and staring blankly at the floor. "She was killed in the first burst of machine gun fire, along with their leader. Only one of them made it out."

"Five people from our State Department killed?"

"She wasn't with the State Department," she mumbled. "That was just...cover. I'm not sure what she did in the field. I only know she spoke Hmong, and knew all about the tribes."

"Hmong? Who the hell are they?" Cramer asked.

"They're small people, but good fighters," she said. "Trustworthy, loyal. Not one has ever gone over to the enemy. Nancy lived with them, during summer vacations, when she was a teenager, working with her anthropologist father. Eventually she got her degree too. After her father died, she took over his work, and we recruited her."

"We? Who the hell's we?"

She looked up at him, anguish showing in her face. "What difference does it make?"

"Dammit, I want to find out how this happened," he snapped.

Margaret shook her head. "Nobody will talk to you, John. You weren't married, or related. You have no official status."

He stood there, feeling helpless. "Can I at least see her?'

"Don't you understand? She didn't get out! She'll never get out!" Margarette leaned forward, bending nearly double, and buried her face in her hands, sobbing.

Cramer left her like that, turned, and walked woodenly away--through the living room, then into Nancy's room--images flooding his mind--things she had said, things she had done. My God, how could he have been so stupid? He should have expected this. There were plenty of clues. The trouble was...he hadn't attached any significance to them.

He remembered the way she acted in the cab in front of his hotel. The way she seemed lost in thought, mulling something over. She knew what she was into, knew it might turn bad. "Life can be short," she said.

There were other signs. The gun in her purse, the time she was dressed in fatigues with a gun strapped to her side--just before the first time they made love, when she came straight toward him, surprisingly aggressive.

She knew this could happen. She simply decided to live what little life she might have left. Now the pieces fit. What a fool! He hadn't caught the meaning of it. Never even thought about it. Only worried that he'd be killed, or wounded, or sent back to the States. How the hell could he have been so self centered?

He stood there, in the middle of her room, eyes fixed on the open closet, focusing on the yellow dress she had worn the first day he saw her. He'd never see her in it again. Never see her smile, hear her laugh, or make a clever remark. Suddenly, tears streamed down his cheeks, and he stood there helplessly, wishing he had died before she did.

That night he had the nightmare. The following night, he had it again.

CHAPTER TWENTY SIX

Idle time plunged him into depression. Sleep became something to dread--his nightmare, now almost predictable in its regularity. The only time he seemed to be able to shake his dark mood, was while he was flying. Only then did he get some relief. Airplanes still commanded his attention, and they became his refuge, so he flew even more now. Flew his ass off, day and night, in a desperate effort to fill his mind, and keep his personal demons at bay.

Though he still flew with precision, once a flight was over, it seemed an empty accomplishment. A well earned, weekend R&R to Hong Kong did little to help. Even the complex demands of the unforgiving ADF approach, skillfully flown off the infamous, Stonecutter's Beacon, failed to bring satisfaction.

After the bizarre, double procedure turn, he broke out at minimums, flying the post, low station leg, head-on, in poor visibility into a sheer, towering cliff, with a huge, cautionary orange and white checkerboard painted on its face. A delayed to the last second, desperation, hard-right turn, brought him onto a steeply angled final approach, that skimmed over towering apartment buildings in a close-in, antenna threatening descent. In spite of its hazards the taxing procedure left him with a--so what--feeling. Even the subsequent tire squeaking, grease job landing, provided little satisfaction.

Cramer sat in the overstuffed chair, with his feet propped up on the sill of the President Hotel's expansive, tenth story window, watching the fascinating chaos of Hong Kong Harbor. Near the far shore, a racy looking speedboat sported a towering rooster tail as it swept past an aging freighter with cargo booms and rust stains on her side. A short distance away, two tugs, with sterns low in the water, pushed against a ship big enough to swallow them. Farther out--the Star Of Hong Kong ferry--her airy, open sided decks crammed with people. Beyond that, a pair of wooden, square sail vessels pitched and bobbed, their masts waving erratically as they cut across the wake of a departing ocean liner.

Over near the squalor of the low rent district, whole families lived on wooden boats, apparently rent free, and somehow making it, their small, aged vessels handed down through generations—fixed, and patched and kept afloat. Fish a little? Smuggle a lot? Nearly all had dogs and cats aboard. Seemed practical. Cats could take care of the rats, while the dogs stood guard and played with the kids.

A knock on the door pulled his attention back to the room. Damn! First pleasant interlude he'd had in weeks, and now this. There it was again, that irritating rap!, rap!, rap!, insistent and invasive. Finally he gave up, and shouted, "It's not locked dammit!"

He looked behind him as the door opened slowly, and his co-pilot, Captain Denny Stillwell stuck his gray, crew cut head into the room.

"Damn, John. You still staring out that window?"

"You got a better view?"

"There's a better one down on the street" Stillwell stepped inside, and closed the door softly behind him. "Let's get out of here and see the town."

"I've already seen it," Cramer grumbled. "Twice. Son-of-a-bitch hasn't changed." He tipped his glass up and drained it, then reached down beside the chair, and picked up his bottle of Canadian Club.

"I guess I could go alone," Stillwell said. "But it'd be nice to have a little company."

"Try the bars," he said as he unscrewed the cap. "You'll get lots of company there."

Stillwell curled his lip and snorted, "Suppose I could call my wife and ask permission. But I already know what she'd say."

Cramer tipped the bottle up vertically, and the last few pathetic drops dribbled into his glass. "Damn!"

Stillwell chuckled. "Now you gotta go. Get your ass out of that chair, and let's go get drunk."

Cramer set the bottle on the floor, put his feet back on the sill, folded his hands in his lap, and stared out the window. "Don't have to get drunk," he mumbled. "I'm already drunk. And it doesn't help. Nothing helps. 'Cause nothing I do, is gonna bring her back."

Williams, Bishop and Steve Davis sat around Cramer's bunk, their shadowy forms barely visible in the darkened interior of hut 124.

The end of a cigarette brightened as Davis drew in a puff, then slowly exhaled. "John," he said softly, "This could be serious. We know you're OK, but if the head-shed finds out about these Goddamned nightmares they may think you're falling apart."

"We've gotta do something," Mark said. "These huts are only a few feet apart. Screen wire, and louvered sides don't dampen much sound."

A bare chested Bishop leaned forward, putting his elbows on his knees, a small roll of fat riding on top of his shorts. "A couple of guys are already running their mouth about the noise you're making," he said. "Wondering if you're losing your guts. Sooner or later, some asshole will say it too loud, and one of the wheels will get involved."

Cramer wiped the sweat off his face, and dried his hand on the sheet. "Dammit," he growled softly, "I'm not having nightmares because I'm afraid to fly. I'm still doing my job."

Steve nodded. "That you are. Trouble is, you're flying so much, a couple of guys are bitching that you're some kind of glory hound, making them look bad by comparison."

"Ah for Christ's sake! How can you win?"

"Take it easy John," Steve said. "We're just trying to find a way to deal with this, before the flight surgeon over-reacts, or someone in headquarters gets involved."

"It could be dicey," Mark said. "If they send you to Clark for observation, and some arrogant shrink decides you've got mental problems, they might even force you out of the service. You've got too much time in to risk that."

Davis reached over, and his cigarette made a faint hissing sound as he dropped it into the slot of an empty beer can. "Let's not get carried away," he said, as he looked up and set the empty aside. "Nobody's declared him nuts yet. Things aren't hopeless. There are a couple of things you guys in here can do to help out."

"What's that?" Mark said.

"Start leaving a radio on low at night," Davis said. "It'll help mask the noise he makes. What would help even more, would be if one of you guys would get up off his lazy ass, and shake him awake, instead of letting him run through the whole fuckin' nightmare."

Mark nodded. "We can do that."

Davis stood up, and started for the door, then stopped short, and paused, obviously about to say something. Seconds later, he shook his head. "No," he mumbled. "No, by God. Won't do that for anybody." He opened the door, and looked back over his shoulder, the tone of his voice still showing a trace of irritation. "I've got to get to bed. My wake-up's in two hours." His voice softened, as he looked down at Cramer. "Hang in there John. Sooner or later, it's bound to get better. Maybe it's a good thing you're going back to Nha Trang. At least up there, you'll have a private room. Watch your ass. I'll see you in a couple of weeks."

CHAPTER TWENTY SEVEN

Dawn was just beginning to break when Cramer came out of the mess in the Nha Trang MAAG compound, feeling the damp air wafting in from the beach, barely a block away. Even from here the air smelled salty. Or...maybe it was just his imagination. He looked around for the rest of his crew. The engineer, Tech Sergeant Culpepper, cool, quiet and competent, and the loadmaster, Staff Sergeant Nelson, a mouthy, part time horse's ass were already sitting in back of the weapons carrier.

Captain Joe Clark, his hung-over, red eyed navigator, and Lieutenant Donovan, the blond, clean cut, and boyishly handsome, new co-pilot were standing beside the vehicle. Both got into the truck as soon as they saw him approaching.

Cramer climbed aboard, and yelled, "Let's go." He grabbed the side-rail, and held on tight as the truck lurched forward, pulled away from the curb, and rolled slowly down the street. Passing through the compound gate, the skinny, kaki-clad ARVN guard saluted, and Cramer returned the gesture, though Clark and Donovan, were looking the other way, and didn't seem to notice.

This morning, a stalled ARVN convoy was blocking the short drive toward the beach, so the driver turned left, and detoured through back streets to avoid the situation.

At the first intersection, they turned left again, and rolled slowly through a badly congested area, with rows of low, squat shacks, lining both sides of the dusty, narrow street.

Lt Donovan, was staring intently, seemingly fascinated by the scene. No mystery there. He had arrived last night after flying directly from the States--making a series of stops at American Military air bases. This must have been his first daylight look at South Vietnam, and for him, the experience was obviously spell-binding.

This morning the back street was busy, teeming with multitudes of strange looking people, moving in a scene presenting an almost bewildering jumble of alien sights, and sounds.

The truck idled quietly along, parting the crowd, as a constant din of unintelligible voices babbled in an unfathomable language. All along the road, women were making breakfast--cooking over small, wood fires, crouched, or standing in front of their hovels with thin, blue smoke rising from the flames, spreading out, and hanging heavily in the fetid, humid air.

A dozen offensive odors assaulted Cramer's senses, and he found himself holding his breath to avoid them. Ahead, cyclo drivers strained their wiry legs, pedaling their small, three-wheeled rigs, picking their way slowly through the congestion.

On the right, a street vendor was doing a brisk business, serving soup in tarnished, tin cups to a small group of people crowding around his steaming rig. As the driver idled past, the odor of bubbling soup wafted over the slow-moving truck, and Cramer sensed the nauseating smell of rancid fish.

In front of one shack, a mother in black pajamas squatted at the edge of the street, holding her naked two-year-old behind the knees. She leaned the child backward, his head against her breast, spread his legs, and he squirted dark runny, feces onto the pavement. Lt Donovan winced, and turned his head to avoid the sight.

The Loadmaster showed a tobacco stained grin, and gave Donovan the needle, "Nice country huh, Lootenant?"

The question had a sneering quality to it, that bordered on insolence, and Cramer moved to soften the remark. "Well, look on the bright side," he said. "At least they're not like those filthy Americans who eat, and shit in the same house."

Everyone laughed, Donovan included, and the incident seemed defused.

The truck continued, weaving its way carefully through the crowd, passing an open sided shack, where in spite of the early hour, two women were already at work in their make-shift laundry. A crudely painted sign with white background, and red letters, advertised in fractured English, "for to wash the clothes."

Farther on, a naked, snot-nosed three-year old, holding a jagged piece of brick in his grubby hand, squatted at the edge of the street, and pounded belligerently on a dead rat.

The people surrounding the truck seemed oblivious to their passing. It suddenly occurred to Cramer that most of them would probably live their entire lives within a few blocks of this squalid area.

"Thank God I wasn't born here," he mumbled. "What a hell of a thing it must be, to live like this." Suddenly he realized, it was the closest thing to a positive thought he'd had, since Nancy's death.

A hundred feet below, the jungle looked dark, and wet as usual. Cramer picked his way through the saddlebacks, avoiding the hills by banking first one way, then the other, as they skimmed below the weather.

"Chudron ahead," Joe Clark called, pointing out the left window. "There it is at ten o'clock."

"Got it," Cramer said.

A column of green smoke billowed upward, indicating that it was safe to land. He retarded the throttles, slowed the plane, and called, "Gear down," then shoved the mixture, and prop controls forward. Lieutenant Donovan leaned down, lowered the gear, latched, and locked it, then looked up, craned his neck, and pointed out the left side of the windshield. "Is that it?"

Cramer nodded. "Not very impressive huh? Just a muddy little slash in the jungle. We've got a lot of them like that over here. Give me half flaps."

As the flaps started down, he banked steeply trying to stay away from the fog on the right, then flew a 270 degree, left hand pattern with his wing-tip skimming only yards above the jungle. He compulsively leaned forward, his head on a swivel, as he scanned the area one more time, looking for signs of enemy activity. After getting full flaps, and turning close-in final, he rolled out quickly, and flared.

She shuddered, just before the wheels thudded on, a hundred feet beyond the threshold. They rumbled along, bouncing, and shaking, fuselage rattling, as reddish brown water splashed from a seemingly endless succession of mud holes.

Finally the tail wheel touched, they slowed to a leisurely taxi, then he spun her around, and parked in the only space available. After that, he set the brakes, shut down engines, and turned off the switches.

While Donovan fumbled with his harness, Cramer got out of the seat, and strapped on his 357. Once out of the cabin, they snaked their way past the cargo--stepping carefully around tie-down straps, holding on to things, with their feet slipping on the sloping, greasy, mud tracked deck.

Several ARVN troops climbed aboard, a few wearing boots, others with thonged rubber sandals flapping on their feet--their uniforms a mottled mixture of faded military, and thread-bare civilian. They milled about aimlessly, tripping over tie-downs, and bumping into things. Sergeant Nelson, growled a string of profanities, and tried to get them organized.

As Cramer stepped off the plane, a huge, deeply tanned Special Forces Captain met them, his sweat-stained fatigues still showing a hint of crease.

Blond, bristle haired, and square jawed, Captain Kiner was a hard driving man, already mid-way through his third in-country tour. Cramer introduced him to Donovan, and the two shook hands.

Kiner hooked a thumb over his shoulder. "Come up to the camp. We'll have a glass of tea while they're unloading."

They walked slowly along the weed-lined path with Cramer scanning the weather. "It's starting to break up," he said. "We ought to be able to get to Bien Hoa without much trouble."

"You're not going back to Nha Trang?" Kiner asked.

Cramer shook his head. "Our two week tour is over. It's back to the flatlands for us."

They entered the small houch serving as a mess, and Donovan gasped, pointing at a white porcelain chest with a silver handle sitting on a crudely made, wooden table. "A refrigerator? I never expected to see one of those in a place like this."

Kiner laughed. "Yeah, we're damn near civilized, lieutenant. We even cook over a fire. Anyway, it's not as impossible as it seems. If you notice, there's a tank, with some tubing attached to it. It runs on gas, and it's just about the most valued piece of equipment we have." He shot a glance at Cramer. "You did bring us another bottle didn't you?"

112

"Sure did."

Kiner opened the door of the small unit. Inside, two partially consumed bottles of pale wine, and six no doubt precious cans of Schlitz crowded a couple of open ration cans, and a glass, screw top, gallon jug of tea.

They sat around a small, oil-cloth covered table made from discarded packing crates, while Kiner took the jug out of the refrigerator, spanned the top with his massive hand, unscrewed the lid, and poured each of them a glass of tea.

Cramer took a sip of the dark liquid, silently marveling at the strength and body of the almost bitter brew. His eyes swept the tiny, make-shift room, constructed from splintered, mis-matched boards, held together by poorly driven, bent over nails. The place reminded him of the fort he had built from packing crates in the back yard, at the farm. He'd worked on it all day, and that evening, his uncle made him tear it down, claiming a fort was not a fitting project for a Christian youth...Bible thumping jerk.

He quashed the memory, snapped back to the present, and watched the huge Captain as he sat down, comparing his appearance to the way he was on previous runs. Three consecutive tours in the bush were beginning to take their toll. The man looked tired.

"Are things getting any better here?" Cramer asked.

"Not a hell of a lot," Kiner said. "Everyone on the A Team is still giving a hundred percent, but we've lost our delusions about making good soldiers out of the ARVN. It's like beating a dying horse."

"What's the Problem?" Cramer said.

"Well for starters, intestinal parasites, TB, and a piss poor diet. They're anemic as hell, and their endurance is low. When we go on patrol, they peter out after no more than a few hundred yards. Iron tablets help some, but not much."

Cramer frowned. "The Army managed pretty well with the Koreans during that war. What's so different about these guys?"

Kiner set his glass down, and gave him a tired look. "Don't get me wrong. I'm not knocking all of them. A few are damned good. But the majority are unenthusiastic at best. They don't trust their leaders. Corruption, and thievery are a way of life over here, and they know that. It's an uphill battle just to motivate them."

"If you don't have good leadership, you don't have shit," Cramer said.

Kiner clenched his lips, and shook his head. "It's almost a no-win situation. We have to watch them every minute. If they get a chance, they sell their weapons on the black market, then claim they lost them--don't even consider the damn things will be pointed back at them the next day." He waved, disgustedly. "Lets talk about something else. How are things with you. You still going with that good looking girl from the State Department?"

Cramer flinched. "No...uh no...she was killed recently." His voice broke, he swallowed hard, and looked down at the dirt floor, struggling to control his emotion.

CHAPTER TWENTY EIGHT

The huge air-conditioner mounted high on the back wall rumbled fitfully, blowing a faint fog into the musty, dimly lit, low ceilinged room.

Colonel Driscole slumped wearily in his chair, his sweaty flying suit feeling cold against his skin, as he watched the sharply dressed Special Forces officer outline the mission on the Command Post map. How the hell could those guys make starched fatigues look so great?

The major tapped his pointer on a spot near a stream. "The river's low. They're in an area that's flat, covered with tall grass, and weeds--with no trees, and no heavy brush."

Driscole squinted skeptically. "How soft is it?"

"According to them, its OK. The river switched channels a few weeks ago. The ground is firm, and the brush is still not much more than waist high."

"How much room would we have?"

"More than enough for a 2500 foot strip, with both ends clear." The major turned to face them, lowered his pointer, held it horizontally across his pelvis, and grasped both ends. "Standard deal, Colonel. They'll have two lights on the approach, and one in the center at the far end."

"A helicopter would be a hell of a lot better," Driscole said.

The major nodded. "Yes sir, you're certainly right about that. Unfortunately, most of our choppers are already committed to a critical operation. Of those remaining, one was shot down, and three others are grounded with mechanical problems. "His face took on a worried look, and he pointed backward, without looking, tapping the map. "Our people are in there, Colonel...cut off, with no way out. We're out of airframes. And damn near out of time."

"There's no way they can hole up and wait?" Driscole asked.

"No sir. They're low on ammo. They've been in one fire fight already. Had to move to divert the enemy. After that, they lost them, then doubled back. It's only a matter of time before they're discovered again."

Driscole shifted in his chair, and turned to his ops officer. "Who has the best chance to pull this off?"

Major Keller looked at the duty officer, and pointed to the phone. "Get Cramer."

Outside the plane, no moon, low ceiling and dark. Nothing but dark. Couldn't see a damn thing. The air blowing in from the open side window, was so humid, Cramer wanted to wring it out. God, what a climate.

The red glow from the instrument panel reflected off Joe Clark's face as he leaned forward, between the pilots and shouted, "We're getting close to the border, John. Descend to 1300. That'll give you a 200 foot terrain clearance."

Cramer reduced power, and engine sound diminished as he reached for the elevator trim and the aircraft sank slowly in the darkness. "What's the ETA for that village?"

"Zero seven."

Lieutenant Donovan twisted in his seat, looking over his shoulder at Clark. "How do we identify the town?"

"It's small," Clark said. "There's no other village for miles. I got a good fix on Tacan before we let down. There's no wind, and no drift. If we pass over a village at the right time, that'll be it. "

Cramer tapped Donovan on the arm. "Keep your eyes out front, Lieutenant. It'll be easy to miss."

Clark shined a red light on his map, then held it forward so Cramer could see. "Our designated landing area is here," he said, pointing. "Nineteen miles beyond the village. Nothing but jungle between."

Cramer took a quick look, nodded, and resumed his instrument cross check. Altitude, airspeed, and heading. All had to be precise. Especially the altitude. Finally, he leveled off, nudged the power up, and engine noise increased.

The chances were that radar wouldn't be operational across the border, but he didn't want to bet their lives on that, so they'd have to stay at 200 feet. Like they said at Hurlburt, if they strayed off course, stars disappearing just above the horizon would be their only warning that a hill loomed ahead. The trouble was...there weren't any stars. Tension built as time dragged. Still no lights.

"Forty five seconds to turn," Clark said. "We oughta be close."

"Roger," Cramer said.

"Thirty seconds...Twenty...Fifteen."

Donovan stabbed the windshield with his finger. "Lights! Dead ahead."

"Gimme a tight left to 215...Now!" Clark shouted.

They roared in, turning over a dimly lit, straw thatch village, passing in a flash, getting a fleeting glimpse of thatched huts, towering sparks, and a startled group of wide eyed, gap mouthed people with upturned faces, crowding around a bonfire. After that, darkness.

"LZ at 16 past." Clark yelled.

Cramer made his call on FM. "Traveler, Traveler, this is bulldog-- Home in six minutes."

A scratchy voice answered, too broken to make out. It would have to do. He wouldn't risk another call. He glanced at Donovan. "What we're looking for is three lights marking the corners of an invisible triangle. Just like they showed you at Hurlburt."

Donovan nodded, leaned forward, and craned his neck, his nose nearly touching the windshield. Minutes later, he pointed, "Lights! But there's only two...no, wait, there's another!"

"Timing's right," Joe shouted. Gotta be it."

116

Hands all over the cockpit. Cramer pushed mixtures rich, retarded the throttles, trimmed, and bled off airspeed as he shoved the props to full increase. "Gear down! Flaps a half."

Donovan twisted in his seat, and reached for the levers.

Cramer shook his head. "Dammit! We're in too close! I'll do a racetrack pattern, and make a longer final." He added power, put a little back pressure on the yoke, and leveled off in the darkness at 300 feet as Donovan called, "Gear down, and locked. Flaps-a-half."

Cramer rolled the elevator trim. "Roger. Keep it in sight, Joe."

"Keep coming just like you are," Joe shouted.

Cramer continued the pattern, cross-checking instruments, and taking fleeting glances outside. Suddenly, there it was, the picture he was looking for. Three tiny lights, seemingly out of place, but gradually moving into position as the parallax factor diminished. He lead the turn, rolled wings level, and called, "Full flaps."

As Donovan lowered the flaps, Cramer closed the throttles, and checked instruments, with the airspeed hovering on the bottom edge of 75. He lowered the nose slightly, trimmed, and nailed the numbers.

They floated inward, engines muttering--props coasting, with warm, damp air buffeting in through the open side windows. The airspeed crept upward, crowding 80. Cramer tugged against the throttles just before the threshold lights swept beneath them. He flared, re-focused on the distant light, held back pressure, and worked the rudder to keep her straight.

Suddenly, she shuddered, then dropped, hit the ground, and bounced. He held the yoke back, worked the rudders, kept her straight, and waited. The second touchdown came with a moderate jolt, followed by a final gentle bounce, as she settled in with the tail wheel touching down.

"Flaps up!"

Screeching brush raked the fuselage, the sound, gradually diminishing as their speed bled off. Finally, he needed a touch of throttle just to keep her rolling.

Close to the end, he slowed his taxi, craning his neck to keep the penlight ahead, in sight. Suddenly it rotated briskly. He unlocked the tail-wheel, held the yoke back, stepped on the left brake, powered up the right engine, and spun her around. After that, he brought up power on the other engine, and taxied a few feet forward, to get out of the hole the inboard wheel had undoubtedly dug. Following that, he checked his heading, locked the tail-wheel, and tapped alternate brakes to make sure the pin had engaged. Finally, he closed the throttles, and both engines settled into a satisfied idle.

"Get 'em aboard Loadmaster," he said.

Donovan leaned toward him. "Our elevators must have taken a beating from that brush Captain. Think we should we check them for damage?"

"What's the point?" Cramer said. "They're free and working. If they're damaged, there's no way to fix them." He turned his head, and looked at Donovan, barely able to make out his boyish face in the dim light. "We're sure as hell not gonna stay here. We'll either make it out...or bust our ass trying."

Donovan nodded, reached to his right and set the cowl flaps, then leaned forward, and peered into the darkness. "It's pitch black out there, captain. You'll have a bitch of a time taking off on instruments alone."

"That signal fire at the other end is what we aim for."

"Don't you want landing lights for takeoff?"

"No lights! There's an NVA unit out there looking for these guys. They might be close."

In back, footsteps banged on metal as someone hurried toward the cockpit. Cramer turned in his seat, looking backward, as a dark image came through the cabin door. The shadowy form stopped, just aft of his seat, and leaned forward, bringing with it the rancid odor of stale sweat, and moldy clothing.

"Captain, I'm Lieutenant Stouffer, the team commander. We've got a severely wounded man with us. The two guys that lit your beacon fire will be here shortly. It'll take them maybe four, or five minutes to flounder through the brush. Can you wait?"

"We came to get you out. I'm not leaving anyone."

The Lieutenant nodded. "Fair enough sir."

Cramer pointed to the bandaged hand hanging from the sling. "How bad is it?"

"Might have been a 12.7," the lieutenant said. "Broke my wrist, spun me around, and knocked me on my ass. It's swelled up, and throbbing now. Red streaks going up my arm."

"We've got some morphine in the first aid kit. You need a shot?"

The Lieutenant shook his head. "Not yet. I've got to keep my mind clear. Our commander was killed, and I'm in charge. Excuse me, Sir, I gotta go back and make sure everything's OK."

As the Lieutenant left, Cramer turned to the front, and checked the rapidly fading beacon fire. Both engines loped quietly now, belching, and popping with that strange, erratic sound that big radials make at idle. Warm, humid air wafted in through the open side window, and finally...here came the mosquitoes, brushing his face, tickling his eyebrows, the hairs in his nose, and the backs of his hands, looking for a break in his repellent. He waved irritably at them, and snorted to clear his nose.

He could smell the river now--picture it in his mind, slow moving, with swirling, muddy currents--filled with leaches, snakes, and God only knows what other vermin. All the rivers in Southeast Asia were like that. What a sorry assed place.

Sweat trickled down his face, tickling, irritating...always something. A mosquito got past the repellant, and landed on his neck, then pierced the

118

skin. He took his hand off the yoke, and slapped the little bastard.

Joe Clark leaned forward in the darkness, his face barely visible in the reflection of instrument lights. "John, your heading after takeoff will be 121 degrees. Estimate the border in fourteen minutes."

"Roger."

Still they sat there--waiting, listening to the engines. Suddenly, a clatter of footsteps hurried forward to the cabin. The loadmaster barged into the cockpit. "Okay Captain, they're all on board."

"Hang on!" Cramer shouted, as he advanced the throttles. The fuselage responded, shaking with a fierce, rumbling rattle as the engines built to peak power. She was roaring now, rattling and shaking, with a bone jarring vengeance. Cramer squirmed, strained against the lap belt, and set himself. A glance outside, one quick sweep of the gages, a final heading check, and he released the brakes. She lurched ahead, jolting over uneven ground, struggling to go, her momentum building slowly. Screeching brush, and rattling sheet metal, added to the roar, as the elevators slowly came alive. Finally, he raised the tail.

"Flaps a quarter!"

Donovan reached back, and worked the lever.

They pounded along now, instrument panel dancing spastically, barely readable in the dim light--soft ground, and dragging brush pulling at them, slowing their progress. Ahead, the beacon fire moved closer, its thin, dying sparks spiraling upward into the darkness. Just before they reached it, Cramer pulled back hard, and she bounced off the ground, lurching upward as they swept through the sparks, and rose into the night.

"Gear up." He paused to gain altitude, then rolled slowly right, picked up his heading, and continued the climb. "Screw the radar," he shouted. "Even if its working, they'll never catch us now. Their sorry-assed Air Force won't be off the ground before noon." He reached across the isle, tapped Donovan on the arm, and laughed, "Hey...I almost forgot...flaps up."

Someone clapped him on the back, cheering in his ear, and he felt a surge of joy. They made it! Made it by God. Got 'em out. Saved those guys. Best mission ever. What a great feeling.

But slowly...slowly, the let down came, and his joy subsided, as he considered the irony. None of those he saved was the one who mattered most. He hadn't saved her. She died out here. Somewhere in this God-forsaken jungle. Just one of thousands who rotted with her. By now, even her name had vanished--already wiped from the grease-penciled, scheduling board, in some air-conditioned office, of an unknown command post.

CHAPTER TWENTY NINE

The two creations of Donald Douglas were parked side by side on the Can Tho ramp, offering a bizarre study in contrast. On the North, a shiny, green and white Air Vietnam DC-3. Beside it, its junky, mud spattered, skid-row sister, a Bien Hoa based C-47, looking like an uninvited relative, home to embarrass the family over the holidays.

The last of the Air Vietnam passengers were just going into the small terminal. Airline pilots in gold-braided uniforms, and Oriental stews with high heels, and immaculately coifed hair brought up the rear.

Cramer and Donovan, dressed in faded, oil stained flying suits, followed them into the noisy, crowded, already sweltering terminal. Cramer pressed his way gently through the crowd, threading through dozens of short, brown people, many with tears of joy streaming down their cheeks as they greeted arriving friends, and relatives.

Lieutenant Donovan, his face flushed, blond hair sweaty, and matted, walked alongside. "I was hoping this place would be air conditioned," he grumbled.

Cramer chuckled. "This isn't Boston Logan, Lieutenant. You ought to be getting used to the climate by now."

"Are you sure he's here?"

"The Command Post said a Huey snatched him out of the swamp, and took him to Can Tho. Unless he decided to turn down the ride, he ought to be here. They said he wasn't hurt."

Donovan pointed toward the far end. "Is that him?"

"Where?"

"Right there. Near the corner. The one in the muddy flying suit."

Cramer grinned. "Yep. There he is, looking natural, with his head tipped back, drinking a beer."

"Isn't it a little early for that?"

"It's a little early to get shot down too. Maybe he figures he's entitled."

"Who's that with him?"

"Beats me," Cramer said. "With hair that long, he's gotta be a civilian."

As they made their way through the crowd, a scowling, mud spattered Davis spotted them, and started in their direction. The long haired civilian, holding a pad in one hand, and pencil in the other, followed him, still trying to engage him in conversation."

As they approached, Davis pointed his thumb backward. "Can you believe this asshole? Son of a Bitch won't take no for an answer."

The gangling, hollow cheeked reporter, his face flushed and weary looking, responded, "I'm just doing my job."

Davis stopped suddenly, and turned, scowling at the man. "Doing your job? Like maybe...Ernie Pyle, or Bill Mauldin, or Edward R. Murrow in WW II."

The reporter nodded. "That's right."

"Right, your lying ass," Davis snarled. "Those guys were on our side. You bastards are on the other side."

"Why do you say that?"

Davis stabbed a finger at him. "Every time you run a story, you sift through the details, pick out what you want, and change the facts to make us the villains."

"Are you saying we lie?"

"No Goddammit. You don't lie. You distort! You don't tell the whole truth. Anything that shows us in a good light, you leave out. Our side is the only one you make moral judgments about. The Commies get a pass no matter what they do."

"Then why not tell me your side of the story?"

Davis waved disgustedly, and turned away. "Piss on you. I don't trust you devious bastards, anymore."

Heads were beginning to turn, and a few of the Vietnamese stopped talking, staring curiously at the muddy, disheveled American flyer.

Davis stepped closer to Cramer, scowling, his features sweat streaked, and mud spattered, a speck of greenery still plastered to his cheek. "You know what burns my ass about these guys? How arrogant they are. They always know more about everything than the poor son-of-a-bitch who's doing the job." He gestured toward the door. "Let's get out of here. I'm ready to go back to Bien Hoa."

"Ok."

The three officers resumed walking, and the reporter followed closely, calling to their backs, "What was your target, Captain?"

Davis looked over his shoulder. "Who said I had a target?"

"If you didn't have a target, what were you doing up there?"

Davis shrugged. "Flying."

"Flying? Just flying?"

Davis stopped suddenly, and turned to face the man. "Why the fuck not? It's a good day for it!" He stepped closer to the reporter, snarling through gritted teeth. "I've had a bad morning, asshole. I don't like getting shot down. It pisses me off to lose my airplane. Get off my back, you Pulitzer chasing prick, or I'm gonna punch your fucking lights out."

The reporter backed up a couple of steps, and Steve turned toward Cramer, and pointed toward the man. "You know what pisses me off about these guys?"

"What?"

"They come at you like they're the biggest fucking deal in the world. Like you ought to be honored just to talk to them. Honored shit! You take the most screwed up pilot in our outfit, and one of these sons of bitches isn't good enough to wipe his ass."

The reporter waved his pad, his obvious fatigue turning to anger. "The

American people have a right to know what's going on over here."

Davis, turned, his color rising. He stepped in front of the man--their noses nearly touching--veins standing out on his neck, and screamed, "Then let the American people fight the fucking war!" He spun on his heel, looked at Cramer, and shook his head disgustedly, as they continued walking. "Do you know who these guys remind me of?"

"Who?" Cramer asked.

"You remember when you were in first grade, and every time you said a bad word on the playground...or punched some irritating little prick in the mouth...or tried to peek up some little girl's dress, there'd be some weasely, whiny little shit who'd run, and tell the teacher on you? Remember that?"

Cramer nodded.

Davis gestured backward toward the newsman. "Well...that little son of a bitch grew up to be a reporter. Boy, I hate those bastards!"

They went out the terminal door, leaving the reporter behind.

Outside, a cloud had drifted over the airport offering the welcome relief of a little shade. Cramer clapped Davis on the back. "You've got a way with words, buddy. Made me feel good to hear that. Too bad you're getting near the end of your tour. I hate to see you go. Why don't you extend?"

Davis shook his head, his irritation obvious. "Can't do it. My wife's already moving into a house in upstate New York." He snorted. "Can you believe it? Ten fuckin' rooms, and we don't even have any kids." He gave Cramer a disgusted look. "But you can bet your ass, we'll have a housekeeper."

"Must be nice to have a rich wife."

"That's what you think. When her family's not trying to control me, she is. Always trying to change me--make me into something I'm not. Even bitches 'cause I cuss too much."

Cramer chuckled, "You? Swear too much? The woman's a crank."

Davis rolled his eyes, and threw his hands up. "Yeah, well, what the fuck you gonna do? Hey! I could put up with that, if she, and her old man would just keep their hands off my career." He kicked viciously at a piece of paper blowing across the ramp. "Damn! I had my heart set on Flight Test School. They sure fixed that."

"Man," Cramer grumbled, shaking his head. "I can't believe it. Liaison to the New York Air Guard? How in hell did they come up with that?"

"Her father had a hand in it, naturally. Political influence. Big brokerage house, real estate, and a half dozen car dealerships--money out the ass. Contributes to every crooked politician in Washington. Lyndon owed him a favor, and Lyndon pays his political debts. Anyway, that's the way politics works, John. Some people get what they want...the rest of us get screwed."

CHAPTER THIRTY

Surprisingly, the Bien Hoa Club was not yet busy, so Cramer walked around the bar and took a stool on the far side, where he could see everyone who came in. Across the bar, next to the wall, Dean Olmer, a nearly naked A1E pilot, tipped up his beer and took a sip, then pursed his lips and swallowed hard, like maybe the brew was not that cold.

Why the hell would anybody be in here dressed like that, Cramer wondered. True, nobody cared, but coming into the club in just your jockey shorts seemed so...unhandy. Even the guys who smoked did it. Had to carry their cigarettes, lighter, and script in their hand, for Christ's sake. Made you wonder what they had against pockets.

As he paid for his CC and soda, Steve Davis, came through the door, looking like an overage college kid on spring break, in that garish, silver palm tree, short sleeved shirt, he'd bought on his R&R to Hawaii. Trouble was, the damned thing looked natural on the guy. What a character. He watched as Steve walked around the bar, and climbed up on the stool next to him.

"How's it going John?" Davis said.

"OK, I guess." Cramer reached out, and punched him lightly on the shoulder. "Your thirty day extension didn't come through, huh?"

"'Fraid not." Davis gave him a sheepish look. "To tell you the truth...I chickened out.   Never asked for it. Caught hell from home, when I mentioned it."

How much time do you have left?" Cramer asked. "A couple more days?"

Davis nodded. "Yeah. That's what I wanted to talk to you about."

"Need help packing?"

Steve waved impatiently. "What's to pack? I've only got two bags." He stared intently, his irritation obvious. "Dammit John, don't make this hard for me. I'm about to do something I don't exactly want to do...but know I should."

"What are you talking about?"

Steve leaned forward, put his elbows on the bar, and lowered his voice. "Look...I know what you've been going through, and I think I might be able to help."

Cramer waved a hand, and shrugged. "I'm OK."

"The hell you are!" Davis leaned back, and jabbed his arm. "Look at you! Everyone knows you've got a problem. It shows. You used to come in here every night, and laugh it up with the rest of us. Now, you don't even smile."

"I haven't been in a joking mood."

Steve leaned forward, and lowered his voice. "I know. But maybe I can fix that. Just promise me you won't get pissed, if I stick my nose in."

Cramer took a sip of his drink. "Okay. Give it a shot."

Davis put his forearms on the bar, and stared intently at him. "Let me build an analogy for you. Suppose you're walking down a dark alley some night, and a mugger comes up behind you, and grabs you in a choke hold. You can't breath, and you're blacking out. What's the first thing you need?"

"I need to get away from that son of a bitch."

Davis shook his head. "No. Not yet. What you need first, is another breath of air. The same thing you were deprived of. There's no substitute for that. If you can't breath, you're shit out of luck."

He squinted. "What's this got to do with me?"

"Everything!" Davis jabbed him on the arm. "John...you lost a woman you were crazy about, and it left a big hole in your life. You've got to fill that hole." He pointed to Cramer's glass. "Will that stuff help? Not much. It may blur the problem, but it damn sure won't fix it."

"So what do you figure will fix it?"

"Only one thing. Another woman."

"What?"

"Another woman!" Davis gripped his shoulder. "Dammit John, you can't fix this problem without another woman. That's the only way you're gonna replace what you've lost. There's no other solution."

"So how do I find another woman like Nancy?"

"You can't!" Steve snapped. "Like everyone else, she was unique. But since you can't get her back...you'll have to settle for a different woman." He back-handed Cramer lightly on the arm. "And I've got one in mind."

"Who?"

"Kim."

Cramer's jaw dropped. "Your girlfriend? Why would you want to give me your girlfriend?

"For Chrissake, John...I'm rotating back. I can't have her, anymore. But somebody will. She's too beautiful to go unattached."

Cramer nodded. "You've got that right. A woman like her...they'll be standing in line."

Davis put his elbow on the bar, looked down and grumbled, "Damn right they will. In a country like this, she's one in a million. Good looks, and lots of money." He paused, then looked up at Cramer, and squinted. "How's that for an attractive combination? Every slick talking bastard in the country will be after her."

"I suppose you're right," Cramer said. "I never thought about it, but why wouldn't she have money. Damn restaurant's always full."

"Shit!" Davis snorted. "That's not the half of it. She's got all kinds of stuff. For starters...real estate, and a garment factory. Makes uniforms for the ARVN. Damn...lend lease check comes from Uncle Sam, right on time, every month. How's that for an angle?"

"Impressive."

124

"Sure as hell is." Davis stabbed a finger at him. "And that's not all. She owns a tailor shop outside the main gate at Tan Son Nhut. Four girls working in there, making civilian suits, and fancy shirts for American GI's. Owns a beer distributorship, too. John, I'm telling you, that woman isn't smart, she's brilliant!"

"Then how'd she end up with you?"

Davis chuckled, and shook his head. "Damned if I know. Never could figure that out." He reached out, and grabbed Cramer by the shoulder, his face turning grim. "Anyway, I'm worried about her. I know she's gonna be looking for someone after I'm gone. Why the hell wouldn't she? She's gotta have a life. What bothers me, she could end up with some guy who's a real bastard. So...I figured if I could fix her up with someone who'd treat her right, a guy who needs someone like her, then maybe I can help two good people at the same time."

"What makes you think she'll go for it?"

"I'm not sure she will. But I know she likes you. A lot." He gave Cramer a wary look. "To tell you the truth, that kinda bothered me."

Cramer squinted. "Then why are you trying to fix me up with her now?"

Davis slammed the side of his fist on the bar. "For Christ's sake John...think! I'm rotating back! Going home. Back to the fucking New York Guard, my rich, snooty wife, and her politically connected relatives." He slid off the stool, and stepped back, still looking glum. "Anyway, if it works out, promise me one thing."

"What's that?"

"Don't write me any letters telling me how good she is in the sack. I don't think I could handle that." His jaw muscles rippled as he clinched his teeth, balled his fists, then turned abruptly, and stalked out the door.

CHAPTER THIRTY ONE

The restaurant was full when he walked in, abuzz with subdued conversation, and rattling dishes at tables being cleared, with a couple of bustling waiters carrying trays of food, palm up, as they walked from the kitchen.

Kim was obviously busy, standing behind the register, explaining something to a waiter he'd never seen before. Today, she was dressed in simple western wear, a plain white blouse, high heels, and short, dark skirt. The outfit looked good on her. No surprise there. Everything she wore, looked good on her.

Rather than distracting her while she was minding the store, he walked back to her private table, and sat down, facing in her direction. This could be touchy. Better to let her take care of business first. Steve said he'd talk to her. If she was receptive, she'd make the next move.

A waitress in an ornate Chinese dress came by, and he ordered a drink, requesting no ice. A warm drink wasn't the best, but even in this place, the ice could be deadly. No matter where you got it, it all came from the same plant. Leaking sewer water, and storm runoff were a bad combination.

As usual, when he was anxious, time dragged. What if she wouldn't go for this? Even worse, what if she was insulted by it? God. On the face of it, the prospect seemed almost bizarre. Even with Steve's blessing, he felt like he was stabbing a friend in the back.

The waitress brought his drink. He paid her, and added a tip. Better not run up a bill. After he popped the question, she might be so insulted she'd throw his ass out.

He watched her, carefully, evaluating her as a person, not just a beautiful woman. Surprisingly good natured, she had a reputation of being good to work for--in a country where benevolent employers were hardly the norm. She seemed so patient, as she spoke to the new man, explaining things, speaking softly, and smiling a lot.

She looked even better than he remembered. True, he didn't get that electrifying jolt when he looked at her, the way he did with Nancy, or Janet Shaw, but she was still attractive. More important, she was here. It was time to face reality. Nancy wasn't coming back, and Janet Shaw was married to some asshole on Cape Cod, so John Cramer was going to have to spend his time with someone else.

Finally the conference was over and Kim looked at him, and smiled. He watched her walking toward him, moving with a grace that was nearly hypnotic.

As she drew near, he stood up, and took the hand she offered. Her skin felt incredibly smooth. Suddenly he realized this was the first time he had touched her. Hopefully, it wouldn't be the last.

"Can I buy the boss a drink?" he asked.

126

Her smile broadened. "Of course."

She turned, made a gesture, and the bartender sprang into action.

She slipped into a seat across from him, and folded her hands on top of the table. "How are you feeling, John?"

"Better."

"I'm glad," she said, looking at him, with those soft brown eyes, and he felt a flutter in the middle of his chest. "Did Steve speak to you before he left?" she asked.

Cramer nodded. "We talked about you. He said maybe...maybe we could help each other get over our losses."

She smiled, reached out, and squeezed his hand. "Steve was a kind, and gentle man. Nancy was a good friend too. But they are gone, and I'm glad you're here."

She lived in a high rise apartment complex where four buildings were situated at the corners of a huge courtyard. Her place was exceptionally well done with a small kitchen, bath, living room, and bedroom, all decorated in contemporary French like some of the better places he'd seen in Casablanca.

She turned on the living room air conditioner, then walked into the bedroom, and turned on another. He stood in the middle of the living room, uncertain what to do next. As she walked by him into the kitchen, she took a couple of glasses out of the cupboard, sat them on the counter, and poured them a drink. He moved into the archway so he could see her better. "I like your place." he said. "How'd you get an apartment this nice in a town like this."

She looked up at him, and smiled. "I own the complex, so I get my choice."

"You own this?"

She nodded, and pointed out the window. "When prices started going up, I took advantage of inflation, sold the two buildings over there, took the profits, and paid off the two on this side."

"Pretty smart."

"Thank you." As she handed him his drink, she looked up at him, and he kissed her, gently on the mouth. She slipped an arm around his waist, and increased the pressure.

Suddenly she was the only woman in the world. His desire surged and he struggled for control, trembling in a wave of increasing ardor. They stood like that, holding on to each other, and kissing ever more passionately, their drinks nearly forgotten. Finally she pulled her head back and smiled at him. "Do you have to fly in the morning?"

"Yes."

"Then you need your rest."

He nodded. "Perhaps we should go to bed."

She gave him a squeeze, and smiled. "Great idea. Why didn't I think of that?"

They walked into the bedroom, and he fumbled with his buttons as he watched her slip out of her clothes. Her white bra, and panties made an striking contrast to her light tan skin, and he wondered why they called the Chinese the yellow race.

She moved toward him, and he took her in his arms, feeling the warmth, the smoothness of her skin, as he pressed his erection against her. It had been nearly three months since he'd done this. He looked down at her and smiled, already concerned that the first one might not last very long.

CHAPTER THIRTY TWO

Even for late fall, it seemed surprisingly cool on the Bien Hoa flight line. The sun was below the horizon, but there was still enough light to read the form without a flashlight. Cramer scanned the page as the lieutenant looked over his shoulder. "Well, obviously we're not going anywhere in this thing," Donovan said.

"Why not?" Cramer asked.

Donovan pointed at the page. "Two red crosses. 'Twenty six cracked rivets left wing, and excessive corrosion in both wings.' Either one is enough to ground the plane. This thing is junk."

"It's been that way since I got here." Cramer said. "This is a VNAF aircraft. It's what we fly. Air Vietnam is supposed to do our major maintenance, but they're too damn busy taking care of their airliners, and making money, to waste time on our stuff."

"Can't our mechanics fix it?'

"How? They'd have to take the wings off. Make major repairs. They don't even have a tool box apiece. Have to share the damn things." He snapped the form shut, turned, and walked toward the entrance. "Forget it. Let's get aboard."

Donovan stayed put, and called to his back, "You're not going to turn it down?"

Cramer sighed, looked back, and gestured toward the door. "We're wasting time, Lieutenant. Let's go. There are people down south who need to get to a hospital."

In the distance, ominous looking lightning flashes, confirmed the reported severe weather in the Can Tho area as Cramer leveled off at 4500 feet, and set cruise power.

Fortunately, there were no reports of hail, but that was small comfort, considering the way things looked. He envied fighter pilots. In a structural sense, fighters were three or four times stronger than transports, so unless they encountered hail, a thunderstorm was, for them, little more than a very bad ride. It wasn't that way with transports. Even new transports. And this one was a hell of a long way from being new.

Over the years, he had read numerous thunderstorm accident reports, relating the mid-air destruction of bombers, tankers, and transports, and admitted to himself that in a corroded, structurally flawed C-47, he was deathly afraid of weather that severe.

Unfortunately, there was no sure way to gauge the intensity of a storm. Those with extreme height or hail, were the worst, but so far, no hail had been reported with this one. That did little to quell his apprehension as they droned onward, and he watched the brilliant display of lightning in the Can

Tho area.

He picked up the approach chart, and handed it to Donovan. "Here. Hold on to this. It'll never stay in my lap in rough air. If I forget a heading or altitude, I'll ask you for it."

Donovan nodded. "Yes sir."

"It's going to be pitch black, rough, and raining like hell down there." Cramer said. "I'll be on instruments. When we break out, let me know right away. If we make the landing it will have to be in the first 500 feet. They only have 3000, and pierced steel planking is a slick son of a bitch when it's wet."

Donovan glanced at the diagram. "They don't show any runway lights Captain."

"They've got flare pots," Cramer said. "They're not much help in weather like this, but they're better than nothing."

The voice of GCI crackled in their headsets. *"Air Evac five seven niner--radar position twenty five miles northeast of the Can Tho Tacan. What are your intentions?"*

Cramer checked the position against his instrument, and answered, "Delta Control, Air Evac five seven niner requesting a Tacan approach to the Can Tho airport."

"Air Evac five seven niner, be advised...Can Tho weather, currently below Tacan minimums--ceiling obscured, estimated 200 feet. Visibility one half mile in heavy rain. Winds zero five zero, variable, zero two zero, fifteen gusting to twenty knots."

"Roger," Cramer said. "This is an emergency air evac flight. I'll use my pilot's emergency authority to make the approach."

"Roger seven niner. You are cleared for a Tacan approach to the Can Tho airport. Report procedure turn inbound."

"Seven niner, Roger."

Donovan leaned toward him, his youthful face barely perceptible in the dim glow of instrument lights. "Captain, I don't think that's a proper use of a pilot's emergency authority. It's supposed to be used only for on-board emergencies."

"Lieutenant...I need a co-pilot, not a fucking lawyer."

"Yes sir."

Ahead, a nearly dark western sky, offered just enough light to define the storm, its huge, ominous shape, sitting there, isolated, seemingly motionless--a murderous mountain of towering black cloud, with jagged streaks of lightning flickering from its bottom, and sinister, inner flashes walking across the middle, and upper levels. Holy cow, look at that lightning--Jesus Christ, the lightning. He'd never seen anything like it.

Here was a thing that could easily destroy them, and he swallowed hard, and clenched his teeth as fear gripped his guts. They were getting close now. He reduced power, slowed to turbulence penetration speed, and

130

tightened his lap belt.

"Turn the cockpit lights on bright," he said. "It'll ruin our night vision, but at least we won't be blinded by lightning."

The cockpit brightened, and their formerly cozy surroundings suddenly appeared tiny, primitive, and hopelessly fragile. Captain Joe Clark, the navigator was standing between them, bent over, gripping the backs of their seats, and peering out the windshield, when they slammed into a wall of water.

She plunged downward, nearly wrenching Cramer's hands from the wheel as his elbows flew up, his pelvis squashed against the lap belt, and the engineer's thermos shattered against the ceiling, sending hot coffee spraying in all directions. Seconds later, she lurched upward, crushing him, driving him into his seat, forcing his chin to his chest as the unsecured thermos ricocheted off the floor, and swept past his head in a wild, crazy, spinning tumble.

She pitched and rolled, jerked and creaked--instruments going wild, altimeter spinning swiftly upward, jerking to a stop, then plunging back down as she floundered and rolled, like a derelict steamer caught in the grip of a savage hurricane. Seconds turned to minutes, and minutes became hours, as fear expanded time, and the roar of the rain never ceased. There seemed no pause, no mercy, no relief.

Water flooded in through the windshield, cascading over his knees, running down his legs, and filling his boots. He gripped the slippery yoke desperately, struggling to hold on, as she jerked, and lurched through a hammering, procedure turn.

Donovan gave the call, his voice made shaky by the pounding they were taking. "Delta Control, Air...uh...Air Evac Five Seven Niner, proced...procedure turn inbound."

"Five seven niner, Roger. Be advised Can Tho radios are inoperative due to a lightning strike. You are cleared to land.

"Roger."

They continued inbound, with Donovan, clutching the checklist in one hand and holding onto his seat with the other. Cramer finally leveled at the prescribed three hundred--still in weather. He rolled the dice, let her sink, and deliberately broke minimums. Nearing 200, Joe Clark pointed left, and shouted above the roar, "There it is! Lights! Ten o'clock!"

"Too early!" Cramer yelled, "Can't be. Tacan shows we're still not there. Must be the town along the river. Wipers!"

No response.

"Goddammit Lieutenant! Give me the fucking wipers!"

Donovan reached out--arm waving, fumbling awkwardly, grasping for the switch. The overwhelmed blades finally responded, sloshing feebly, back and forth in the torrent of water pounding the glass. Lightning flashed, in their right rear quadrant, and Cramer caught a glimpse of thrashing tree tops a hundred feet below.

Donovan stabbed his finger against the glass, and shouted, "Runway in sight! Straight ahead!"

Cramer looked up as a dull amber blur rushed toward them, split in the middle then eerily morphed into twin rows of faintly flickering, washed out yellow.

"Half flaps."

He closed the throttles, and she wallowed in, touching down, almost gently. He shoved the yoke forward, spiked her on, and they skidded, and slid over rain washed steel. Gradually she slowed, the tail came down, and he added a touch of brake. Finally, with less than 200 feet remaining, he had her stopped. He slumped in the seat, thankful for the rest. "You got it," he said. Donovan grabbed the wheel as Cramer let go, and massaged the cramp out of his arm.

In the distance, lightning flashed as both engines died, and they shut off the switches. Cramer looked toward the terminal, seeing a pair of ambulances start toward them, followed by an open-bed, six-by-six, filled with dark, slumped over figures, huddled in back.

He set the brakes as the crew unbuckled, then left his seat, with cold water squishing between his toes as he walked to the rear. By the time he reached the door, the ambulances were already slowing to a stop.

He held on to the door frame, stepping carefully, descending the ladder, with the cold splash of rain soaking his upper body. Once on the ground, he turned, hurried along the wing's trailing edge, then stooped down, and made his way to shelter under the wing tip.

Ambulance headlights showed weakly through the rain, lighting the scene as ARVN soldiers, and Vietnamese medics struggled with stretchers, taking eight casualties from the first vehicle, seven from the second.

Back at the terminal, pale yellow light stabbed into the night, as a door opened, and dark silhouettes hobbled out, walking toward the plane with halting, pain-filled steps. The men approached slowly, a couple, helped by others as they struggled along, slack jawed, with eyes glazed over, their wounds made obvious by disheveled looking, red stained bandages. One bare chested man, had a band-aid under his collarbone, and walked unassisted. As he passed by, Cramer noticed a much larger patch covering the exit wound high on his shoulder. Bringing up the rear, a glassy eyed troop, with a missing left foot, was supported by a medic under each arm.

Cramer turned to Donovan. "It's going to be a long flight for those poor bastards. They've lost a lot of blood, and they're soaking wet. No rear door, no cabin heat, and all that cold air blowing inside? We'll be lucky if some don't die of exposure before we get them to Tan Son Nhut."

Donovan shook his head, dismay written on his youthful face. "My

God, Captain. Why'd they send us on a mission like this? Didn't they have anything better?"

Cramer snorted, "Welcome to low budget, back-burner warfare, Lieutenant. You won't see much first class equipment over here. Washington's saving the good stuff to fight the Russians."

CHAPTER THIRTY THREE

Cramer put his shaving gear into the kit, wrapped the towel around his waist, and left the Officer's latrine, feeling the warmth of the rising sun on his bare skin. He walked slowly, his unlaced flying boots flapping against his legs, as he made his way back to the hut.

Just beyond the fence, a bird sang, its cheerful, lilting call, a fitting match for his mood. Last night's mission had somehow brought him back to life. His depression was gone. Nearing hut 124, he shifted the kit to his left hand, then reached out, and grabbed the door handle with his right. The rusty spring twanged as he opened the screen door, and stepped inside.

FNG, Captain Chuck Simpson, tall, with a prominent nose, and permanent scowl, stubbed out his cigarette, and looked up, as he entered. "Bad mission last night, huh?"

Cramer took the towel off, and threw it in the laundry basket. "Where'd you hear about it?

"Had breakfast with Joe Clark at the club." Simpson's face twisted into a crooked grin. "It's been a long time since I've seen a navigator that shaky. Said he couldn't believe you made that approach." The grin faded into a wary, skeptical look. "Is that kind of shit SOP in this outfit?"

Cramer reached up, and laid his shaving kit on the locker, top shelf. "Nothing's SOP in this outfit, except doing the job." He picked a tee shirt off the clean laundry stack, and pulled it over his head. "Anyway, it wasn't like we had a choice. People were dying. They needed a hospital. Seemed like the right thing to do." He kicked off his boots, and stepped into a clean pair of Jockey shorts, then reached over, grabbed a fresh flying suit off a hanger, stepped into that, and zipped it up. "What the hell," he said, as he slid his feet into his socks, "we got away with it. Twenty two ARVN who might otherwise have died, got to the hospital. Hopefully in time."

"Clark seems torn between outrage, and admiration," Simpson said. "Says after they kick your ass for being so stupid, you oughta get the DFC."

He grunted as he leaned over, and put on his boots. "A transport pilot in a fighter group, getting the DFC? You've got to be kidding. You want medals in this outfit, you gotta kill people, and tear up stuff."

Simpson raised his eyebrows. "Well....maybe you can do that. I hear they're gonna put guns on one of our C-47s."

He tied the second bow, then straightened up. "You expect me to believe that?"

"I'm serious, John." Major Keller says they've got some kind of special gun. Claims they've already tried it back in the States."

"Sounds like one of those crazy-assed jokes they cook up in the club when everyone's shit-faced."

"Maybe. But suppose it's true?"

Cramer slipped his wallet into his pocket, mulled it over for a second, and shrugged. "Okay...suppose it is true. With just one airplane involved, there won't be many pilot slots open. What the hell, there's only one way to be first in line." He reached for his gun belt, strapped it on, and headed for the door.

He climbed the shaky entrance ladder, squeezed between the doorframe, and the strange looking gun-mount, stepped onto the cargo deck, and stood there, staring in disbelief.

A strange arrangement to say the least. Three multi-barreled Gatling guns, were firmly bracketed in massive aluminum mounts, with the aft gun pointed out the open rear doorway, and the two forward units protruding from adjoining, left side windows. A tech sergeant in sweat stained fatigues, was bending over the middle gun, working on something.

Cramer cleared his throat to get his attention. "Does anyone actually believe this will work?"

The Sergeant bumped his head, as he straightened up. "Damn!" he grumbled, as he briskly rubbed the hurt. Seconds later, he bent over, with his flying suit hanging loosely from his lanky frame, and retrieved his cap. "Excuse me, Captain," he said, as he straightened up, then nodded toward the gun. "Damn right it'll work. She's been tested at Eglin, and we've already used it on a couple of targets over here." He smoothed his thinning hair with quick slapping motions, put his cap back on, and managed a crafty smile. "Want to try it?"

"I'm not sure," Cramer said. "Frankly, the concept sounds ridiculous. On the other hand, those little bastards have been shooting at me for months, and I'm fed up with being a victim. I'm ready to try anything that'll give me a chance to shoot back."

The sergeant pointed his screwdriver, waggling the end to emphasize his point. "Captain, this thing works! You ought to see it in action. Each gun fires six thousand rounds a minute. With all three on line, you get three hundred shots a second! Right now, we're shooting one in five tracer, and the son-of-a-bitch puts out so much fire it looks like a red blizzard."

Cramer laid his hand on the shiny gray, streamlined canister behind the gun barrels. "Is this the magazine?"

"Yes sir. Each one holds fifteen hundred rounds. Enough for fifteen seconds of firing. Believe it or not, that's a lot. Most of the time they shoot in short bursts. After several shots, we have to reload."

"How long does that take?"

"A few minutes. But that's not a problem. After the first two guns fire out, the pilot switches to the backup. He shoots that one, while we reload the empties. We hand crank 'em in, so it goes pretty fast. Usually, we don't even have to go off target. By the time the third gun is fired out, the first two are ready again."

"They tell me you shoot it while flying in a circle."

"Yes sir. That's another advantage. A fighter can only shoot while it's inbound to the target. That's no problem for us. When this thing circles a target, she's in a position to fire about eighty percent of the time."

"Sounds like it might work," Cramer said.

"You gonna sign up captain?"

"I'd like to. Down in the Delta, the VC are attacking villages nearly every night. Wiping out whole families. Maybe this thing could make a difference." He glanced absently out the doorway. "I lost my family when I was a kid...still remember what that was like."

The Sergeant raised his eyebrows. "Back home, the TV news don't talk much about civilian casualties on our side...unless, they come from friendly fire."

"Civilian casualties are bound to happen," Cramer said. "In any war. Especially when politics forces you to do all your fighting in a friendly country."

The Sergeant's face twisted into a disgusted look. "They never mention that on the six o'clock news," he said, shaking his head. "I'll tell you Captain, you can't believe the crap those networks are saying about this war. It's a damn shame."

"I don't even want to think about that," Cramer grumbled. "Can't do a damn thing about it. So...anyway...you think this thing's gonna work?"

The Sergeant nodded. "We've already proved that, Captain." He tapped the bracket with his screwdriver. "Try it. You'll see. This son of a bitch shoots so fast, it's unbelievable. Don't even sound like a gun."

Cramer squinted, "What's it sound like?"

"Like some kind of demon roaring from the depths of hell. Just sixty beats a second makes a low bass tone, and each one of these guns shoots a hundred shots a second." The sergeant put the screwdriver in his hip pocket, cupped both hands around his mouth, tilted his head up and gave a long, deep moan, "Wooooooooo, she goes." He hunched his shoulders and shuddered. "Man, it sounds weird. First time you hear it...somebitch makes your skin crawl."

"A thousand rounds a minute?"

"Sure...if you only use one gun." The sergeant's eyes narrowed as he cocked his head, and grinned broadly. "This thing will get your attention, Captain, 'specially if you're on the ground. Talk about spectacular. A reporter from Stars and Stripes was in one of those villages we saved. Claimed she shot tracers so fast, she looked like a fire breathing dragon."

"Clever way to put it."

The sergeant gave him a crafty look. "One of our fighter pilots read the piece, and came up with a smart-assed remark. Tried to make fun of her. Called her Puff The Magic Dragon. We threw it right back at 'em. Painted the name on her nose." He chuckled, "Right below the pilot's window."

"I thought they didn't allow nose art anymore," Cramer said.

"They don't. But who gives a big rat's ass? So far nobody's complained. Anyway, it won't make no difference. By the time Headquarters gets their ass out of joint, everybody will know who she is."

Cramer's eyes swept over the three gun system, marveling at the practicality of the arrangement, wondering why no one ever thought of it before. "Puff The Magic Dragon?" he mumbled softly. "Got a nice ring to it."

The sergeant reached out, and ran his rag over the gun canister, wiping the already shiny surface with gentle, caressing strokes. He squinted at Cramer, and gave him a welcome aboard smile. "Might as well give it a try Captain. You want to save villages? Mark my words. This old wreck's gonna save a lot of 'em."

Bien Hoa was the only base with American fighter planes in the South, and by now the VC obviously knew that. Enemy tactics were simple--launch a surprise attack, fight like hell for half an hour, then withdraw to a safe distance, just before the strike planes got there. After the fighters expended their ordinance, and departed, the enemy would reinitiate their attack, and sometimes overrun a village before additional help arrived.

The gunship, introduced a new factor into the equation--staying power. Carrying its own flares, thousands of rounds of ammunition, and several hours of fuel, she had the means to save a village, and keep it safe until dawn.

In a country the size of South Vietnam, slow cruise speed was not a significant drawback for the newly, but grudgingly dubbed--FC-47. By orbiting leisurely in the central Delta, it was in a position to respond immediately, and could cover most southern villages in a matter of minutes.

Time no longer favored the enemy, and for them, temporary withdrawal no longer worked. When the VC broke off an attack and left, so did the lumbering old plane--but only far enough to make it appear that it was gone. Once the VC resumed their assault, the rattling old gunship returned, ripping into their ranks with a savage blizzard of flaming tracer.

The news spread quickly. Requests multiplied, and they worked her hard. In the following weeks, the clanking old derelict amassed an amazing number of flying hours, as her sleep deprived mechanics, made an around-the-clock effort to keep her aloft. Cramer flew her every time he could, day or night, reveling in the chance to strike back at an enemy who had previously shot at him with impunity.

Dawn was just beginning to break, as he stood at the counter, filling out his strike report, and Don Wilson's huge frame came through the door. The odor he brought with him, smelled like home. "Old Spice?" Cramer asked, "Where the hell did you get that?"

Wilson grinned sheepishly as he walked around the end of the counter, and sat his satchel down. "My wife sent it to me in her last Care package." He chuckled, "Hey, what can I say? The woman loves me." He pointed to the report. "How'd it go last night?"

"Shot up every round on board," Cramer said. "After we suppressed the ground fire, I raked the bushes one more time, just to make sure."

Wilson took his cap off, looked at it, and ran his thumb contentedly over the new oak leaf. "Sounds good," he said quietly. He laid the cap carefully on the counter, looked up and smiled. "Why don't you take a couple of days off, John. The other guys are complaining you're hogging the airplane."

"Okay with me, Major. If you need me, I'll be at the restaurant or my girl friend's apartment."

Wilson smiled. "Fine. But let's not make this an open ended arrangement. Be back here, ready to go, day after tomorrow."

"What time?"

"An hour before sundown oughta be about right."

The restaurant was busy, when he entered--every table filled, with the large room rumbling in subdued conversation. In the rear, the muffled clanking of plates confirmed that the kitchen help was hustling to keep up with demand. Nice place. Even this busy, it was still well run, clean and efficient. It was remarkable how the crowd had changed since he first came in. Formerly catering to high echelon Vietnamese, and Europeans, the clientele was now, almost exclusively American.

As usual, Kim was in her customary place, keeping an eye on things, through the decorated glass partition. She smiled, as soon as she saw him. He slid into a seat next to her. She reached over, gripped his hand, and he felt his pulse quicken.

"It's good to see you," she said, softly. "I was beginning to worry you weren't coming back."

"Sorry," he said. "They've been flying me a lot. I just couldn't make it in. Phone lines off base, never seem to work."

He watched her as she sipped her tea, stunningly beautiful, her movements, gentle, graceful, and elegant. "Steve told me you spoke four languages," he said.

She smiled demurely. "Vietnamese, Chinese, English and French, though I seldom use French anymore." She closed her ledger, pushed it carefully aside, then looked away, and added wistfully, "Most of the French are gone now."

"Yeah, I suppose a lot of them have left." Cramer said. "Their colonial empire is falling apart. I still see a few on the rubber plantations. There's one up at Nha Trang, running a bar, but you hardly see any in the small towns. Still, even with them gone, I don't think I've ever seen a country with a more diverse population than Vietnam."

She gave a little--so what--shrug. "That's hardly surprising. Our history has been...interesting. At one time or another, we've been overrun by nearly everyone--Chinese, Siamese, French, Japanese, and now," she added with a smile, "even the Americans."

"Who was the worst?"

Her face turned grim. "The Japanese."

"Why do you say that?" he asked.

She looked down at her tea cup. "They raped at will. They killed for sport. I was not yet born, but the older women still tell their stories with bitterness."

"What about the French?"

Her expression softened, as she looked up. "The French brought us our first glimpse of the world outside of Asia. They made many improvements...and kept the profits."

"How about the Americans?"

"You have not been here long, but already, you have taught us a valuable lesson."

"What's that?"

She reached out, and her look turned somber as she squeezed his hand. "Never...never fight someone else's war."

CHAPTER THIRTY FOUR

APARTMENT 3-C
OTIS AIR FORCE BASE
CAPE COD, MASSACHUSETTS

Janet Shaw stood in the kitchen archway, watching Stan dump the old cubes into the sink, then reach into the bucket, and drop a handful of fresh ice into his glass--his movements so practiced, they seemed almost automatic.

He'd changed a lot in the last couple of years. His blond hair was still thick, and wavy, but the formerly trim torso was showing signs of an enlarging liver, with his complexion, becoming increasingly mottled, and splotchy. He'd been drinking in the daytime for nearly a year now, mostly one or two before lunch. But whenever he had the day off, he was bombed by mid-afternoon.

Even though he wasn't scheduled to fly, he leaned forward, and looked up, squinting through the small kitchen window, scanning the overcast, with a pilot's typical pre-occupation with the weather.

"Still bad," he grumbled. "God, I'm sick of this place. Damn weather's always rotten up here." He looked over his shoulder, his increasing intoxication made obvious by slurred speech and rising belligerence. "It's not bad in Florida," he said. "Not in Panama City, by God. Sun shines every day there."

"Stan," she said softly, "I've already told you...I'm not going."

He looked down at the counter, and picked up the Scotch. "Why the hell not? How's that going to work? I'll be at Tyndal, and you'll still be up here." He looked up at her, and scowled. "Maybe you haven't noticed, it's a hell of a commute from the Florida panhandle, to Cape Cod."

"I'm aware of that."

He looked back at the counter, poured three fingers of Scotch, then set the bottle down. "How come you suddenly decide you don't want to leave Otis?"

"There's nothing sudden about it. We've been discussing this for weeks. I'm not resigning my commission, and I'm not going with you."

Stan tipped the glass up, took a sip, and coughed, his features flushing as he slammed the drink back on the counter. "For Chrissake Janet! What's the problem? You'd still be a nurse. You can always get a job in a civilian hospital."

She struggled to keep her voice down. "The only thing I'll get in a civilian hospital is low pay, and verbal abuse from arrogant doctors. At least in the Air Force, I'm an officer. I'm not giving that up to follow a man who chases every skirt he sees."

He waved irritably. "Aw what the hell are you talking about? Nobody means as much to me as you."

"You have a strange way of showing it."

He took another sip, and shrugged. "Okay, so I fool around a little. Hey, I didn't think it bothered you that much."

"Why? Because I didn't shriek, and scream and tear my hair? At first I wanted to. But now...now, I don't care anymore." She picked her bag off the end table, and turned toward the door. "I've got to go. My shift starts in twenty minutes."

"Dammit Janet," he called to her back. "We're at a crucial point here! It's too late for me to get out of this assignment. What do you expect me to do?"

She reached out, grasped the doorknob, then turned, and looked back at him. "I expect you to get your things together, and move into the men's BOQ. Tomorrow, I'll move into the women's. Housing is short up here. Somewhere out there, is a real family that needs this apartment."

CHAPTER THIRTY FIVE

The engines droned peacefully at cruise power, as Cramer reached over, and adjusted the panel lights. Outside, the Delta was nearly dark, the visual distinction between tall-grass swamp, and soggy, brush choked land barely discernible. Ahead, muzzle flashes were visible at 11 O'clock, and a couple of hundred yards to the right of that, more flashes with tracers streaking outbound toward the action on the left.

Lieutenant Than, the ARVN interpreter stood behind him, headphones on, monitoring the village frequency on the portable FM. Than leaned forward, and shouted in Cramer's ear, "He say many VC firing now. Much shooting. Two people dead. One child dying. Ammunition low."

"Tell him we're on the way," Cramer said. "Got the tracers in sight. We'll be there in a couple of minutes. "He adjusted power, and switched to interphone. "Get ready with the flares. Put the two forward guns on the line. I'll save the rear one for backup."

"Roger sir."

Lieutenant Donovan leaned toward him, and shouted, "Shouldn't we turn on our position lights Captain?"

"Leave 'em off," Cramer said. "The chances of running into another airplane are damn near nil. The gunfire will help mask the sound of our engines. Without lights, we may be able to get in position before the VC even know we're here."

Than gripped his shoulder. "Chief say, VC move closer. Soon kill everybody. You shoot. You shoot."

Cramer turned his head, and looked up at him. "Ask him if he's shooting any tracer."

Than made a long call in Vietnamese, paused, then talked again, seemingly forever, as Cramer called on interphone, "Ready in back?

"Roger sir. Flares ready. Forward two armed."

Than leaned down, and shouted, "He say only VC have tracer. You shoot. You shoot."

Cramer winced, and turned his head slightly. Good God! What the hell did that man have for supper? His breath smelled like a stockyard. He adjusted heading, turned to the right of the VC position, and waited patiently, as she lumbered into position. Once there, he called "Flares now."

"Flares away."

He reached over and changed intensity in the gun-sight pipper, dimming the glow of the opposing, red dot crescents. Finally, he opened the side window fully, hearing an increased roar of the engines, feeling the warm, muggy draft. Seconds later, the flares lit, and a mile wide circle of tall grass, and scattered brush suddenly had daylight thrust upon it.

He scanned the area, surveying the ground fire, double checking to make sure. Finally, he rolled in, stabilized her in a moderate left turn, put the pipper where he wanted it, touched the button, and the guns came alive.

"Wooooooooooooooo...an eerie, ear-splitting, ghost-like moan reverberated through the plane. He held her there, cross-controlling, feeling himself sliding sideways in the seat--gradually feeding in opposite rudder, slowing the turn, with a blizzard of tracer streaking downward--two seconds--three seconds--four seconds, five--as a long, wide swath of enemy fire, winked out, and stayed dark.

Finally, he released the button, the guns fell silent, and she wallowed sickeningly as he rolled her out of the grossly, uncoordinated turn. His inner ear rebelled, screaming to his brain, that his visual senses were lying. He swallowed hard, ignored the conflict, and focused on the gauges.

A long string of excited Vietnamese came over the radio, as Lt Than leaned forward. "He say, 'very good shooting! Very good shooting. Shoot more. Shoot more!"

Cramer looked over his shoulder, and shouted, "Roger. Tell him to keep his head down, hug his kids, and save his ammunition. This time, we caught the little bastards in the open. I'm gonna kill 'em all."

He turned his head, and looked down, watching the tiny figures—in a panic driven retreat--splashing their way through the marsh in a frantic quest for safety in the jungle. If they made it, tomorrow they'd be back. No by God. Not this time. He rolled into a bank, gritted his teeth, touched the firing button and tore 'em up again.

The sun was long since down, but there was still enough light in the hut to see. Bill Bishop stubbed out his cigarette, then grabbed the pack off the table and lit another, tilting his head to one side, blinking defensively as the smoke rose past one eye. "You still going with that Chinese girl?"

Cramer nodded.

Bishop gave him a sly grin. "I don't blame you. A guy could lose his head over someone like that."

"She's an unusual woman," Cramer said. "Easy going, smart, and a whiz at business. Nothing gets by her. Her English is damn near flawless and she's fluent in Vietnamese, Chinese and French."

Bishop squinted, and shook his head. "How the hell can anyone master four languages?"

"Beats me. I had trouble with Spanish."

Bishop tipped his nose up, and gave him a skeptical look. "Does she know you're getting close to the end of your tour?"

He glanced down, and folded his hands on the table. "I haven't had the guts to tell her. Tried to...but I...I wasn't sure how she'd take it."

"You could volunteer for another tour."

"Too late for that," he said. "I got my new assignment yesterday."

Bishop tossed his empty into the trash, stood up, and walked over to the cooler, then reached in, rattled the ice, and brought out another beer. "Maybe you could get out of it," he said, as he wiped his hand on the leg of his flying suit, and walked back to the table.

"It's hard to do that," Cramer said. "Anyway, it's a really good assignment. C-130s out of Charleston, South Carolina. There's a bonus attached. A year from now, they're supposed to convert to the new C-141. Looks like I'll get to fly them too."

Bishop sat down, popped the beer tab, took a sip, and wiped his lips with the back of his hand. "Man! That'll round out your resume. I've heard great things about both planes. Talk about a career boost."

Cramer turned his palms up. "Dammit! I hate to leave. But its hard to throw away a chance like that. Anyway, there's something else to consider. Look at the situation here. Civilian transportation is becoming increasingly unreliable. If the war keeps heating up, I could be twenty miles from Kim, and never get to see her."

Bishop leaned back against the wall locker, and stretched his legs out. "Not only that, they could transfer you to the other end of the friggin' country."

"Sure could. Who can predict what's going to happen over here. Anyway you look at it, I'd be stupid to turn down that assignment."

"Have you told her?"

He shook his head. "No. I'm...I'm taking the coward's way out--gonna tell her the last week I'm here. At least that way, the time we have left won't be turned into an extended wake."

The restaurant had been closed for nearly an hour, the help had already gone home, and still she was quiet. Cramer scraped his plate, finished his sweet and sour pork, then downed the last of his wine, and looked at her. Something was obviously wrong.

"Want me to carry the dishes back to the Kitchen," he asked.

She shook her head. "They can take care of them in the morning. Let's go home."

Back in the apartment, they had a couple of drinks, but her pre-occupation elsewhere was obvious. When they finally went to bed, she responded enthusiastically to his lovemaking, but afterward, seemed troubled. She lay on her back, saying nothing, staring vacantly at the ceiling, the covers barely covering her navel. He wondered if she had somehow learned he would soon be leaving.

Finally, she turned over, crowded against him, and propped herself up on her elbows, as she looked down at the sheet. "I won't be able to see you after tonight, John." she said softly.

144

The words hit with a jolt. He turned his head, and looked at her. "Why not?"

"Tomorrow I must go to France."

He raised his head, and stared at her. "France? Why the hell would you go to France?"

"To be with my husband."

His jaw dropped. "You never told me you were married."

She continued looking downward, avoiding his gaze, as she ran her hand slowly back, and forth, over the sheet. "Two years ago my husband took our children to France," she said, her voice quivering. "He wanted to start a new business in a country where they could be safe." She blinked, wiped her eyes, drew in a deep, trembling breath and added, "I stayed behind to run things, until I could sell our holdings. Now they are sold, and I must go to my family."

Cramer lowered his head to the pillow, gripped his brow, and stared at the ceiling. "My God! How could I live with you this long, and know so little about you?" He turned his head, and looked at her. "You've got a husband? I never even suspected. Who is he? What's he like?"

She swallowed hard, and kept staring down at the sheet. "He's an older man. Years ago, he helped my parents when they were desperate. When I was sixteen, he asked to marry me. They agreed."

"They just...gave you to him?"

She shook her head. "It wasn't like that. It was not a bad thing. My parents were concerned for my future." She looked at him, somber faced, blinking back tears, her voice shaky. "Don't think bad of them. You don't know what it's like to live in a country like this. To have no other choice. All over Southeast Asia, there are only two kinds of people. The users, and the used. For women in particular, Vietnam offers a difficult life."

"What's your husband like?"

"He's a good father, and a good husband, even though he suspects I do not love him." She smiled wistfully. "In spite of that, he is quite pleased. When he left Vietnam, all we owned was the restaurant. He says I have done very well."

"I don't understand this. Why...why would he take your kids with him? Most men wouldn't do that."

"He took them because he feared if he did not, I would not follow."

He stared at her. "My God! You mean...this is it? It's over? Just like that? "

The moisture in her eyes spilled over, and his irritation vanished. He reached out, and drew her to him. She curled up, and lay her head on his chest, sobbing, her tears splashing against his skin.

What a hell of a situation. She was leaving, and he couldn't follow-- even if she wanted him to. He was tied down. Locked in. Owned, body and soul, by the Air Force. What a way to live. What a brutal business. Betty was right. One way or another--someone's always leaving. Someone's always saying good-by."

The rising sun filtered through the Plexiglas skylight, making a long bright spot on the far wall. Cramer sat silently on the edge of his bunk, forearms resting on top of his thighs, hands clasped loosely together.

In one of the nearby huts, the Armed Forces Radio station was on, and Petula Clark was belting out "Downtown." It was one of his favorites, but this morning, the cheery, upbeat lyric seemed at odds with his somber mood. This was it. The big day was finally here...his last in-country. Like it or not, he was going back.

For a while, he'd had a home here. One big rowdy family, where everyone looked out for the other guy. It was a good outfit. No matter how bad it got, someone would always jump in, and risk his ass, just to save yours.

Actually, there seemed little reason to stay now. Most of his friends were already gone, and those remaining, would be leaving soon. Both of the women who had been part of his life were no longer here, and soon, even their memories would begin to fade.

Still, it was hard to deal with. In sixteen years, of all the units he had served in, this was the one that felt like home. Here, they had demanded more, forgave less, and taxed him to the limit, in an endless series of life-threatening tests that filled him with pride, and gave him a deep sense of accomplishment.

There were times when he had yearned for this moment, wondering if he would live to see it. But now that it was upon him, it seemed as though it had come too soon. He would leave here shortly, and when he did, the people he served with would disappear from his life, their unique, incandescent personalities, sliding backward into his past, until even their memories were nearly gone.

He wanted to stop the clock, slow things down, pause to savor the spirit, the essence, the soul of this place, and the people in it. But the sun still rose, and time still passed, and soon, he would have to go.

The twang of the screen door spring invaded his thoughts, as Mark stepped into the hut, popping the last of a donut into his mouth, and licking his fingers. Williams let the door go, and it banged twice before staying closed. He chomped a couple of times, and swallowed with obvious difficulty. "Well, the big day's finally here, huh John?"

Cramer nodded. "Maybe I should have done it your way. Look at you, a month into your second tour, and you like it better than ever."

Mark grinned. "Sure do. If it stays like this, I'll be here until it's over. Had breakfast yet?"

146

"Naw, I'm not hungry."

"Me neither. I just...had some coffee, and a donut."

Williams moved away from the door, walked toward the center of the room, and tossed his hat on top the mosquito netting over his bunk, then turned around abruptly. "What the hell, I know it's early, but we could have a drink before you go."

Cramer stood up. "Sure, let's have one. It's not like we do this every day."

They walked over to the cooler, reached in, and plopped some ice into their glasses. Cramer grabbed a bottle of VO off the shelf, and poured them each a generous portion. Mark sipped, swallowed hard, and shuddered. "To tell you the truth...damn stuff doesn't taste that good after a donut."

Cramer chuckled, "Glad I didn't have one. Wouldn't want to waste this."

"How you gonna get to Tan Son Nhut?" Mark asked.

"Donovan's bringing a weapons carrier," he said. "I could have flown over on the courier of course, but I wanted to take one last ride through the countryside."

Williams gave him a wry smile. "Sort of a final grand tour, huh?"

"Yeah. Wouldn't want to miss that scenic drive through the slums along the Mekong, now would I?"

"Nothing better than a trip through a picturesque city."

Cramer smiled. "You got that right. Litter in the streets. Tangled traffic. Wood smoke mixed with exhaust fumes. Grime streaked buildings--rats scurrying into dark corners--sidewalks filled with little bitty, funny looking people."

"Pleasant memories. What a treasure." Williams punched him lightly on the shoulder. "John, you've got the soul of a friggin' poet. This shit hole won't be the same without you. Well anyway, you're off to better things...flying Herky Birds out of Charleston. How 'bout that? Think you'll like it?"

"I dunno. Trash hauling, is trash hauling. At least I'll see a lot of the world. They tell me those guys go everywhere. Europe, Africa, the Middle East, South America. Now, they're even coming over here."

Squeaking brakes, and the sound of scruffing gravel broke into the conversation. Seconds later a truck door slammed, with a metallic bang.

"Gotta be Ken," Cramer said. He tipped his head back, gulped twice, and set the glass down. Mark finished his, and both of them watched as the front door opened, and Donovan barged in.

"We have to make it quick, Captain," Donovan said. "They want the truck back by ten. How many bags do you have?"

Cramer pointed toward his bunk. "Just those three,"

"Is that all?"

Cramer shrugged. "What the hell, I was only here for a year."

Each one grabbed a bag, and walked through the sparsely furnished room--their steps echoing loudly off the bare wooden floor. Once outside, they hurried down the walk, passing by the sandbagged bunker, then finally, stopped at the rear of the truck. One, by one, Donovan threw the bags over the tailgate, then turned, walked around the vehicle, opened the door, and slid behind the wheel.

Suddenly, events became a blur. Cramer turned woodenly, stuck out his arm, and shook hands with Mark. "Well, nothing that's good lasts forever, huh?"

"Take care, John."

"You too."

They looked away, trying not to show their emotion. Cramer turned, walked forward, and climbed into the truck, then closed the door, and draped his arm out the window.

Donovan gunned the engine--cleated mud grips spun into action, and a spray of gravel flew behind them. The truck lurched forward, and pulled away.

Cramer twisted in his seat, leaned out the window, and looked back, waving at Mark--sensing their paths would never cross again. He shifted his gaze, took one last look at hut 124 fading in the distance, and the significance of the moment finally hit home. A page had turned, a chapter had closed--an important part of his life was over, and he realized with a deep sense of regret, that he'd never pass this way again.

CHAPTER THIRTY SIX

CHARLESTON AFB, SOUTH CAROLINA

Lt Col Jenner, slim, gray haired, and nearly fifty, leaned back in his chair, and said, "OK, Captain, it's settled. We'll check you out in the squadron instead of sending you to C-130 school in Tennessee. That way you won't have a commitment to stay in the Herky Bird, and there'll be nothing to prevent your going to C-141 school when we change over to the new plane."

Major Robbins' round, sun tanned face broke into a smile. "We can send you through the three week, maintenance ground course to familiarize you with the 130. After that, you'll fly a few trips as third pilot, upgrade to co-pilot, and a few months later, move into the left seat. By that time you'll know the MAC system."

Cramer could hardly conceal his surprise. No one in SAC would have dared circumvent the system in such a manner.

Jenner scanned the records, and looked up. "I notice you're not married."

He shook his head. "No Sir. Not any more. My wife divorced me when I was in SAC. Said I was gone too much."

Jenner and Robbins laughed.

"Well, its nice you got that out of the way." Robbins said. "If she hadn't left you then, she'd damn sure do it now. I've got to be honest with you, Captain, once you're checked out, you're not going to see much of Charleston.

"He's right about that," Jenner said. "We operate all over the world. But even when you're here, you'll be busy. Besides learning the airplane, and MAC rules, there'll be volumes of foreign regs, and a bunch of political procedures to study."

"A lot to watch out for," Robins said. "In addition to our military commitments, we also support the State Department. Unfortunately, a lot of countries we go into are unfriendly, and there's only one way to keep your ass out of trouble in places like that." He pointed his finger and scowled. "Be polite, and read. Read Goddammit! Read! Get your whole crew involved. Study your foreign clearance guide, and check every notice you can find."

Jenner nodded, and gave him a grim look. "It may only be a torn piece of paper, thumb tacked to some fly specked bulletin board in an unfriendly country, but you damn well better not ignore it. It could be the only notice you'll get of something that could destroy your career. Dismiss it...you and your whole crew could end up in a stinking jail somewhere. Might take months to get you out."

Jenner stood up, reached across the desk, and stuck out his hand.

"Anyway Captain, welcome aboard. Grab a quick lunch, and get back here as soon as you can. We'll put you on one of our local, afternoon transition flights, and get you started."

What an outfit! Totally different from the iron assed, unforgiving environment of SAC. Here the snarl factor was low. The profane tongue lashings, and abusive critiques common in SAC were considered bad form in this command.

Here there were no career threatening exercises, no alert, no readiness tests. Certainly, they gave check rides, but in this command, a failure was deemed little more than an indication that additional training was needed. The difference, was understandable. SAC was charged with the daunting task of keeping the Soviet Union at bay. MAC simply hauled people, and cargo--apparently, damn near everywhere.

Naturally, there was a down-side. Since failing a test was seldom career threatening, MAC check rides, were surprisingly even tougher than those he'd experienced in SAC.

The new airplane was a pleasant surprise. Compared to worn out C-47s, the C-130 seemed like a flying palace--air conditioned, with modern instruments, it was surprisingly light on the controls, and a delight to fly. In spite of its size, it could operate off of airstrips nearly as short as those the C-47 could handle.

During the next three weeks he completed aircraft familiarization. After that, flying training increased, and he flew a heavy schedule of day, and night transition flights. Each mission called for numerous takeoffs, landings, and instrument approaches, all made intentionally difficult by an endless stream of simulated emergencies. Off duty time was spent with his head buried in the books.

Once his checkout was complete, the Squadron made good on its promise to keep him moving. Time off was brief at Charleston, and non-existent overseas. They'd told him he'd travel, and travel he did, going on line as a qualified co-pilot, flying long overseas routes, logging countless, boring hours on autopilot, suspended--seemingly motionless--thirty thousand feet above a blue, rippled void that stretched from horizon to horizon.

At other times, on multiple, back to back, short-leg runs, it seemed he lived in perpetual motion, stopping only to grab a bite, snatch a few hours of sleep, and file a new clearance.

Missions took him to an amazing variety of places--in the Caribbean-- Puerto Rico, the Canal Zone, and tropical, melodic Trinidad. In South America--Paramaribo where only the casino, and Governor's mansion were fit to live in. Down the line came ultra-modern Brasilia, the wide, beautiful beaches of Recife, darkly tanned girls speaking only Portuguese, and a local currency that inflated at an astonishing rate.

On mid-Atlantic trips he stopped at Bermuda, and the wind-swept Azores, then continued on, subsequently landing in Spain, Morocco, Libya, Egypt, and Saudi Arabia. In spite of the stops, on this trip, monotony ruled, with the cruise altitude view alternating between endless waves, and barren desert.

On southern Atlantic runs into Africa, Ascension Island provided a stark study in bizarre topography, its eerily arid moonscape, broken by centrally located Green Mountain, where clouds forming in the upper regions supplied moisture to bright green, surprisingly productive, farms. Down the line, the Congo's depressingly filthy chaos made the next day's stop in flower bedecked, ultra modern, Johannesburg, a welcome return to first class living.

On trips to this hemisphere, in spite of its increasing intensity, the war in Vietnam seemed little more than a remote conflict. It wasn't just the distance that obscured it, it was the attitude of the other airmen. Many, seemed to have little, if any interest in the war.

It wasn't that way for him. Rounding out his perspective by reading local English language newspapers, when available, he developed an enhanced appreciation for the world situation. The Communist menace seemed everywhere, insidious, pervasive, and always threatening. In nearly every country he visited, there was some kind of terrorism, insurgency, or Russian threat under way. Unfortunately, most of his fellow crewmembers, had not yet experienced a Vietnam tour, and many seemed unconcerned about the Communist incursions.

Granted, on this side of the earth, there were other things to worry about. An ever-changing operational environment--sensitive borders, diplomatic quagmires, and the constant struggle with exotic names, and languages. A man could only concentrate on so much.

He seemed perpetually in motion. Lonesome became a way of life. Other than a tentative camaraderie with temporary peers, his social life all but disappeared. In this command, more than any of the others, he missed having a family. Now it seemed, life offered no close relationships, no social stability. In spite of being constantly surrounded by a crew, lasting friendships were impossible to develop, since the people he served with, were seldom together for more than a week.

During a trip, getting acquainted, was a tentative thing, with only sporadic opportunities for personal discovery. Once underway, whenever there was time, each man revealed just a bit of his background, making wary, generalized statements, that over time, slowly revealed his character, background, and personal values.

Most of the information was exchanged during pre-flight, after level-off at altitude, or following arrival, during bus rides into town. The process was fraught with risk. If a man talked too much, complained too often, or expounded at length, he ran the risk of appearing self-centered, whiny, or even a braggart.

In the end, the social exchange had little lasting value. Back at Charleston, once a trip was over, the crew was dissolved, and its members entered their respective pools. Following a short crew rest, they'd be separately alerted, randomly re-assigned, and scattered in all directions.

Native populations were a lost cause as far as company was concerned. Only rarely did foreigners speak English, and polite conversation was seldom possible. Even during Cab rides into town, small talk was normally out of the question, restricted to short, simple phrases and the mispronounced name of some second rate hotel. He saw dozens of attractive women, but beyond the boundaries of the airport, few spoke English, and sign language seldom worked. Eventually, after scores of misunderstandings, he grew tired of the frustration, and simply gave up talking to local girls. What the hell was the point? He wouldn't be there long enough to shake hands anyway.

The heater roared as the crew bus pulled to a stop in front of Rhein-Main Airlift Command Post. Pilot Flight Examiner, Captain Dan Roberts, thirty, balding, and perpetually cheerful got off first. Cramer followed him into the building, relieved to be out of the cold.

As they approached the counter, a red eyed duty officer with five o'clock shadow, and that end-of-the-shift look, picked a folder out of the rack, laid it on the counter, opened it, then turned it around so they could read the paperwork.

The Duty Officer squeezed his eyes, and blinked, as Cramer and Roberts leaned forward. "Good news guys," he said wearily, "You hit the jackpot. Oslo, Norway."

Robert's mouth dropped open. "No shit?'

The briefer looked up, and shook his head. "It's hard to believe, but the State Department wants you up there for three days. Make sure your class A's are in good shape. They mentioned orientation flights for the natives, guided tours, and formal receptions."

Cramer looked at Roberts. "Oh my God. I can see it now. Gorgeous, six foot blonds, with short skirts and loose morals."

Roberts chuckled, rubbing his hands together. "Cramer, you're gonna have to screw up really bad to bust this checkride."

After briefing, they checked the weather. Famous throughout the line, the German forecaster gave his usual over-dramatic presentation--heavily accented, smaltzy expressions, exaggerated gestures, pregnant pauses, and a dramatic, voice rising, heel clicking, map slapping flourish at the end. What a performance. On his best day, comedian Sid Caesar couldn't have done better.

152

The upshot of it was...the weather was rotten. The usual winter situation for Europe, so Cramer could expect a challenging operational environment for his Aircraft Commander's checkride. Oh well, at least there'd be a couple of nights to spend on the town, hopefully in the company of tall, blond and leggy Norsewomen. What an opportunity.

Arriving during a winter storm, he made a rocky, VOR approach, finally breaking out into a narrow, valley at 500 feet, descending between hillside rows of modern Scandinavian homes with high pitched roofs--a breathtakingly beautiful, snow blown scene that Currier and Ives would have killed for. The elegance of the view, only heightened his expectations. This time surely, adventure and romance were definitely in the making.

Cramer paid his bill in American dollars, then picked up his tray, left the cafeteria line, and searched the expansive room for the rest of his crew. What a terminal. Polished hardwood floors, towering modernistic windows and fine Scandinavian sculptures. Damn Norsemen spared no expense to impress their visitors. Finally, he spotted his navigator and check pilot, sitting at a long table near the windows.

He walked over, set his tray on the table, and took his seat. Dan Roberts, smiled at him. "Well, look on the bright side. At least you passed your check ride. No need to be totally disappointed."

Cramer put his napkin in his lap, and reached for his knife, and fork. "Disappointed is hardly the word." He stared down at his tray, and shook his head. "What an outfit to work for. We come in here thinking we're gonna have a couple of nights on the town, and before we can shut down the engines, we've got a message to haul ass for Athens."

Roberts listlessly stabbed a meatball. "I guess we're lucky they gave us time for lunch." He stuffed the morsel into his chubby face, chewing as he talked in a muffled, mumble. "Oh well, lighten up. At least we'll eat well. No peanut butter and crackers today, huh guys?"

Cramer looked down at his tray. "Yeah, this is great. Meatballs and mashed potatoes. Now there's some exotic shit for you. I feel like I'm back on the friggin' farm."

Lieutenant Edwards, the navigator, thin, dark haired and boyish looking, took a sip of coffee, sat his cup down, and scanned the nearly deserted room. "I was really looking forward to this trip," he said wistfully. "Thought maybe this time, we'd have a chance to see something besides the airport."

Cramer snorted, "A country full of beautiful women, and what do we see? One middle aged, overweight Amazon in the serving line."

Roberts looked up, and nodded toward an approaching man dressed in a dark, pin stripe, three piece suit, with a briefcase handcuffed to his wrist. "That's gotta be our passenger."

"I wonder how much money he's got in that satchel?" Edwards said.

"Can't be money," Cramer grumbled. "Friggin government's not that careful with money."

Roberts chuckled, "Take it easy, John. So you didn't get laid this trip. It was still a nice run."

"Nice for you," Cramer said. "You married guys got it made. Go home to mamma, get your ashes hauled, and play with the kids. Me? I park my ass in a deserted BOQ room, do my laundry and maybe get to watch a little television before I go out again. How the hell can a man have a home, and start a family with a schedule like that?"

CHAPTER THIRTY SEVEN

Captain Ben Harris, the lanky, crew cut Charleston duty officer laid a stack of papers in front of Cramer as he sat his bags down in front of the counter. Harris smiled, his gold tooth shining. "Congratulations John. Your C-141 school date finally came through. You can kiss the Herks good-by."

Cramer gave him a thumbs up, smiled, and winked. "Two months in Oklahoma City? I'm looking forward to that. What's it like to spend that much time in one place?"

Harris squinted. "Hard to get used to, I guess. Eating at regular hours. Getting up, and going to bed at the same time. Same classroom two days in a row. How can people live like that?"

Cramer chuckled, as he picked up the papers. "I'll let you know. Give you a few pointers when I get back."

In Oklahoma city, he lived off base, among dozens of other pilots in an upscale housing development with manicured grounds. Billeted two to each apartment, they enjoyed carpeted, attractive rooms, with modern furniture and pastel colored walls. In spite of the genteel living, his social life was limited, as he once again put professional ahead of personal.

Times at Tinker were hectic, filled with daytime classes, fast paced simulator sessions, and after the first few days--flying. Other than the classroom, and flightline, he saw little of the bustling base as he concentrated on getting the most from his training.

Off duty, he buried himself in his books, or sat through extra simulator classes watching other pilots and learning from their mistakes. The extra effort paid off, and he once again finished near the top of his class.

Back at Charleston his aircraft commander's local check, lasted more than eight hours, and covered nearly every emergency listed in the 60 page, red bordered section of the encyclopedia sized, pilots hand book.

During the flight, two emergency riddled, instrument approaches, with subsequent landings, were made at each, of four, widely separated airfields. En-route between bases, the cordial check pilot relentlessly quizzed him on systems, procedures, and additional emergencies. Following the fast paced, eight hour, ordeal, he showered, left half of his first drink sitting on the night stand, collapsed into bed and fell into a nearly catatonic state.

Three days later he departed on his Aircraft Commander's line check--a trip to Southeast Asia, with stops at Dover, Delaware, a rest over night in Elmendorf AFB Alaska, followed by another RON in Yokota near Tokyo. The following day he flew into Saigon. An hour later he was turned around, headed back east-bound, and entered crew rest at Clark AFB, in the Philippines.

The next morning began with a long, over-water leg which ended in

Alaska, where he again stayed overnight. After crew rest, he spent the next twenty hours leap-froging through Canada and the States and finally reached Charleston. During the grueling trip, his check pilot asked literally hundreds of questions, on C-141 performance, MAC regulations, ICAO rules, weather, and crew co-ordination.

Throughout the trip, every take-off, approach and landing had been endlessly nit picked, and critiqued down to the last detail. They might have been civil, and soft spoken in MAC, but the cordial, low-key bastards were uncompromisingly thorough.

Following his checkout, Cramer looked forward to the standard MAC routine, traveling to various continents, with most trips earning him from one to three days of crew rest. Finally, by God...*finally*, there was time for a social life.

A dozen Sand Pipers hurried up the grade on long, spindly legs, doing their best to stay ahead of the foam as the surf rolled in, washing quietly over the gently sloping beach.

Cramer hid behind his sunglasses, watching her daintily sample her cognac. Fine looking woman. Tall, trim and blond, with the kind of face that could make it big in Hollywood.

He remembered the first time he saw her, standing in the middle of the Charleston gallery, sipping champagne--surrounded by her stuffy academic friends. He had stared at her, almost mesmerized. When she finally glanced his way, and their eyes met, he felt a flutter of excitement in the middle of his chest.

Out here, the sunlight gave a faint, reddish tinge to her hair, and she looked even more beautiful. He remembered how good her bare skin felt next to his.

She sat her glass on the table, and spoke just loud enough to be heard above the sound of the surf. "How was the trip to Rio?"

"About like the others," he said. "We had a room on the fourth floor with a balcony overlooking the water. Nice place. We could see the whole length of the curve in the beach--ate breakfast there both mornings."

"I envy you," she said. "Europe one week, Africa the next, then South America or the Middle East. Where are you going next time?"

"I don't know. Probably Southeast Asia. I make a trip there at least once a month."

"Not your favorite place is it?"

He picked up his glass, and shook his head. "No--too many memories. But...the trip over and back is OK. Alaska, Japan and Okinawa are fine. Thailand's not bad either, but Vietnam is as crappy as it ever was."

He wanted to change the subject and get back to them, but couldn't think of a subtle way to do it. Finally he just plunged right in. "Are you going to see David while I'm gone?"

She nodded, and he got a sinking sensation in the middle of his chest.

"I'm not sleeping with him," she said. Our relationship is not at that stage yet. He may have a PHD, but he's not as worldly as you." She grinned. "Nor as sexy."

"That oughta give me an edge," he said.

She raised her eyebrows. "It does. At least for now. But I remember what it was like when Carl, and I, were married. After awhile the animal attraction fades, and you have to be compatible in other ways, or it just doesn't work."

She took a drink from her cognac, set her glass down, and looked at him. "David and I have a lot of the same interests--the same tastes--in the arts, in politics. All our friends are from the academic community." She shook her head. "I don't understand...it's not supposed to work this way. Can someone be in love with two people at the same time, for different reasons?"

He struggled to hide his irritation. "Apparently. Dammit Linda, I don't mean to sound callous, but the answer is yes. It happens all the time. All over the world. That business about there being only one woman for every man, and a man for every woman, is a bunch of crap."

She gave him a wry smile. "You're such a sensitive idealist."

He tipped his drink up, and finished it in two gulps, feeling the slight burn in his throat as he sat the glass down, and looked at her. "Well, it's the way things are. When you consider the population world wide, for every man there must be at least 10,000 women, and vise-versa. Regardless of that, society, convention and the law, all say that sooner or later, you have to make a choice."

She gave a frustrated little wince. "It's difficult to do that. I have a lot in common with David--he's gentle, kind, and refined."

"Oh...and I'm a crude, drunken lout, right?"

She laughed, reached out, and slid her hand up his arm. "No. No you're not. You're considerate, and intelligent, but, just a tad rough around the edges." She cocked her head slightly, and smiled. "You're also the most attractive man I've ever met."

"Then what's the problem?"

"Well for one thing, you plan to stay in the Air Force, and I'm not sure I want to live that lifestyle." She picked up her drink, drained it, put the empty glass back on the table, and gave him a sultry smile. "Anyway, why don't we go to bed and talk about something else? Or did you rent this room just for the view?"

CHAPTER THIRTY EIGHT

CAPE COD, OTIS AFB HOSPITAL

Out in the hallway, an orderly pushing a wheelchair with a grumpy looking patient aboard, rolled past the doorway, as Captain Janet Shaw sat in the hospital lounge, scanning the latest copy of *Air Force Times*. Beside her, Captain Dorothy Zanier, chubby, dark haired, and brainy, drained the last of her coffee, sat the cup on the end table, leaned forward, and stubbed out her cigarette, her white, sausage like fingers gripping the butt firmly as she ground it almost vengefully into the glass. "How come there's no gray in your hair?" Zanier said.

Janet kept her eyes on the paper. "Why should I have gray hair? I just turned twenty six."

"Don't rub it in." Zanier leaned toward her, tipped her head back, and peered through the bottom of her bi-focals. "Anything interesting in the times?"

"Umm...nothing so far," Janet said. "I was looking to see if anyone I know got promoted."

"Like you perhaps?"

"Not likely. I barely have two years in grade. Wait a minute...what do you know...John Cramer's on the Majors list. How about that?"

"You said that sort of wistfully. Was there something between you two?"

"Not really." Janet turned her head, and smiled. "Come to think of it, maybe there should have been. We both ended up divorced. He's an attractive man."

Zanier gave her a baleful smirk. "There's nothing worse than a missed opportunity. Oh well...I've got to get back." She grasped the chair arms, grunted, pushed herself to her feet, and brushed the ashes from her skirt. "If you get a chance, how about the Club for lunch?"

"Fine."

A minute later, Janet folded the paper, and laid it on the coffee table. After leaving the room, she turned down the hallway, and began walking toward ward three. Ahead, Dorothy stood in front of the bulletin board, her head tipped back at an almost extreme angle as she looked through the bottom of her glasses. As Janet drew near, Dorothy pointed at the sheet posted prominently in the center of neatly arranged directives.

"Take a look at this?"

"Janet looked up, scanning the fresh notice.

"What do you think?" Zanier asked.

Janet shrugged, as she concentrated on the paper, trying to unravel the terse, abbreviated military phrases.

SUBJECT USAF AUGMENTATION PLAN 167...PATCHUP

Due to increasing casualties in SEA, HQ USAF has requested medical personnel volunteers for PCS & TDY assignment to augment personnel already participating in operation WHITE EAGLE and SILVER DOVE. Selected applicants may anticipate PCS & TDY assignments in following locations: CLARK AFB PHILIPPINES, KADENA AFB OKINAWA, YOKOTA AFB JAPAN, as well as TAN SON NHUT, DA NANG & CAM RANH BAY, VIETNAM. Interested parties should contact Personnel Officer for further details.

"I love the way they write these things," Zanier grumbled. "All those short phrases, all the caps on exotic sounding places. Who the hell do they think they're kidding? This thing's nothing but a lure."

Janet looked at her, and smiled. "You're right. You know what? It worked." She turned abruptly, and started toward the Admin Office.

"Are you nuts?" Zanier called to her back. "They'll work your tail off over there." Her voice rose as Janet continued walking. "Makeshift showers. Lousy food. Tyrannical doctors. Hospital tents, muddy, blood soaked fatigues...you...you...Dammit, Janet. Wait a minute! I'm coming with you."

CHAPTER THIRTY NINE

CHARLESTON AFB, SOUTH CAROLINA

Cramer reached for the thermos on the end table, and poured himself another cup of coffee. The rules said no coffee pots, or hot plates in BOQ rooms, so what the hell could he do. A man had to have something. This was the only home he had. And...it looked like it might stay that way for the foreseeable future. He kicked his boots off, put his feet on the coffee table, and took a sip of the lukewarm brew.

In spite of a still torrid relationship, the situation with Linda seemed to be going nowhere. Apparently, from her viewpoint, she had the best of two worlds. She used him to satisfy her considerable sexual appetite, while she held David Packard at prim, and proper arms length, in an apparent ploy to impress him with her chastity, and lofty moral standards.

The routine was obviously working well for her. While he was out of the country on trips lasting a week or more, she spent her time with Packard, living a snobbish, social climbing lifestyle in the academic community. But once a trip was over, she shared crew rest days with him, making the passionate most of another counterfeit honeymoon. There was little doubt she was strongly attracted to him. All he had to do was rent a motel room, and call her. She'd be there in record time, shedding her clothes in a scattered trail as the door closed behind her. Following that, they'd spend the next couple of hours in bed, enjoying each other's bodies. A few hours later, they'd do it again. But once their ardor was temporarily sated, time seemed to drag.

The problem was, they shared few common interests. When he talked about airplanes, or the military, her eyes glazed over. When she spoke of Shakespeare, Chaucer, or Van Gough, she simply bored the hell out of him. He tried to seem interested, but suspected she knew he was faking it.

Granted, most men would have reveled in the situation, immersed in a torrid romance with a beautiful, financially independent woman who made few social demands. The trouble was, he wanted more. He was tired of being an orphan, dammit. A man with no permanent bonds. A man with no home.

Unfortunately, it looked like she was unwilling to be the solution to his problem. Certainly she was attracted to him--she showed that in bed. But that probably wouldn't be enough in the long run. Eventually when the animal attraction diminished, and he became less of a sexual novelty, satisfying her long term goals with David might well become her only priority.

Cramer walked back to the bed, naked--with her drink in one hand, and his CC and soda, in the other. Linda sat up, leaned back against her pillow, and let the covers slide into her lap. Her breasts, moderately sized and beautifully shaped, pointed outward, the nipples blushed.

He handed her the cognac, placed his drink on the night-stand, arranged his pillow, then sat on the bed, leaned back, and stretched out without bothering to cover up. He took a drink, and put the glass down. "I better call in. They may have something for me tomorrow."

She nodded, and took a sip. As he reached for the phone she laid her hand on his leg, her wrist nestling in his pubic hair, her fingers gently stroking the sensitive skin on the inside of his thigh. He looked at her suspiciously.

She giggled. "Go ahead, I won't bother you."

He chuckled. "C'mon now, we've got to serious up here. I'm about to make an official government call."

She answered in a small voice. "Okay."

He put the phone on his stomach, got an outside line, and dialed the number. It answered on the second ring. "Fourteenth MAS scheduling. Sergeant Draper speaking."

"This is Major Cramer. Do you have anything for me yet?"

"Yes sir. You're scheduled for a trip to Mildenhall tomorrow. Briefing at 1400 local."

"Well that's nice," Cramer said. "England's simply lovely in February. Nothing like snow blowing around your ass, especially when it's mixed with freezing rain."

"Yes sir," Draper said. "I know what you mean. We did our best. Had you on a trip to Spain, but Colonel Benton bumped you, and took it himself."

"What a sweetie," Cramer chuckled. "I'll remember that the next time the Colonel needs a checkride."

"Hey, that's right Major, I just noticed your tag on the board. You're a Pilot Flight Examiner now. Congratulations."

Linda tickled the inside of his leg, and he snickered. "Thanks...uh how about putting me down for Southeast Asia, next trip. I haven't been to the zone this month." He chuckled again as she tickled him harder.

"I'll do that Major. You sound like you're enjoying your crew rest."

Linda tickled him again, wiggling her fingers, and he laughed out loud and grabbed her hand. "Yeah...I...I've got cartoons on television. That Bullwinkel is a riot."

The first morning back at Charleston, he spent in squadron operations, reading a plethora of notices, new rules, older regulations and, the MAC manual of operations. Three hours into the study, he reviewed selected sections of the six inch thick, *Foreign Clearance Guide.*

Once the books were closed, he ate lunch in the club. After a satisfying meal of fried oysters, baked potato and slaw, he checked with scheduling, and found he was slated to depart for Southeast Asia, day after tomorrow. Alert time was scheduled for late in the evening.

Suddenly there was room for opportunity. He drove back to his room, and dialed Linda's number. She answered on the second ring.

"I know it's short notice," Cramer said, "but I was hoping we could see each other this evening. Do you have anything on the book?'

There was a pause on the other end of the line. Finally, she answered, "I was going to the gallery, with Marsha, and Ted, but if I rode with you, we could just meet them there."

He hesitated, nearly turned off by the destination. "Well, okay. Yeah, sure, that sounds good. It'll be our only chance to see each other for a week or so."

"Fine. Pick me up at seven."

Cramer's eyes swept the expansive room. Biggest damn loft he'd ever seen. A lot of space to hang pictures, and they'd used nearly all of it. A local artist's work was being featured, and there were more than fifty people in the crowd. He reached for his wallet, and laid a twenty on the portable bar, then looked up to see blond headed, Sergeant Wilson in a white jacket, with gold braid. The outfit looked surprisingly good on him. Reminded Cramer of a Nazi admiral, in one of those WWII movies. He decided to keep that to himself.

"Moonlighting Sarge?"

Wilson's eyes crinkled at the corners, as he nodded and gave an embarrassed smile. "Yes sir. We broke down in Incirlik last week. I got in a poker game with the guys to pass the time. Lost my ass. Now I have to moonlight to pay back what I borrowed from the family Christmas fund."

"Hell of a note. Hope it didn't cause too much trouble on the home front."

Wilson wrinkled his nose, and shrugged. "Naw...she's pretty understanding. I just don't want to disappoint the kids."

"I can understand that. Give me a glass of your best white wine. Make mine a double CC if you've got it."

Wilson poured the wine, then reached for the whisky. "Didn't know you drank doubles, Major."

"I don't usually, but I'll probably need something extra to insulate me from all this...culture."

He picked up the drinks, looked around for Linda, and started in her direction. She looked good in that pale yellow dress, but he had to wonder why she wore it. She had great legs, and long dresses simply didn't do her justice. As he approached, she stood with her head tipped back, lips pursed,

162

scrutinizing a splattered, multi-colored, rough textured, monstrosity, in a polished brass frame.

He handed her a drink, and nodded toward the canvas. "What's this crap?"

She answered without looking at him. "Don't be crude. Its called Chaos."

"Damn sure looks it."

Linda flashed him an irritated frown, then turned her head, and pointed at two men across the room. "There's David. Let's go say hello."

"Wonderful," he grumbled. "Crappy art, and a chance to talk to your old flame. Looks like a great evening."

He started walking slowly. Linda fell in beside him, leaned over, and put her hand on his arm. "Don't be cross. And be nice to the young man talking to David. That's Vernon Teems, a California artist. He's really, I mean *really* talented."

He looked suspiciously at the tall, slightly built man, with a high forehead, and thinning red hair. Teems gestured effeminately as he spoke, flopping his hand like his wrist was broke.

Cramer leaned toward her. "Looks like a pansy to me."

"Don't be crude!"

He snorted, "How come I'm crude, because he's a pansy?"

Linda stopped walking, grabbed his arm, and said in a low voice. "Why not act civilized for a change? He's homosexual." She waved her hand, and gave a little--so what--shrug. "He's...he's gay."

He leaned down, and said softly, "I don't give a damn what he likes to call himself. He is, what he is. Politician or pansy, it makes no difference. I don't trust anyone who has to re-invent the English language before they can describe themselves in a decent manner."

She gave him a withering look, and snipped, "They prefer to be called gay!"

Cramer scowled back at her. "How can anyone call that, gay? Queer, maybe. Strange, perverted, certainly, but it's sure as hell not gay."

The color rose in her face. She gripped his arm, and grumbled, through pinched lips, "For God's sake, John. This is a festive evening. Don't ruin it for me."

He shrugged. "OK, I'll be good."

An emaciated looking David Packard, dressed in a black tux with the traditional bow tie, managed a little wave as they approached. What a pompous, stuffed shirt. That damn pencil thin mustache, and slicked back hair, made him look like something out of a 1930s movie. What the hell did she see in that guy?

Cramer returned the greeting as cordially as he could. Linda brightened, apparently flattered by the subdued, but obvious friction between suitors. After he and Packard shook hands, Lynda introduced him to Vernon Teems.

Cramer gripped his clammy, hand, and afterward, Teems stepped back, turned to Packard, and mumbled something from the side of his mouth.

Linda got that prissy look, and purred in a loud voice, "Vernon is quite a student of the arts, John. He already has his PHD."

Cramer took a sip of whiskey, and nodded. "That's impressive."

Not surprisingly, the conversation centered on art, and he stood there, feeling out of place, taking short interval sips from his drink in a futile effort to make time go faster.

Obviously, these people worshiped celebrity. Supposedly famous names from the art world were bandied about with elitist relish. Techniques of traditional painters were snobbishly evaluated, as well as the meaning of works by various abstractionists. Cramer's droll contribution about the artistic genius of cartoonist Al Capp, was met with testy looks, and dead silence.

Finally, he tipped his head back, drained his glass, and excused himself. Janet had hardly touched her drink, and as far as the others were concerned, to hell with them. Let the snooty bastards buy their own booze.

The place was packed now, and he threaded his way carefully through the crowd, doing his best to avoid jostling anyone, and spilling their drink. Several of the men already had rosy cheeks, and were gesturing grandly, and talking loud. Obviously, GI's didn't have an exclusive franchise on getting drunk.

Surprisingly, the bar was temporarily vacant, and Sergeant Wilson smiled as he approached. "Another double Major?"

"Better make it a single," he grumbled. "I don't want to end up involuntarily horizontal in the middle of this bunch. At least one of them belongs to the Legion of The Languid Wrist."

Wilson's grin broadened, and he poured a single this time. After an absence of several minutes, Cramer returned to his artistic purgatory.

Time dragged while the cultured great critiqued damn near anyone who ever daubed a brush, or drew a line. He stood there, fidgeting, curling his toes inside his shoes, and wondering when it would end. Apparently not soon. Eventually, he headed back to the bar, got in line, ordered another drink, and promised himself that Hell would indeed freeze over before he attended another one of these events.

By the time he returned, the group had apparently set aside it's lust for art, and had embarked on saving the world. Evidently, Vietnam was now the subject, and he steeled himself for the predictable. Before long, Vernon the mince, advanced another over-educated observation.

Teems tipped his head back, and stared haughtily down his nose. "Linda tells us you've been deeply involved in the Vietnam conflict, Major."

"Still am," Cramer said.

Teems screwed his face up in a spiteful look of disapproval.

164

"According to her, you've actually killed people over there."

"Only the right people."

"Oh, and who might that be?"

"The bastards who invaded the sovereign country of South Vietnam."

Teems cocked his head to one side, and smirked, "There's been no invasion. An infiltration perhaps, but no invasion."

Cramer, stared back at him. "If you think there's a difference, then you're too damn stupid to be voicing an opinion."

Teems flushed, stepped closer to David Packard, tipped his nose up and snapped petulantly, "You're nothing but a hired Killer!"

"Maybe so," Cramer growled. "But at least I'm not an anus licking, feces fornicating, penis sucker."

"Oh my God!" Linda gasped.

"What's the matter?" Cramer said. "I didn't use any profanity."

CHAPTER FORTY

The phone on the night stand woke him with a nerve jangling vengeance. He rolled over in the dark, and yanked the receiver off the cradle before it could ring again.

"Major Cramer," he answered gruffly.

A cheerful female voice on the other end answered, "Good evening Major. This is the 734th Military Airlift Command Post alerting you for your trip to Southeast Asia."

"Thank you," he mumbled. "I'll be down there shortly."

He hung up the phone, swung his legs over the edge of the bed, and put his feet on the cold floor. The glowing dial of his watch on the nightstand, showed eleven o'clock. A lousy hour and a half. Not much sleep to start a trip on. He reached up, snapped on the light, stood up wearily, grabbed his shaving kit, and walked to the bathroom. A splash of cold water cleared his thoughts, and he focused on the prospect of yet another trip to Southeast Asia.

The situation in Vietnam was changing rapidly. Other than the jungle and shitty weather, nothing was the way it was in '64 and '65. Places that used to be nothing more than drop zones, were now major installations.

Today, the war was open. Gone were the clandestine outfits flying cast off junk. Now the guys had first line equipment--jet fighters, and bombers-- air conditioners--well stocked exchanges. Warehouses, bulged with equipment. It was nothing short of amazing. In the early days, you couldn't get a tube of toothpaste, let alone a parachute, or a new flying suit.

And the medals...great Jesus the medals. When he was there, guys who should have been awarded the Silver Star, didn't even get a "thanks," or "nice job." Now, it seemed every pilot who finished a tour without kicking the Wing Commander in the nuts, or fucking up royally, came home with a chest full of ribbons.

On the other hand, it was a different war now--hotter than a two dollar pistol. Especially for the guys flying north. Heavy triple A, and SAMs out the ass. Losses were climbing. There wasn't much doubt those guys earned every decoration they got.

He reached for the towel, dried his face, then went into the room, and donned his flying suit. The gold oak leaves on the shoulders had been there for a few months, but they still made him feel good when he looked at them. Sure, he'd get used to it after a while, but for a man who started at the bottom, being a field grade officer was a big boost.

In spite of himself, he compulsively reached over, and turned on the television. Big mistake. There it was, some lacquered-up little broad mouthing the standard Liberal crap about Vietnam being a civil war that we shouldn't be in.

She smiled smugly. "Today, opposition to the war was reflected in the reaction of students at a Florida university."

The picture changed to an auditorium where rioting students were shaking their fists, screaming, and throwing things at a college official, and a South Vietnamese general standing on stage.

Cramer looked closer. He knew this man. Respected him. Early in the war as a junior officer, he had flown numerous infiltration flights into the North, dropping off clandestine teams that fought the Communists on their home ground. Later, he became a fighter-bomber pilot, distinguishing himself with his aggressiveness, and courage.

Now, here he was--confronted by football players, and an unruly mob of American students--nearly all a head taller than him. Cramer watched, fascinated by the spectacle. There were two kinds of courage at work here. The general's--steely, tempered and hardened in battle. The students'--the collective, counterfeit courage of the mob. No brave souls there. Let danger threaten, one would bolt, and the others would follow, tumbling over one another like frightened rabbits, in a frenzied panic to save themselves.

The uproar continued, with the general standing his ground, his contempt obvious. He was half their size, and they hated him. Hated him for the courage he had, that they couldn't match. But they hated him from a distance, by God. Not one climbed up on the stage to confront the man directly.

The camera switched back to the reporter.

"The disturbance continued for nearly half an hour," the news-lady added with obvious relish. "Finally, the school administrator simply gave up, and called off the General's address. School officials declined to say if they planned to schedule another attempt."

He reached over, turned down the volume, and viewed the disturbance. Wads of paper, rotten fruit, and even a roll of toilet paper bounced on stage, leaving behind a lengthening trail of white as it rolled toward the back, while the students screamed and shook their fists. Still the general stood there, ramrod straight, a contemptuous look on his stoic face.

Cramer continued watching, his irritation growing. "Welcome to America, General," he grumbled. "How do you like our freedom of speech?"

Finally, he reached out, punched the button, and darkened the set. After that, he stuffed his shaving kit into his AWOL bag, zipped it shut, turned out the light, and locked the door behind him. At the bottom of the stairwell he entered the lobby, noting that Sergeant Miller was behind the counter.

Noticeably sharp in dress, and highly intelligent, the trim, darkly handsome Miller was a soul mate of sorts. With just a small difference in luck, they might have changed roles. Also an ex OCS attendee, Miller had been eliminated from officer training, after he had punched out a particularly obnoxious upper classman. Often, when he was on the desk, Cramer would sit in the lobby just to chat with him.

"Evening Major," Miller said. "Uh just a minute sir." He reached under

167

the counter. "I've got a letter for you. Hand delivered." Miller smiled. "And, I might add...by a very attractive lady."

Cramer reached across the counter, and took the envelope. The handwriting looked familiar, and there was little doubt about what was inside. If it was good news, she would have called. "Thanks," he said. "Been expecting this."

He crossed the BOQ lobby, sat down in one of the overstuffed chairs, and held the letter in front of him for a moment, mentally weighing its likely significance. Why bother to read it? He already knew what it said. Education be damned. She was the most predictable woman he had ever met. Finally he took out his pen knife, slit the top of the envelope, removed the paper--unfolded it, and noted wryly, that it began with the classic, ominous greeting.

Dear John,

I wish there was a better way of saying this, but I simply can't think of one. Even after that ugly scene in the gallery, this is a heart wrenching decision. You're an attractive man, but frankly, I know I'll never fit into the military lifestyle. Being married to someone as dedicated to his job as you are, would be a never ending ordeal. A husband who is home little more than a few days a month, is not my destiny.

I've agonized over this for weeks, even considered asking you to leave the Air Force, but realized that at this stage of your career, that would be an unreasonable demand.

Certainly, we both felt a powerful physical attraction to each other. But that's not enough for a lasting relationship. You love the military, but the arts, and academic community are where I belong. Therefore, I've decided to accept David's proposal, and accompany him to Columbia. It's a marvelous opportunity. I look forward to the cultural atmosphere that only a place like New York can offer.

Please believe me when I say that for the rest of my life, I will have fond memories when I think of you. Good luck, and God bless you. I sincerely hope you find a woman as good as you deserve.

Linda

He sat motionless, staring at the page. Finally he looked up at Sergeant Miller.

"Bad news?" Miller asked.

"I suppose so." He gave an off-hand wave, and shrugged. "Actually, I was expecting it. Right now, I'm trying to figure out why I'm not more upset. Like you said, she's an attractive woman. Unfortunately, the way she sees it, instead of wasting my life in airplanes, I should have been studying art, or the friggin' opera."

Miller chuckled, "Frankly Major, you don't seem the type."

"You've got that right."

Finally, he tore the letter into small pieces, dropped it in the nearby wastebasket, then rose to his feet, and picked up his bag. "Well, she's got her destiny, I've got mine." He forced a smile, and nodded at Miller. "See you in a few days, Sarge."

"Be careful, sir. Have a good trip."

Cramer left the building, descended the steps, and walked to his Buick parked a few spaces away. He opened the door, and climbed in, scarcely noticing the new car smell. As he backed out of his space, he noticed the officers club parking lot next door was nearly full.

Well why not? It was Saturday. Yeah, Saturday night, and tomorrow...they'd all be home. Maybe with a hangover, but still home. Sunday morning with their families. Their wife and kids, their dogs and cats. Talking about going on leave to see Grandma, and Grandpa.

Suddenly, loneliness washed over him, and he wondered who he'd be crewed with this time. Would he know any of them? Probably not. Just another trip, with another bunch of strangers. On the other hand, maybe he'd get lucky. Maybe there'd be a familiar face among the crew. Someone he knew, or even liked. Someone he could talk to.

Cramer entered the Squadron Ops building, and walked down the hall, with the sound of his heels clicking on polished, square tiles. Air conditioned and clean, with pastel colored walls, it was a pleasant place to start a trip.

He passed a couple of doors on either side then came to the wide expanse of the scheduling room. Behind the counter, a round faced, heavy set, Mexican-American duty sergeant turned away from the status board, and smiled. "Good evening Major. Figured you were about due. Got another trip to the zone huh?"

Cramer stopped short, leaned on the counter, and looked at him. "What are you doing back there Sarge?"

Quintana grinned sheepishly. "Busted my last flying physical--high blood pressure. Flight Surgeon grounded my ass."

"Damn! That's tough. Is it permanent?"

Quintana tossed his pencil on the counter and shrugged. "Depends on me, I guess. Gotta get my weight down. But, what the hell, at least my wife likes it better this way. Now I'm home instead of being gone most of the time."

"Yeah, they sure like that don't they? The question is, how are you taking it?"

Quintana leaned on the counter, a look of desperation on his face. "Major, I'm about to climb the fucking walls. I'm just not used to this...this, staying in one place all the time."

"That's gotta be tough."

"Sure is. Off duty, I'm at loose ends--constantly getting in my car to go somewhere--go to the store for milk--to the drug store for aspirin--to the Seven Eleven for a magazine." He shook his head. "Dammit, I can't sit still. And those kids. Jesus, the kids are driving me nuts! I'd like to kick that flight surgeon in the balls."

Cramer gestured toward his waistline. "Well...you look like you've already lost some weight. That ought to help."

Quintana patted his belly. "Yes sir, fifteen pounds already. Now my wife complains 'cause I won't eat her cooking anymore. Hey, if this keeps up I'll starve if that's what it takes to get back out on the friggin' line."

A phone rang at the far end of the counter. Quintana excused himself, and moved to take it.

Cramer looked at the status board, searching the Aircraft Commander's column for his name. With this outfit, there were plenty of places to go. Seemingly everywhere. Europe, Africa, South America, and now, because of the current world situation, Southeast Asia, the destination with the longest listing. Finally, he found his tag under the SEA column, and scanned down, curious about who he'd be crewed with this trip.

Major Bill Grey was listed as co-pilot. Nice break. He actually knew the man--slightly. Flew a short run to McGuire with him a couple of months ago. Grey had finished a Southeast Asia tour as an F105 pilot a few months back, and the one white dot on his blue name tag showed that he had already upgraded to first pilot.

Captain Dan Sullivan would be his navigator. He smiled and mumbled softly, "Damn, I'm on a roll. I actually know both of these guys." Finally, satisfied with the listing, he turned, walked down the hall to retrieve his bags, and get on the crew bus.

It was overcast, and totally dark, as they pulled up to the front entrance door of the middle C-141 in the back row. As the bus door opened, the irritating scream of the huge transport's aux power unit assaulted Cramer's ears. Hidden in the left wheel well, the small, jet engine powered the electrical, and hydraulic systems while the plane was on the ground. Wry, conventional wisdom claimed its true purpose was to convert jet fuel into noise.

After the bags were loaded, he climbed the stairs on the back side of the entrance door, stepped inside, passed the small galley on his left, and went up the ladder to the upper deck cockpit.

Inside the cabin, dials, gauges, and gadgets populated the walls and panels of each crew position. Lights glowed everywhere, some steady, some blinking.

God, he loved this airplane. Air conditioned throughout, system redundancy was lavish, with four engine driven generators, each capable of running everything electrical on the plane.

170

Lockheed had bestowed an awesome array of communications equipment on the 141, six com-nav radios, a doppler navigation computer, plus radar for map reading, and thunderstorm avoidance.

With a maximum gross weight of 325,000 pounds, she'd climb 4000 feet per minute--and come down even faster. With throttles closed and the spoilers deployed, she could fall out of the sky at 20,000 feet per minute and recover in 1500 feet with no excessive G forces.

Unlike previous transports he'd flown, she was completely dependable, with not one single, treacherous quirk. Best of all, she could be converted into an airborne hospital in just forty minutes.

He stopped at the engineer's station, checked the maintenance forms, then went to the left pilot's seat, and performed his brief preflight. After that, he walked to the rear of the cabin, and descended the cockpit ladder into the cargo area.

Ninety feet to the rear, underneath the majestic, upswept tail a motorized cargo loader was parked between the gaping clamshell doors. The loadmaster, waved directions as another pallet of cargo was pushed on board. Above the sergeant, a ten foot square, pressure door, was temporarily stowed against the ceiling, waiting to seal the cargo compartment so it could be pressurized.

Once the navigator, and co-pilot, had finished their pre-flight, they came downstairs, and joined him. All three left the plane, boarded the crew bus, and rode to the Airlift Command Post.

Located in a cavernous room, ACP was invariably a busy place. World wide, ACPs seemed nearly identical--like they'd been made from the same mold--medium gray tile floors, and pastel green walls. Across the back wall, a huge, back-lighted, status board showed tail numbers, names of aircraft commanders, destinations, and the next scheduled stop for each of scores of aircraft currently scattered around the world.

Cramer leaned on the counter, as Major Krebs, the duty officer approached. Krebs, red headed, crew cut, and perpetually good humored, opened his briefing folder, spread the documents, and smiled. "You must be on someone's shit list John. You never seem to go anywhere in the daytime."

Cramer grinned back at him. "So, how come you're on this shift?"

"I'm building up brownie points so I can get on the Embassy run." Krebs rearranged the papers. "Well anyway...let's see what you have for your trip to the inscrutable Orient." He pointed to the heading on the first sheet. "Boring start. First you'll take five passengers, and six pallets of cargo to McGuire Air Force Base, where you offload the human beans and grab some shit bound for Southeast Asia."

"Sounds familiar."

Krebs nodded, and pointed to the next form. "Your first scheduled crew rest is Elmendorf. Take your coat. I hear it gets cold in Alaska. After you get there, you enter our ball busting, hyper efficient, crew stage system, and leap-frog your way to the Far East. Any questions?"

"Just one," Cramer said.

"What's that?"

"How come I gotta fly west, to get to the far East?"

"Dammit, John. Don't ask me those tough ones."

CHAPTER FORTY ONE

They'd spent precisely twelve hours in crew rest before departing for Yokota, and Elmendorf was well behind them. Presently, they were skimming through thin, widely scattered cirrus--wispy, feathery clouds that swept toward them with awesome speed, whisked silently by, and disappeared behind them.

Bill Grey, the co-pilot was in the rear of the cabin, probably asleep in the lower bunk, as Cramer sat reclined in the seat, legs stretched out, with his feet on the rests above the rudder pedals, and the autopilot doing the flying. All things considered, the job was going well. His private life, was another matter. Obviously, his affair with Linda was finished. Once again, it seemed, his career had wrecked his personal life. The conflict seemed never ending. Unfortunately, any kind of resolution would be tough to manage.

A change in profession was out of the question. With seventeen years already invested, the loss of retirement benefits seemed an unacceptable price to pay. Besides that, he loved this job. Anything civilian life had to offer would be second best. Being a military pilot had become part of his identity. It was who he was. Somewhere he had to find a woman who understood that. Other men did. Why couldn't he?

A sleepy eyed, Bill Grey, needing a shave, sat down in the right seat and strapped himself in. "How's it going?" he asked.

"We're slightly ahead of flight plan," Cramer said. "Everything looks normal. I'm talking to Clark on 11226. The next pilot report is due in twenty minutes."

After Grey took over, Cramer left the seat, and took his turn on the bunk, grabbing the curtain, and drawing it around him, creating his own private sanctuary, shielded from the outside world by the steady hum of fan-jet engines. He laid his head on the pillow. What a great place to snooze. Seven miles above the ocean, hauling ass, and now he was sacking out. Talk about beating the system. There was one other thing he liked about it. He'd never had his nightmare while sleeping here. Didn't have it often anymore...but he *never* had it here. Wonder why? He stretched contentedly, and drifted off.

The engineer's voice jarred him awake, "Major Cramer, we're one hour out."

He rubbed his eyes. "Okay Sarge." Damn! An hour, and a half didn't last long. He propped himself up on one elbow, and drew back the curtain. Daylight in the cockpit. Not bright, but still, light enough to see. He scooted over to the edge of the bunk, and put his boots on, then stood up, stepped over, and opened the cockpit door. Cool air, increased engine noise, and the roar of the slipstream greeted him, enveloping him with the familiar sounds of the cargo bay.

Downstairs in the small lavatory, he stood in front of the urinal and relieved himself as he looked around the small cubicle. An undersized aluminum sink, and flushable commode, made up the fixtures, and he marveled at how far airborne comfort stations had come since he first started flying. Sure beat wall urinals, and shit cans you had to empty after every flight.

Few military planes had such refined facilities, and he smiled, as he recalled the droll MAC credo that stated, "People who fly airplanes without air conditioning, and flush toilets are barbarians."

Back in the cockpit he strapped himself in, put his headset on, and scanned the panel. "Nav, what's your ETA for Diago?"

"Diago intersection at three one, Sullivan said. It won't be long now."

Yokota Airlift Command Post. Not much to look at. Grey floor. Pale green walls, three telephones, a half dozen file cabinets, a long counter and the usual wall to wall, aircraft status board in back.

A departure briefing folder lay open, in anticipation of their arrival, as Cramer, Grey and Sullivan approached the counter, following their required, twelve hour crew rest. Cramer turned the paper work around, and scanned the top page. Wham! Destination--Bien Hoa. It never failed, a rapid-fire sequence of unforgettable images flashed through his mind--Nancy, and Kim. Steve Davis, and hut 124--the Bien Hoa club, and Puff the Magic Dragon.

A short, smiling, sandy haired captain approached on the other side of the counter, and Cramer mentally changed gears, forcing his mind to focus on the present.

The captain spread his hands on top of the formica, and chuckled, "You're gonna love this load, Major. Forty-eight guard dogs going to Bien Hoa. I just debriefed the incoming crew. They said the plane is wall to wall dog shit."

"Terrific!" Cramer growled. "A load of dog shit, and a trip to Bien Hoa in the same package."

"You've been to Bien Hoa?"

He nodded. "Spent a lovely, fun filled tour there in '65. I try not to dwell on it though. Sweet nostalgia chokes me up."

"Sounds like a fun place," the captain said. "Anyway...after you get there, you'll have to figure some way to wash the plane out, 'cause from what I hear, it's one hell of a mess."

Cramer rubbed the back of his neck, and struggled to hold his irritation in check. "Just how in hell are we supposed do that? he grumbled. "Where the do we get the water? Do they have a wash rack at Bien Hoa now?"

The briefer opened his hands, and shrugged. "I don't know Major. Just... just do the best you can."

"Why didn't they contract this son of a bitch out to the civilian airlines?" Cramer fumed. "The stews could have cleaned up the dog shit, and everybody'd be happy."

After briefing, they checked the weather, filed their flight plan, and went downstairs to the small, wood-frame snack bar. Howard Johnson's it wasn't.

Cigarette smoke, and the gut churning odor of burning grease hung heavily in the crowded room. The acoustics were bad, and the place reverberated with tangled conversation, rattling plates, and the spitting sizzle of hamburgers, and bacon being scorched to death on an overheated grill. Bad scene for a hangover.

Tired looking Air Force mechanics in greasy fatigues, and flight crews in multi-zippered flying suits dominated the room. In the far corner--a pair of civilian contract, 707 airline pilots in gold braided suits, sat with four, painted up stews in short skirts, and high heels, the lot of them looking like society snobs in formal wear, come slumming to some neighborhood tavern, in a grimy, factory town.

Grey leaned toward Cramer. "Maybe the stews would like to pick a little housekeeping money cleaning up after our doggies."

Cramer chuckled, "I wouldn't mention it, if I were you. This place is too small to hold a riot."

It was just beginning to get light in the east, as the headlights went out, and the approaching jeep rolled to a stop on the Bien Hoa ramp. A slim, boyish looking, non-rated second lieutenant with horn rimmed glasses stepped out, and saluted. The officers on the crew returned the greeting.

Cramer shined his flashlight on the forms, handed the young officer the in-bound paper work, and said cheerfully, "Good morning, lieutenant. Welcome to Dog Shit One. Your first test of the day is...how are you gonna handle the clean up?"

The lieutenant gave him a baffled look. "Clean-up?"

"Yes dammit, the cleanup," Cramer grumbled. "That's not the flight crew's arm pits you smell. Hear that barking? Those mutts haven't been walked since they left the States. You ought to see the inside of that plane. It's wall to wall dog shit. It's got to be washed out." He stabbed his finger toward the young officer. "And you're the guy whose going to have to figure out how to do that. Any ideas?"

The lieutenant's mouth worked, but nothing came out. Finally he sputtered, "Sir...I...I...haven't the faintest idea!"

"Do you have a wash rack here?"

"No Sir."

Cramer threw his hands up, and looked at Grey. "That figures."

Grey turned away, and looked up at the stars, as Cramer turned back to the lieutenant. "Okay. Tell you what...call for a fire truck, and have them wash down the deck from front to back." He shook his finger in the Lieutenant's face. "Front to back, mind you. That's important! Not the other way around. We don't want every piece of electronic equipment in the cabin shorted out. Our loadmaster will supervise. While they're working on that, you can give us a ride to the Officer's Club."

They sped along the ramp, then slowed, and the lieutenant turned down the same bumpy road, Cramer had traveled with Major Keller at the beginning of his tour years ago. Little had changed. Same mud puddles, tall trees choked with sinister looking vines...and of course, the ever present smell of urine.

Suddenly, the vehicle lurched--headlight beams waving as it splashed through a series of deep puddles, wallowing over the bumps. Cramer gripped the windshield, and seat frame, doing his best to keep from falling out. In back, Grey and Sullivan held on desperately, their asses pounding a dusty, worn out seat cushion. "Dammit, lieutenant!" Cramer grumbled, "Slow down. There's no hurry. It'll take them an hour to wash out that plane."

Beyond the old VNAF area, it appeared not much had changed. The entrance to the American compound looked the same, and the diesel generator still roared from the same location--though the place did seem smaller than he remembered. His excitement built. It was like coming home.

As they stopped at the gate, Cramer returned the guard's salute, and told the lieutenant. "We'll walk from here. Pick us up at the club, after the airplane's clean."

"Yes sir."

He strolled leisurely along the walk, with Sullivan, and Grey following. The air seemed unusually fresh this morning. Small wonder. After hours in close proximity to dog shit, even mildew smelled fragrant.

Surprisingly, the compound looked exactly as it did when he left, and Hut 124 was in remarkably good condition. He smiled, and pointed proudly. "My old homestead."

"Nice neighborhood," Grey chuckled. "Striking architecture."

They turned left at the crosswalk, and Cramer stopped abruptly, staring, open mouthed. The sign over the door said Officers Club, but the building looked completely different.

176

"What's the matter?" Sullivan asked. "It's open, isn't it?"

Cramer stood there, running his eyes over the unfamiliar sight. "Yeah. Yeah, I guess so. It's just that it's so...so much bigger."

Once inside, he stopped abruptly, and looked around. "Where the hell is the bar?" he grumbled. He spun around, surveying the room, and waving his arm. "Look at this!" he snapped. "They put glass in the friggin' windows. The fans are gone. They fancied it up. Son of a bitch looks like some...over-glitzed bar on Miami Beach." He pulled his sweaty flying suit away from his chest, fanned the fabric, and squinted at Grey. "Feel that? Damn place is air conditioned. My achin' ass. Air conditioned!" He pivoted slowly, gesturing--voice rising. "Plush upholstery. Thick carpets. Fancy lights!"

"So what?" Grey said. "Looks like any other club."

Cramer turned on him, snarling, "Of course it does Goddammit! They changed the son of a bitch. Changed everything. What a bunch of pricks!"

He turned, and stalked down an unfamiliar hallway, then turned again as the others followed. After the third turn, he stopped, and looked around, helplessly.

"Where's the Goddamned dining room?" he shouted. "I'm lost. Lost in the club at Bien Hoa. Can't even find my way around in this...lavender and lace, son of a bitch." He spun around, his arms wide-spread. "Look at this. Used to be a two-room shack! The wildest fucking club on the face of the earth. A joint. A dump. A piece of shit. But it had character. It had balls! Now look." He sputtered, "It's... it's like some kind of tea room for a bunch of rear echelon faggots. If the old guys could see it, they'd burn this overdressed son of a bitch to the ground."

Down the hall, a door opened, and a bald, overweight, sleepy looking master sergeant put his shirt on as he hurried toward them. "What's the problem sir?"

Cramer lowered his voice. "Sorry, it's just that I...I can't find the dining room."

The Sergeant finished buttoning his shirt and nodded to his right. "Follow me sir. Actually, we're not quite open yet, but no matter, we can take care of you."

They walked behind the sergeant, made a couple of turns, and finally, came to the dining room. If it hadn't been for the tables, Cramer wouldn't have known what it was.

Even the procedures had changed. Now, instead of going through a serving line, they were shown to a table. A gum cracking Vietnamese girl suddenly appeared, with menus in hand, acting like she had been trained in some Chicago diner. She took their orders with maddening efficiency, fielding the suggestive banter of Grey, and Sullivan, with equally suggestive sass, and hardly a trace of accent. Minutes later, instead of screwing everything up, she returned, with exactly what they wanted. How the hell could you figure that?

He ate mechanically, oblivious to the taste. Halfway through the bacon and eggs, he laid his fork down, and his eyes swept the unfamiliar room.

Look at what they'd done to this place. Look at how they'd changed it. This was once the watering hole of the wildest, most unusual group the Air Force had ever put together. Its rough hewn structure, a reflection of a hard core, Spartan heart--the organizational soul of a poorly equipped, but dedicated unit with a reputation for delivering incredible results from damn few resources. Now look. Damn thing was like a some...monument to the self indulgent--a rear echelon, hangout for high powered clerks. What a piece of crap!

He felt robbed. Cheated, by God. He'd looked forward to this, but now? Nothing. Here, he could have been back home again. Rekindled the fires of intrigue, excitement and adventure. The war, the friends, the times he'd had, it could all have come alive. If only for a little while. But all that was gone. Destroyed by a bunch of strangers, in a war he no longer recognized.

His eyes slowly swept the room. "Damn those bastards," he grumbled, bitterly. "Goddamn 'em to hell. Why'd they have to change it? Why couldn't they just leave it the way it was?"

CHAPTER FORTY TWO

TURN-AROUND POINT

TAN SON NHUT AIRPORT, SOUTH VIETNAM

The humidity was high, and the temperature was already beginning to climb, as Cramer, and his other two officers walked away from the plane. A huge forklift roared by, towering above them, the clank of its empty fork adding to the irritation of the acrid odor coming from its diesel exhaust.

Two other C-141s, and a couple of C-130s were parked nearby, surrounded by cargo pallets temporarily spotted on the sprawling ramp. Trucks, and self propelled cargo loaders roared through the scene in a seemingly endless procession. Jet engines, and auxiliary power units added to the din, building a noise level that was higher than a boiler factory on a busy day.

Ahead, beyond the command post, several huge, steel paneled warehouses with gaping doors, were stacked to the ceiling with equipment, and supplies.

Cramer shook his head. "This has to be the most oversupplied conflict in history. If they keep bringing this crap in, the whole damn country is gonna sink."

"That may be the best solution," Grey said.

"Oh well, at least nobody's going without."

Cramer opened the door to ACP, and once inside, thick insulation and a noisy air-conditioner, completely blocked the noise of the ramp. He leaned on the counter, and nodded to the duty officer, a surprisingly young, dark haired major in starched, freshly pressed fatigues. Damned guy looked like he was going on parade. Obviously there was something to be said for cheap laundry service, and fighting the war from an air conditioned office.

"Hi," Cramer said. "We brought in 484. What's the load outbound?"

The Major selected a portfolio from the out-basket, opened it, turned it around, and pushed it toward the crew. "You've got 81 pax. Marines rotating back," he said, with an air of boredom. "There'll be 15 bodies loaded behind them."

Cramer tensed. Bodies--caskets--it made no difference. The mention of either, still flashed him back to that terrible day in the Indiana cemetery. Suddenly, he realized the duty officer had asked him a question.

"Huh?"

"I asked if you were ready to haul passengers," the major said irritably. "Is your airplane clean?"

"Damn right," Cramer snapped. "You can bet your ass it's cleaner than anyplace those marines have been for the last year."

"Okay, fine, here's your folder. Have you been in here before?"

Cramer nodded. "Probably before you were a captain. Anything new since last month?"

"No," the briefer added, with civility finally creeping into his voice. "But, better make sure you stay above 5000 feet in the area to the East. There's a lot of activity out there."

Cramer nodded, signed the stack of papers, then handed them back. By the time they got to the airplane, the marines were already seated, and the last of the silver coffins was being loaded behind them.

A short time after level off, Cramer identified the Henchung VOR, and locked the autopilot onto the signal. Bill Grey folded a small tabloid sized paper, and held it over the pilots aisle stand. "Have you read the *Air Force Times* yet?"

He shook his head.

"Go ahead," Bill said. "I'll mind the store."

"Thanks." Cramer slid his seat back, propped his feet up, and leisurely scanned the paper, reading each article until he had the gist of it, before moving on to the next. Ten minutes into the read, he turned a page, and looked at the first of three, small-print columns. Suddenly he tensed--read the last line again--then re-read the heading, just to make sure. He closed the paper abruptly, dropped it on the console, and punched the interphone. "You've got it."

Bill nodded absently, as Cramer released his belt, swept off his headset, then turned, and squeezed by his seat. Once past the engineer, and navigator stations, he fumbled open the cabin door, scrambled down the ladder, turned, and ducked into the crew latrine, locking the door behind him.

He sat down on the toilet with the lid closed, fighting to control his breathing, his hands trembling, a pounding in his chest, and temples. It had to be a mistake. But he knew it wasn't. The *Times* didn't made mistakes. Not in that column. He'd read it twice, just to make sure. There it was under Missing in Action--Davis, Steven B Maj. It wasn't hard to figure out what that meant. Damn few ever came back from that column. Steve Davis was dead. He knew it. He could feel it. But how? Why?

He hadn't heard from Steve in years. They'd lost contact with each other, like everyone does in the military when people are scattered in all directions. He must have gone back for a second tour. Maybe he hoped to find Kim again. Or maybe he just wanted to get back in the war. The reason didn't matter. The result was the same.

Missing in action? Damn small comfort, from mighty small odds--slim to none. Steve was the closest thing to a brother he'd ever have, and now he was gone.

He reached out, gripped the edge of the sink, and laid his forehead on white knuckles, swallowing hard, staring vacantly at the gray floor. Probably it would help if he could cry. But somehow, he couldn't. All that came out were a few tears, and a low, half-strangled groan.

CHAPTER FORTY THREE

YOKOTA AIR BASE, JAPAN

It was a typical Tokyo winter afternoon, with an indefinite ceiling, and the usual industrial haze choking the air. Inside the plane, with the heaters off, cold soaked aluminum, and the draft coming through the open entrance door, the temperature was falling. The passengers had boarded the busses, the co-pilot, navigator, and engineer were still up front, and the loadmaster was outside, talking to the driver. Cramer stepped off the cockpit ladder, and turned toward the nearly empty cargo bay.

In the rear, fifteen aluminum coffins were still in place. He felt irresistibly drawn to them, unable to ignore the pull of the tragedy they represented. He walked slowly aft, approaching them hesitantly, stepping softly, as though his presence might somehow be intrusive.

Finally, he stopped in front of them, and stared at the plain aluminum containers, stacked three high, on pallets. Eventually, the bodies they held would be transferred to civilian caskets in funeral homes all over the United States. After that, the empty receptacles would be returned to the military, and used again, and again, a situation made grimly clear by the placard on each, which cautioned, "Reusable container. Do not destroy."

The practicality of the arrangement was obvious, but he nevertheless felt troubled by the seemingly heartlessness, and efficiency of the policy.

His eyes swept slowly over them. Inside each aluminum container was someone's son, husband, brother, father, nephew, grandson, great grandson-- or possibly--all of the above. Whatever their final destination, the lives that had been connected to them by family, and friendship, would be forever saddened.

For them, military protocol was strict. They were always loaded ahead of everything except live passengers. No cargo, no matter how vital was deemed more dear, and no one was allowed to lay any object on top of them. The flight crews meticulously conformed to those rules. It wasn't much, but it was all they could do.

Behind him, he could hear the navigator, and co-pilot shuffling down the cockpit ladder, but still, he stood there, contemplating the changing scenario that brought the men before him, to this point. There were forty times as many Americans in country now, as there were when he arrived in '64.

They had Americanized the war, and the casualty rate was climbing. Now, on nearly every trip out of Vietnam, there were several bodies on board his plane.

Back home, the selection to serve was no longer restricted to volunteers. In the ground forces, draftees filled the ranks--America's cannon fodder, gleaned from high school drop-outs, hot rodders, factory workers, farmers, and clerks.

Almost none came from snobby Northeastern colleges, or radical California universities. In modern America, the socially privileged, and politically indignant, were called to a higher purpose than serving their country. After all, someone had to stay home to pass judgment, and demonstrate. That way, cowards were able to claim noble motives, and the draft, could be honorably dodged.

In the last few years, everything had changed. Vietnam was no longer a clandestine war. In-country, headquarters had proliferated as the number of troops increased, and the once dominant Special Forces were now all but lost in the massive buildup of conventional units. If there were any unique organizations like his old group still there, he couldn't name them.

His old Bien Hoa unit was now unrecognizable. It had been the most intense, and memorable thing in his life, and now, it was gone, leaving him with a deep sense of loss.

The aluminum containers stacked before him, were a symbol of the price that was being paid for those changes, and they filled him with an ache that he knew would last for a long time. Here they were, the good and honorable men, who had been caught up in a conflict between an American Right that demanded that they go, and a self righteous Left that condemned them when they did.

In World War II, and Korea, these men would have been heroes--but not today. Now, our media, and the American left, screamed they were the enemy. It wasn't fair. It wasn't right. He reached out, gently laid a hand on one of the coffins, and was nearly overcome by a deep, and bitter sense, of America's betrayal.

There were a dozen officers in the place, a couple in class A's, the others in flight suits, as Cramer stood in the stag room, bellied up to the horseshoe shaped bar, clutching his third drink.

On his right, above the bend in the lacquered wood, a highly polished, brass bell hung, awaiting to announce the next man's intent to buy a round. On his left, above the open end of the bar, two black velvet portraits of attractive, bare breasted women, done in flesh tones, made a fitting highlight to an otherwise stark decor. Rumor had it, that each of the women had been the wife of other officers stationed at Yokota. Man-o-man. That artist must have been some kinda salesman.

On his right, Grey, and Sullivan, were talking, but the subject didn't appeal to him, so the opportunity for conversation was limited. Basketball. Their obvious fascination with the sport was baffling. How the hell could anyone be interested in games with a war going on?

Sure he was cranky. But he didn't know why. Something was bothering him, but he couldn't quite put his finger on what it was. Nothing seemed to roll off his back anymore. Little things bothered him more than they used to. Had to be the war. There seemed no respite from it. Even on trips to Europe, the Middle East, Africa, and South America, the conflict followed him, crowding into his mind through television news, the radio, magazines, and papers. Frequent trips back in-country kept it all fresh, and alive.

Back in the States, the unrelenting anti-military tirade spewing from the media only added to his frustration. To hell with it. He needed a change in scenery. He tossed down the rest of his drink, and put his glass on the bar, then turned to Grey, and Sullivan. "I've got an errand to run. I'm going off base for a while. Anybody want to come along?"

Both men shook their heads.

"I'll be back shortly," Cramer said. He left through the rear door, and took the sidewalk around to the main club entrance. Out front, it was surprisingly busy, as private cars, and cabs, created a minor traffic jam while officers in mess dress, and ladies in fancy gowns, streamed inside. Obviously, a formal function was scheduled for the evening.

He recalled how much Sandy had enjoyed those gatherings. She was attractive no matter what she wore, but in a formal, she was absolutely elegant. He shook his head, wiping out the image. To hell with that. No point dwelling on it. He felt bad enough already.

After a short walk, he passed the main gate guard station, and crossed the highway, dodging through oncoming traffic. On the far side, the sidewalk was narrow, the edge, less than an arms length from traffic, and his hair blew, as vans, and busses roared by at 60 miles per hour.

On his left, the architecture was standard Japanese, faded paint, weathered wood, touches of bamboo, with everything looking small and cramped. Behind the windows, shelves were stacked, filled with goods calculated to appeal to Western tastes, though most of the colors were excessively bright. Apparently, Orientals saw colors differently than Caucasians--or, maybe it was just a matter of taste.

Finally, he stopped at a small window, and admired the display--a white Boeing 707 with the red logo of World Airlines, a military C-130, and a C-141. Carved from wood, from 12 to 16 inches long, they were masterpieces of miniaturization, with every tiny inspection plate, access panel, and hatch faithfully reproduced.

He opened the door, and squeezed inside as the Japanese behind the counter bowed politely. Cramer looked him over, five-four, and surprisingly thin for a Japanese. Had on a dark, buttoned vest, with an open at the neck, white shirt. His five o'clock shadow correctly showed the time of day, and a long ash on the cigarette between his lips was already bent by the demands of gravity.

Cramer handed him a receipt. "I'm here a little early, but I thought I'd stop by, and see if my model was ready."

184

The man grasped his cigarette with a 3 fingered, underhand grip, and the ash finally separated, fell to the glass counter, and splattered in a dusty, star shaped deposit. "Very sorry," the man said. "Next week be ready. For sure."

"Okay. I should be through again in a couple of weeks. I'll check with you then."

Once outside, he headed back to the club, still feeling somber. After stopping at the gate, the Japanese guard checked his ID, then casually handed him a folded piece of paper. He unfolded the strip, and read the type-written message. "Tomorrow afternoon, at 2 PM in front of the main gate of Yokota Air Base, you are invited to join an anti-Vietnam war demonstration."

Inside his head--something exploded. Anger surged as he clenched his teeth, crumpled the paper, rose on his toes, flung it to the pavement, and screamed at the guard, "God damn your fucking demonstration, you little Communist bastard!

The guard recoiled, back-peddling, open mouthed, and obviously frightened, feeling behind him for the doorway. He darted into the guardhouse, locked the door, and flattened himself against the far wall.

Cramer twisted the knob, and kicked the door viciously, rattling the glass. "Come out you little Communist bastard!" he screamed. "I'm gonna tear your head off, and stuff it up your fucking ass!" He drew back his fist, intending to smash the glass, reach inside, and unlock the door. But suddenly, he noticed the look on the guards face. Bewilderment! The guard didn't write that note. He probably couldn't even read the damn thing.

He let go of the knob, and stepped back, clenching his fists, and grinding his teeth. Well, somebody wrote the son of a bitch. And even worse...someone went along with it. And it wasn't hard to figure who that was. The Base Commander! That's the asshole he wanted to talk to.

Demonstration be damned! He turned, and stormed down the street, his rage building, muttering oaths, balling his fists, and swinging his arms, throwing short-reach punches as strobe-light images flashed through his mind--lying anchors, scheming networks, and those anti-war, Communist loving cocksuckers in Hollywood. Liberal bastards had a lock. A full control grip on all communication. Accentuated the negative--overlooked the positive, made up facts, and ignored the truth--maligned our troops, while those draft dodging cowards crawled across the line into Canada.

And how 'bout that asshole Bobby Kennedy? Telling people to give blood to the Viet Cong. That's right, Bobby--you silver spoon, surf wading, bastard--give 'em blood, fix 'em up, make 'em well, so they can pick up gun, and kill more Americans. Never mind that your sainted brother's the one who sent us there."

The crowd parted as he neared the Club, people staring, obviously shocked. "Fuck 'em," he grumbled, gritting his teeth. "Fuck 'em all." He reached out, yanked open the door, and stormed inside, stalking down the hall. Screw that coat and tie bullshit. After he made this call, causal dress would be the least of his worries.

He barged into the phone room, where several women sat on their overdressed asses, snickering petty gossip, and sucking up drinks. Piss on 'em. Let 'em look.

He snatched up the phone book, and fanned the pages. The Base Commander--that's the son of a bitch he wanted to talk to. Who the hell was he? He fanned the pages harder. Goddammit! Why couldn't you ever find a name in a military phone book? Why the hell'd they make 'em that way? If civilian books were this screwed up we'd still be using smoke signals.

Suddenly, there it was. He reached out, spun the dial, and went through the number. Beep--beep--beep, the irritating sound jabbed his ear like a needle thrust. Busy! Busy by God! Wouldn't you know it? Gate guards handing out communist bullshit on an American air base, and this pompous prick's probably on the phone to his broker in 'Frisco.

Seconds later, he tried again. Still busy! He slammed the receiver into the cradle, and the older broad looked at him, and snapped, "What's your problem mister?"

He balled his fist, shook it in her face and snarled, "The problem is, lady, some asshole guard is handing out invitations to a Communist demonstration on an American Air Base."

The woman laughed, and waved her hand. "That's not important. They do that all the time. We just ignore it. "

"Not important?" he barked. "Not important, your ass! It's a damned sight more important than who wore what, to your silly assed party. Or who's screwing who in the Goddamned squadron." He waved disgustedly. "Aw what's the use? I'm wasting my time talking to some dizzy, social climbing twat."

Her jaw dropped, and she sputtered, "Now...now wait minute! I don't appreciate that kind of talk. I've a good mind to report you."

"Lady, you've got no friggin' mind at all. Take your Goddamn report and shove it." He threw the phone book into the corner, and stalked out. What the hell was the point? Even this close to the war, people didn't care. If their kid wasn't being killed, or their ass wasn't in the line of fire, nobody cared.

Goddammit! Somebody had to. Somebody had to listen. He gripped his hands, swung his arms, and ground his teeth. Something was wrong dammit! Broke inside. He was fed up. Caution gone. Reserve depleted. A drink! A drink, by God. That's what he needed. Go to the stag bar. Talk to the pilots. They'll understand. Drink. Scream. Pound the fucking bar. Raise holy hell. Unload it! Shake it loose. Let it go. Goddammit, he had to do something. He'd kept this bottled up for all these years, but tonight, by God, tonight, he was gonna tell 'em all!

186

CHAPTER FORTY FOUR

Someone shook him, breaking into the cemetery scene of his perennial nightmare, and he opened his eyes to a dark figure bending over him.

"John! Dammit, John! Snap out of it. You're making so much noise you're going to wake the guys in the next room."

"Okay," he said. "Okay. I'm alright...I'm...I'm out of it now."

Grey, leaned over, snapped on the lamp, and the sudden upward thrust of light illuminated his troubled features with an eerie, reverse shadow effect. He lowered his arm, and stepped back. "That must have been one hell of a dream," he said.

Cramer wiped the sweat from his face, and dried his hand on the covers, then threw them aside, sat up, and swung his feet to the floor. "It wasn't that big a deal," he said, looking down at the carpet. "Just a damn nightmare. I...I dreamed I was falling."

"Must have been one hell of a drop," Grey said. "You kept it up for two or three minutes."

He squeezed the back of his neck, and groaned. "Man, I feel like shit."

"I can believe that," Grey said.

"Not just the headache," he said. "It's...its like it's the end of the world, or something."

Grey sat down on the edge of the other bed, and gave him a sympathetic smile. "The flight surgeon calls it post alcoholic depression. If ever there was a worthy candidate, it's you. Man, you were something." He gestured theatrically. "The star of the stag bar! You raised hell for more than an hour. Cussed Hollywood, the draft dodgers, and every TV newsman except Huntley, and Brinkley."

He gripped his forehead, and winced. "Glad to hear I didn't give Chet, and David hell. I like those guys. They don't pass judgment--just give the news."

Grey chuckled, shook his head, and smiled. "Man! Anyway you look at it, that was one hell of a performance. Got several rounds of applause."

He rubbed the back of his neck, and groaned. "If you think I was wild in that bar, you should have seen me before I got there. I almost blew it."

"How so?"

"Tried to punch out the gate guard."

Grey's grin changed to a shocked, look of disbelief. "You're kidding!"

He leaned back, and stretched, feeling the tendon's ache and the joints pop. "Fraid not." Finally, he managed a weak smile. "Good thing the little guy locked himself in that guardhouse. He saved my career. This isn't World War Two. The Air Force would be a mite upset if one of its field grade officers punched out a Japanese guard."

"That ass chewing you wanted give the base commander wouldn't have made your day either." Grey said.

"Ain't that the truth? Thank God his line was busy." Probably wasn't even his fault...the message I mean." He took a deep breath, shook his head and sighed, "I don't know anything about the status of forces agreement over here. He could be totally helpless to prevent that."

Grey gave him a baffled frown. "Why'd you blow up like that over a stupid message?"

"It caught me by surprise," Cramer said. "For Crissake! Who'd expect that on an American Air Base?" He leaned forward, put his elbows on his knees, and stared at the floor. "Actually...I suppose it was a lot of things. A bad string of events. Started when I was reading the Times. Found my best friend's name in the Missing in Action column." He looked up at Grey. "You know what that means. Odds are fifty to one, he's dead. Steve was like the brother I never had--and now he's gone." He lowered his head, and pressed his fingertips against his eyelids. "What they did to the Bien Hoa club didn't help much either. That place was like home to me. And those empire building bastards changed it. Made it look like some kind of...resort for headquarters weenies."

"C'mon, John. They just...wanted a nice club."

"Man, you don't need fancy shit in a war. What a waste!"

Grey cocked his head, and squinted. "Is that what's really bothering you?"

"I suppose not," he said, staring into the distance. "The hardest thing to take, was bringing back those bodies. Hearing about casualties is bad enough, but seeing them stacked up dead, three deep on pallets, like so much cargo, is tough to take." He paused, searching for a way to put it in words, and finally looked back at Grey. "Those were real men, for God's sake. From all over the country. There'll be hundreds of people at those funerals."

Grey nodded, his face grim. "And after they go home they can watch some overpaid anchor man bad mouth the military."

He pressed his fingertips against his temples, and winced. "You got any aspirin?"

"Sure." Grey rose, and walked over to a bag sitting on top of the dresser. He zipped open a side pocket, reached inside, and came back with the bottle.

Cramer dumped out three tablets, and nodded toward the open bottle of Kirin beer on the night stand. "Yours or mine?"

"It's mine, and it's warm," Grey said. "But you're welcome to it."

Cramer picked up the bottle, held it up to the light, and sighted through it. "Hmm, half full." He popped the tablets into his mouth, tipped the bottle up, and drained it in long thirsty gulps. Finally, he looked at his watch. "Glad we got that extension. Still a few hours before alert. Hope this next leg goes better than the last."

188

Major Martinez, the Yokota ACP duty officer, opened their flight folder, turned it around, and pushed it in front of them. Martinez put his hand on the back of his neck, and squeezed. The reflection of the overhead lights shined through his crew cut, as he rolled his head around. "Damn aspirin didn't do a bit of good. Must be coming down with something."

Cramer chuckled, "Yeah, I came down with the same thing last night."

"Whatever it is, don't give it to us," Grey said. "We want to get home on time, huh John?"

"Won't matter to me," Cramer said. "One BOQ room is about like another."

Martinez re-arranged the papers, and pointed to the top line. "Well, anyway...you'll have aircraft number 50222. It's an air evacuation flight to Elmendorf. There'll be a medical team, 61 patients, and two emergency leave pax on board. The senior medical officer is a Captain Taylor. She'll brief you on any seriously ill, or altitude-sensitive patients."

Martinez paused, raised his eyes from the paperwork, and looked at Cramer. "I remind you...that on all air evac flights, the senior medical officer, and not the aircraft commander is in charge of the aircraft. In short Major, that female captain owns your airplane."

Cramer nodded.

"Whoa!" Grey said, scowling. "The nurse is in charge?"

"That's the way it is," Martinez said.

"Is she a pilot?" Grey snapped. "What the hell is this?"

Martinez shook his head. "No, dammit, she's not a pilot. And yes, by God, make no mistake about it, she is in charge! She's a flight nurse who's had considerable additional medical, and practical training. You may outrank her, major, but don't give her any crap."

Grey waved irritably, his color rising. "What the hell does she know about running an airplane?"

"Very little. That's not what she's there for. She's expected to run her medical team efficiently, and handle medical emergencies." Martinez stabbed his finger at Grey. "Don't make this a contest, Major. You'll lose! She has a tremendous responsibility on her shoulders. She needs your support. You guys still get to point the damn thing, and make it go, but she has final approval over the operation."

"Bill hasn't been in MAC very long," Cramer said. "This is his first air evac."

"Fine," Martinez grumbled, tapping the paperwork. "But he has to recognize the special nature of these missions." He gave Grey a testy look. "We've never had a problem with this policy. I'm sure Hollywood could invent some high drama for a situation like this--tremendous clashes between the towering egos of macho pilots, and bitchy nurses. The fact is, nothing like that has ever happened. Why should it? You're all after the same thing. Get the wounded back to the States as safely, and comfortably as you can."

"There are some advantages," Cramer said. "Air evac has priority over all other aircraft--including airliners. Any route or altitude we ask for is ours. Any request we make will be granted. They'll give us special treatment along our entire route."

Grey, looking sheepish, shrugged. "Hey, I'm sorry. It was a knee-jerk reaction. Forget I said anything."

After the briefing, they finished their paper work, filed the flight plan, and went downstairs to the snack bar for a quick meal.

By the time they arrived at the aircraft, it was noticeably colder, with the visibility not much more than half a mile. Damn, this country was gloomy in winter. Oh well, at least the patients were already on board, and the large rear doors were closed. After climbing the steps, all three officers went directly into the cockpit, and Cramer checked the maintenance status.

The engineer opened the form, and pointed to an entry. "They found a minor problem on number three," he said. "The line chief says it shouldn't delay us. They're working on it now."

Cramer nodded, then stepped around the engineers station, edged over to the window behind the co-pilot, and looked outside. Two maintenance stands were locked down near the inboard engine, one in front, and the other on the side. Number three cowling was open and the two mechanics standing on the inboard stand, were working feverishly. Below them a thin, gray-haired maintenance chief with an arm full of stripes, paced the ground like a caged animal. There was good reason for his concern. Air Evac flights were closely watched. All the way to headquarters in Illinois.

Cramer looked at the engineer. "Tell the scanner to let me know when they finish."

"Yes sir."

He turned, walked over to the cabin entrance door, descended the ladder, and scanned the rear of the plane. Full load. A portable, airline type comfort pallet, containing two bathrooms was locked down on the right side, with a full galley on the left. Behind that several upholstered airline-type seats faced rearward. Behind those, rows of litters, four high, each with a patient strapped in place, were secured to both sides of the fuselage—with, no doubt the most serious cases in the middle two levels for easier access. Most of the wounded were immobile, either asleep or sedated, though a couple seemed fully aware of their surroundings, and were looking around.

An Army sergeant, and an Air Force captain, evidently the emergency leave passengers, sat in the front row of airline seats. He walked past them, stopped in the aisle between the aft seats, and looked into the litter section, searching for the senior medical officer.

Three male enlisted medics were hustling back and forth, along with

190

two nurses. Both women had their backs to him, but as they moved, he could see that one was a first lieutenant, and the other a captain. He walked toward the senior officer. As he passed by, the eyelids on one litter patient opened briefly, fluttered, then closed again.

From the back, the senior nurse looked familiar, and he suspected they might have worked together before. When she turned around, the effect was stunning. Holy cow. Even after four years, there was still that electrifying jolt. It was Janet Shaw. Beautiful face, trim figure, short black hair, and perfect smile--a woman who still made him literally catch his breath.

Her name tag read Taylor, but he knew that was wrong--hadn't seen her since the Cape, by God, but he knew Janet Shaw when he saw her--lived next door to her for more than a year. Maybe she'd borrowed a jacket from another nurse.

She smiled in obvious recognition, and extended her hand as he approached. "John. It's great to see you. I saw your name on the paperwork, and couldn't believe it. What a nice surprise."

"Man, talk about surprised. I saw your name just now, and didn't even recognize it."

She shrugged, and gave a little offhand wave. "Oh, that. I went back to my maiden name after Stan and I were divorced."

His heart skipped a beat. "I'm sorry to hear that," he lied, then added, "Wow, you look terrific. How long have you been in air evac?"

"About a year. It's more challenging than working in a hospital, but it has its rewards." She gave him a wry smile. "I certainly get plenty of flying time."

He nodded. "I'll bet you do. Speaking of flying, do you have any patients who can't stand a high cabin altitude?"

"No," she said. "Several have severe wounds, but for now, they're stable."

He was reluctant to end the conversation, but it was obvious she was anxious to get back to work.

"Hey," he said. "If you get a chance, come up to the cockpit later, and we'll talk awhile."

She reached out, lightly touched his arm, and winked. "I'd like that. I'll make it up there sometime during the flight. That's a promise."

"Great. I'll see you later."

Outside, both mechanics were fastening number three cowling back in place, as the glowering line chief offered his version of encouragement. "Button that son-of-a-bitch up." he shouted, "And get those stands out of the way so these people can get out of here."

"Okay, Sarge, we're almost finished."

"Fister," the line chief barked, as he pointed. "Go around front, and get that tool tray. I don't want wrenches scattered all over the ramp when you move that stand."

"Okay, Sarge." The young airman stepped quickly to the front of the engine, stooped, gathered his tools and dropped them into the tray. As he stood up, he spun around, and the tray swung outward, colliding with the engine nose cone. Tools flew in all directions, some clattering to the ramp, others spilling into the engine intake, and bouncing erratically into a forest of fan blades.

"Holy shit!" the line chief shouted. "Watch what you're doing. The last thing these people need is to have a wrench processed through one of their engines. Get those tools out of there. Now!"

"Okay Sarge." The young airman dropped to his knees, grasping frantically--stuffing pliers, sockets, and open end wrenches into his pockets. "Good God." he mumbled. "Why'd I have to screw up on this guy's watch? I'll be on his shit list for months."

Eventually, everything was retrieved, and he moved his head from side to side, peering around fan blades to double check. Once sure nothing remained, he turned, and climbed down the stand."

"Did you get 'em all?" the chief growled.

"Sure did Sarge. Got 'em all. Every damn one."

Outside, the scanner paced the ramp, flipping his long, interphone cord, playing it snake-like, on the concrete, as he called, *"Pilot this is scanner. Looks like maintenance is wrapping it up. They're moving the stands out of the way."*

Cramer squeezed his mike button, "Okay fine." He looked across the aisle stand, as Grey finished strapping the knee board on his right leg. "Check on our clearance, Bill."

Bill nodded, "Roger," and keyed number two UHF. "Yokota Clearance Delivery this is Air Evac five zero triple two, standing by for clearance."

"Air Evac five zero triple two, you are cleared to Elmendorf Airport via Atsugi departure, direct Shimofusa, direct Ami, Victor twenty two Diago, flight plan route. Contact departure control on three six three decimal eight after takeoff, over."

Cramer shook his head, and squeezed the command switch. "Yokota, this is triple two. The forecaster reports high westerly winds aloft. I requested a north departure to avoid mountain wave turbulence that's almost sure to be present on the downwind side of Mount Fuji. Some of these people are in bad shape. I don't want to bounce them around."

"Roger triple two. Be advised the surface wind is out of the south at 10 knots, can you accept that much tailwind on takeoff? Over."

"Affirmative."

"Roger sir, standby one."

192

A minute later clearance delivery resumed their transmission.

"Air Evac five zero triple two is cleared to the Elmendorf Airport via Nicho one departure, direct Diago, flight plan route. Contact departure control on three six three decimal eight after takeoff, over."

"Triple Two, Roger."

Outside, on the ramp, the scanner turned to face number one engine, as the left outboard was started first, with the sequence progressing from left to right. By the time number three was selected, both engines on the left wing were running, and the airplane was enveloped in a maelstrom of noise.

"Starting number three," Cramer said.

"Number three clear sir."

Cramer pushed the starter button, the control valve opened, a hurricane of air blasted into the starter, and the engine began spinning up. He watched the gauges, his attention focused on number three N2. At ten percent, he moved the Fuel and Start Ignition Switch to run--the ignition fired, fuel in the burner cans ignited, and engine speed jumped with a sudden upward surge.

Seconds later, a small, blackened, badly scarred object rode a roaring, superheated wind, blasted from the tail pipe, and bounced away, unnoticed, behind the plane.

CHAPTER FORTY FIVE

Outside, it was nearly dark, with a billion unblinking stars already visible in the cold, dry air of the stratosphere. What daylight remained wouldn't last long as they flew ever deeper into the earth's shadow at 500 miles per hour. Unfortunately, short days weren't the only problem on this route. The North Pacific was a big, lonesome place, and the still distant Aleutian Islands were widely separated. Vast areas of this part of the ocean didn't see a ship at all during this time of year.

Cramer leveled off, thumbed the elevator trim and punched the magic button. The autopilot dutifully took over, and he stretched his legs under the instrument panel, laid his feet on the cable guard, and looked around. Man! What an airplane. A great way to travel. Especially in the Arctic. There was nothing this bird couldn't do. Her anti-icing systems were a match for the worst weather, and mechanically speaking, system redundancy was almost lavish.

He picked up his en-route chart, unfolded it, and looked it over, once again reviewing his emergency landing options--a mixed bag, at best. The Coast Guard station at Casco Cove would be a poor choice, with an always icy runway, only 6300 feet in length. Below the approach diagram, a terse notice warned, "For Emergency Only."

Farther on, rocky, windswept Shemya, was cold and barren, though it did offer Tacan, VOR and GCA approaches to its 10,000 foot runway. But it often had wicked crosswinds, and he remembered it as slick, and treacherous from one of his earlier C-130 trips.

Two hundred miles to the southeast of Shemya, Amchitka boasted a 9100 foot runway--but no instrument approach. And winter weather was seldom good enough for a visual attempt. According to the forecast, today wouldn't be an exception. He could forget about that one.

Three hundred fifty miles beyond Amchitka, Adak Island, offered the last of the pitifully few, imperfect choices--a naval air station with a 7800 foot runway. Between them all, a vast, desolate expanse of freezing ocean, where weather changed with alarming speed.

Near the top of the chart, a black saw-toothed line warned of the dark menace of Soviet territory, with a notice threatening in bold print, "Aircraft infringing upon non-free flying territory may be fired on without warning." Air Evac or not, relations with the Soviet Union were as threatening as ever, and a military plane venturing into Soviet airspace would almost certainly be shot down, regardless of its proclaimed mission.

Finally, he folded his chart, laid it aside, and scanned the horizon. By now, it was totally dark with stars shining brightly. They were flying in clear air, above a solid under-cast, well into the flight, approaching Shemya.

He had flown this route often--including a number of Air Evac flights. But this time, things were different. This time, Janet was on board. Just thinking about it, gave him a flutter of excitement in his chest.

She looked as good as ever, and her disposition was still just as sunny. And now, she was single. He felt like turning cartwheels. Being crewed with her? What a stroke of luck. There had to be a way to take advantage of that.

Maybe he could talk her into going into Anchorage after the flight, or better yet, to the club, for dinner and drinks. The problem was, he didn't know her schedule. Never knew what those nurses did after a flight. Flight crews went one way, the medical teams another. Would she have free time? He'd have to stay flexible. If he blew this chance, he might never see her again.

Things were going smoothly, well into the flight now, with boredom setting in--the crew, listening to the radios and struggling to stay awake as the autopilot did the flying.

Fifty miles east of Shemya, nicks turned to cracks, and cracks became longer as a tiny fissure crept across a battered compressor blade on number three. Suddenly, the blade twitched. The twitch grew to a flutter, that quickly became a blur. Seconds later, the blade ripped from its base, shot through the cowling, and pierced number four engine, slicing through a catalogue of vital parts, before exiting the outboard side, and expending the remainder of its awesome energy in a descending curve, that finally ended with a tiny, splash, seven miles below.

In the cockpit, white vertical lines suddenly shot off scale, and the plane yawed violently. Cramer bolted upright, reached for the controls, punched off the autopilot, pushed on the rudder, and canceled the yaw.

"Losing power on number four," he said, reaching for the rudder trim. "High fuel flow...must be a leak."

"Yes sir. Looks like..."

A screaming blast echoed through the cabin, cutting the engineer short, as the fire warning horn blared, and the master fire warning light flashed its frantic message, Fire! Fire! Fire!

Grey silenced the horn, as Cramer pulled the glowing T-handle, and punched the extinguisher button. "Engine fire in flight Checklist!" he called.

"Roger."

They worked together, quickly, smoothly, clicking off items as they dealt with the problem.

"Engineer's check complete sir."

"Roger," Cramer said. "Scanner, advise the medical team we've lost an engine. We're past the point of no return, so we'll continue on to destination."

"Roger sir."

Cramer checked his panel, trimmed the controls, and put her back on autopilot. Not much to worry about, actually. She'd run just fine on three. Plenty of power. Other than an occasional, out of trim adjustment, there'd be no problem.

"Pilot, this is engineer. I've got an indication of vibration on number three."

Cramer snapped his head around, and looked back over his shoulder. "I don't like the sound of that!"

Sergeant Pace leaned toward his panel, a squint accentuating the deep lines in his weather beaten face. "I don't know, Major. It's still within limits." He straightened up, and turned his head, giving Cramer a doubtful look.

"Okay, keep an eye on it," Cramer said. He looked across the isle stand. "Bill declare an emergency, and request flight level 330, then get the weather for every suitable alternate. You can forget about Shemya. When I talked to their tower a half hour ago, they had a 40 knot direct crosswind."

Grey slipped a ballpoint out of his arm pocket, and looked at him. "You know this route a lot better than I do, John. Which fields are the best choices?"

"The forecaster said the weather may be marginal at Elmendorf, so check 'em all," he said. "Anchorage International, Eielson, Adak, Cold Bay, King Salmon, and Kodiak."

"Okay," Grey said.

Cramer looked back over his shoulder. "Engineer, how's number three look now?"

"Holding steady sir. Near the vibration limit. Can't feel it in the cockpit, but the gage shows it's there." He turned his head, and gave Cramer a grim look. "Don't think it was like that before."

"Okay, keep an eye on it. I don't want to make a precautionary shutdown if it's not necessary. We'd have to give away too much altitude to do a two engine cruise. In the long run, we'd end up burning more fuel."

"Makes sense Major. We're OK on petrol for now, but with the destination weather looking the way it does, we don't want to waste any."

"You got that right." He keyed the interphone. "Loadmaster, ask the Senior Medical Officer to come forward."

"Roger sir."

"Okay," Cramer said. "Nav, if things get worse, we may have to go into one of the alternates. Some will be poor choices because they couldn't handle the patients. Regardless of that, be ready for anything."

"Roger Sir."

He looked over his shoulder at Sergeant Pace. "Engineer, let's plan on the worst, and stay ahead of the game. When you check three engine cruise for fuel consumption, look up the two engine rate too. When the time comes, make out a takeoff and landing data card, for both two, and three engines." He turned his attention back to his panel, as the engineer responded, "Roger sir."

Janet Taylor came into the cockpit, sat on the edge of the jump seat, and put on a headset. She leaned forward, reached out, and touched his arm. "What happened, John?"

He shifted in his seat, and looked back, trying to ignore the zing he got from the sight of her. "We lost an engine. May have trouble with another. Possible alternates are Anchorage International, Adak, Cold Bay, King Salmon, Kodiak and Eielson. Which ones look the best to you as far as the patients are concerned?"

She pursed her lips, and gave him a thoughtful look. "The only good choices are Elmendorf, Anchorage, and Eilson, in that order. Unless we could make it to McChord."

He shook his head. "McChord's not a good option. We'd lose our jet stream tailwind if we took a more southerly course. In addition to that, if we get down to two engines, the altitude we'll be forced to give away might actually increase our fuel consumption. In that case, we couldn't make McChord at all."

Bill Grey interrupted. "I've got the weather."

"Shoot."

"Adak and Cold Bay have high winds, well over the max allowable. Kodiak is below minimums, and forecast to stay that way. King Salmon is at minimums now and forecast to go below that in the next hour."

Cramer snorted, "We can forget those."

"Elmendorf is four hundred overcast, and a mile with light snow," Grey said. "Winds zero two zero at fifteen gusting to twenty. Anchorage is about the same. Both are forecast to stay above minimums for the next few hours."

"How about Eielson?"

"Three hundred obscured, and three quarters of a mile. Trouble is...they're forecast for two hundred obscured, and a half mile in the next hour, possibly going to zero zero within the next two hours."

"Looks like Elmendorf is still the best choice," Cramer said.

Grey nodded. "The way things are going, I hope it's not the only one."

Janet leaned forward, and put her hand on his arm. "I've got to get back, John. Let me know if there are any more problems." She released her seat belt, turned, and walked out of the cabin.

Just as the door closed behind her, the airplane shuddered violently. The Navigator's book thudded to the floor, as instrument panels danced spastically, with a high frequency chatter. Cramer punched off the autopilot, and moved to take control--the yoke pounding against his hand.

Outside, number three jerked, wobbled, and hammered, as mounts snapped, hoses sheared, cables ripped from the pylon, and a rainbow streak of fluids spewed behind the engine.

Fasteners failed, cowling buckled, and sailed backward, bouncing off the inboard flap. Number three twisted, wrenched from her mounts, and fell away, disappearing behind them. The plane lurched, and fish tailed, wallowing like a fatally wounded beast. In back, hospital supplies, IVs and a jumble of junk bounced around as a bewildered medic rolled off his back, and Janet struggled to her knees, then pulled herself up. The loadmaster called, "My God Major...Number three! It's gone!"

Up front, Cramer wrestled the yoke, worked the rudder, and fought for control. She fought him back. Screaming horns, flashing lights, one engine dead--another one gone. She was coming apart. Breaking up! Seven miles above a freezing ocean--and it didn't look like he could save her.

CHAPTER FORTY SIX

Cramer shoved everything to red line, stood on the rudder, and trimmed furiously, trying to take the strain off his leg. Finally, she stabilized, and he called for the checklist. The crew responded, clicking things off in clipped, deliberate tones as they worked their way back from the edge.

He glanced across the isle stand. "Bill, tell Anchorage we're starting a two engine drift down. We'll stay as high as we can manage. I'm slowing to point five five Mach."

Grey squeezed the switch. "Anchorage Control, this is Air Evac five zero triple two. We just lost a second engine. We're drifting down. Don't know what flight level we can hold. We'll be slowing to less than three hundred fifty knots, over."

"Roger triple two. Break! Arctic Air, One Four Eight, turn left to a heading of 180, temporary vector around descending emergency traffic. Break! Jayhawk Two, is cleared present position direct Dillingham VOR, Jay five one one to Elmendorf, over.

"Arctic Air, One Four Eight, Roger."

"Jayhawk Two, Roger."

Cramer set normal rated thrust on the two remaining engines, and keyed the interphone. "Loadmaster, you okay back there."

"Roger sir. Things got bounced around a bit, but everyone's on their feet, and taking care of things."

"Fine. As soon as you can, take a look at that aft pressure door, and make a thorough check for any other damage."

"Roger, Sir. I've already spotted one problem. When number three engine cowling blew off, it must have hit the inboard flap. The trailing edge is bent, and ragged."

"Okay. When I get squared away, I'll come down, and take a look. In the meantime, make sure everyone who isn't working, straps in." He looked back over his shoulder. "Engineer, after a wrench that severe, the fuselage may be warped. Better run the cabin altitude up to 12,000 feet. We need to take some of the strain off the aft pressure door. If that son of a bitch blows, it'll clean out this fuselage like the barrel of a shotgun."

Cramer descended the ladder, and walked around the comfort pallet, surveying the passenger compartment. Further back, the medics were hustling between patients, but from a housekeeping point of view, very little was out of place--one discarded glove lying in the aisle, a tissue box with a boot print in the middle of its crumpled top, and that was about it. From this vantage point, damn place looked almost normal.

He stepped over to the right side, and peered out the window offering the best view. Didn't look normal now. Number three was gone! Flat-ass gone, the pylon bent and ripped at the bottom with a three foot piece of cable trailing backward in the slip-stream, its frayed end vibrating furiously, in a frenzied, high frequency flutter.

The loadmaster moved in behind him, pointing to the jagged, trailing edge of the right, inboard flap. "Knocked hell out of it huh, Major?"

Cramer nodded, as he surveyed the damage. "I've got to wonder if the flaps will work when the time comes." He pointed out the window. "If this section hangs up, the asymmetry prevention system may lock all of them in place." He paused for a moment, evaluating the problem, then turned toward the loadmaster. "Everything else okay?"

"Yes sir. Pressure door looks normal."

"Good. If it didn't blow under higher pressure, it ought to hold now. Keep an eye on things. I'm going back to check with the senior medical officer."

"Yes sir."

He walked toward the rear, eyes searching the scene until he spotted Janet bending over a litter patient. When he reached her, he put his hand on her shoulder. "How are things back here?"

She looked back at him without straightening up. "Everything's under control. How's the airplane?"

"Number three engine tore off the mounts, and knocked hell out of our flaps. So, we may have a no flap landing, in addition to having two engines out. As usual, the weather's rotten. Elmendorf is near minimums, and all the alternates are socked in. Other than that, everything's great."

"Doesn't sound good."

He shook his head. "Be prepared for the worst. Better set your cabin up for a crash landing. It might turn out that way. Well, I've got to get back upstairs."

"Okay John."

He turned, and walked slowly forward, his eyes scanning the interior. Nearing the forward bulkhead, he reached for the cockpit ladder, then paused, sensing a loose end that needed tying up. It might be a personal, but he wanted it taken care of.

Normally, Air Evac crews separated once a mission was over. Medics went one way, the flight crews another. Often neither group encountered the other again. This time, he wanted things to be different. If he lost touch with Janet, he might lose track of her entirely. This could be his only chance to make sure that didn't happen.

He turned abruptly, and walked toward the rear. Janet looked up, saw him coming, and walked forward to meet him.

They met in the middle of the bay. He looked down at her, and smiled sheepishly. "Uh--look, is there any way we could get together after the flight? You know, go to the club, and have a drink, or maybe dinner or something?"

She smiled up at him. "Sure. I can meet you somewhere after we land. It may be a couple of hours before I can get away, but name the place, and I'll do my best to make it."

"How about the main bar in the club...say three hours after we land?"

"I can probably make that. She gave him a little poke in the ribs. "Promise me you'll wait if I'm late."

He winked at her. "You can depend on that." He stepped back. "Well, I've got to get up front. There are a lot of problems to solve before we have that first drink."

"Pilot, this is Nav. Estimate St Paul island at zero three. I'll work up an estimate for Elmendorf."

"Okay. Use the speed we have now. Looks like we can hold 25,000.

"Roger."

Janet came into the cockpit, sat on the jump seat, put on her headset, and leaned forward. "Things have calmed down in back," she said. "Bring me up to date on how it's going up here." As Cramer looked back over his shoulder, she added, "Don't sugar coat it, John. I need straight answers."

He motioned for Bill Grey to take over, then loosened his shoulder harness, turned in his seat, leaned an elbow on the arm rest, and looked back at her. "Events are beginning to gang up on us," he said. "The weather at Elmendorf is near minimums, and it looks like all suitable alternates are down." He gestured toward the engineer's panel. "As far as the airplane is concerned...a lot of things aren't working. Still, it's not hopeless. The two remaining engine driven generators should give us all the electrical power we need, and the only hydraulic system we've lost is one half the power to the ailerons, rudder and elevators."

"Will that be a problem?" she asked.

"Probably not. The remaining system should be adequate for control. The landing gear should operate normally, as well as the brakes, and spoilers. On the other hand, flap action is questionable. We'll have enough pressure, but the damage to the right inboard section could make them lock out."

"How so?"

"The damaged part may jam the inboard section. If it does, the asymmetry prevention system will lock out further movement of all sections. In that event we'll be faced with a no-flap landing, in addition to the directional control problems associated with two engines out on one side."

Cramer winced, loosened his lap belt, and shoulder harness, and twisted further around in his seat in an effort to relieve the crick in his neck. "Let me explain this a little better," he said. "A no-flap landing in a C-141 is a demanding procedure even under ideal conditions. It requires much higher than normal approach speed. It also requires an unusually high angle of attack to compensate for the loss of lift. On flare out, the sink rate will be increased, and on touchdown the bottom rear portion of the fuselage will be only inches away from dragging on the runway."

"Sounds risky."

He nodded. "It will be. At best, be ready for a hard landing. I won't be able to soften the touchdown by raising the nose much higher for flare-out. Raising it a few inches more than would normally be required under these conditions will probably cause the bottom of the fuselage to scrape on the runway. But that won't be the only problem. On touchdown, the droop of the wings, and the fact that they're swept back, will cause the tips to be close to the ground. During a no flap landing, a bank angle of only five degrees will drag a wing tip on the runway. A bank of eight degrees will cause an outboard engine to drag as well."

"I don't like the sound of that," she said.

He paused, and took a deep breath. "Unfortunately, that's not the end of the bad news. It looks like we'll have a strong crosswind on landing. That's going to be tough to deal with. I can cancel the drift by flying in a crab during approach, but I can't land that way."

"Why not?'

"Landing in a crab could blow the tires. Might cause landing gear failure as well. It could also put an excessive side load on the engines and rip them off the plane. Botch it completely--she could roll up in a ball, and explode."

"Is there any way to prevent that?"

"Maybe." He raised his right hand, mimicking the profile of a plane, then cocked it at an angle. "In order to cancel drift during approach, I'll have to fly in a crab during the early part. Just before touchdown I'll need to align the fuselage with the runway, and change the crab into a slip." He straightened his hand, and lowered the left side. "I'll do that by lowering the upwind wing, and applying top rudder. But, if I put the wing down more than a few degrees, the tip will drag, and possibly the outboard engine as well. There'll be almost no margin for error. A higher crosswind, or a minor mistake will almost guarantee disaster."

"Any other problems?"

"I'm afraid so. During approach, and landing, visibility will be marginal at best. With the weather, and extreme aircraft attitude, the visual references I normally use will be distorted, and blowing snow will be reflected in the landing lights, making things even harder to see."

She leaned forward, looking doubtful. "How many landings like this have you practiced?"

He shook his head. "None! We can't practice stuff like this. It's too risky."

She drew back, her expression changing to deep concern. "Do you

202

think you can do it?"

He took a deep breath, and looked down at the aisle stand. "It'll be a tough go. Throughout the approach, and landing, every change in power, will affect the balance between trim, wind, asymmetrical engine thrust, and directional control. All of those factors will change constantly, and will have to be dealt with as precisely, and quickly as possible." He looked up at her. "Anyway you look at it, Janet...this landing is gonna be one hairy son of a bitch. You asked for a straight answer. That's about as straight as I can make it."

Bill Grey scribbled the last of an incoming message on his knee board, and looked across the aisle stand, his face grim. "Elmendorf is 300 obscured and 3/4 in snow. Wind zero one zero at fifteen, gusting to twenty."

Cramer gave him a guarded look. "Not as good as I'd hoped for. But...we'll do our best. In the meantime, might as well check the flaps. If they're not going work, I want to find out now. I'll slow to flap placard speed, and give them a try." He retarded power slightly, waited for the speed to bleed off, and said, "Give me ten degrees."

Grey reached out, nudged the handle, and the master caution light instantly flashed, as a logo on the annunciator panel warned, "flap asym."

"So much for that," Cramer said, as he re-applied cruise power, and pressed the rudder harder. "No flaps for landing. Damn!" He thumbed the electric trim buttons, canceled out the pressures, then turned his head, and stared absently out the windshield. "If that crosswind gets worse, I'll never get this son of a bitch on the ground in one piece. Tearing off a wing tip will be bad enough, but if number one touches down...there's going to be hell to pay."

"Sure will," Grey said. "The turbine may disintegrate. At best, the damn thing will more than likely throw shrapnel all around the plane of rotation. Some of it's bound to penetrate the fuselage."

"You're right about that," Cramer said. "A couple of years back a C-130 starter came apart, and two passengers were killed when flying shrapnel tore into the fuselage. A disintegrating turbine would be a lot more destructive than that." He keyed the interphone. "Loadmaster, go to the window directly opposite the red turbine stripe on number one engine cowl. As of now, that's a danger zone. Clear everyone out of an area at least 3 feet forward, and aft, of that line--more if you can manage."

"Roger sir."

He re-focused his attention on Grey. "Call Elmendorf ACP. Tell them we anticipate possible severe aircraft damage on landing. In addition to the crash crews, request all the qualified medical people they can spare. They may be offloading these patients from a burning wreck."

CHAPTER FORTY SEVEN

Pulsating position lights swept by them a half mile on the left, as the turbo-prop, Air-Sea Rescue C-130 banked steeply, tightening its turn to complete the intercept, and fall in behind them. Cramer called on company frequency. "I show us passing Nerka, Rescue One. Glad to see you're with us. Think you can you keep up?

"We'll do our best triple two. Right now we've got a panel full of needles crowding against red lines. Are you still planning on Elmendorf?"

"Roger. There's no better choice anywhere in the North Pacific or Canadian area. Standby, and I'll double check with ACP".

"Roger."

He squeezed the mic switch, and keyed company. "Elmendorf ACP, this is Triple Two, any luck with a better alternate?"

"Negative, Triple Two. The crosswind at Kenai is worse than it is here, and Ketchikan has a 25 Knot direct tailwind on their precision runway. Both airports have shorter runways than Elmendorf, and they're covered with glare ice. You'd have zilch for braking action.

"What's the latest on Eielson?"

"They're zero zero, and the GCA just went out. The ILS will be down for modification for another week. Their wind is nearly calm, but without a precision approach, you'd probably never see the runway."

"Okay, thanks for trying. Are the crash crews standing by?"

"Affirmative triple two."

Six foot four, gray haired and lanky, Major Jack Thibodaux, the Elmendorf ACP duty controller picked up his coffee, took a swallow, winced, and sat the cold brew down. He glanced up at the scheduling board on the far wall. It was still there. Problems like this didn't solve themselves. He scanned the info on the top line--next in--C-141--50222--pilot--Cramer.

Thibodaux turned to Master Sergeant Lambert, his NCOIC. "Two engines out on one side, and a no flap landing. I hope this guy's good. It'd be damned risky in daylight, and good weather. In the dark, with a low ceiling, blowing snow, and a gusty crosswind?" He shook his head. "I'm glad I'm not flying this one. Wish it was over. It's bad enough for any MAC plane to be in this fix, but an air evac flight...Jesus!"

Sergeant Lambert rubbed the salt, and pepper bristles on his round face, and looked at him with bloodshot eyes. "Things like this make me glad I'm not flying the line anymore. Maybe my wife was right after all."

Thibodaux leaned back in his swivel chair, laid one arm on the desk, and propped his feet up on the wastebasket. He took the toothpick out of the corner of his mouth, and tossed it into the ash tray. "We're under the gun on this one Sarge. They're watching this all the way to the top. If we screw it up, it's off with our heads. What have we missed?"

"I can't think of anything Major."

Thibodaux ran his fingers into his hair, scratched, and squinted. "We've done everything in the book, but something's still nagging me?"

"What else can we do Sir? We've finished all the emergency procedures."

"Remember that incident we had last winter? When a C-130 almost creamed a moose that strayed onto the runway?"

"That's the only time it ever happened."

"So? We damn sure don't want it to happen tonight." Thibodaux picked up a pencil, and tapped the phone on his desk. "Call the Air Police. Tell 'em to get two vehicles. Put a man with a rifle in each of them. One car on the ramp, the other on the north side parallel taxiway. If they see a moose, shoot the son of a bitch before he has a chance to wander onto the runway."

Lambert turned his head slightly and squinted. Thibodaux threw the pencil down, and spread his arms. "C'mon! Don't give me that look. Hell yes, I know it's an unlikely scenario, but dammit man...we gotta do something!

CHAPTER FORTY EIGHT

"Air Evac five zero triple two--Anchorage control. Radar position five zero miles southwest of Elmendorf. Cleared descent to fifteen thousand."

Cramer looked at Grey, pointed downward, and pulled the power back.

"Triple two, leaving flight level two five zero now," Grey said.

"Triple two, Roger."

"Descent checklist," Cramer called.

"Crew briefing," Grey responded.

"This will be a GCA to runway zero five at Elmendorf," Cramer said. "Field elevation is 213 feet. Decision height--375 feet. Missed approach will be as directed by GCA. If we miss the first approach, I'll stay at Elmendorf, and try another GCA. Navigation, and communication radios are set."

"Triple two, Anchorage approach, maintain present heading, cleared further descent to five thousand."

"Triple two Roger."

"Crew, prepare the cabin for a possible crash landing," Cramer said. "Make sure everything is tied down."

She came down like an express elevator, nose steeply angled, seemingly falling from the sky. Nearing five thousand, they were cleared further descent to three. At level off, Cramer re-set power, and the exaggerated, asymmetrical factor made itself known as she slewed awkwardly, wallowing in an uncertain, corkscrew fashion--a once docile, and obedient servant, now squirmy, cantankerous, and uncooperative.

He mulled over the problems, dividing his attention between flying the plane, and planning ahead, then glanced across the aisle stand. "The easy part's over, Bill. From this point on, there can't be any mistakes. With no flaps, the nose high attitude, will make it hard to judge height above the runway. If we break out, there'll be just seconds to decide whether to land or not."

Grey gave him a solemn look and nodded.

"What if you have to go-around?" The engineer asked.

Cramer glanced over his shoulder, "It'll be tough," he said. "If I miss the approach, we'll be at low altitude, in weather, and I won't be able to use more than partial power. May not have enough rudder to handle that."

Major Thibodaux stopped pacing, picked up the phone, and punched the button for Approach Control.

"Elmendorf Approach Control."

"This is ACP, where's triple two now?"

"Seventeen miles out, we'll hand them over to GCA shortly."

"How's it look?" Thibodaux asked.

"The wind has shifted, and picked up a little. Three six zero--twenty-- gusting to twenty five."

"Have the crash crews been notified?"

"Affirmative. We'll call you if anything happens."

"Ok. Fine." Thibodaux hung up the phone, then picked up a pencil, and leaned over the C-141 performance handbook, squinting as he followed the lines in the crosswind landing chart, carefully factoring in estimated gross weight, wind direction, and gust factor.

"Damn!"

"What's the matter?" Nichols asked.

"The chart shows the crosswind's barely in the acceptable range."

"Then it's OK." Nichols said.

Thibodaux kept his eyes fixed on the page. "No. No it's not. This diagram is made for a normal landing--a landing with flaps." He laid his pencil down, and looked at Nichols. "Damn crosswind's too high for a no-flapper. This guy's in a hell of a fix. Boxed in, with no way out. If he puts his wing down far enough to cancel the drift, the tip will drag, probably an outboard engine too."

"Suppose he shallows the bank?"

Thibodaux shook his head. "Can't do that. Damn wind will blow him off the other side of the runway." He took a deep breath, looked back at the chart and added, "Hate to say it, Sarge, but it looks like they're screwed. I don't think they're gonna make it."

Cramer leveled off, and nailed his altitude, feeling the huge plane wallow as he adjusted power, and trimmed. His eyes swept the gages, in endless fluid cycles, mind racing as he mentally converted GCA's terse mono-tone instructions into timely action. "Anchorage Approach, triple two, level at three thousand." he called.

"Roger, triple two, radar position one five miles southwest of Elmendorf. Current Elmendorf weather--three hundred obscured, one half mile in blowing snow. Wind--three six zero at twenty, gusting to twenty five, contact Elmendorf GCA on two seven three decimal five."

"Roger, triple two going to two seven three decimal five."

Grey leaned across the aisle-stand. "Crosswind's worse, John. Too damn high. What are you going to do?"

Cramer shot him a glance. "I'll do the best I can."

Grey nodded, then reached down, and changed frequency. "Elmendorf GCA...Air Evac five zero triple two, heading zero one zero at three thousand over."

"Roger triple two, this is Elmendorf GCA, continue heading zero one zero, this will be a dog leg to final approach for runway zero five at

Elmendorf. Your lost communication procedure is as follows, climb to 3000, proceed to Hobbs intersection, hold northwest, contact Anchorage approach on three six three decimal eight, over."

"Triple two, Roger."

"Air evac five zero triple two descend to one thousand six hundred, perform landing--cockpit check, over."

"Triple two, out of three thousand, for one thousand six hundred."

Cramer reduced power, and nudged the trim. Passing through 2500, the first jolts from terrain induced turbulence hit them with aggravating, hammering little chops. By the time they leveled off at 1600, she was rolling noticeably, and becoming increasingly harder to handle. He called for the Before Landing Checklist, added power to maintain 166 knots, then moved the rudder, high-pressure override switch to the override position.

"Triple two, now intercepting final approach course, ten miles from Elmendorf, turn right, heading zero four zero, maintain one thousand six hundred, stand by for Final Controller."

"Triple Two Roger."

"Air Evac five zero triple two, Final Controller, how do you read, over."

"Five square," Grey responded.

"Roger, GCA reads you loud, and clear. Do not acknowledge further transmissions unless requested to do so. Turn left heading zero three five. Maintain sixteen hundred."

GCA droned on in a steady monotone, verbally nudging them back, and forth, with a series of small heading changes as Cramer slowed to two engine final approach speed.

"Ten seconds to glideslope."

He reduced power, re-trimmed, and eased into the descent, his eyes sweeping the panel in a steady, rhythmic pattern. Initially, he nailed everything, but erratic wind, inevitable drift, and increasing turbulence took their toll, as the controller warned, *"Heading zero two eight, now going 10 feet below the glide path."*

He adjusted pitch.

"Twenty feet below glide path, heading zero two two."

He added power, changed pitch, pressed the rudder harder.

"Twenty feet--now thirty feet below glide path, heading zero two four. Holding thirty feet below glide path..."

He gritted his teeth, crammed the power, and stood on the rudder.

"Thirty feet below glide path heading zero two two--now adjusting twenty feet below glide path heading zero one eight--ten feet low, heading zero two four--back up, and on glide path, heading zero two two..."

A pulsating glow formed in the windshield, as Grey shouted, "One hundred feet to minimums!"

"Approaching GCA minimums,"

Rapid fire, lead-in-lights, invaded his peripheral vision, zapping repeatedly toward a still hidden threshold. He stayed on the gauges, corrected heading, and held the speed.

"Runway one o'clock!," Grey shouted.

"Lights!" Cramer shouted, and the world burst from the darkness, blinding white, in brilliant slashes of streaking snow. Suddenly, there it was, one faint row of wavering green. He closed the throttles, lowered the wing, and they swept beyond the threshold, left wing low, and drifting right, with snow packed concrete rushing up to meet them. The left mains hit with a neck snapping jolt. Tires flattened, struts bottomed, and the wing tip crumpled, as the position light shattered, and was swept away.

Number one touched, the left wing bowed, and a torrent of sparks sprayed from the turbine. She bounced, lofting upward--control wheel hammering against his hand. Number one wobbled, wrenched, tore loose, and tumbled--end over end, as it disappeared behind them.

She hung there, yards above the runway, seemingly forever, nose too high, left wing low, and drifting right with the warning horn screaming. Suddenly she shuddered, fell back in, and rocked to the right.

"T handle one," Cramer called. "Fire extinguisher."

Grey pulled the handle, and punched the button, as Cramer popped the spoilers, and a long line of panels snapped erect on top of the wing. Their speed ebbed slowly. Close to the edge, he tested brakes, feeling the anti-skid respond, as the pedals throbbed against his toes. Once below 80, the lift diminished, and braking action improved.

"Engine failure checklist complete, "Grey said."

"How's it look loadmaster?"

"Number one's gone Major. Flat-ass gone!"

"Any fire?"

"No sir, that left with the engine."

They slowed below 60, and Cramer glanced at Grey. "The taxiway's too narrow for ambulances, fire trucks and the airplane too. Tell the tower we'll offload on the runway. Shouldn't be a problem with no one behind us."

Finally, he braked to a slow taxi, pulled in close to the red cross busses, eased to a stop, and reached for the parking brake. "Damn!"

"What's the matter?" Grey asked.

"God only knows. For some reason, the brakes won't lock." Fatigue washed over him as he took a deep breath, and shook his head. "Aw, to hell with it. I'll sit here and hold them. Give me the Engine Shutdown Checklist."

Outside, the Artic wind howled, buffeting the plane as a line of vehicles stopped behind the clamshell doors, yellow lights flashing, headlights dimmed by the storm. Doctors, nurses and medics spilled off a bus, their heads cocked low, in a futile effort to avoid the sleet. They huddled together, beneath the upswept tail--backs to the storm, shivering, teeth chattering, hands tucked into armpits, and stamping their feet as the ramp slowly lowered. Finally, a couple of medics, grabbed the trailing edge, and swung themselves aboard.

Up front, the Fire Chief stopped behind the jump seat, and leaned toward Cramer.

"You've got a lot of damage, Major," he said, "Including a couple of fuel leaks in your left wing. Better shut 'er down as soon as you can."

Cramer looked back at him. "Ok. The emergency lights should be enough for the people in back. I'll stay here, and hold the brakes until the tow vehicle hooks up. Engineer, kill the power."

"Roger sir."

The scream of the aux power unit changed pitch, and wound down, as the cockpit darkened. Suddenly, the emergency exit light on the rear bulkhead came on, illuminating the cabin in a faint, ghostly glow.

Cramer slumped in his seat, and looked out the windshield--feeling emotionally drained, and suddenly sleepy. Behind him, connections clicked, zippers zipped, and someone coughed, as the front office crew disconnected equipment, stuffed it into their bags, then shuffled to the door, and climbed down the ladder. Bill Grey was the last to go, clutching his helmet bag, and code books close to his chest as he squeezed by his seat. Finally, Cramer sat alone in the gloom, guarding the brakes.

Out front, a huge, yellow tow vehicle moved in close, all but disappearing under the nose. On the left side, medical vehicles slowly pulled away, single file, headlights stabbing weakly into the storm. Cockpit temperature plunged, as Cramer sat there, feeling the cold creeping in, listening to the throb of the tow vehicle engine, and the muffled clunk of the tow bar being attached.

He stared wistfully as the last of the tail lights disappeared in the storm. Janet was onboard one of those buses. Would he see her again? Maybe not. Air Evac was short handed. Maybe she'd have trouble getting away. Maybe she wouldn't make it at all.

Behind him, footsteps hurried up the crew ladder, and he looked backward, seeing a parka clad enlisted man step through the door, and stop behind the jump seat.

"Okay Major, I'll take over now."

210

Cramer grabbed his personal equipment, and slid out of the seat, crouching low to keep from bumping his head.

The sergeant stepped back, making room for him to pass as he shook his head. "God Major, I don't know how you can look so calm. To tell you the truth...I didn't think you were gonna make it."

Cramer smiled as he brushed by the man. "Neither did I, Sarge. Neither did I."

CHAPTER FORTY NINE

Impressive by any standards, the Elmendorf Officer's Club was large, and spacious, it's furnishings reflecting the impeccable taste of a top-flight decorator. The main dining room was already crowded when Cramer walked by, and a band was scheduled in the ball room, so it was a good bet the place would be busy until closing. And why not? Weather be damned, it was still the best night spot north of Seattle.

He walked into the spacious, dimly lit bar, and sat down at a table near the entrance, so he could see whoever came in. The room was crowded--bar full, as well as most of the tables. When the waiter arrived, he ordered a coke. No booze yet. There'd be a lot riding on the next few hours, and he didn't want to be bombed, if Janet showed up late.

Minutes later, he got up, left the half finished Coke, walked to the door, and was pleasantly surprised when he saw her enter the club. He walked down the hall to meet her.

She turned, and smiled, as he approached, dark eyes shining, complexion blushed by the cold, her short black hair barely disturbed as she pushed back the hood of the parka. "Hi," she said softly, and a flutter of excitement stirred in his chest.

"You look great," he said. "That's a good combination--a woman who's punctual, and looks good too."

She smiled. "Helps me beat the competition."

Cramer chuckled. "You don't have any competition."

She checked her coat, and they headed to the main bar, then made their way to a corner table. When the waitress came, Janet asked for a whiskey sour, and Cramer ordered the usual CC, and soda.

She turned her head, as her eyes swept the room. "It's amazing," she said. "In here, everything seems so calm. It's hard to believe we were in that much trouble." She smiled, leaned toward him, and gripped his arm. "The pressure on you must have been enormous."

He moved the glass chimney, candle holder over to the side, so he could see her better. "Things had to be tough on your end too," he said. How'd your critical cases make out? Lose anyone?"

She shook her head. "No. But it's a good thing the busses were waiting. It's always better for the patients in a hospital."

"You people do a fantastic job," Cramer said. "It's a well organized, operation."

She nodded, and looked down at her hands. "Even with 400 nurses involved, things are running smoothly. As soon as casualties are stabilized, they're put on board a C-141. The last thing some of those guys remember is getting hit in Vietnam." She looked up and added softly, "When they wake up, a day and a half later, they're in a hospital in the States."

"It's obviously working well," Cramer said. "Even the press can't find

212

fault with it. Maybe that's why they never mention the operation." He shook his head, and grumbled, "A story that big? With that much human interest? You'd think someone would notice, and give you credit. Damn press never talks about anything that's going right."

She reached out and put her hand on his arm. "Let's forget the press for tonight. I don't know about you, but I'm starving!"

"Okay," he said. "As soon as we finish our drinks, we'll head for the dining room."

"Sounds good to me."

Soft music by Mantovani set the mood, and thick carpets cushioned their way, as a waiter led them to a table set with polished silver, and fine dinner ware. Huge by any standards, the club dining room had a wide expanse of windows covering the back wall. In better weather they would have had a spectacular view of the brightly lit suburbs of Anchorage. No matter. Tonight he wasn't interested in the view outside.

After they were seated, Janet smiled, and looked around the room. "I eat here every chance I get. This place has an elegance that's hard to resist."

Cramer chuckled, and gave her a sheepish grin. "Yeah, it is nice. But to tell you the truth, I usually go downstairs to the casual bar."

They finished their drinks, and after studying the menu, Janet ordered the Alaskan King Crab. He chose Salmon steak. When the meal was served, it was pleasant to the eye, and exciting to the palate. Afterward, they talked over coffee, until the dining room closed.

Following a short trip to the rest room, they met in the hall, and he pointed toward the bar. "Care to dance?"

"I'd love to," she smiled, and his chimes rang again. He looked at her, almost mesmerized. God, she was something.

"Scheduling released me until 1400 tomorrow," She added. "I'm ready to make a night of it."

They made their way past several tables, and finally found one vacant. When the drinks arrived, he tossed his down, while Janet sipped slowly. Conversation was difficult, because of the band, but they talked anyway. Finally, the music switched to dreamy, and they got up to dance.

Once on the floor, he held her closely, feeling her pressing against him, soft and graceful--her face even more beautiful in the subdued lighting. There was a kind of anonymity in being lost in a sea of people and he followed his instincts, and kissed her. She responded readily, holding it for a long time.

When the band took a break, they returned to their table, and talked. Eventually, he realized time was running out. He looked at her, and made his pitch. "I'd like to find a way for us to see more of each other," he said.

"That would be nice," she said. "But how can we manage that?"

"I've got a lot of leave time built up," he said. "Almost ninety days. I'll have to take some by the first of July, or lose thirty."

She sat her glass down, leaned forward, and folded her hands on top of the table. "I'm in the same boat. Got so involved with my job that a vacation didn't occur to me. The leave just"...she waved a hand and shrugged,"...built up."

Cramer looked down at his glass, and tilted it slowly back, and forth, watching the melt maintain level. "Suppose...suppose we each take fifteen days, and agree to meet here?" he said. "I could get jump orders, give a checkride on the way up, then sign out on leave when I get here." He looked up at her. "Could you work out something like that?"

"I don't see why not."

"Good," he said. "Say we do that a couple of times between now, and the end of summer. "He opened his hands, and added with a shrug, "No matter how it works on the personal level, it wouldn't be a total loss. There's lots to see, and do in Alaska. It ought to be enjoyable. A nice vacation for both of us. By the time, summer's over we'll know how it's working. "

She reached out, and squeezed his hand. "Sounds good, John. I like it."

He drained his glass, and set the empty aside. "Over the next couple of years we'll accumulate two more months of leave," he said. "We could use ten days at a time, and see each other fairly often." He leaned forward, and gave her a hopeful look. "No reason it can't work. It's not like we're strangers."

The corner of her eyes crinkled. "True. We've known each other since Otis."

It was bitterly cold, by the time they left the Club, but at least, the wind was dying. They made their way slowly, stepping carefully through six inch snow, guided by street lights, talking as they walked, their breath trailing behind them.

Finally, they went up the steps to the women's BOQ, and took refuge inside the warm foyer. On the wall, near the inner door, a sign warned sternly in bold red letters, "Male guests not permitted beyond this point."

She turned toward him, and he took her in his arms, and kissed her. His pulse quickened. Finally he broke the embrace, and looked at her.

"Think you could sneak me in for a night cap?"

She smiled up at him, "It's an appealing prospect, but I can't take that chance. Uncle doesn't like for his single female officers to co-habit in government quarters."

"Ok. Tell you what...as a consolation prize, how about having breakfast with me at the club in the morning, say about nine?"

"I'd like that."

"Want me to call you for wake up?"

She smiled, and shook her head. "I'll be up. Meet you there at nine sharp."

"Terrific," he said. Then he kissed her again.

Finally, she broke the embrace, drew her head back, and looked up at him with that gentle smile, her dark eyes warming his heart. "If we're going to make it to breakfast on time, we'd better call it a night." She said.

Cramer chuckled. "That's a lot more common sense than I'd hoped for...but, Ok. See you in the morning."

"Good night John."

As he left the building, cold air hit with a vengeance, and he walked quickly, hands stuffed deeply into his pockets, shoulders hunched, his hormones in turmoil. "Damn!" he mumbled, shivering. "Ben Franklin had it right--A man in a passion, rides a mad horse."

Inside his building, the hallway felt mercifully warm, but his room was surprisingly chilly. He turned on the light, adjusted the register, then pulled back the covers, and began to undress. On the desk, a complimentary copy of the Anchorage paper lay, awaiting his inspection. He snatched it up, then slipped into bed, feeling the shock of cold sheets against his skin. He propped himself up, pulled the covers under his arms, and scanned the publication. Of all the English language newspapers he had read, world wide, this was his favorite. In spite of its big city format, it still had a frontier flavor about it, and the numerous articles about life in the bush, were invariably interesting, and well done--human interest at its most compelling.

Fifteen minutes into the read, the knock on the door was so soft, he barely heard it. He lowered the paper, and listened. There it was again. This time, a bit louder.

"Just a minute." He threw back the covers, slipped into his pants, and reached for the door. As soon as he turned the knob, a shivering, rosy-faced Janet, once again dressed in her flying suit, pushed into the room, and kicked the door shut behind her.

She held up her briefcase, and smiled. "Don't look so surprised. This is official government business. I'm here for a post flight conference with my pilot. How's that for a cover story?

Cramer chuckled. "Sounds logical to me. What...what made you change your mind?"

She gripped his arm, and flashed him a determined smile. "I let you get away back at Otis. Been kicking myself ever since." She turned away, stepped over, and sat her briefcase on the desk, then opened it, and pulled out a handful of papers.

She looked back over her shoulder, and smiled. "Might as well set an alibi scene," she said. "In the unlikely event we're interrupted." She scattered a few papers on top of the desk, then unzipped her parka, took out a pen, and dropped it on top of the documents. After that, she stepped back, and surveyed the arrangement. "There," she said with obvious satisfaction. "That looks official." She turned, and smiled at him. "You know, all this subterfuge may not be necessary. Can you believe it? There aren't any signs in this building saying, 'No Females beyond this point."

"He chuckled, "Must be an oversight. Anyway, there shouldn't be a problem. I'm spill-over. After we got to the BOQ office, I was the last one to register. They had to open this building just to give me a room. The way the weather is...it's not likely anyone landed behind us."

She took off her gloves, unzipped her parka, and nodded toward the door. "Better lock that, anyway. And turn up your radio, just in case."

"In case of what?"

She sat on the bed, kicked off her boots, and smiled up at him. "In case it gets noisy in here." She slid her slacks down, pulled them off, and swung her legs up on the bed. Holy cow. Look at those legs. She always had great legs. He reached up, unfastened his pants, and almost tripped as he kicked them off. Dammit! Take it easy, he reminded himself. No need to hurry. Your gonna have all night.

CHAPTER FIFTY

ELMENDORF AIR FORCE BASE

An apparently dying, orange colored sun hung just above the horizon, casting long, early afternoon shadows across the snow covered landscape. Ahead, the line of cars moved slowly, a couple of them with cold engines, and thin white smoke still coming from their exhausts. The engine on their rental car was barely warm as Cramer returned the guard's salute, drove through the main gate, and headed for Anchorage. More than likely, they'd be in town before the heater was much help.

Well, cold or not--at least he'd made it. Hell of a thing. Almost late for his own wedding. Barely had time to speak to her, before the function began. Good thing they had it in the Base Chapel.

At first, the Chaplain seemed a bit nonplussed about his showing up in a flying suit, but...he made a nice recovery, and the brief ceremony went well. Cramer glanced to his right, feeling a flutter of excitement in his chest. Man, what a sight. She always looked great, but this afternoon, she was absolutely stunning. "That fir collar frames your face like a picture," he said.

Janet beamed, slid across the seat, and slipped her hand under his arm. "Thank you," she said. "So...now that the nuptials are over, fill me in on the news, back in the States." She looked up at him, her expression concerned. "Did you go to your aunt's funeral?"

He nodded. "Yeah. Yeah, I did. Changed my mind. After it was over, I was glad I went."

"How'd it go?"

He gave her a quick glance, then looked back at the highway. "It wasn't as bad as I thought. There were more people there, than I expected, but the big surprise came later. In the lawyer's office."

"Surprise?"

He nodded, keeping his eyes on the road. "Turns out the judge never gave them clear title. To the farm, I mean. They had a lifetime deed--a consolation prize for raising me. After their deaths, the property rights reverted to me."

"Sounds logical."

"I suppose so," he said. "But evidently, the arrangement caused them a lot of concern over the years."

"Why would they worry about that?"

"Who knows? he said, shaking his head. "They worried about everything."

Traffic ahead slowed for a red light, and they rolled to a stop behind a blue pickup, with a white, camper top. He looked at her and added, "According to the neighbors, they thought I might somehow take the place away from them."

"You wouldn't have done that, would you?"

"Of course not. They earned the right to live there. Took care of me. That was the deal."

Janet nodded toward the windshield. He took the cue, saw that traffic was pulling away, accelerated to catch up, and gave her a quick glance. "Anyway, it's over now. Seems hard to believe we actually own the place."

"What are you going to do with it?"

He snorted. "I'm not gonna farm it, that's for sure. You won't catch me working that hard. I rented the land to an old school chum."

"The house too?"

He nodded. "Sure. It's so rundown, he has to fix the roof, before he can use it for storage."

"That's sad." She looked up at him, her expression solumn. "You were born there."

"Yeah, I know," he said, "But, somehow...it never seemed like home after my parents were killed. Without a family, a house is just..." he shrugged, "a house." He reached for the dash, and adjusted the heater. "One more thing," he said. "She had a small bank account. Two thousand dollars. Not much for a life of hard work." He gave her another quick glance. "I told them to give it to her church. She would have liked that."

She squeezed his arm. "Good move. I'm glad you did. Well..." she took a deep breath, "anyway, I hope you're saving the best for last. How'd the interview go?"

"Great! Hey, Southern's a good airline. I'll have to sit in the right seat, and read to the old man for a couple of years, but their growing fast. Their co-pilots have been upgrading to Captain quicker than most."

She chuckled, and nudged him in the ribs. "You're keeping me in suspense, Cramer."

He smiled, and looked at her. "The domicile won't be a problem. That's one reason I wanted Southern. We can live in Fort Walton Beach."

She beamed. "That's terrific! So...when do you have your retirement ceremony?"

"I'm not going to have one. Told them to forget it."

She tipped her head slightly, and gave him a doubtful look. "Can you do that? Retire without a ceremony?"

He nodded. "Sure. It's not required. But, I did remind them to send my check every month."

"That sounds like you." She looked up at him, her expression concerned. "Have you had the nightmare lately?"

He smiled, and shook his head. "Not since you agreed to marry me."

"Well that's encouraging." She looked out her window, squinted, lifted her hand, and shaded her eyes as the bright orange reflection of the setting sun bounced off the picture window of a passing house. She looked back inside, and lowered her arm. "Anyway, I hope you're right about Eglin, I've never been there. Don't know a thing about the hospital. I hear it's big."

He gave her a nod. "Big base, big hospital. But, don't worry. You'll love it in the panhandle. Ft. Walton is terrific--beaches are never crowded-- whitest sand you've ever seen. Even beats Bermuda."

"Well, at least it'll be warm." She laughed, and waved at the barren trees, and snow covered yards. "Will you look at this? Some people go to Rio, others to Florida, or the Bahamas--or maybe even Mexico, but not us. We travel thousands of miles from different directions so we can get married in Alaska. In the middle of winter!"

"Ah why not? It's a fine place, and it's really not that cold. It'll be great. We'll get used to it in no time."

"I guess you're right." She patted his leg, and smiled up at him. "Besides, we probably won't spend much time outdoors anyway."

They laughed, and he felt a surge of joy in his chest. Finally, he had someone. And she was terrific. He was going to have a home. A real home. And suddenly he realized...he'd never be lonely again.

A TRIBUTE TO SOME PEOPLE

"Air evacuation of wounded from Vietnam to the United States was one of the most successful military operations ever conducted. From 1965 to 1971...84,841 battle casualties were Air Evacuated—of that number, nearly half were moved with some device or appliance—cast, IV tube, etc which complicated their care. Seventy five percent were not ambulatory at the time of movement, and nearly one thousand were unconscious. Despite the huge numbers of patients involved, only eight were determined to have a condition which deteriorated in flight, and only one died. None were lost due to aircraft accident." Ref. Roger D. Launius & Cecil L. Reynolds: Office of Military Airlift Command History:

A TRIBUTE TO A PLANE

After the introduction of Puff The Magic Dragon, and the follow-on side firing gunnery planes it inspired, in over 6000 engagements, no Vietnamese village was ever again overrun while it was under the protection of a gunship. Ref. GUNSHIPS, Squadron Signal Publications, by Larry Davis. Page 13.